The
FALCON
OF
PALERMO

Maria R. Bordihn

GROVE PRESS
NEW YORK

Published simultaneously in Canada
Printed in the United States of America

FIRST GROVE PRESS EDITION

Library of Congress Cataloging-in-Publication Data

Bordihn, Maria.
The falcon of Palermo / Maria R. Bordihn.
p. cm.
ISBN-10: 0-8021-4232-X
ISBN-13: 978-0-8021-4232-0
1. Frederick II, Holy Roman Emperor, 1194–1250—Fiction.   2. Holy Roman
Empire—History—Frederick II, 1215–1250—Fiction.   3. Holy Roman Empire—
Kings and rulers—Fiction.   4. Palermo (Italy)—Fiction.   I. Title.
PS3602.O735F35 2005
813'.6—dc22   2004057399

Grove Press
an imprint of Grove/Atlantic, Inc.
841 Broadway
New York, NY 10003

06 07 08 09 10   10 9 8 7 6 5 4 3 2 1

For Zell,
with Love and Gratitude

Acknowledgments

My gratitude goes to Harriet Sutin, Christopher MacLehose, D. L. Nelson, Libby Husemeyer, and Stuart Sundlun, for their invaluable help.

POLAND

HUNGARY

R. Danube

SILESIA

Liegnitz

Prague

Vienna

AUSTRIA

EMPIRE

MARCH OF TREVISO

Aquileia

Trent

Milan

Augsburg

Staufen

Brunswick

R. Elbe

R. Weser

THURINGIA

DENMARK

R. Rhine

Hagenau

Aix La Chapelle

DUCHY OF LORRAINE

Constance

Basle

St. Gall

COUNTY OF BURGUNDY

SAVOY

Lyons

Paris

ENGLAND

London

FRANCE

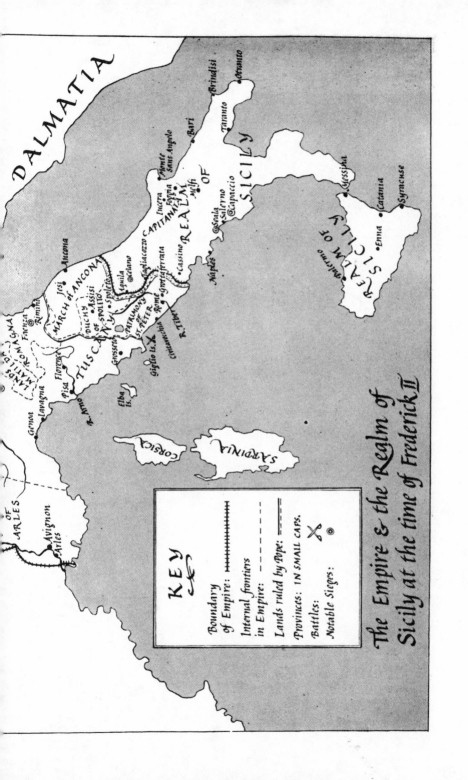

The Empire & the Realm of
Sicily at the time of Frederick II

KEY

Boundary
of Empire:
Internal frontiers
in Empire:
Lands ruled by Pope:
Provinces: IN SMALL CAPS.
Battles:
Notable Sieges:

DALMATIA

Brindisi
Otranto
Bari
Taranto
SICILY
Monte
Sant'Angelo
OF
Foggia
Lucera
REALM
Melfi
Capaccio
Salerno
Scala
CAPITANATA
Cassino
Gaeta
Naples
Gagliacozzo
Grottaferrata
Assisi
Aquila
Celano
Messina
REALM
OF
SICILY
Maltino
Catania
Enna
Syracuse
MARCH of ANCONA
Ancona
Jesi
DUCHY OF SPOLETO
Spoleto
PATRIMONY
OF
ST-PETER
Rome
R. Tiber
Civitavecchia
Faenza
Rimini
LANDS of MATILDA
ROMAGNA
TUSCANY
Florence
Grosseto
Giglio Is.
Pisa
R. Arno
Genoa
Lavagna
Elba
Is.
CORSICA
SARDINIA
OF
ARLES
Avignon
Arles

Prologue

PALERMO, AUGUST 1194

The executioner raised his ax. The blade descended, severing the head with a flawless stroke. Blood spurted from the trunk, then ebbed to a trickle; the executioner wiped the blade with a rag before reaching for the head and holding it up to the crowd gathered in the square outside the royal palace. They didn't break into cheers today. In silence they stood in the fierce August sun, staring at the body slumped against the block.

The Emperor Henry turned away from the window. "He's got a way with an ax, that headsman."

There was a faint distaste on Walter of Palear's sallow features. Perhaps, he thought, I've seen too much of Henry's methods. The man had not been a criminal, but a member of the Sicilian nobility, who had rebelled against the emperor's harsh rule.

Henry looked down at the square again. The crowd was dispersing slowly. He pursed his lips. "What do you make of that rabble, Walter?"

The chancellor cast a thoughtful look at his new master. "Your Grace," Walter said, "I must tell you frankly that you cannot rule Sicily through fear alone. The Sicilians see you still as a stranger. They resent the increased taxes, the shipbuilding levies, the lands you've given your German barons. If the common people were to unite with the nobility . . ."

"Damnation, Walter, as part of the Empire Sicily will be greater than ever, greater than under the Normans. It will be my granary, feeding my army as I conquer Byzantium. Think of it. One realm, from the Bosporus to the Baltic."

And he's capable of it, too, Walter thought with reluctant admiration. Since becoming emperor, Henry's name had become a byword for ruthlessness. The rebellious German princes, the king of France, even Richard the Lionheart, had all been bested by him. He was a strange man, this German emperor who had wedded their queen. He looked much older than his twenty-nine years. Bearded, of medium height, with a muscled body, and an already deeply lined forehead, he was a man of Spartan tastes, indifferent to wine, women or the trappings of wealth. Ambition was his only passion.

Henry sat down, his brow furrowed. He wiped the sweat off his forehead. After a moment, he asked: "Where's the letter to the empress? Constance must come to Sicily at once. Add a postscript, telling her to come south without delay. Once they've got their queen back, your people might become more docile, and I can get on with building my fleet instead of wasting time with traitorous whoresons such as that one." He jerked his head toward the square. "Particularly if the babe is a boy. Not that I can understand why the Sicilians are so loyal to the Hautevilles. After all, they, too, were foreigners not so long ago."

Walter stared at him. "But my Lord, the empress, in her condition, at her age . . . By the time your letter reaches her, it will be September or even October. To travel from Germany over the Alps in winter is dangerous. Would you risk . . ."

Henry waved his objections away. "Constance is as strong as an ox. She's a Norman, after all. Write the addition yourself. I want her arrival to take everyone by surprise."

Walter nodded. The price of remaining in power was compliance with the emperor's will. He dipped the quill into ink, ready to render Henry's blunt summons into elegant Latin. It never ceased to amaze him that this harsh man, who ruled half of Europe, was the son of the affable and cultured Barbarossa. It was Sicily's misfortune that the last of the Hautevilles was a woman. True, they had begun as adventurers, like all great dynasties, but what a cosmopolitan culture had they created, what tolerance had they shown their subjects. Henry would do well to take their example to heart if he wished to rule Sicily without the sullen resistance they had both just witnessed.

When he had finished, Walter read the postscript to Henry.

"Very well," the emperor said curtly. "Dispatch it at once. I need her here before Christmas."

JESI, ADRIATIC MARCH, DECEMBER 1194

A dusting of snow lay on the red-tiled roofs and ramparts of Jesi. On this second day of Christmas, townspeople, their cloaks of coarse homespun wool wrapped around them, thronged the narrow streets, pushing and shoving their way to the marketplace. There, an enthralled audience surrounded Berengaria, Jesi's most respected midwife. She shook her head. "I tell you, it was horrible. How the poor thing struggled, shivering despite all her fur rugs, for a day and a night. That child wouldn't come." The women shuddered, remembering their own searing pains, the screams and blood and deaths of so many childbeds.

"I never thought she'd live, in that icy tent, and her first babe, too, at nearly forty. Oh, we forced hot wine mixed with henbane down her throat, tried all we could to help her push the child out. From time to time her screams would turn to deadly silence. She'd just lie there with closed eyes. Then she'd start to moan again and we'd give thanks that she was still alive. During the night they sent for a Saracen physician."

The old midwife spat and drew her dark cloak closer around her. "But it was through the mercy of the Virgin, whose Son, too, was born at Christmas, that the empress and the little prince were saved. I tell you . . ."

Fanfares sounded. An expectant murmur ran through the crowd in the marketplace.

"Gesù, it really is a miracle, look, there she is, look at her." Berengaria pointed at the bishop's palace on the far side, rising above the great red and green tent still standing in the piazza. A wintry sun pierced the clouds, gilding the facade of the palace. Above the portal, the open loggia, its balustrade hung with tapestries, was thronged with courtiers and churchmen parting to make way for the empress. Constance advanced until she stood at the parapet. She was wrapped in a fur-lined mantle of blue brocade. Her fair braids were entwined with ropes of pearls, coiled on her head to support her crown.

The townspeople broke into jubilant cheers. Constance raised her hand
and smiled. Only her pallor betrayed the effort she was making. She turned
to her friend Matilde of Spoleto. "Give me the child," she said. She took
the swaddled infant and held it up. Then, with an age-old gesture of infinite grace, she parted her mantle and held the child to her exposed breast.
The little prince began to suckle hungrily. A roar of approval went up from
the crowd. "*Viva! Viva! Viva Costanza! Viva la figlia di Ruggiero!*" they chanted,
throwing their caps into the air and stamping their feet.

I was right, she thought. Just as every instinct of statecraft had told
her that she must subject herself to giving birth in a tent, before the
nobility of Jesi, to quell the rumors that her pregnancy was fictitious, so
she had known that she needed the common people's approval of her
son's legitimacy. And here, on the Adriatic March that separated Sicily
from the Empire, they acclaimed her as her father's daughter, not as
Henry's wife.

Pride welled up within her, and a fierce love for this child she had so
longed for. To bear her first child at nearly forty was almost a miracle.
She looked down at him, at the thin fuzz of auburn hair. She could feel
the warmth of his little face pressed against her breast. Frederick of Sicily . . . She whispered his name, dizzy with happiness. Suddenly weakness engulfed her. She felt her knees buckle; everything around her
began to spin in a kaleidoscope of shapes and colors. She swayed, trying
to hold her balance. Her ladies rushed to support her, lifting the heavy
ceremonial mantle. Hands reached out and took the child from her.
Someone shouted for a litter.

Constance steadied herself on the balustrade. "Leave me," she said in
a shaky voice. Summoning the last of her strength, she squared her shoulders, shifting the weight of her cloak. Her head held high, one hand at her
throat, she left the loggia, followed by her retinue, with the little prince in
the arms of Matilde. Behind her, the bells of Jesi pealed in celebration.

THE CHAMBER IN the bishop's palace was dimly lit by oil lamps, the thick
crimson curtains drawn.

"Drink this, it'll warm you and make you sleep." Matilde held out a cup
of steaming wine.

Constance sat up and drank while Matilde plumped up the pillows behind her back. The hot, spicy wine warmed her cold and exhausted body. "Thank you." She smiled at her friend.

"I wish I could have spared you this dreadful journey," Matilde said. She brushed a strand of hair from Constance's forehead. "Henry's selfishness could have killed you, and the child, too."

Constance had to smile. It wasn't often that Matilde gave vent to her dislike of Henry. The fact that Matilde's husband held the duchy of Spoleto from Henry tended to curb her tongue. "Don't fret, it doesn't matter any more. The child is strong and I am alive, and we're going home to Palermo."

Matilde, folding garments and putting things away, didn't reply.

Constance watched her as she moved about the room amid open traveling chests, placing her rings, her crown, and the gold necklet with the enameled reliquary back into an ebony jewel coffer. Dear Matilde, so thoughtful, so loyal. She, too, was no longer young; she must be nearly fifty. Matilde's hair was streaked with gray, and her movements had lost the suppleness of youth. When they had first met, years ago in Germany, Matilde's hair had been the color of ripe corn. How glad she had been to have found a friend. A bitter smile twisted Constance's lips as she recalled her unhappiness when she arrived in Germany as Henry's wife. She hated the drafty castles and icy, long winters, so different from the sunny Sicily of her youth. She had longed to be back at her father's cosmopolitan court in Palermo, with its urbane Christian, Jewish and Muslim courtiers and scholars. The German barons, in contrast, were unlettered ruffians.

The only one who had been different was the old Emperor Frederick, Henry's father. Redheaded, red-bearded, imposing and jovial at the same time. The common people, who loved him, nicknamed him "Barbarossa" because of his flaming beard. How he used to make her laugh, telling outrageous stories in elegant Latin, and always treated her with courtesy and kindness. Partly, no doubt, because she would bring the Hohenstaufen the crown of Sicily, but also, she thought, because he genuinely liked her.

What would he have made of the manner in which his grandson had been born? Constance closed her eyes and felt herself again being jolted along in the hide-covered wagon in which she had travelled from Germany. She remembered her panic when she had felt the onset of birth pains, weeks early.

Thankfully, they had been close to Jesi, whose bishop had ridden out to welcome her. Constance remembered with amusement the consternation on the good bishop's face when she had refused the comforts of his palace and instead ordered her great tent to be erected in the marketplace. The heir to the Empire, she had told the bishop rather sharply, between deep breaths, as she anticipated the next wave of pains, must be born in public.

Her little son had reddish hair; would he resemble the old emperor? Or would he take after her husband? Henry was taciturn and brusque, lacking his father's charm. I have never loved him, Constance thought, I don't even like him much, but he has given me what I have always wanted: a child and an heir for Sicily. He has served his purpose.

And if her son were to take after her father? A smile curved her lips. That would be the greatest gift of all. Please, oh Lord, she pleaded, let him be a Hauteville king rather than a Hohenstaufen emperor. Keep him safe, far from the dangerous rivalries of German imperial politics. Many obstacles lay in the path of Henry's ambition to have their son elected as the next emperor. With the Lord's help, these might still prove insurmountable, even for Henry.

Constance yawned. The poppy juice in the wine was beginning to take effect; she felt tired, so tired.

"Matilde, I think I will sleep now."

Matilde came over. "I'll just go and look in on the little one, and then I'll come back and bed down here. Sleep well, dearest." She brushed Constance's cheek with her lips and walked to the door, closing it quietly behind her.

ROME, 1204

Berard of Castacca disliked Rome, its crowds, its decay, and the corruption of the papal court. The young, burly bishop of Bari was wet and irritable as he followed a wheezing chamberlain up worn steps to the pontiff's apartments. Torrential winter rains had been falling on Rome for three days. The streets, crowded and fetid at the best of times, were awash in mud and debris from overflowing sewers. He and his escort had been drenched when they reached the Lateran.

He did not relish the prospect of meeting the pope again. While he respected Innocent's principles and his much-needed reforms, there was a ruthlessness about him that disturbed Berard. The pope had only recently appointed him to the see of Bari; why had he summoned him now from the Adriatic, and in the worst traveling season?

The old chamberlain stood aside with a bow, letting Berard into the papal study. Although it was only early afternoon, tall wax candles lit the chamber, casting their shadows over the sumptuous wall hangings. In the fireplace at one end of the room, a slow-burning fire gave off a feeble warmth.

The pope, tall and gaunt in his purple robes, rose. "Ah, Berard, I see the air of Apulia agrees with you. I hear the people of Bari are pleased with their new shepherd."

Berard inclined his head. "The merit isn't mine, Holy Father, the Baresi are likeable. They fish and grow olives and their sins are small and few. It will be pleasant to grow old in the shadow of Saint Nicholas."

"I'm afraid that is not to be. I need you elsewhere." The Pontiff laid a hand on Berard's shoulder, "I have a new honor to confer upon you, my son. I am appointing you archbishop of Palermo. You will become the youngest archbishop in the Church."

Berard groaned inwardly. He had only just established himself in Bari, far from the intrigues of the curia. Becoming the youngest archbishop didn't tempt him a jot if it meant becoming embroiled in the Sicilian problem. After a moment's hesitation, he said, "Your Holiness, this is entirely unexpected. I . . . I don't know what to say."

"Don't say anything. I have restored some order on the island, but the situation there is still far from stable. Young Frederick is my ward. I need someone to watch over the interests of the boy and those of the Church. I need a man I can trust, who understands the Sicilians. Your family has old ties to the Norman nobility. During the king's minority, you will be part of the regency council. And your erudition . . ."

"Your Holiness, I'm not at all qualified. A young king needs a mentor with far more experience, an older, wiser . . ."

The pope waved his protest away. "Your exceptional erudition makes you eminently suitable to supervise the young king's education, which has been neglected."

Resistance was useless. Berard bowed. "I shall endeavor to justify the great trust you are placing in me, Holy Father."

The pontiff smiled. "Good. Cardinal Savelli, who has just returned from Palermo, where he has been legate, is expecting you in the chancery. You will leave for Palermo as soon as your successor arrives in Bari. Report directly to me, in monthly dispatches." Innocent extended his hand.

Berard kissed the fisherman's ring and turned to leave.

"And Berard . . ."

"Yes, Your Holiness?"

"See to it that Frederick's religious education is taken in hand, too." He fixed Berard with a hard look. "Too much toleration exists on that island. Saracens everywhere, even at the court itself. It will be your duty to protect the young king from their influence."

"I shall do so to the best of my ability, Your Holiness."

It was dark when Berard finally left the Lateran with his escort. In the torchlight, their horses threw ghostly shadows onto the deserted streets. Although the rain had stopped, a sulfurous mist engulfed the mansions on either side, pitted and pockmarked by age and neglect. Berard felt profoundly dejected. After his long meeting with Cardinal Savelli he relished the prickly honor Innocent had bestowed on him even less.

He would certainly take his cook; after what he had heard about conditions in Palermo, there was no telling to what depths the culinary standards there might have sunk.

THE SLEEK PAPAL galley forged through the waves, propelled by a strong northeasterly wind.

Berard stood on the heaving deck of the ship, one hand raised to shade his eyes from the glare, and watched the approaching landfall. For years now the Sicilian problem had been a major preoccupation of the papacy. The whole of southern Italy had been drawn into the conflict; Sicilian lords loyal to pope and king had been pitted against those who had sided with the German usurpers.

As he stood in the blowing wind, Berard reflected on the ill fortune that had dogged Sicily since the emperor's sudden death. Queen Constance assumed the regency, ruling with surprising ability for a woman.

One of the first acts of her reign had been to sever all connections with the Empire and expel her husband's German lords. But three years later she, too, died. On her deathbed, in a desperate attempt to protect her infant son, she made Sicily a papal fief and appointed the pope regent during Frederick's minority.

Despite this, after her death Sicily was invaded by German barons. One of them, once Henry's close adviser, claimed that he, not the pope, was the rightful regent according to the emperor's testament. The four-year-old king became their prisoner. They ruled with the aid of mercenaries and the complicity of many of the Norman-Sicilian nobility. The child survived because the usurpers needed him to justify their rule.

Pope Innocent had employed the time-honored weapons of the Church in his fight against the invaders: excommunication and negotiation. Finally, the last usurper was captured by the bishop of Catania, Walter of Palear. This powerful prelate, chancellor of Sicily already in the days of the Emperor Henry, had changed sides several times; now he held the reins of power again, ruling Sicily in the boy king's name.

Berard sighed. Walter of Palear was the only man capable of recovering the lands still held by rebels. He was certain to resent a papal legate looking over his shoulder. The ten-year-old Frederick himself might be a problem. According to Cardinal Savelli, the boy was headstrong and uncouth. He had been neglected, his education provided in a haphazard fashion by an elderly tutor. After first being imprisoned, Frederick was eventually allowed to do as he pleased. There were rumors that he had been allowed to run wild in the streets of Palermo, befriended by the common people. Berard could well imagine how he would take to being told that he must behave with the decorum required of a young king.

He would find out soon enough what his charge was like. The harbor of Palermo had come into view. The town was built around a crescent-shaped bay, its waters shimmering blue in the afternoon sun. Stately palm trees, church towers, and minarets stood outlined against the purplish background of the mountain chain embracing the town. The buildings of Palermo, like its inhabitants, were a medley of Byzantine, Arab, and Norman influences, blended together gracefully with brick and mortar and painted in every conceivable hue of yellow and red, from pale lemon to deep ocher and shell-pink to Roman terra cotta. On the outskirts, at the foothills of the mountains,

Palermo was fringed by lush orange and palm groves, emerald fields of young wheat, and orchards of peach and almond trees.

The only thing Berard found disturbing were the minarets. He didn't approve of converting Jews and Muslims at swordpoint, but it was a king's duty to promote Christianity. That the Normans were negligent in this respect was well known; the whole of Europe knew of the oriental tenor of life at the court of Palermo. King Roger, Frederick's maternal grandfather, had kept a harem of Saracen girls. He had also gathered about him great scholars, turning Palermo into a center of culture and learning. Perhaps the palace library is still intact, Berard thought with a stab of excitement, if the invaders haven't plundered it, too . . .

He felt more cheerful now that he had seen the town, even at a distance. The galley had slowed down. They'd soon be docking. With a last look at the bay, Berard went below. Inside their cabin, Berard's elderly chaplain was still lying fully dressed on the narrow berth. "Will we be landing soon?" he asked in a hopeful whisper.

"Shortly, Gregory. The men are already taking the luggage up. Come, let's get you up."

The chaplain, infused with new life at the prospect of dry land, straightened his gown. Tightening his belt around his sparse frame, he cast a pointed glance at Berard's windblown hair.

Berard passed a comb through his curly black hair and smoothed his beard. He picked up his cloak, a mantle of wine-colored camlet, and fastened it with a jeweled clasp. He fingered the uncut ruby set in its center. "This should impress them. Apparently the treasury is permanently short of money. The crown jewels are pawned to a Jewish moneylender, from whom they are redeemed for important ceremonies."

"I thought the wealth of the Normans was legendary."

"The Emperor Henry took most of it. The German freebooters stole the rest. And since there's no strong government, scarcely anyone pays taxes these days."

"Come, let's go on deck." He took Gregory by the arm. "Some fresh air will do you good. Once we meet the king, you can talk arithmetic to him. I'm told he's very keen on it." Berard found that he was looking forward to meeting young Frederick of Sicily.

* * *

FREDERICK SQUATTED BESIDE the old silversmith in the bazaar. He watched as the gnarled brown hands of his friend deftly hammered tiny squares of silver into leaf-shaped pendants for an anklet. The old man was sitting cross-legged on a dusty rug in front of a workbench.

"How long will it take you to finish it, Massoud?" Frederick asked in Arabic.

The silversmith smiled. "Soon, little king, soon. Then maybe a beautiful dancing girl will come and buy it, and I can go home, and my wives will give thanks to Allah." The old man sighed. "And maybe not. Times are hard, not like the old days. When your grandfather King Roger was alive, there were more than a hundred dancing girls in the palace alone. And they all bought expensive anklets and armlets and earrings and all sorts of baubles."

Frederick's eyes widened. He loved to hear the old man speak of the past.

Massoud said, "In those days even Christian churchmen had their own troupes of dancing girls. And they did more than just dance for their lords, I promise you!"

Frederick lost interest. He knew all about whores and dancing girls, everyone did. He also knew about venal priests. His attention drifted to the bustle around them. He loved the bazaar, its sounds, sights, and smells.

Massoud's shop was in the lane of the gold- and silversmiths. The vaulted roof was intersected at regular intervals by skylights through which the sunlight filtered into the lanes and alleys below. In summer it was pleasantly cool under the high vaults, and in winter the bazaar was sheltered from rain and wind. The open-fronted booths served both as shops and as workrooms. Frederick listened to the hum of the jostling, bargaining crowd. Itinerant water carriers, melon vendors, and sweetmeat sellers praised their wares to the passersby. Heavily burdened donkeys plodded behind their owners. From the lane of the spice vendors wafted the scents of cloves, cinnamon, and sandalwood, mingled with the pungency of pepper, cumin, cardamom, and saffron.

Suddenly, the crowd parted, making way for a group of people. With a start, Frederick recognized his tutor William and several palace guards. For an instant, he considered flight. Too late. "Massoud," he tugged at the old man's sleeve, "They're here again!"

The silversmith looked up. The group had halted near his booth. In their midst stood a stranger in a magenta cloak with a jeweled clasp. Massoud nudged Frederick. "Look at that ruby!" he whispered.

Frederick sighed. This was worse than he'd thought. This was definitely not the escort the palace normally sent to look for him.

William scurried forward. "Frederick, we've been looking all over for you." The old man's wispy white hair was even more disheveled than usual, his voice high-pitched with reproach. "His lordship, the new archbishop, has just arrived from Rome. When you were nowhere to be found, he insisted we search for you!"

Frederick got up with deliberate slowness. He stuck his chin out. "I'm old enough to go where I want. I'm the king and I'm not returning to the palace yet. Tell him," he nodded toward the bearded prelate, aware that he was close enough to hear every word, "I'll receive him later."

William was turning to the archbishop with an apology when the latter stepped forward with two large strides. With surprising grace for such a large man, he sketched an elegant bow before Frederick. "Your Grace, I am Berard of Castacca, the new archbishop of Palermo. Since you are not inclined to return to the palace, let us remain here. If you would care to show me around this bazaar, I would be delighted." He smiled broadly, "I've never been inside a bazaar before."

Frederick felt a flicker of remorse. This new archbishop did not seem as stuffy as the other churchmen who made his life a misery. At least, remaining here, he would be spared William's recriminations for a while. He tightened his belt. "If your lordship would follow me."

"Splendid," the archbishop said. "Perhaps we need not tire Master William with our little excursion. I'm sure he would prefer to return to the palace."

William departed with two of the men-at-arms, leaving the others to follow them.

At first, Frederick answered the archbishop's questions unenthusiastically. After a while, though, he warmed to his novel task as a guide to a stranger who seemed interested in everything and actually listened. The archbishop halted at a sweetmeat seller's. He pointed to a pyramid of pink translucent cubes: "Ah, *lukum.* Made from pomegranate juice. The Saracens in Apulia make it, too. And look! Almond pastries!" He asked the old woman, "Are they fresh, mother?"

"My son made them this morning. Here, my lord, try one."

The archbishop popped the white oval into his mouth. "Hm. Delicious. Give us a dozen each, in two parcels."

Frederick stared, mentally counting, as the archbishop fished coins out of his purse. No wonder such delicacies were never seen in the palace.

He handed him a parcel. "May I offer this to Your Grace?"

Frederick nodded. He quickly stuffed a sweet crumbly morsel into his mouth. It tasted of honey and rose water. He ate another and another.

As they ambled through the bazaar, it crossed Frederick's mind that the archbishop might have some hidden motive for his friendliness. He discarded the thought immediately. Everyone knew that he was unimportant, that the powerful one was Walter, the chancellor.

"Now LET's HAVE the names of each pope since Honorius II, and the high points of their reigns."

Frederick grimaced, "Ugh, popes!"

"A king must know his history," William said. "This will be the last question for today. Then you may run along."

"If I answer well, will you tell me the story of the Normans?"

"But you've heard it a thousand times. You can recite it by heart."

"Please, William. I love to hear you tell it."

William sighed. "If I have to . . ."

Frederick reeled off the facts. "Gregory VII, pope from 1073 to 1085. He humbled the Emperor Henry IV at Canossa, forbade clerical marriages and renewed the prohibition against lay investiture. Clement III, antipope from 1085 to 1100, was made pope by the emperor, in rivalry to Pope Victor III . . ."

As he listened, William's eyes wandered from the shade of the schoolroom to the sunshine outside. How he loved this tranquil spot. Even the dusty weeds and cracked tiles did not diminish its beauty. The small chamber in which they were sitting, tiled in brilliant blues and greens, opened onto a large courtyard. At one end, there was a circular fountain whose stone lions spewed water into a long pond covered with water lilies. Lemon and orange trees hedged with lavender reflected themselves in the water. Under the eaves, fat pigeons cooed to each other.

William's gaze returned to the boy, resting fondly upon his pupil. Frederick's shock of auburn hair was as unruly as always. He was as brown as a peasant, his nose freckled from too much sun. His blue-green eyes were almost too luminous for a boy, and his tunic was grubby. Frederick continued to prefer short tunics to the long ones the new archbishop had suggested.

Frederick, like most boys, had a lazy streak. The lives of the saints and Church history bored him. Because he hated practice, his penmanship was dreadful. Fortunately, he was interested in logic, astronomy, and mathematics. History, particularly that of the Caesars, brought a glow to his cheeks. Despite William's exhortations, Frederick never read his psalter, sneering that it was child's stuff. Worried about the boy's lack of devotion, William often reminded him that Queen Constance used to read her psalter every day, but even that did not help. Once, when he upbraided him for his truancy from Mass, the boy had snapped, "What's the point? God has forgotten me anyway."

William sighed. If only the queen were still alive. God knows, he'd done his best to teach him, but, unlike most of his fellow students at Bologna, he had not taken religious orders; he was not expert in theology. The new archbishop had appointed a chaplain for Frederick, an erudite young priest named Adalbert. He at least would be able to answer those disconcerting questions about dogma.

William halted his reverie. Frederick had completed his litany without a single mistake. He was looking at him expectantly, elbows on the table. The table was littered with wax tablets, styluses, books, and an abacus. Sheets of paper, a cheap newfangled invention of little solidity, lay about, covered with Frederick's scrawl.

"You promised me a story!" Frederick prodded.

William leaned back against his bench. "Aah, the Normans. They were the bravest, most unscrupulous daredevils ever to ride across the face of the earth. They had a thirst for power, for gold, and for women. And look what they've achieved," his liver-spotted hand swept the courtyard. He was half-Norman himself.

"The Normans were Vikings, or Norsemen, hence their name. For a long time, they raided the coasts of Europe and England, terrorizing the West. In their swift longboats they traveled even inland, up the rivers, pillaging, burning, and taking captives. As soundlessly as they had come, dark shadows in the night, they would be gone until the next raid. They were great flaxen-haired men who wore their hair streaming down their backs. Some of them, attracted by the mild climate and rich soil of France, began to covet land as well. A number of them settled on the northwestern coast of France. They took local wives, they renounced their gods and became Christians. Soon, they called themselves Normans. Normandy became a duchy under a Norman duke, the most famous of whom was William, who conquered England. At about the same time, in the little village of Hauteville lived a minor Norman baron named Tancred d'Hauteville. He owned the village and the mill, and commanded ten knights. He had twelve sons and three daughters born to him by two wives, but far too little land to share between them. He . . ."

"But how could such a glorious family come from a miserable hamlet?" Frederick chewed his lower lip.

"Always remember, my son," the tutor said, "no man is so noble that he doesn't have a humble ancestor. As I was telling you, Tancred d'Hauteville had this brood of ambitious sons without a patrimony. At that time, most of Apulia was held by Byzantium. The rest of southern Italy was controlled by the Lombards. They looked toward Apulia with covetous eyes."

"What about Sicily?"

"Patience, I'm coming to that," William said. "The Lombards were not strong enough to wrest Apulia from the Byzantines. They spread the word that they'd welcome foreign knights who were prepared to fight hard. In return, they would be given part of the conquered lands. When Tancred's sons heard this from some pilgrims returning from Palestine, they could hardly wait to buckle on their armor.

"Over a period of several years, all except two of Tancred's sons rode into Italy. They fought bravely, if not always honorably. They reaped their rewards. Some received manors; others owned strings of towns. All were outstanding fighters. Two were exceptional: the eldest, Robert, and the youngest, Roger. Within a short time Robert, with the help of his fellow Normans, had succeeded in ousting the Byzantines from Apulia. He then turned on the Lombards, proclaiming himself Duke of Apulia. Robert and his brother Roger now cast their eyes on Sicily.

"The island had long been ruled by Saracen emirs from North Africa who raided all along the Italian coast, even into Rome itself. The pope promised to reward the Hautevilles if they dislodged the infidels. And they did. The two brothers conquered Sicily. Roger became count of Sicily. His son, also called Roger, was crowned by the pope as the first Norman king of Sicily, joining the mainland and the island into one kingdom. And because he was your grandfather," William shook his head, "you can never sit still. It's the restless blood of your Viking ancestors!"

Frederick looked disappointed. "You forgot Sichelgaita."

The old tutor smiled. "Sichelgaita was an extraordinary girl. She was the sister of the prince of Salerno. She was beautiful and wild and unlike any other woman I've ever heard of. Robert married her, repudiating his Norman wife in favor of a more becoming alliance. But then he fell madly in love with her and she with him. Sichelgaita rode into battle beside him, long hair streaming, her lance poised in her right hand, the bloodcurdling Norman battle cry on her lips. She must have looked a little like you, and been just as stubborn," William said.

Wistfully he added, as if speaking to himself, "Once, long ago, when I was tutor to the lord of Ferrara's twin daughters, I knew a girl who was just like that: but she was destined to marry a prince . . ."

For a moment, William's deeply lined features appeared smoothed, a sparkle in his watery eyes. Then his eyes clouded over again and the glimmer of a long-lost youth vanished. He patted Frederick's head. "Run along now, my lad. I'm going to take my nap. Can I trust you not to slip out to your heathen friends while I doze under my palm tree? "

A look William knew only too well flashed into Frederick's eyes. "They're not heathen! They believe in God just as you do!"

William watched him walk away and sighed.

WALTER OF PALEAR flicked a speck of dust from his russet sleeve. "My lords," he said, surveying the council table, "this provocation will not go unpunished."

The members of the regency council began to talk all at once. The rebels' recent assassination of a royal bailiff after a period of relative calm had started a new round of aggression in this long war of attrition.

Although Berard had disliked Walter on sight, he could not help but admire his competence. He was arrogant, but his decisions were sound. Of the seven council members, three were abbots of large monasteries, one of them the octogenarian abbot of the great abbey of Monreale. The only member of Berard's age was Alaman da Costa, a Genoese *condottiere* in charge of the soldiery. With exception of the Genoese, appointed by the pope, they were all Walter's men, although the abbot of Monreale, when he roused himself, could speak his mind with great firmness. Now, as if in confirmation of Berard's thoughts, after a brief debate they all agreed with the chancellor.

"Well, what do *you* say, my lord of Castacca?" Walter's tone was acerbic. He had made it clear from the beginning that he viewed Berard as an irritation. He didn't hide his annoyance if he came across Berard in the chancery. Whenever Berard approached him on matters concerning Frederick, he was dismissive, almost curt. Walter was clearly not impressed by Frederick. His hands were full enough as it was, he had said, without having to play nursemaid too. The boy was always making trouble. Once he was of age, he would be taught to rule. In the meantime, William looked after him, and so could Berard, if he wished to.

"I think," Berard said into the sudden silence, "that we should stay our hand. Our first priority is to hold our parts of the island. We are short of men to protect Palermo and Syracuse. If we weaken our defenses to attack the rebels, we could jeopardize the lands we have already recovered."

Walter smiled thinly. "True, my lord, but you forget that it's not a major attack I'm planning. A swift raid to destroy the crops and burn a few villages. Homeless and hungry, the villeins will abandon their lords and join us. Gradually, the rebels' base will shrink."

"Innocent people will suffer."

"Such, my lord of Castacca, is the way of the world. I must re-establish the crown's authority. Yours is the only dissenting voice. My lord da Costa, I'll await you after vespers in the chancery."

The council chamber emptied. Berard found himself walking behind Walter's tall spindly figure. He walks fast for a man of his age, Berard thought, slowing down to avoid him.

"Ah, my dear Berard." Alaman clapped a hand on Berard's shoulder from behind. He grinned, jerking his head toward the vanishing russet cloak. "The uncrowned king . . ."

The swarthy Genoese fell in beside him. Large and affable, with appetites to match, he was, despite his braggadocio, a fine soldier. Berard invited him from time to time to sup with him. Alaman was good company and loved to gossip, although he stuffed himself with the delicacies produced by Berard's cook with a barbarian lack of appreciation for their excellence.

"I'm going to see Frederick," Berard said. "Would you like to join me?"

Alaman shrugged. "Why not? After all those old buzzards in there, the little scamp will be refreshing."

Berard sighed. "I think the boy's lonely. I try to see him whenever I can."

"You may be right, although with all his grubby Saracen friends, he can't be *that* lonely. Perhaps you should stir him toward more suitable playmates. Engage some noble young pages . . ." He spread his large hands. "I've no children, not even a wife, so I don't know much about such matters. . . . Old William seems to think he's quite clever."

Berard stepped into the courtyard, and squinted up at the sun. "It's too late for the schoolroom. He might be in the tiltyard at this time." As they turned a corner, they heard the boy's voice.

FREDERICK RUMMAGED IN the quiver until he found an arrow less squashed than the others. He smoothed the feathers and fitted the arrow. His brow was furrowed in concentration. He readjusted his feet several times, making sure they were in line with the target, before drawing the bowstring. The arrow hit the straw man in the middle of his chest. The target already bristled with arrows. A few lay on the ground.

Berard and Alaman stood on the parapet above the tiltyard, watching. Alaman nodded as another arrow found its mark. "Not bad, not bad at all." He laid a hand on Berard's arm, "I think I'll leave you. I must prepare our

little excursion to the rebels. Walter will want to know every detail . . .
Greet the scamp for me."

"WELL DONE, FREDERICK," Berard called, coming down the steps, "You're
becoming a great marksman!"

Frederick looked up. He shook his head. "You don't understand, Your
Grace. In real life they move. I'll never be able to kill them fast enough
when they're running and ducking all over. The other day, I tried it on a
hare, and I lost four arrows and the hare!"

Berard suppressed a smile. "I assure you, I fully understand." He
stretched out his hand. "Give me the bow."

Berard took aim, bending to adjust to the target. His arrow lodged
within a hair's breadth of Frederick's last shot.

Frederick's eyes widened. "By the beard of the Prophet! I thought
priests were all useless." He crimsoned. "I . . . I am sorry, Your Grace, I
didn't mean to . . ." He stared at his sandals.

"It's all right." Berard ruffled his hair, "But you'll have to improve your
manners, Frederick. Not for my sake, but for your own. If you want your
people to obey and respect you, you must cultivate the manners of a king.
And as for a Christian king swearing by a Muslim prophet, I am sure you
yourself can see the unsuitability of that."

Frederick bit his lower lip. "Yes, Your Grace. But I'm also their king, and
they are my people, too, you do understand that, don't you?"

"Yes, Frederick, I do." Berard sighed. It was true. After three months in
Palermo, Berard was beginning to find it impossible to reconcile reality with
Innocent's order to keep the boy from infidel influences. They were every-
where, they were part of the island, they were part of Frederick's heritage.

He took Frederick by the shoulder. "Come," he said, "I'm sure you've had
enough practice for today." He glanced at the head falconer, who doubled as
tilt master. "I'm taking the king for a walk, Fakir."

The old Saracen salaamed. "I shall wait here, my lord."

Frederick walked beside him. After a moment, he said, "I'm sorry I was
rude. But why did you become a priest? Couldn't you have been a knight?"

Berard smiled. "It's a long story, my son. My father was a Lombard
nobleman. He had three sons, but only one title. My eldest brother

inherited that, my second brother died on crusade, and I was destined for the Church. My father bought me a rich living that would enhance the prestige of our family. When I was eight, I was sent to study with the monks."

"And the monks taught you archery? What else did they teach you? Can you joust and hawk and swim?"

Berard shook his head, laughing. "No, the monks didn't teach me any of that. My father's falconers taught me to hawk. My middle brother was a knight. In fact, he was quite famous. He used to win tournaments and much gold, as far afield as France. It was he who taught me archery. I never took to the sword, though. The clang of steel on steel has always sounded barbarous to my ears. And as for swimming, water terrifies me." He patted his stomach, "In any case, with my girth, I'd sink like a stone."

"What was your mother like?" Frederick asked, his voice suddenly tight.

Berard shot him a sympathetic glance. "She was a Norman, like your mother, a gentle lady. She was pleased when I entered the Church. She used to say that although the Church isn't perfect, it is far better than the temporal world. At first I was very unhappy, but I realized later that she had been right. She died when I was eleven. In the end, the Church became my mother."

Frederick nodded. They ambled along the dusty paths of the gardens, past mossy old fountains and empty water channels. Ancient gardeners as withered as the gardens they tended were sweeping the paths. As they passed the rose garden, Berard halted. The bushes were straggly from neglect, the few blooms small and deformed.

"Did you know," he said, pointing to the grid of rose beds, "that your grandfather had these roses brought from Persia?"

"Alexander's Persia?"

"Yes."

Frederick's eyes lit up. "When I'm grown up, I'll be a new Alexander. I'll have the remaining Germans all thrown into the sea, in great sacks with stones and a viper apiece!"

Berard's eyes widened, "But you're half German yourself."

Frederick scowled. "No, I'm not." He drew himself up. "I'm the son of Queen Constance, and the grandson of Roger the Great. When I'm big, I'll be like him. There'll be peace and all my people will have enough to eat.

I'll have dancing girls, and mews full of Ger falcons and wise Saracen friends to help me rule."

Berard nodded. He'd been told by William that Frederick never spoke about his father or his German heritage, of which he knew virtually nothing.

"Hm. And what about the Christians at your court?"

Frederick broke off a laurel twig and began to chew it. "Oh, they'll be allowed to stay, but not Walter or some of the others." He cocked his head at Berard. "*You* can stay. You *will* stay, won't you?"

"For a while, yes, Frederick. But I must go where Pope Innocent tells me to go."

"But when I'm of age, and rule, I could order you to remain here, couldn't I?"

"If you'd appointed me, yes. But I've been appointed by the pope. You see, it's complicated, and I'll explain it to you one day, but both the pope and the king can appoint bishops."

Frederick nodded. "That's easy. I'll just reappoint you, and then you'll be my archbishop."

"All the same, I may have to leave one day," Berard said gently, "I may not be able to be your archbishop."

THE SUN BURNED down on the harbor. A smell of caulking tar and fish hung in the air. Seagulls cawed and dived, squabbling over the entrails being thrown into the sea by the fishermen gutting the night's catch.

The two boys dangled their bare feet over the old Saracen jetty. Frederick picked up a pebble. He grimaced as it hit the water. He searched behind him, found a flatter one. This time he swung his arm as far back as he could. The stone flew through the air, hitting the inky water at the far end of the harbor, beside the sea wall, where it was deepest.

One of the fishermen let out an approving whistle. Frederick grinned. "I could do better, Omar, but this son of a mule here won't let me stand up. Says I spoil the fish he never catches anyway."

The younger boy jerked his line out of the water. He glared at Frederick. "I'll never catch anything because you can't sit still. Even fish have eyes." He wound the string carefully around his cane and picked up his empty basket. "Let's go to my home."

Frederick narrowed his eyes. Who did Mahmoud think he was, to give him orders? Then he shrugged. It wasn't worth a fight. Moreover, Fatima might have baked bread. She often did, Mahmoud's aunt, the day before Fridays. Saliva shot into his mouth as he thought of hot bread.

As they passed the squatting men, slicing open the fish with deft movements, Mahmoud cast a longing look at the baskets full of shimmering, scaly silver, soon to be strung and dried. Frederick gave one of the fishermen his widest smile, "Venerable father of Ali, couldn't you spare just one of those for my poor friend?"

The gray-bearded fisherman laughed, "You're the king of beggars, Frederick, worse than all the beggars of Palermo together. Here," he reached into a pannier, took a handful of sardines and flung them into Mahmoud's basket.

Frederick inclined his head. He swallowed, "We thank you, father of Ali."

They walked in silence, keeping to the shade along the mosque's enclosure. From the other side of the faded crimson wall came the scent of orange blossoms. They could hear boys' voices reciting the Koran. Frederick watched his feet push up little puffs of ocher dust, coating his toes. He was afraid to raise his eyes, to wipe them, afraid Mahmoud would notice. The king of beggars . . . The old fisherman, who was his friend, had meant no harm, yet he could still feel the fierce ache inside him, where the words had found their mark.

"LITTLE FALCON!" FATIMA'S muscular arms closed around Frederick. His face sank into the yielding vastness of her bosom. The comforting, familiar smell of female sweat and old, smoke-soaked clothes filled his nostrils. Female sweat was different, sweeter. For a moment he could hear the rhythmic slapping of wet cloth on stone in the laundry yard, the women's chatter, remembering the days when Fatima had worked in the palace laundry.

"Let me look at you, little Falcon." Fatima rested her arms on her hips, a large ugly woman with tender eyes and a hairy upper lip. "You're still too thin. I'm sure this new archbishop pockets most of the money for your food, just as the old one did."

Mahmoud proffered the basket. "For you, Aunt."

"Allah bless you. I will fry them nice and crisp. There's no more salt till Uncle gets his wages, but there's fresh bread."

Frederick glanced at the flat round loaves in a basket on the table. He could *smell* their warmth. Fatima must have just returned from the public ovens. He said, "I like him. He sometimes invites me to eat with him. Some of the food's awfully fancy and William goes on and on about manners, but the sweetmeats, Fatima . . ." He rolled his eyes to the ceiling.

The mustache twitched doubtfully. "Hm." She sliced pockets into two loaves, filled them with vegetable stew, and handed them to the boys. "Here, eat."

Frederick bit into the soft bread. The tasty gravy of stewed cucumber, garlic, and chickpeas ran down his chin.

It was cool and dim inside Mahmoud's home. Mahmoud was an orphan; he lived with his uncle and aunt. The muezzin's quarters were two cramped rooms inside the mosque's archway. Although there was only a single tiny barred window, from it, if one stood on tiptoe, one overlooked the great courtyard with its orange trees, water channels, and alabaster fountain.

Fatima took a dented cooking pot and the basket of sardines. "I'll go to the cookhouse and fry these before they spoil in this heat." To Mahmoud she said, "Will you lead your uncle up at noon?" Five times a day, Fatima led her blind husband, who was much older than she, up the spiral staircase inside the minaret. She was his only wife. Although Fatima never bore him a child, the muezzin had been too poor to take a second wife. He was a kindly man, who had allowed Fatima to take her sister's son into their home. He treated Mahmoud as if he were his own child.

They followed her outside. Frederick glanced at the sundial over the gateway. It was nearly midday. He jerked his head at Mahmoud. "You had better wake him. It's almost time for prayer."

Mahmoud nodded. He made as if to go, then halted. "Thanks. For the fish. And for not telling."

Frederick shrugged. "It is nothing. One day, when I am really king, you'll have an honored post in the palace." He turned, "I'm going inside."

Frederick crossed the courtyard. He washed his face, hands, and feet in the ablution fountain. The mosque's interior was cool, a vast expanse of

serene emptiness, its wooden roof upheld on a forest of graceful mis-
matched marble pillars. In a corner beside the *mihrab,* surrounded by cross-
legged boys, sat a man with a straggly orange beard.

Frederick placed his hand on his heart. "*Salaam aleikum,* great teacher."

Ibn el Gawazi glanced up, then inclined the emerald turban that proclaimed him a hajji. "*Aleikum es salaam,* O King." He smiled, "I am glad you
have not forgotten your old friends, but you will be unpopular with Master William. You know he . . ."

"Allah is great! There is no god but Allah, and Mohamed is his prophet!"
A splendid voice flowed from the courtyard through the open archways.
"Come hither to prayer! Come hither to salvation!" Four times the muezzin repeated his summons. Frederick imagined the frail old man in his
long, ash-colored tunic, facing in turn east, west, north, and south. Christians rang bells, Jews blew a trumpet, and the Muslims employed a human
voice to call their people to prayer. How similar they were, Frederick
thought, biting his thumb, as the imam took up his position before the
mihrab.

Frederick watched Ibn el Gawazi and his pupils turn toward Mecca.
They prayed, now touching their foreheads to the floor, now standing or
kneeling, following the imam's lead. He would have liked to pray too, but
he could not. They were his friends, but he wasn't part of them. He did
not belong in the palace chapel with its mosaics and wilting lilies, its interminable harangues about sin, its priests who knew everything. Ibn el
Gawazi, a far greater scholar than those Christian priests, often and
unashamedly confessed his ignorance.

After the prayers, Ibn el Gawazi dismissed the other boys. "Come," he
said, smoothing his hennaed beard, "Walk with me to my house. Do you
still remember the Five Pillars of Islam?"

Frederick straightened his shoulders. "Of course, great teacher. The
shahadah, or profession of faith. The five daily prayers. The annual *zakat.*
Fasting during Ramadan, and for those who are able to do so, the Hadj to
Mecca."

"When is a man exempt from some or all of his daily prayers?"

"If he is ill, on a journey, or at war."

"Apart from abstaining from food and drink, what else must a man not
do between sunrise and sunset during Ramadan?"

"Lie with his wives."

"What about the *zakat*? Is it also levied on a man's house?"

Frederick's mind raced. Grains and fruit, camels, goats and horses, gold and silver, those he was sure about. But a house? He couldn't remember. It had been a long time since he had sat with the other boys in the mosque. Now he had to spend most of his days in the palace. Was it just to tax a man's home? He decided to take a chance. "No," he said. "Only movable property." He searched Ibn el Gawazi's profile. Had he noticed?

The Saracen gave a small smile. "As king, when would you use *zakat* to conciliate those of wavering loyalty, and when would you send them to the executioner?"

Frederick stopped. "If they didn't obey me I'd have their heads cut off. I'd never buy loyalty with gold."

Ibn el Gawazi's dark eyes held his: "There are times, young king, when the headsman's ax is the only remedy. But there are other times when it is necessary to appease your foes, even if your pride suffers. The only thing that matters is the final result. Remember the double truth. If the danger is great enough, it is permissible for the strongest man to unwind his pride like a turban and cast it off."

Frederick nodded. He understood, yet how he longed to punish those who had made him suffer. As if in a far-off dream, he heard again the sound of splitting wood as the German invaders burst into the tower by the sea where William and a few loyal courtiers had fled with him, hoping to escape by boat. He felt himself a child of five, being flung over the shoulder of a flaxen-haired giant. He remembered kicking and beating his fists on the man's back, howling to set him down, screaming that they had no right to touch him, that he was the king. The soldiers' mocking laughter rang in his ears.

They walked through the empty streets of the Muslim quarter in the searing midday sun. Frederick, lost in his thoughts, started when they reached the blue door in the white wall. They entered the scholar's small garden. A fountain bubbled beside the garden's only tree, a gnarled pomegranate. In its shade stood a bench, its tiles worn and cracked. A pebble path led to the house, whose peeling paint proclaimed its owner's poverty. Although Ibn el Gawazi's fame reached as far as Cordova, Cairo, and Baghdad, he eked out a living by teaching the sons of wealthy Saracens and by writing treatises on logic, rhetoric, and dialectic. He taught the poor boys of the Muslim quarter for free. His family—once court physicians and astronomers—were impoverished now.

Frederick halted on the threshold. He looked up at the scholar: "I'm going to tell the archbishop that I wish you to come to the palace and teach me. You will be well rewarded."

Ibn el Gawazi smiled. "And do you think he will permit it?"

"Yes. He's not like William. I will tell him that you can teach me to talk my enemies into becoming my friends."

The Saracen laughed. "I think Allah has taught you that already."

PALERMO, JUNE 1208

The two figures bent over the chessboard in the shady gallery above the palace gardens were engrossed in their game. In the stillness of the afternoon, the only sound was the cool splashing of water from a nearby fountain.

"Check," said Frederick, moving his ivory rook.

William, seated across from him, let out an oath. "Well done, Frederick, you've put my king in a nice little predicament here."

"If only I could do that to others as easily, and not on a chessboard, either."

William, taking no offense, nodded in sympathy before concentrating on the game again.

Waiting for William to make his move, Frederick's eyes wandered to the streets below. Palermo was deserted at this hour. The carved fretwork shutters of the flat-roofed houses were closed against the assault of the sun. The town was dozing in a heat-induced torpor, awaiting the evening to resume its bustle until the small hours.

Frederick hated these soporific afternoons. As soon as he came of age, he'd change everything, bring order into the chaos that was Sicily. The treasury was bankrupt, the officials corrupt, the barons untamed. Even Berard, who thought that most of his other plans were futile dreams, agreed with him on this. If only time would pass more quickly . . .

The thud of a chess piece brought Frederick back from his reverie. "Right, William, let's see your defense." He stared at the board for a moment. "Hm, I think I've found a way to get at you."

William threw up his hands in mock despair. "I'm about to be defeated by the greatest tactician since Julius Caesar."

"I wish I had just a fraction of his legions. The men I could muster would've made Caesar roar with laughter."

Frederick moved his queen. "Between the chancellor, who treats me like a child, and the rebel barons in their mountain aeries, they've got me wedged between Scylla and Charybdis."

A deep voice said from the doorway, "That may not be so for much longer."

Frederick glanced up to see Berard striding toward them. "You're back!" He leapt up. "We'll finish this game tomorrow, William." He patted his tutor on the shoulder before turning to embrace Berard.

Berard put an arm around him, steering him towards the gardens. "I have some wonderful news from Rome." Berard's brown eyes shone. "Let's go outside, where the walls have no ears." Although William could be trusted, there were spies everywhere.

As they walked down the steps, Frederick said, "It's good to see that at least someone moves about at this hour. Not a soul stirs in the palace till vespers. Even William would much rather doze under a palm tree than play chess with me. When I'm fifteen, I'll move the court to the mainland you've told me about, where the air is dry and fanned by a breeze. Where . . ."

Berard grinned. "I know. All the things you'll do when you come of age. The Lord have mercy on us. None of us will be safe, and it's only another year."

"How was Rome?"

"Crowded. Dirty. Filled with scheming cardinals. We docked at noon. Knowing that you'd be about, I came straight here." He drew a parchment, sealed with the keys of Saint Peter, from his pocket. "Here, read this. This time, the Holy Father has answered our prayers."

"Ha," sneered Frederick. "He's allowed the barons to mock his authority for years, and as for what he's permitted them to do to me and my kingdom . . ."

Berard sighed. "You know that the only weapon at Innocent's disposal has been negotiation, and with it, in the end, he's achieved considerable success."

"Yes, I know," Frederick said, kicking a pebble out of the path, "but it doesn't change the fact that the pope always sees to the interests of the Church first."

"Read the letter."

Frederick scanned the letter, then handed it back to Berard. "I've told you I won't marry her. I'll have none of his pet project. I don't want a wife, and certainly not one as old as this one. I don't care if the pope has squeezed a better dowry out of her brother." Frederick grimaced, mimicking revulsion. "Berard, how could you? You're supposed to be my friend. It wouldn't even do the dynasty any good. I'd never be able to breed heirs on her. Imagine bedding a wife as old as this. Ugh." He shook himself like a wet dog.

"You did not finish reading, or you would have changed your mind. In addition to the original dowry, the king of Aragon has agreed to give his sister five hundred Aragonese knights, armored, each with a squire and three horses."

"What?" Frederick grabbed the letter. Excitement gripped him. Thoughts raced in his mind. With five hundred well-equipped knights, he could reestablish control over his country. He read on in feverish haste. After he finished, he leaped into the air with a triumphant shout, waving the parchment like the banner of his new host. Grabbing the beaming Berard by the arm, he whirled him around in a wild jig.

"Enough, Frederick, enough!" Berard's flat black hat fell off and rolled into a flower bed. He retrieved it from among the lilies. Placing it carefully back on his head, he smiled: "I told you it was good news. May I write to the pope, conveying your acceptance?"

Frederick laid a hand on Berard's arm. "I know how hard you must have worked in Rome to bring this about. No, don't interrupt me," he raised his hand. "I know you're going to say it was all the pope's doing, but although I'm young there is one thing I know: no pope will ever be as true a friend to me as you. I shall not forget it."

Berard stood still. He stared at him as if he had never seen him before. Then, slowly, he went down on one knee. Taking hold of Frederick's hem, he brought it to his lips, bowing his head. "My liege," he murmured, "may God grant you success and wisdom."

Tears shot into Frederick's eyes. It was the first time that anyone, without an ulterior motive, had paid homage to him. As he looked down on Berard's bowed head, he felt himself imbued with new confidence. The fears and doubts of the past vanished. He knew, in that moment, that he would succeed. He would rebuild his kingdom and safeguard his people. Yet he knew that it wasn't the Aragonese dowry that had caused this sudden certainty. It was something else: God had finally remembered him.

He raised Berard to his feet. For a moment he looked into the archbishop's brown eyes. He saw love there, and respect. He kissed him on both cheeks, not caring that the other should see the tears in his eyes.

Together, in silence, they climbed the marble steps to the loggia. Behind them, the westering sun set the horizon ablaze in splendor.

THE NEGOTIATIONS DRAGGED on all through the autumn and winter of that year. Envoys traveled back and forth between Palermo, Rome, and Saragossa. Finally, at the beginning of the new year, Frederick signed the marriage contract. Frederick, who had come of age in December, was now ruler of Sicily. The pope had relinquished his regency, although the kingdom remained a vassal state of the papacy.

The Sicilian nobles, realizing that their indigent boy-king had turned into a man, allied to the powerful kingdom of Aragon, reconsidered their position. Invitations to the wedding festivities had been sent to many of the barons. Most decided to accept the proffered olive branch.

"IT'S ABSURD. AND irresponsible." Walter's voice was trenchant. "To spend so much gold on a wedding when the exchequer is up to here in debt!" The chancellor reached to his neck. He fixed on Frederick. "You, my boy, had better learn the first lesson of governance, and learn it fast: husband your resources. Without thrift, the wealthiest kingdom will bankrupt itself. And Sicily is far from rich."

Frederick glared at Walter, "I didn't ask your advice. I was merely informing the council." He narrowed his eyes, "And don't you ever address me like that again."

The chancellor's face muscles twitched. He picked up his hat, turned, and stalked out of the chamber. Silence fell on the chamber. The councilors glanced at one another.

They've been waiting for this, Frederick thought. And they're waiting to see how I'll react. He sat down. With all the calm he could muster, he said: "My lords, precisely because I am aware of the precariousness of our position, I intend to dazzle the barons with the lavishness of the celebrations. This is not profligacy but an investment in the future." He added pointedly, "My lords, you have my leave to go."

The councilors bowed and shuffled out of the chamber. Only Berard and Cardinal Savelli, the papal legate, remained. Berard whispered to the white-haired cardinal. The other nodded. They approached Frederick, who was furiously pulling on his gloves.

The cardinal spoke: "A word with you, please."

"Arrogant old vulture!" Frederick exploded. "I'll teach him to insult me. My grandfather would've had his head for this!"

"Not so loud, Frederick," Berard pulled him into the window niche. "You still need him. None of us has his experience."

Cardinal Savelli nodded. "Do not offend him too openly, Your Grace, it would not be wise."

They're right, Frederick thought. He couldn't do without Walter. Not yet. Not for a while. He felt as if he were choking. Taking a deep breath, he said, "Tell him to apologize. I'll make a show of forgiving him, but I won't forget."

He glanced at the pope's ambassador, the white-haired, rubicund Cardinal Savelli. The second churchman he'd ever liked. "Thank you for your concern. That, too, I shall not forget."

THE ORANGE SILK curtains stirred in the evening breeze. Frederick put the book down; it was futile to continue straining his eyes in the twilight. His attention had been straying from the text anyway. Instead of concentrating on the book, his mind had been wandering to the wedding.

When he thought of his bride his mouth curled down. Of all the nuisances he had to contend with, this was no doubt the most infernal. It was a king's lot to marry for the good of his country, but it still irked him. The Aragonese fleet bearing the five hundred knights and the future queen of Sicily was expected any day. Frenzied preparations were in progress. Wherever one set foot, tapestries were being hung and furniture moved about. Servants staggered past with piles of linen, bundles of candles, chests, trestles, and panniers full of God knew what. Musicians, dancers, and acrobats practiced all day long amid disjointed snatches of music. The whole fuss grated on Frederick's nerves.

He rose and went over to the perch in the corner. At her master's approach, the peregrine, tethered to her perch, stretched her neck out. Stroking the soft brown plumage Frederick marveled, for the hundredth time, at the intelligence in those jet-black eyes whose sight was so superior to that of man. The bird had been a New Year's gift from Berard. Because she was far more docile than his other falcons, he kept her in his apartments and even took her, sitting on his fist, to the interminable church services he was forced to attend now.

"You want to go hunting, my beauty, don't you?" he murmured, caressing her. "So do I, but we must both be patient. When all this to-do is over we'll go hunting, and you can show me how clever you are." Pressing his cheek close to the small head and the mighty beak, he inhaled the clean, furry smell of her feathers; it gave him comfort.

A movement behind him made him wheel around. A servant girl carrying a burning taper had padded on bare feet into the chamber and was lighting the lamps. Seeing the relief on his face as he recognized her, she smiled. "Did my lord think an assassin had crept into his chamber?"

Despite her impudence he couldn't help noticing that her teeth were magnificent, gleaming white in the dark oval of her face. She was one of the new Saracen servants who had been hired for the arrival of the Aragonese, and uncommonly pretty.

It annoyed him that she had surprised him petting the falcon. He sat down behind the table and pretended to busy himself with the writing implements. But while his hands toyed with inkhorn and quills, his eyes followed her. As she went about the room, trimming the wicks with a little pair of bronze scissors before lighting oil lamps and candles, her bangles tinkled softly. Unbidden, the memory of his only experience with a girl came back. Color rose in his cheeks. The hasty coupling with a dancing girl provided by Fakir, his head falconer, had been followed by acute embarrassment. Whenever they went hunting, he had to endure Fakir's banter. The old falconer, who had taught him to hawk since Frederick could barely sit a horse, felt entitled to such familiarity. According to Fakir, Frederick was surrounded by old Christian priests, who were thus doubly disqualified from understanding the needs of a virile young man. A king needed a harem.

Afraid the whole of Palermo might hear about his inexperience, he had since declined Fakir's offers to provide him with further "target practice," as the Saracen termed it. Now, however, Frederick found that all he could think of was the girl. She was much prettier than the other one had been. He wanted to reach out and touch her.

The girl slowed her movements. When she reached the desk, she raised her dark liquid eyes to him. Then she bent over the lamp, slowly lighting the little wicks on the bronze tiers. She was so close to him that he could smell her. Her scent was a mix of wood smoke, sweat, and female that made him dizzy.

"What is your name?" he asked, trying to sound casual.

"Leila, my lord." The softness of her voice robbed the guttural Arabic syllables of their harshness.

Frederick rose and stretched out a hand. "Come here," he whispered in her language. She hesitated. Then, taking a deep breath, she blew out her taper and came toward him.

He encircled her waist with his hands, pulling her to him. Standing on tiptoe, she offered him her lips. He kissed her, slowly at first, then more urgently, holding her against him with an iron grip, as if the strength of his embrace could assuage the fierce ache within him. His lips wandered down, following the line of her throat. His fingers fumbled with the tiny brass buttons on her blouse.

Leila disentangled herself. "Come, my lord," she whispered, taking him by the hand and leading him to the canopied bed in the corner.

As they lay together afterward, he raised himself on one elbow to look at her. Softly tracing the contours of her body, still damp from the sweat of their bodies, with his index finger, he admired the pliant roundness of her flesh, so different from his own hard muscular form. The girl, obviously unsure whether to linger or leave, looked up at him. "Did I please my lord?"

He nodded. His wandering finger was exploring the silken skin on the inside of her thighs, had found the warm, yielding moistness within her. He began tentatively to stroke her. She moaned with pleasure. Encouraged, Frederick continued his rhythmical stroking. Her eyes were closed now and her breath was coming faster; suddenly her body convulsed, then slackened. She gave him a radiant smile. Frederick realized what he had witnessed. So women could be pleasured like this, too.

Leila giggled, pointing. He burst into laughter. "Oh, the royal scepter has risen again." He took her hand and clasped it around himself. As her hand moved steadily, her long hair brushing across his chest in a soft caress, Frederick fell back on the bolster, abandoning himself to her.

When later, drowsy and drained, he lay beside her, he was filled with surprise. How much pleasure men and women could give each other. And it needn't be hasty or furtive. Yet, according to the Church, he had just committed the sin of fornication. Perhaps Fakir had hit on a truth when he said that the old men who ruled the Christian Church were so far removed from real life that their teachings did not reflect God's will but their own ignorance.

A FLOTILLA OF galleys was anchored in the bay of Palermo. In the bright morning sunshine the red and gold arms of Aragon fluttered from their riggings. The biggest of the vessels had just docked and its gangplank was being let down.

Frederick, standing on the quay, scanned the crowded forecastle. A group of lords and ladies under the main awning was coming down the gangplank, led by a dark handsome man with an arrogantly beaked nose.

"That must be the other brother, the Count of Provence," whispered Berard, stepping forward with Frederick and Walter to greet them.

Walter, after introducing the count to Frederick, launched into a mellifluous speech of welcome. While listening absently to Walter's elegant Latin, Frederick's eyes were drawn to the count's splendid scabbard. He tried not to stare at the rubies and amethysts and pearls.

Count Alfonso said, "My lord Frederick, may I present my sister Constance?" A cloud of pale blue silk curtsied before him. Through the veil on her bent head he could see that her hair was a rich hue of gold.

Mechanically, he extended a hand to raise her. With slender fingers she lifted her veil and smiled at him.

Frederick looked into luminous gray eyes fringed by dark lashes. Her face, although somewhat long, was unlined, with a straight, aristocratic nose and a warm, generous mouth, showing a row of perfect white teeth. Not only isn't she old, she's lovely, Frederick thought, astonished. He managed to say, "My lady Constance, I welcome you to Sicily."

"I am pleased to be here, my lord." Constance stretched out her hand. She broadened her smile, and Frederick realized with alarm that he was meant to kiss her hand. As he did so, he was aware of his clumsiness. He had never kissed a lady's hand before. Constance gave him another smile, squeezing his hand almost imperceptibly before lowering her veil. She's an angel, he thought, his heart thumping.

The grooms pushed their way through the crowd, bringing the horses. They mounted and began a slow progress through the crowded streets toward the palace. Frederick felt light-headed, as if he had drunk too much unwatered wine. Clearly, his bride was a great success. Berard had given him an approving wink. Even Walter wore something resembling a smile.

Riding at the head of the party beside her brother, Frederick pointed out the sights of Palermo to him. The count kept on asking prying questions that would have irritated Frederick at any other time. But now he patiently answered, smiling. Yet, despite his excitement, he kept on glancing back at the ships in bay. When would he see the five hundred knights and the gold?

ALFONSO WAS BEGINNING to lose patience. He drummed his fingers on the ledge of the huge fireplace he was leaning against. Women! Sweet Jesus, they could be so maddening, yet without them life would be terribly dull.

He'd followed his sister to her apartments as soon as the banquet had come to an end. It was their first opportunity to be alone since they'd arrived in Palermo, and he wanted to talk to Constance. Now, instead of dismissing her servants, she was giving them lengthy instructions on the unpacking of her traveling chests.

Alfonso selected a peach from a platter piled with fruit and settled down to wait, observing his sister. Constance, clad only in a linen shift, was sitting at a table littered with the paraphernalia of female adornment. Without her brocaded gown and her jewels, she looked very vulnerable. He felt a pang of protective love. The poor girl had suffered so much. Becoming queen of Hungary had brought her nothing but misery. He remembered how for months after her return to Aragon she'd suffered horrendous nightmares that even the most learned doctors were unable to prevent. Night after night she'd relive her husband's and her little son's murder, her escape from the nunnery into which her husband's brother had forced her, and her flight across Hungary.

At last, the women curtsied. Alfonso waited for the door to close before asking, in a tone designed to play down the weightiness of the question: "What do you make of him?" He'd been wanting to ask this all day, since he'd first set eyes on Frederick. Beneath the awkward boyish charm he'd sensed a will of steel, like that of a prized Toledo blade. He found the young man unsettling. This was not the docile ward of the pope he had been led to expect.

Constance took out the last pin from her hair, letting it tumble down her back. She looked up at him. "I don't know," she said. "There's something appealing about him. He's certainly far more mature than an ordinary youth of fifteen." She thought for a moment. "But he's also much less civilized." She picked up a comb and passed it through her hair. "Did you see the way he eats? He wipes his hands on the tablecloth and throws bones to that dreadful dirty Alaunt."

Alfonso laughed. If these were her only objections, then all was well. "Well, he may not be the paragon of virtues the Holy Father made him out to be, but at least he doesn't belch. What can you expect of a boy who has grown up surrounded entirely by men? I am told that he spends his days in the chancery or hawking, and reads Roman history half the night."

He placed the peach pip on a pewter plate, careful not to soil his fingers. "I'm sure that like a thoroughbred, his blood will tell with some training. All he needs is some feminine influence to refine him a little." He laid a hand on her shoulder. "You'll do that in no time at all."

"It may not be so easy; I've been told by the archbishop, who is obviously fond of him, that he's as stubborn as a mule. If even his friends say that about him . . ."

"Did the archbishop say that?"

"Well, not exactly. He said that I should be patient with him, as he is a bit headstrong."

"That," Alfonso agreed, "is a tactful way of saying that dear Frederick is used to having his own way. Nevertheless, I am convinced that your gentle persuasion will work wonders."

"Do you think he'll grow to like me, even though I am so much older than he is?"

"Judging by the way he looks at you already, I would say that he'll be besotted before the week is out."

Amused at the thought of a fumbling youth smitten by his elegant sister, Alfonso went over to the open window, left unshuttered to allow the cool of the night to enter. The bay of Palermo shimmered in the moonlight like a sheet of beaten silver. "Look at this view," he called over his shoulder.

Joining him, his sister gazed into the night. The air was fragrant with jasmine. Torchlights flamed on street corners and flat rooftops, where people sat and enjoyed the cool of the evening. A distant sound of drums and tambourines floated in the air, coming from the Muslim quarter.

"It reminds me of Granada," she said. "Do you remember when I accompanied you on an embassy to the caliph? The gardens in the Alhambra had fountains just like these. I was but a child, but I remember thinking they were the most glorious gardens I had ever seen, even though they were Muslim gardens on Christian soil." Constance laid her head on his shoulder and sighed.

"What is it, my precious? I'm sorry it had to be Sicily, but with our help Sicily will revive."

"It's not that. I was just thinking how much I missed you and Pedro when I was in Hungary. Having you here it is almost as if we were children again. Poor Frederick, it must be sad to have no brothers or sisters, no family at all. I'm lucky to have two wonderful brothers. You will stay for a while, won't you?" There was a hint of anxiety in her voice.

"Yes, my sweet. It will take some time to settle the knights in. And I promise to visit later on—not, you understand, to clasp my lady sister to my heart, but just because the Sicilian peaches are the best in the world."

He put his arm around her and gave her a reassuring hug. "I think I should let you get some sleep." He brushed her hair with his lips.

THE WEDDING DAY dawned, a cloudless August morning. By noon the city was sweltering. Since sunrise townspeople and country folk had been jostling each other for the best places from which to view the pageant. Immense crowds lined the streets. They crammed the rooftops and hung from every window. The mansions along the royal route were festooned with tapestries and garlands of flowers. Church bells began to peal. As the procession came into view the people broke into frenzied cheering.

Mounted heralds, the arms of Sicily and Aragon on their surcoats, led the way on horses with flower-bedecked bridles. Behind them, on foot, appeared Saracen musicians, playing tambourines, pipes, and sackbuts. The crowd gasped as line after line of Aragonese knights rode past on their great warhorses, banners flying, their black armor glinting in the sun.

At last, shouts of "*Il re! Il re!*" rang out. Frederick, on a white stallion under an emerald canopy upheld by six turbaned Saracens, gripped his reins tighter. He shifted his shoulders to balance King Roger's magnificent vermilion mantle. The cheering swelled to a deafening roar. Flowers began to rain down. For the first time, the people of Palermo were acclaiming him in a procession. How many remembered him as a boy, scrounging roast chickpeas from the street vendors? They were his people, his kin. A bond more powerful than blood.

Behind him the crowd cheered Constance. As they turned a corner, he glanced back over his shoulder. She looked lovely. In pale lemon, a gem-studded circlet securing the veil on her flowing hair, she waved to the crowd. "*Federico e Costanza! Federico e Costanza!*" the people now chanted, stamping their feet. "*Federico e Costanza! Federico e Costanza!*"

The procession swept into the cathedral square. To the sound of trumpets, he and Constance ascended the steps toward the altar that had been erected before the bronze doors. There Berard awaited them with the officiating clergy.

A herald stepped forward. Unrolling a scroll with the great red seal of Aragon, he read out the terms of the marriage settlement. Those within hearing distance gasped in astonishment. Berard shot him a quizzical look. Frederick smiled back nonchalantly. He watched the barons, clustered nearby, and caught them exchanging glances. Good, he thought. Let worry gnaw at those traitors. The reading had been his idea. Within minutes the news would spread through Palermo. He had selected and coached the herald himself, doubling the number of knights and the gold.

Berard took the ring from a silver paten and blessed it. "In the name of the Lord, I bless this ring and this union between Aragon and Sicily."

Taking the gold band, Frederick slipped it on and off three successive fingers on her hand, saying: "In the name of the Father, the Son, and the Holy Ghost." He then pledged her his troth: "With this ring I thee wed and with this gold I thee endow."

Constance gave him a glowing smile. He took her hand and kissed it, letting his lips linger. She blushed, and lowered her eyes.

The public ceremony now ended and the invited guests entered the cathedral. After the glaring heat in the piazza, the interior, fragrant with incense, was cool and restful. Frederick and Constance knelt before the altar. Berard gave each a lighted taper. He extended his pallium, a stole of white lambswool, symbol of his episcopal authority, over their bowed heads. After Mass was over, a priest emerged from the sacristy bearing a silver casket tarnished by age. Whispering to Constance to remove her circlet, Frederick opened the casket, lifting out of it a crown of Byzantine design, in the form of a scarlet skullcap studded with gems, with two long jeweled pendants hanging on either side. Though his hands were steady as he placed it on Constance's head, his voice trembled: "This was the crown of my mother. May you wear it for many years in happiness."

A murmur of surprise ran through the congregation. Constance sank to her knees. She looked up at him, her eyes moist. "Thank you, my lord. May I be worthy of this great honor."

Frederick smiled. "Come," he said, extending his hand. Together they walked down the nave, out of the cool dimness of the cathedral into the sunshine outside.

*   *   *

THE INTENSE HEAT of summer had given way to long golden autumn days. Preparations for the campaign to flush out the rebels on the mainland had begun. The army would leave at the end of the short Sicilian winter.

Frederick threw himself into the process of learning how to equip and train an army: he observed the Aragonese knights feint with Saracen swordsmen to learn the Muslim way of warfare, inspected barrels of dried sardines and strings of cheeses in the storehouses on the waterfront, watched armorers temper hissing steel in vats of cold water. He clambered about requisitioned ships, talking with muscular sailors and wrinkled ship-wrights hammering the old hulls into seaworthiness. When no one could find an adequate supply of army tents, he suggested that the palace silk works produce them instead of weaving the gorgeous fabrics for which they were famed. He pored over maps with Alaman, Berard, and Alfonso. During the afternoons, while the court came to a standstill, he worked with his secretaries.

Frederick glanced at the hourglass. He had promised to take Constance hawking and it was already past the fourth hour. He beckoned to the tall Saracen guarding the door. "Mahmoud, send word to the queen that I'll be there shortly." His childhood friend had turned into a brave and loyal man with broad shoulders. Mahmoud's attention to detail was the only vestige of the careful, shy boy he had once been.

Frederick signed the last parchment and handed it to a black-gowned secretary to sand and seal. He was about to leave when the sentry outside announced the archbishop.

"Escort his lordship in." If Berard had come all the way to the summer palace, it must be important. They greeted each other with a hug.

"Sit down." Frederick said. "I won't be able to see you for long, though. Constance has been waiting for hours. What news do you bring?"

Berard gave him a folded parchment. "A letter from His Holiness, Frederick. I'm afraid it's not good news. I've had a letter from him myself."

Frederick broke the seal and read in silence. When he put the letter down, his lips were pressed together. "So Innocent thinks he rules Sicily, too?"

"Frederick, I told you the pope wouldn't accept your appointment of bishops without his consent."

Frederick slammed his palm onto the table. "Damnation, Berard, you know better than anyone that a bishop wields immense power. Bishops govern cities, administer justice, collect taxes, at times even command armies. How can I not have the right to appoint the most worthy, loyal man to the post? What does the pope in Rome know about who the best candidate is? Or is the most suitable man the one who has paid the highest bribe for the appointment, who will look after the interests of Rome?"

Seeing Berard's face, he added, "I'm sorry, Berard. I know that not all churchmen are like that, but you know that many are corrupt. They fornicate, line their pockets with bribes, and openly practice simony. Small wonder that the people don't heed their preaching any more."

Frederick slumped in his chair. He passed his hand over his eyes. The papacy was encroaching from all sides like a relentless tide. How was he ever going to free himself?

Berard leaned forward. "I know how you feel, and you are essentially right, but this is a legal matter. According to your mother's concordat with the papacy, when she recognized the pope as suzerain of Sicily, she agreed to Rome's right of veto in the election of Sicilian bishops."

"Are you saying, then," Frederick asked, "that I must accept the pope's decision?"

"I am."

"That means that by forcing me to accept a bishop of his choice in every diocese, the pope will effectively be ruling Sicily?"

"No, but he can certainly exert considerable influence," Berard admitted.

Frederick leaped up. He began to pace. "Innocent thinks he rules Christendom like a Caesar. He treats the kings of Europe as proconsuls, graciously tolerated so long as we do his bidding. . . . Look how he humiliated poor John of England. This jackal on the papal throne is getting far too big for his embroidered slippers . . ."

"Frederick!"

Frederick stopped pacing. He stared at Berard. All anger had gone out of him. He felt empty. A pawn, he thought, that's what I am. First of the Germans, now of the pope. Nothing but a pawn. He sat down. "What shall I do, Berard?"

"Be patient. Don't antagonize the Holy Father. Try to persuade him. Innocent is only trying to protect the Church and uphold her principles. I'll go to Rome if you wish, plead your case."

Frederick wasn't listening. A thought had occurred to him. Yes. It might be possible . . . "I could of course curtail the power of the bishops. Replace them in their secular functions with a body of trained officials, loyal only to the state, as the Romans had . . ."

Berard shook his head, exasperated. "Frederick, you can't change the world. Where would you get such officials? Since the fall of Rome the Church alone has kept learning alive. Bishops trained in the cathedral schools have been running the Christian world for eight hundred years."

"The Romans had better roads, better bridges, safer cities, and their justice system has not been matched. Why? Because they were superior beings?" Frederick paused. "No. They succeeded because they didn't throw up their hands and cry that it was the will of God."

"The Roman world may or may not have been better," Berard said, "but it's gone forever. You've inherited an excellent administration. Many of the Byzantine and Saracen systems used in Sicily are descended from Rome. Be content with that."

"I don't want to be content. I want to do better. I'll train my own officials, in my own university. I'll establish a secular one, where no pope can interfere . . ."

Berard sighed. He shook his head. "There's no point in arguing with you when you're in this sort of mood."

Frederick rose. "Well, at least there's one papal appointment I don't regret," he put a conciliatory hand on Berard's shoulder. "Since you've come all this way, won't you dine with us tonight? I'm giving a banquet for some newly converted barons. Observing them at close quarters will be interesting."

"I'll be delighted. You've done wonders here."

Frederick laughed. "If only retiling and regilding didn't cost so much . . ." He had begun to restore a summer residence of his grandfather's, built in the middle of an artificial lake on the outskirts of Palermo.

Calling to Mahmoud to see to the archbishop, he strode down the steps toward Constance's apartments.

*   *   *

THE OPEN PAVILION was filled with laughing, drinking guests reclining on divans arranged along the walls. From the screened musicians' gallery came the sound of lutes and mandolins. As the evening progressed and the muscat wine flowed freely, what had started as a formal banquet, with many of the guests uneasy, was turning into a lively gathering.

"Frederick's wine is going down rather well with these lords, don't you think?" Alaman da Costa grinned.

Alfonso of Aragon stared at his table neighbor. "Yes, they seem to be enjoying themselves," he replied coolly. There was something piratical about the man. Alfonso would not have put a buccaneering past beyond him. That was perhaps why Frederick liked him. Against Alfonso's advice he had entrusted Alaman with rebuilding the Sicilian fleet . . .

Trumpets sounded. A troupe of dancing girls whirled into the pavilion. As they began to dance, conversations came to a halt. Swaying to the strains of an Arabic song, they seemed to float above the marble floor, their graceful movements accompanied by a flutter of gossamer skirts in a rainbow of colors.

Alfonso, seated on the dais beside Frederick and Constance, watched the scene over the rim of his cup. Surely this wasn't the court of a Christian monarch, but the palace of an oriental potentate. The Saracen girls in their seductive costumes, dancing to the soothing music; the turbaned eunuchs serving dainty delicacies to reclining guests; the golden mosaics on the walls, its tigers and palm trees gleaming in the torchlight; and in the distance, through the horseshoe arches, the moonlight playing upon the lake—Christian kings didn't live like this. Yet he had to admit that the evening compared favorably with the raucous banquets he had attended at other courts, in smoke-filled halls full of unwashed barons devouring huge joints of venison.

His eyes followed one of the dancing girls, watched her long black hair swing to and fro with the music, her arms raised as if in an incantation. Desire stirred in him as he watched her undulating hips. They were gorgeous, these Saracen girls. No doubt about it. He almost regretted refusing Frederick's offer. Only yesterday, this boy, barely into manhood, had suggested that he needed female company to cheer him, as he found him a bit morose lately. The remedy his brother-by-marriage had proposed had been an infidel dancing girl.

How often had Frederick succumbed to their charms? Surely he wouldn't dream of having a Saracen mistress? Alfonso told himself that Frederick was inexperienced and so besotted with Constance that there was no danger, at least for the time being. And yet with Frederick one never knew.

He drained his cup. The wine was a trifle too sweet, but clear and strong. The dancers, at the end of their performance, were rewarded with enthusiastic applause.

Alfonso's eyes came to rest on Frederick. He was laughing, sharing a joke with a radiant Constance. In the few months since he had first met him, Frederick had changed a great deal. At first, Frederick frequently asked his advice, particularly about military matters. Now he did so less and less. Alfonso was certain that every detail of this spectacular Eastern feast had been planned by him, right down to the hastily regilded ceiling. It was Frederick's subtle way of letting those who counted know that he meant to emulate his grandfather Roger in every way, including that of demanding total submission from his barons.

And Constance, bewitched by her young husband and his exotic country, was encouraging him. She had polished his manners, his language, and his appearance. There was something faintly ridiculous about the way his beautiful, self-possessed sister had succumbed to this young man's charm. Alfonso found himself frequently irritated by the two of them.

"They seem very happy, don't they?" Berard, seated on Alfonso's left, had followed his eyes. Frederick was offering his wife a sugared date, putting it between her lips.

Alfonso nodded. "I must admit that I've been pleasantly surprised at the success of this match."

Berard smiled: "They deserve their happiness. The ways of God may be strange at times, but they are just."

Alfonso was about to say something when a murmur ran through the crowd.

Frederick, in a long saffron tunic, his purple mantle fastened with Berard's ruby clasp, had risen and was descending from the dais. The guests stood and bowed. With a smile and a wave of his hand he put them at ease. One by one he spoke to them, finding a pleasantry for everyone. Most of the barons on the island, and one or two from the mainland, were gathered here tonight at his invitation. Considering that until recently many had been traitors, Alfonso had to admit that it was a superb performance. Having made his way across the hall, Frederick came to a halt at the other end. He remained there for some time, talking to an elderly man in a plain blue gown with a high pointed hat, like an astrologer's.

Alfonso turned to Berard. "Who's that graybeard he's talking to?"

"Oh, that's Jacob Anatoli, a famous Jewish scholar. Frederick admires him greatly."

Alfonso's black eyebrows shot up. "What, he invited a Jew?"

Berard nodded.

"I can't believe it, even if he must borrow money from them . . ." Alfonso shook his head. The Jews, too cunning and wealthy by far, took shameless advantage of the Church's ban on moneylending. While most educated people didn't believe the stories of well-poisoning and ritual murder that periodically erupted in frenzies of Jew-killing, they still despised the Jews. They had, after all, crucified the Lord. "I hope this doesn't reach my brother of Aragon's ears. I wouldn't like the king to get a wrong impression."

"My dear count," Berard said, "Frederick needs the support of all his people if he is to rebuild his country. There are many prosperous Jews in Sicily. He has to show tolerance."

Alfonso nodded. Berard was placating him. He signaled a page to refill his cup while he watched Frederick return and sit down beside Constance.

Frederick said, "What a sight, these traitors all eating my salt like loyal subjects. Look at the one over there, talking to Walter." He whispered something to Constance that Alfonso couldn't hear. They both laughed. The object of their derision was the fat Count of Caserta, far gone in his cups, who was telling Walter a story. He was gesticulating wildly, stabbing the air to make a point between hiccups, oblivious to the look of growing distaste on the chancellor's face.

"By spring," Frederick said to Constance, his eyes glittering, "the rest will all be dead or on their knees. And this lot will have given back every stolen *braccia* of land."

Alfonso saw Constance shiver. She drew her shawl about her shoulders as if to shield herself. What had frightened his sister? Was it the dangers of the coming campaign, or the merciless hatred in Frederick's eyes? Alfonso felt a flicker of unease. The wine is getting to me, he thought. There was no cause for alarm. Good fortune was favoring Frederick. The barons here tonight appeared reconciled. And most of the rebels on the island had recently taken an oath of fealty.

Yet it remained to be seen how long this truce would last. As for the unrepentant barons in mainland Sicily, only defeat would reduce them to obedience.

CONSTANCE SAT IN the window seat, a book open in her lap, and looked out to the sea. The sun was setting over the water, the last streaks of orange turning to gold. She never tired of watching the sea, or the view of Palermo at her feet. Soon it would be Christmas. What would a Christmas court be like in a climate so mild?

A commotion made her glance down. Frederick and a party of Aragonese rode into the bailey. Hounds barked, grooms ran about, holding bridles, dragging mounting blocks. Bags of feathered game were carried to the kitchens. In the background, the falconers remained on their horses, their charges on their fists, waiting for everyone to disperse before taking the falcons to their mews.

Frederick slid off his horse, ignoring the groom who rushed forward to help him. With a laughing remark to Alfonso, who was carefully adjusting his cloak before stepping onto the waiting block, Frederick disappeared from view with purposeful strides. He was always in a hurry.

Constance smiled. How typical. They were so different, and yet she loved them both. Whenever she saw that head of curly auburn hair, she felt a surge of joy. Almost against her will, she had fallen in love with her new husband. At first, she had simply been flattered. He was so obviously in love with her that she found herself returning his smiles, responding to him out of kindness, almost without being aware that her gestures were becoming real. Frederick treated her as her first husband never had. He tried so hard to please her, he laughed and joked with her, he even asked her advice. On several occasions he had actually followed her counsel. Her experience as regent of Hungary after Almeric's death, before his brother had seized the throne, had stood her in good stead after all.

The courtyard had all but emptied now. Frederick often came unannounced at this time of day. Perhaps he would come now. She called to one
of her ladies, who was working on an embroidery in the chamber. "Have
the fire lit, Sancha." While the winter days of Palermo were mild, the evenings could get chilly. "And have some wine and cheese brought up, too,
in case the king should come," she called after the girl, who had gone to
summon a servant.

Frederick was totally ignorant of the etiquette of marriage. He'd
laughed when she pointed this out to him. Never, he said, would he be
able to wait to see her. And he would certainly not send some pompous
steward to announce his arrival hours in advance. As if to make his point,
he had taken her into his arms, in front of her ladies, and kissed her on
the lips.

The thought of Frederick's kisses, his lovemaking, brought a flush of
shame to her cheeks. Some things she couldn't even bring herself to con-
fess to her chaplain. The next morning she'd kneel in prayer, asking for
forgiveness. He touched her in places where no decent woman should
allow herself to be touched. Instead of satisfying his need quickly, in the
position the Church decreed as the only natural one, he toyed with her like
a doll, savoring every moment and prolonging her indignity. She sighed. It
was the only shadow on her happiness and she didn't want to think about
it now.

She was crossing the room when Frederick appeared in the doorway,
still cloaked and spurred. He embraced her. Her ladies withdrew hastily.

He glanced at the book in her hand. "What are you reading?"

"A new French romance about the knights of the Round Table.
Alfonso's wife Blanche sent it. It's a wonderful story, written in verse."

"Let me see." He paged through the beautiful calligraphy. "Why don't
we have a reading of it tonight at supper? You tell me it's the latest
fashion."

Constance suppressed a smile. Although Frederick was terribly curious
about details of life at other courts, he tended to assume a mocking air
whenever they were discussed.

"That would be nice, my darling, but don't you think you should change
first?" she smiled, brushing a twig from his windblown hair. He had a
charming raffish look about him when he wasn't assuming his new role of

remote Byzantine monarch. She ran her hand along his unfashionably clean-shaven, bronzed features.

Frederick threw off his cloak. He let himself fall onto the settle. Patting the cushion beside him, he said, "First, come and sit here." He raised her face, his eyes darkening. "You look lovely." She drew back. She knew that look of his only too well. "The servants will be here to light the fire any moment," she said quickly, removing his other hand from her waist.

"All right, my prim and proper Spanish queen," he said with mock exasperation. "But tonight I'll keep you awake all night."

Two serving women came in with a load of firewood and a brass tray with food and drink. Constance got up, poured a cupful of wine, and handed it to him.

"Ah, just the thing for a tired huntsman." He stretched his legs in their muddy boots and gave a sigh of contentment.

"Why don't you play something for me? I love to hear you play your harp," he begged, taking another sip of mulled wine while sinking deeper into the bench cushions.

She went to fetch her harp from the corner. As the fire began to crackle, the soothing strains of the music echoed through the growing twilight of the room, filling her with contentment. She had found a new life, a sense of belonging.

WITH THE END of the winter rains came the season for warfare. The combined Sicilian and Aragonese forces were encamped in a city of tents outside Palermo, ready to leave for Messina, from where they were to take ship to the mainland. The campaign was to be led jointly by Frederick and Alfonso.

A farewell banquet was held in the great hall to celebrate their departure. A troubadour's rich voice filled the hall with a Provençal song of courtly love:

> *The love reigning within my heart*
> *Keeps me warm in harshest winter . . .*
> *I do not want the empire of Rome,*
> *Nor be elected pope,*

If I cannot return to her,
For whom my heart burns and cracks;
And if she does not cure my ills
With a kiss before the New Year,
She'll kill me and condemn herself.
I am Arnaut who gathers the wind
And hunts the hare with the ox
And swims against the incoming tide.

As the last plangent note of his lute died away, conversation resumed around the long tables.

Frederick was fond of these singer-poets, who had come to Sicily in Alfonso's retinue. Used to the languor of Arabic music, he found the Provençal verse lyrics, with their tales of courtly love and heroic exploits, refreshing. He had even attempted, not very successfully, a few verses of his own. He raised his goblet to Alfonso. "Here is to the man who will lead us to victory." Instead of drinking, he handed the cup to Alfonso.

The Aragonese knights roared their approval at this honor. Alfonso, who looked already a little flushed, took a deep draught before returning the silver cup with an inclination of his head.

Fanfares sounded. A procession of dishes appeared, carried in by vermilion-turbaned Saracens. A roast peacock, reassembled and decorated with its own feathers to resemble the living bird, drew murmurs of admiration. There were pheasant and swan, too, decorated in similar fashion. Great mounds of flat unleavened bread and spiced vegetables swayed past on huge platters.

Alfonso leaned over to Frederick, about to say something, when he suddenly clamped his hand to his mouth. He jumped up, a panic-stricken expression on his face. Clutching the tapestry behind him for support, he swayed briefly before crashing to the ground in a splatter of vomit. A horrified murmur went up from the assembly. Everyone clustered about the count, who was doubled over, gripping his belly.

Constance bent over him, her face ashen. She wiped his mouth with a napkin. Frederick called for a physician. His squires lifted Alfonso and carried him to a chest by the wall. He was shivering, his teeth chattering.

Silence descended on the guests as they stood around the count, waiting for the physician. Walter voiced what everyone was thinking.

"This might be poison. Poison meant for the king."

Constance looked up at Frederick, her eyes wide.

It was true. He had shared his cup with her brother. Reading her thoughts, Frederick flashed her a reassuring look, shaking his head.

The tall, distinguished figure of Ibn Tulun, Frederick's physician, made his way through the press of bodies. After he had been given a detailed account of the events, he insisted on knowing what the count had eaten and drunk. Only then did he turn to the groaning man and begin to examine him. When he raised himself his dark features were grim. He sought Frederick's eyes. "Your Grace, a word with you. In private, please." He gestured to Alfonso's squires. "Carry his lordship to his bedchamber and see to it that he is kept warm. I'll attend to him after I have spoken with the king."

"Well," Frederick asked as soon as they were behind closed doors in the guardroom, "Is it poison?"

"No, my lord, it's not poison. It's worse."

Worse than poison? Frederick's heart sank. Ibn Tulun wasn't given to exaggeration. "Well, what is it? If it's not someone trying to assassinate one or both of us, why are you so glum that you've lost your voice?"

"Your Grace," the Saracen began, "unless I am mistaken, and may Allah grant that I am, the sickness that has struck the Queen's brother is called *kholera*. It kills most of those it touches, and it spreads like Greek fire."

Frederick paled. "Have there been other cases?" he asked, his voice tight.

"I have heard reports of what I took to be common dysentery, from the town. Without examining the patients, I cannot say, but it never comes singly."

"How can we stop it from spreading to the army?"

"My lord, we are not sure how this sickness is contracted." Ibn Tulun spread his hands. "There's little we can do to stop it from reaching the army except forbidding them contact with the town."

"Do whatever is necessary, no matter how much effort it requires. Move the whole army to another town. You have full powers to take the most effective measures." He grabbed the physician by the arm. "I'm going to call an urgent council meeting. But first go to the count. Report to me in the council chamber."

Frederick turned to go. He stopped. "And don't tell the queen how ill her brother is."

Ibn Tulun bowed. "I'll do my best."

As he clattered down the spiral staircase, the physician following behind, Frederick felt a terrible, icy fear knotting his stomach. If this spread to the army, it would be the end of all his hopes, the end of his kingdom.

DEATH HUNG OVER the city like a pall. Day after day the bells of Palermo tolled for the dead. Relay prayers were said in the churches, imploring God to turn the evil away. The miraculously preserved body of Saint Rosalia, Palermo's patron saint, was carried through the streets. As the procession passed, the citizens fell to their knees, crying out to their saint to intercede with God on their behalf. And still, by the hundreds, the people of Palermo continued to die.

The stench of death and decay filled the pillared hall of the palace. Men lay on straw pallets in rows on the marble flooring, retching into basins, gripping their bellies while their bowels emptied themselves into the already sodden straw. At the first outbreak of the disease in the Aragonese camp, the highborn among them had been moved to the greater comforts of the palace. Within days the lodgings were overflowing and the great hall was converted into an infirmary.

Sadness was written on Ibn Tulun's face as he took the weakening pulse of a blue-eyed young giant whose blond hair was dark with sweat. The delirious man was muttering incoherently. They were infidels, to be sure, but they were still Allah's creatures. He had dedicated his life to wresting men from death, but this time he was confronted by an enemy he could not vanquish. Most of them would not live. These muscular knights, who towered over the smaller, darker Sicilians, were even more vulnerable to this dreadful disease than the local population. Within hours of the first outbreak in their camp, the Aragonese had begun dropping like oaks felled by a woodcutter's ax.

Beside him a priest was administering the last sacrament to a dying knight, frantically gabbling through the rite. The man's life was fading rapidly. Ibn Tulun, glancing up, caught sight of a woman in the doorway. The queen. He rushed down the row of pallets. "Your Grace," he bowed, "I implore you, do not enter here. This is no sight for you and your ladies."

Constance's eyes widened as they swept the hall. The stench of excrement and vomit was overpowering. He could see the fear in her eyes. She hesitated. Then she squared her shoulders. "I know, Ibn Tulun, but they're my people. My ladies can stay behind."

Ibn Tulun looked at this petite Frankish queen with new respect. Her drawn features and the dark shadows under her eyes attested to her exhaustion. Yet she had come, leaving her brother's bedside. "As my lady wishes." He gestured for her to go ahead.

Constance stepped into the hall, clutching her cloak. She approached the nearest pallet. The knight, who had recognized her, tried to raise his head from the bolster.

Constance bent down. She took his hand.

"Your Grace, at first I thought you were an angel. I . . ." His voice trailed off. He sank back.

"Don't tire yourself. The king and I are praying for you. Prayers are being said in all the churches. God will hear us."

The man's face suddenly contorted in a grotesque grimace. He closed his eyes, convulsed by cramps, oblivious to all but the searing pain.

Ibn Tulun touched her elbow, "You cannot help him now, my queen. Let us go on."

By the time she had finished making the rounds of those who were conscious, saying a few words of comfort, Constance was as white as chalk. Her eyes brimmed with tears. She clutched his sleeve. "You must give me something to steady me. I have to go back to my brother. I don't want him to guess what's happening here."

"I have just what you need."

He escorted her to a little recessed anteroom in which his instruments and medicines were kept and made her sit down on a stool. Picking up a vial of clear brown liquid, he measured some of it into a beaker and held it out to her. She took a deep gulp and nearly choked.

"Drink it, it will make you feel better. It is rather raw, but very effective."

She swallowed some more. "It doesn't taste as bad as most medicines. What is it?"

"It's called burned wine. The monks at the medical school in Salerno invented it by boiling wine and catching the vapors. They call it distillation. Too much will make you sick, but a little will raise your spirits. I also use it to wash wounds. They heal much better."

Constance got up. "I must go back to my brother. He was sleeping when I left."

"Sleep is a great healer. I shall come and see the count later. You must get some rest, too, my lady."

"We won't forget what you are doing. As soon as he is better, my brother will see to it that you're suitably rewarded."

Ibn Tulun salaamed. "My lady is most gracious."

He escorted her back to where her two attendants were huddled on a bench, waiting.

ALFONSO WAS STILL sleeping when she returned. A stooped Jewish doctor was holding up a beaker of her brother's urine, examining it. He and his Saracen colleague began whispering in Arabic, their heads held together like conspirators.

"Go and hold your confabulation in the anteroom!"

Before they had even completed their hasty retreat, Constance regretted her curtness. She was overwrought from fatigue and worry. Alfonso was going to recover. Ibn Tulun himself had said that he had only come down with a light case. She dipped a cloth in the vinegar and water in a basin beside the bed. As she bent over her brother, about to wipe the sweat from his forehead, she stopped, staring. The skin over his cheeks was taut and stretched like brittle parchment. His cracked lips had a bluish tinge. Like the dying knights . . . He's going to die, she thought.

Until now she had clung to the belief that death would bypass him. For three days and nights she had not moved from the sickroom. She had allowed herself only snatches of sleep on a pallet at the foot of his bed, as if by her presence she could keep death at bay. Now, as she looked at him, she felt her remaining strength ebb away. She hung her head, the cloth still in her hand. It was useless.

"My lady, you must get some rest. Please let me keep watch for a while." Her maid's voice was pleading, insistent. Too weary to speak, Constance nodded.

Juana took her by the arm and steered her towards a settle. "I'll bring you some broth, and then you must sleep."

The girl was a peasant from the hills above Saragossa, yet she had proved more resourceful in adversity than her highborn ladies. Constance leaned her head on the wall and closed her eyes. She was tired, so tired that even her anguish had lost its sharpness, become blurred. Her whole body was numb with fatigue; all she wanted to do was sleep.

Someone was shaking her by the shoulder. "Wake up!" Frederick shook her again, this time more urgently.

She jumped to her feet. Alfonso's bed was surrounded by people. With a start she recognized Berard, in his ecclesiastical robes, bending over her brother. Frederick put his arm around her. "Constance, he's dying,"

"In the name of the Father, the Son, and the Holy Ghost . . ." Berard was anointing Alfonso's eyes, mouth and hands. He invoked the archangels Michael and Gabriel. An acolyte swung a censer. Another held a crucifix aloft.

"Alfonso!" Constance struggled in Frederick's grip.

Berard straightened up. He turned to face her. "Your Grace," he said, "your brother is dead."

"No!" she screamed, "No!" She took a step forward and swayed. Berard caught her. He laid her across the bed, at her brother's feet.

THE CASTLE OF Catania towered above the sea walls and the harbour. To the east, toward Messina, Etna's snow-capped cone dominated the horizon. Despite repeated volcanic eruptions, Catania was a thriving city. To the wheat that already grew here in Greek and Roman times, the Saracens had added sugarcane, dates, almonds, oranges, and lemons, all used in the sweetmeats for which Catania was famed.

The two men walking on the ramparts in the light breeze couldn't have been more dissimilar, yet they walked with the same brisk determination.

Alaman cast a sidelong glance at his companion. What amazing sangfroid this young man had. His army had been decimated in the Palermo epidemic. His wife's brother and most of the knights he had married her for were dead, his resources almost exhausted. Some of the barons had again risen against him, taking advantage of his weakness. Yet he was working at restoring Sicily's prosperity with an energy that even Alaman found hard to match.

All morning Frederick had negotiated with a Genoese delegation, persuading them to help expel the Pisans from the Sicilian ports where they held a trade monopoly, obtained during the years of anarchy. The crown was losing substantiality and desperately needed income from tolls and customs dues.

"Frederick, if you want Genoa to help you oust Pisa, you'll have to offer more than trading rights and the satisfaction of striking a blow at their rivals. It will require large bribes. Where will you find the money?" he asked.

Frederick stopped. "From the greatest thieves in Sicily."

Alaman raised his bushy black brows: "How?"

"You remember my edict that all landowners must submit their title deeds for ratification? A great many of them were forged. In fact, large portions of land belonged to the royal demesne. The barons were in a quandary: if they didn't comply with my order, they were guilty of treason. If they did, many would lose vast tracts of land. In the case of minor offenders I took back the crown lands, leaving them what had been theirs and punishing them with only a fine. After this, many of the big landholders complied as well. But not the greatest magnates."

Alaman nodded. "And how are you going to force those to submit?"

"By arresting them for treason. The difficulty is laying hands on them. When they move from their impregnable mountain aeries, they do so escorted by small armies."

The older man shook his head, "Even if you succeed, you'll have an uprising of barons."

"No, I won't, because the major barons will be in jail, and the small fry will have lost their courage." Frederick smiled. "I've suggested a little ruse that might just work . . ."

A man in a chain-mail hauberk was coming toward them. He bowed.

"Your Grace, an urgent message from the governor of Messina." The man beamed at Frederick. "Your orders have been carried out. The conspirators have been captured."

Frederick grabbed the parchment the man held out. A smile spread across his face as he read. "Two of them taken at Sunday mass. Anfuso of Roto ambushed in his mistress's bed . . . The last one got away, but we've got his eight-year-old heir as a hostage . . ."

Frederick slapped Alaman on the back. "Just as I thought. They became careless, thinking I was hiding in Catania, powerless without the Aragonese." With a glint in his eyes, he added, "Maybe stealth will get me further than might."

He fished a gold coin from his pouch and handed it to the messenger. The man stammered his thanks at so generous a reward, bowed, and withdrew.

Alaman squinted at Frederick in the sunlight. "Was that not a trifle large a gift in view of the treasury's penury?"

"Oh, you Genoese are incorrigibly mean, even worse than the Tuscans." Frederick smiled. "The poorer you are the more generous you should be. No one follows an impecunious king!"

He took Alaman by the shoulder and steered him to the courtyard. "Before rumor spreads, I'm going to draft letters to the Sicilian bishops, explaining the arrest of these traitors. They'll be read from the pulpits of every church."

He added with a grin, "And after that, I'll go and see if I can make my lady wife drink some of that miracle-working wine of yours! Maybe your wine and my news together will put a stop to her mourning. She might even grant me her favors again!"

FREDERICK HELD OUT the cup, "Come on, Constance, have some of this. Alaman gave me a barrel. It's a rare wine from Cyprus."

Constance took the goblet obediently and drank.

Frederick looked at her. She was pale and drawn. Since they'd arrived in Catania two months ago, she'd sat day after day in this window seat, garbed in black, staring out at the sea. She barely ate, and when she wasn't here, she spent hours in the chapel, praying for the souls of her brother and

her dead countrymen. Curled up on her lap was the little white dog
Alfonso had given her as a New Year's gift.

Frederick took the animal from her and put it down on the floor. He sat
down and took her hand. "Listen, my precious, I'm calling a council session
tomorrow and I would like you to be present. I want you to know about
matters of state. You could just sit in on them every now and then, and
afterward give me your impressions. You know I value your counsel. What
do you say?" He gave her his most winning smile.

She squeezed his hand. "You don't have to do that to cheer me up.
You're trying so hard to lift my gloom. It's not fair. Your loss has been as
great as mine, yet you bear it so much better. I'll make an effort, I promise. It's just that I hurt so badly . . ." She smiled through her tears. "My
beleaguered, golden boy, so in need of troops I can no longer bring you."
She ran her fingers through his hair.

It was the first time in weeks that she had touched him. He drew her
to him, his whole body aching with his need. He wanted her desperately,
but didn't want her to withdraw, to shut him out again. He kissed the salty
tears off her face. Reaching for the wine cup, he took a sip himself before
offering it to her. "Here, have some more wine." She drank, then lifted her
luminous gray eyes to him. A faint color had risen in her cheeks.

Alaman knows what he's talking about, no doubt from personal experience, Frederick thought. According to Alaman, nothing kindled the flame
of passion in a reluctant woman as effectively as the wine of Cyprus, birth-
place of Aphrodite.

TO HER SURPRISE, Constance discovered that she enjoyed attending council sessions. The first time she arrived with Frederick, Walter of Palear had
said, "Women have no business here." Although his irritation annoyed her,
she pretended not to notice.

Constance's mind wandered from the matter being discussed, her eyes
sweeping the room. In Catania the council gathered in the castle's great hall.
Despite the black hangings, the hall was bright and airy. Sunshine fell on the
mosaic flooring through the arched windows facing the sea. Two huge blue
ceramic vases filled with almond blossoms stood on the floor. Here, as in

Palermo, the floors were not covered with rushes. It pleased her. Floor rushes, no matter how many aromatic herbs one mixed with them, smelled, bred lice and fleas, and encouraged people to spit into them.

Her attention returned to the session. Many of the routine items were dull. Others, however, she found fascinating. Walter of Palear was saying, "The new German emperor took an oath before his coronation that he'd restore to the papacy land in Italy claimed as the patrimony of Saint Peter. He also took an oath that he would respect the inviolability of the papal fief of Sicily."

Garbed in a gown of dark crimson velvet, as austere and patrician as his narrow face, the skin yellow and creased like old vellum, the black eyes sharp and observant, the chancellor was still, despite his age, a formidable figure. Even Frederick had told her he was indispensable. The chancellor, in turn, had begun to treat Frederick with less condescension.

Walter folded his hands on the table. "What worries me is that there are signs that he may not keep his promises. The question is, which one will he break?"

Berard shook his head. "Why would the new emperor worry himself with Sicily? He'll want to consolidate his position first."

Constance had always found the imperial election system confusing. The Empire wasn't hereditary but elective. Although the emperor was chosen by German princes-electors, it was only after he had been crowned by the pope in Rome that his status was formally recognized. This strange custom went back to Charlemagne. The Empire was in essence German, but conquest and marriage had broadened it to include Austria, Burgundy, and northern Italy.

Constance watched Frederick. Was he thinking about his father? Or the civil war that had raged in Germany for years, pitting Saxon Guelfs and Swabian Ghibellines against each other? At last, the war-weary German princes unanimously accepted Otto of Brunswick as emperor. Pope Innocent had crowned him in Rome, approving their choice. There was peace. Germany and the Christian world rejoiced.

He's probably not thinking about any of it, she thought. Frederick's lack of interest in German affairs puzzled her. He was, after all, half German himself.

"What gives you the impression that the emperor is about to break his oaths?" Frederick asked.

Walter pursed his lips: "The Pope is worried. Otto is gathering a large army south of the Brenner. Why would he want an army in northern Italy, if not to use it against the Papal States?"

"That's a very good question," Alaman da Costa said.

"Nonsense. He'd never dare defy the pope," Frederick said. "As Berard has pointed out, his first priority must be to consolidate his position. If he were to break his assurances to Innocent, he'd be excommunicated. Germany would erupt in civil war again. He can't be that stupid."

"I agree," Berard said, "but there is still the question of the army he's supposedly gathering in Italy. How reliable is your information, Walter?"

The chancellor smiled thinly. "My dear Berard, I never worry about information that is not reliable. Otto is giving out that he's calling a Diet of princes in northern Italy and needs troops for their protection against the untrustworthy Lombards. That is patent nonsense. You don't need an army for—"

"I'll tell you what he's doing," Frederick interjected. "He's going to teach the Lombards a lesson. They've always resisted imperial rule. That's the explanation for this massing of troops."

They all stared at him. Walter nodded slowly. "You may be right. I hope you are."

"Well, I need some fresh air." Frederick rose.

He extended a hand to Constance. "Will you come for a ride? I want to fly that new falcon your royal brother sent me."

"I'd love to." Mention of her other brother always brought back thoughts of Alfonso. However, riding with Frederick was a rare treat these days. He was so involved with affairs of state that she rarely had a chance to be alone with him.

Frederick intercepted Alaman da Costa. "What about you, Alaman? Since you've been on my council you've not been getting enough exercise. Come with us." Frederick punched him in his bulging middle. "If you're not careful, you'll run to fat in my service."

"That, my lord, is the mixed blessing of those who serve the great." He glanced at Frederick's trim waistline. "Unlike the great themselves. I'll join you in a little venery with pleasure."

Constance watched Frederick slap him on the back. "Come on, you old pirate, let's escape these walls." Frederick enjoyed the admiral's company, despite his questionable antecedents. It was rumored that in his youth he had been a corsair, before acquiring respectability as an admiral of the Genoese fleet.

Frederick bounded down the spiral staircase. Constance followed. She didn't like the Genoese. His irreverent manner, his drinking, and his conspicuous womanizing annoyed her. And Frederick was so young . . .

AT THE END of summer the court returned to Palermo. Desolation pervaded the city. Many houses were boarded up. The usually vociferous Palermitans crept about their business in silence. The very air was still, as if in mourning. Not a leaf stirred in the heat. A merciless sun beat down on dust-covered trees and shrubs.

Frederick, who hated black-draped halls, funerary masses, and the absence of entertainments, ordered the court's mourning to end on the last day of September. Constance, who considered this an affront, showed her displeasure by continuing to wear black after everyone else donned bright clothes again.

The success with which he had recovered large tracts of land from the magnates compensated Frederick in some small measure for the loss of the Aragonese. For the time being, he accepted that his authority extended only over the island of Sicily. He now devoted himself to improving it. While the Council of Familiars was left to run routine affairs, Frederick spent hours closeted with experts and advisers, finding new ways of increasing the treasury's income. The tiny Sicilian fleet had begun to grow under Alaman's supervision. The Pisans had been ousted from their trading monopolies, and Frederick was drafting new customs rules that would give the crown a share in every bale of silk or cask of pepper that entered or left a Sicilian port.

In the midst of all this welcome activity a new problem had appeared. For days he turned the matter over in his head, before reaching a decision. Then, for several days, he postponed implementing it, delaying the moment when he knew he had to do so. Finally, he summoned her.

*   *   *

"I'LL MAKE PROVISIONS for the child. If it's a boy, I'll take him into my household when he's old enough."

Seeing Leila's eyes, he said, "I'll give you a generous dowry. You can go home to your people and marry a rich merchant who'll count himself fortunate to have such a beautiful wife."

"Go home? But I don't want to go home. I'll be no trouble, I promise. The queen will never know. She never knew, in the year gone past, did she?"

They were standing in his privy chamber, close to the large table at which he often worked. Dreary gray light filtered through the opaque window glass, reflecting the rainy December day outside.

She must go. He'd summoned her to tell her that. When she had first told him that she was going to have his child, he had been elated, but then the idea of Constance's reaction if she ever found out filled him with dread.

With her face uplifted in supplication, her dark eyes brimming with tears, she was achingly beautiful. The memory of her caresses flooded him. He suddenly wanted her, wanted to crush her mouth with his, sink his body into hers. He took a step forward. "Come here, Leila, for the last time," he said, stretching out his hand. She threw herself into his arms with a cry. She covered his face, his chest, his hands with kisses. Her hands traveled over his body, driving him to madness. He picked her up and threw her down on the bed. Too late he remembered that he should have been gentle with her, that she carried a new life.

There was a commotion outside the door and an exchange of angry voices.

Frederick sat up. The sentry's voice, insistent, "I cannot disturb the king." Another voice, high-pitched, said something unintelligible.

The door was flung open. Frederick reached for the bedcurtains. Too late.

Constance burst into the room. With one glance she took in the crumpled clothes on the floor, his naked body, shielded by a piece of the bed curtains he was holding before him in a futile gesture and the girl, one naked shoulder showing from under the sheet, her disheveled hair streaming down her back, her eyes wide with fear.

Constance's face, white as chalk, registered a number of emotions all at once: shock, disgust, and anguish. Without uttering a word, she turned on her heels and ran out of the room. Frederick had difficulty breathing. He pulled the bed curtains together with a jerk, hoping that the sentry outside would have the sense to close the door to the anteroom.

He slammed his fist into the bolster. "That son of a whore!" He was going to have the fool's head who let Constance push him aside. The guard knew that Leila was inside. Queen or no queen, he had orders that no one was allowed past the antechamber.

"Merciful Lord," he groaned, "what will I say to her?"

WHEN FREDERICK ENTERED her apartments, Constance was sitting by the hearth working on an embroidery, her face a marble mask. Her ladies had been dismissed. She didn't look up at the sound of his footsteps, nor did she acknowledge his presence.

He drew a deep breath. This was going to be even more difficult than he had imagined. "Constance, I am truly sorry, believe me. I had no wish to hurt you," he said into the void above her bent head. The needle continued to fly in and out of the linen with mechanical precision, adding tiny stitches to an arabesque of blue silk threads.

He touched her shoulder. "I am speaking to you, Constance. Please listen to what I have to say."

She lifted her head and gave him a long, cold stare. "I don't want to hear anything. Go away." She bent back over her needlework.

Frederick flushed. He had never apologized to anyone in his life. Here he was, standing like a fool in front of his wife. He had come to make amends, had been prepared for recriminations, for tears, but he had not expected to be dismissed like a servant. His remorse made way for blinding anger. With a sweep of his hand he ripped the embroidery from her hands and sent it flying across the room. The little silver scissors on her lap fell to the floor with a clatter.

Constance jumped to her feet, the haughty indifference gone, her eyes blazing. "How dare you walk in here and knock things about! How dare you even speak to me! You should be ashamed of yourself, a Christian king fornicating with a Saracen! Go back to your infidel whore where you belong!"

Frederick stared at her. Then his eyes narrowed. So that was his real sin in her eyes.

"Constance," he said, icily calm, "they are my people, too. Whatever your priests in Aragon say about consorting with Muslims does not apply here. This is a different country with different rules. As its queen, you had better learn them fast."

"That may be so, but it does not give you the right to fornicate with them. According to the pope, it's a mortal sin."

He glared at her. "To the devil with the pope. I rule here, not he. And don't lecture me on theology, I've enough priests doing that. I came here to tell you that I'm sorry I hurt you, that I was going to send the girl away. Well, I've changed my mind, now that I see that you love your precious Church and its hypocrisy far more than me. You're not jealous, you're just upset because I didn't pick a Christian as my mistress!"

Frederick turned sharply, pausing in the doorway to call over his shoulder, "And as for fornicating, you'd better learn something about that, too. The heathens are far better at it than you." He stalked out, slamming the door behind him.

"Oh Mother of God, what have I done?" Constance buried her face in her hands. Frederick had misunderstood her. Of course she was jealous. The sight of that naked young girl in his bed had filled her with more hatred than she'd thought herself capable of.

He had come to ask her forgiveness, said he was prepared to send the girl away. That was more than she'd expected, more than any other man would have done. And in her stupid pride she had insulted him, driven him right back to that girl. She must tell him that he was wrong, that she loved him. She must beg his forgiveness, explain that she had been crazed with jealousy. She flung the door open, oblivious of the guards' stares, and rushed down the long arched gallery toward the staircase that led into the courtyard.

FREDERICK WAS CROSSING the courtyard in the rain when the sound of running footsteps made him look up. Constance, without a cloak, her hair uncoiling as she ran, raced along the gallery. "Frederick! Wait! Please wait!" she shouted.

Just as she reached the top of the stairs, she lost her footing on the wet marble and stumbled. A scream echoed through the courtyard. In a blur of mauve cloth and tumbling hair she crashed down the stairs.

He rushed to her. "Please, Oh God, do not let her be dead. Don't let her die." He knelt beside her inert form. He lifted her head. Her eyes were closed. A thin trickle of blood ran down from a gash on her forehead, mingling with the raindrops falling on her face.

IBN TULUN DREW the coverlet back over the still unconscious Constance and straightened his back.

Frederick grabbed the physician by the arm. "For mercy's sake, tell me the truth! Will she live?"

The Saracen nodded. "I don't think she has any internal injuries. She should regain consciousness soon. When she does, you must not tire her. But she may lose the child."

"Thanks be to God." Frederick drew a deep breath. Then, as the physician's last sentence struck him, "What did you say?"

"The queen may lose the child. At this early stage of pregnancy, a fall almost always provokes a miscarriage."

"She is with child?"

"Yes, Your Grace. I told her so this morning when she called me to her. She was so overjoyed that she said she was going straight to you to give you the news."

Seeing the look of astonishment on Frederick's face, he asked, "She did not tell you, then, my lord?"

"No, Ibn Tulun, she did not tell me," Frederick said, "she had no opportunity." He turned to the wall, his shoulders hunched, shaking.

"FREDERICK?"

At the sound of her voice, he spun around. He knelt beside her. "Constance," he whispered, "Beloved. I thought you'd never wake up. I was so afraid I would never hear your voice again." He took her hand and pressed it to his lips.

A smile spread across her face. "I ran after you. To tell you that I do love you. I was afraid you would never believe me, would never forgive me for treating you the way I did. Will you forgive me?"

"Of course. Don't talk about it, you mustn't weary yourself."

Her eyes clouded over. "You'll send her away?"

He nodded. "I promise, but you must get some sleep. Ibn Tulun said I was not to exhaust you."

"Did he tell you . . . about the child?"

Frederick nodded, afraid to tell her what else the physician had said, hoping she'd not think of it.

"Did he say whether I will lose it now?"

Frederick smiled. "He said you'd be fine as long as you rest." Let her not fret, let nature decide its course without causing her any unnecessary worry now.

With a sigh of relief, she closed her eyes.

He kissed her on her forehead, where the linen bandage left the skin free.

IN THE WALLED garden below the queen's apartments, the afternoon sun was warm. A distant bell tolled vespers. Constance lowered her psalter. She sighed with contentment. God had been generous to her. The earth, like her body, was quickening with life. Bulbs were pushing out of the wintry soil, lured by the warmth. The almond tree in the corner had burst into snowy blossoms. Near her bench, a little green lizard, its throat palpitating, was soaking up the warmth on the lichen-covered path.

Constance folded her hands protectively over her rounded belly. After marrying Frederick, she'd begun to fear that she'd never conceive again. Frederick had never broached the subject of heirs. Yet, she had known that sooner or later, he or one of his councilors was bound to do so. Perhaps, she'd thought in anguish, I'm too old. And then had come that fateful rainy day. Against everyone's expectations, she had not lost the child after her fall. She'd remained in bed, strictly following Ibn Tulun's injunctions not to move, for two weeks. After that, she had never felt better in her life.

She smiled to herself as she recalled Frederick's protectiveness when she'd first risen from her bed. He had forbidden her to ride, to dance, even to carry her harp across the room. The sight of him, fussing around her, was so comical that one evening Berard, that most tactful of men, burst out laughing. After that, Frederick stopped regulating every aspect of her life.

As her body grew heavier, she often came to sit in this peaceful little garden to dream. Sometimes her eyes would fill with tears at the memory of her dead baby son. She chased away those black thoughts. It was the future that counted. Would it be a boy? She prayed with all her heart that it would.

Frederick talked constantly about his son. His choice of a name had surprised her. He was to be named Henry. Why he wished to name his heir after a father he never mentioned was one of the many mysteries of his character. The possibility that his firstborn might be a girl hadn't even entered his mind.

There was a flash of color at the far end of the garden. Someone was coming up the path. A little regretfully, Constance saw Juana appear, a blue cloak over her arm.

"My lady, you forgot your mantle. You mustn't catch a chill."

Constance was amused by the girl's clucking concern. When most of her Spanish ladies had returned to Aragon after the epidemic, Juana had risen to a position far above that of a maidservant.

"The king's back. He's asking for you, my lady."

"Then we can't keep him waiting, can we?" Constance smiled, rising from her stone seat.

FREDERICK EMBRACED HER. He held her at arm's length. "You look wonderful. Has my son been behaving himself?"

Constance nodded, smiling. She pulled him to a couch. "Come, tell me about Messina. How's the fleet?"

Two servants brought in refreshments. While they arranged wine and sweetmeats on a table, Frederick paced up and down. His face was somber, the cheer gone.

As soon as they were alone, Constance put her hand on his arm. "Frederick, what's wrong?"

They sat down on the cushioned divan that was arranged, in oriental fashion, along one wall. Frederick stared at the floor tiles. "It's the emperor. He's broken his word to the pope. He's refused to return the promised lands, and is about to invade the papal territories in Tuscany." Frederick sighed. "There's worse. He's been in contact with the barons of

Apulia. They've invited him to become their overlord, obviously thinking that a distant emperor is better than a nearby king."

Constance stared at him. Her stomach knotted with fear. "Does that mean . . . ?" Her voice faltered.

Frederick nodded. "Yes," he said, "it means war. He'll march into Apulia, then Calabria. With the principal barons behind him, he'll take those mainland provinces from me with little effort. We'll have him on our doorstep." Frederick put his arm around her. He pressed her shoulders.

After a moment, she asked, "What will you do?"

Frederick sat down. He picked up a sugared date from the platter. "I've been trying to guess what's going on in Otto's mind. There's no doubt that one of his reasons for wanting Apulia is that he sees me, the last Hohenstaufen, as a threat. I've sent an embassy to him. I have explained that I have no interest whatsoever in my German inheritance. I've offered to renounce my claims to the duchy of Swabia, which is rightfully mine now that my uncle Philip is dead."

Constance frowned. "The duchy of Swabia?"

"The ancestral Hohenstaufen duchy. I have no chance of ever taking possession of it anyway. The emperor would never allow a Hohenstaufen king of Sicily to possess a duchy in the Empire's heartland."

"Do you think he might accept?"

Frederick shrugged. "I wish I knew. Berard and Walter think I'm wasting my time. He may need gold. I've offered him ten thousand gold bezants, in several installments, if he guarantees the treaty with suitable hostages."

Constance gasped. "You offered him *what?*"

"Yes, yes, I know," he said. "I can't raise it alone, but the pope's coffers are well filled. To get Otto out of southern Italy, Innocent would mortgage Saint Peter's itself. I might have to pledge a few towns for the loan."

He went on with a rueful grin, "The pope's as scared as we are. It's quite funny. He supported the Guelf faction to avoid precisely this, and now his worst nightmare is looming on the horizon—the fusion of Sicily with the Empire and the complete encirclement of the Papal States. If Sicily became part of the Empire, the pope would be naught but the emperor's pawn." Frederick laughed.

Constance looked down on her hands in silence. She saw nothing to laugh about.

FREDERICK'S SON WAS born on the last day of July, in the early hours of the afternoon. The din of the celebrating crowd, which had been gathering outside the gates since sunrise to await the birth, penetrated even behind the thick walls of the lying-in chamber. The people of Palermo danced and sang in the streets. They're celebrating not only the birth of my heir, Frederick thought, watching from a window, but also a return of the old order, a promise of peace and prosperity. If only they knew . . .

To his intense annoyance, he had discovered that birth was the exclusive domain of women. Pacing up and down the anteroom, tormented by Constance's muffled screams, he sent for Ibn Tulun. The physician had explained that no man, not even a doctor, was allowed to attend a birth. During the long hours of waiting, his thoughts turned to Leila's child. With a pang of regret he realized that he had never seen the boy. He had shrugged the feeling off. She had been well provided for. As for the boy, he would take him into the royal household when he reached the age of twelve.

When he insisted on seeing Constance after the child had been born, he was made to wait yet again, till she had been prepared. When finally he was permitted to enter the lying-in chamber, a hush fell on the women crowding the room. The chief midwife came toward him, her wrinkled face beaming. "My lord, you have been blessed with a strong, lusty prince." She handed him the swaddled infant.

He gazed down at the tiny red face. His son. His son and heir. The baby had a thin golden fuzz of hair, his mother's color. He was fast asleep. Frederick picked up one miniature hand and studied it. It was perfectly formed, pink, with tiny fingernails. He kissed the hand, which smelled of the honey with which they rubbed newborns. Handing his son back to the midwife, he turned to the great bed, its crimson hangings drawn back and raised into their covers.

Propped up on cushions, Constance smiled at him, pale but luminous. They had brushed her hair and braided it with pearls. An embroidered chemise of aquamarine silk had replaced her birthing shift. He could smell rose water. Women were extraordinary. One moment they sounded as if they were dying, and then they looked like this. Frederick bent down and kissed both her hands. "And how, Madam, does it feel to be the mother of the next king of Sicily?"

Constance laughed. "Wonderful. Almost as wonderful as being the wife of a man who always gets what he wants."

Frederick shook his head. "Not always, alas." He bent down and whispered, "Do you know that you look magnificent? Childbirth suits you. If it weren't for all these gawkers, I'd kiss you properly, a promise of things to come."

Constance shook her head. "Oh, you."

Frederick turned to a page behind him. He took a small ebony casket from the boy and handed it to her. "Open it," he said eagerly.

Constance lifted the latch. She gasped. On a cushion of blue silk lay a large oval brooch: an agate cameo of a Roman lady set in gold filigree, surrounded by two concentric circles of pearls. She held the brooch up to the light. "It's magnificent. Is it Roman?"

"It is indeed. The cameo is said to have belonged to the Empress Helena, the mother of Constantine. The setting is new. I thought it would make a fitting gift for another royal mother."

"It must have cost a fortune," she whispered.

"Old Mordecai reluctantly parted with another loan," he whispered back. "One more doesn't matter. One day the Jews will sell me to the Venetians as a galley slave."

Constance shook her head. He was incorrigible. His generosity would undo all his efforts. She'd never understand him. He scolded servants for throwing away candle stubs that were still usable and carefully scrutinized the chancery's accounting books, yet he gave his friends princely gifts, and had now bought her an ornament worthy of an empress.

Frederick kissed her forehead. "I must go now. Everyone is waiting to offer their congratulations. After that, Abu Talib should have finished casting the horoscope. I can't wait to see what the stars portend for him."

Constance leaned back into the pillows. She was filled with happiness. God had replaced her lost son and her brother with a new life. With his help all else would right itself, too.

*　*　*

"SUN, VENUS, MERCURY, and Jupiter in Leo, all in conjunction, in the tenth house of the nativity. Leo being the sign of royalty, this is a most auspicious configuration for a future king, my lord." The astrologer gave a toothless smile, his pointed hat bobbing.

Frederick asked, "Well, what else do you see? And what do you mean by the tenth house?"

The astrologer pointed to the large square on the parchment, which was divided into twelve equal divisions. "You see this square, and the divisions within? Each represents an area of life and character and is called a 'house.' The seven planets—Sun, Mercury, Venus, Mars, Jupiter, Saturn and the Moon—are found in different houses according to the exact moment of birth. Depending on which house a planet is situated in, it affects the individual in a different manner. Added to that are the aspects, or angles of degrees, at which the planets stand to one another, and whether they are easy or difficult. Naturally, the planets are either malefic or benefic, depending on their nature."

Frederick nodded, "Yes, but go on, explain the rest to me."

The astrologer squinted at the chart. It was covered with planetary signs and lines in black ink. "The prince will be tall and handsome, full of pride and self-confidence. Mars in Aries will make him bold, a fine warrior and popular with the ladies." He tilted his head to one side. "He might be a little headstrong and impulsive, my lord. Because Mars can be both benefic and malefic, you should guard against this from early childhood."

"Which planets are malefic or benefic?"

"The great malefic is Saturn. Mars is the lesser malefic, but he can also be benefic, depending on his sign, position, and aspects."

"Is stubbornness going to be Henry's only fault? Come on, Abu Talib, don't tell me only what you know I want to hear, tell me the truth."

The astrologer touched his right hand to his forehead, his lips and his heart. "But I am telling you the truth, my lord."

"Aha, reading the stars?" Berard's rich baritone echoed through the chamber.

Frederick beamed at him. "Henry's horoscope seems very auspicious."

"May I have a look?"

"You know about astrology? I thought you churchmen put your trust in God alone." Frederick grinned.

"In my younger days I used to be quite adept at it. There's nothing unholy about reading the stars. They only reveal the Lord's will."

Berard glanced at the chart. "Hm, a lot of Leo, in a very prominent position. I see what you mean."

Frederick watched him, saw a passing frown. "What is it?"

"These planets in Leo in the tenth house are all in square to Saturn. And Saturn is in the first house."

Berard turned to the astrologer. "What do you make of it, Abu Talib?"

"Your Lordship, there's no need to worry. Like most high-spirited boys the prince might have a little difficulty obeying his father. It is nothing that a little discipline will not put right."

Frederick grinned. "There you are. A true son of mine!"

"As long as I'm not expected to drum sense into him," Berard replied, "I don't mind. I don't want any more of the gray hairs I got attempting to do that to you as a boy!"

Laughing, Berard and Frederick left the chamber.

As AUTUMN APPROACHED, a stream of messengers and informers came and went between the few remaining loyal towns of Apulia, the palace of Palermo, and the Lateran in Rome.

Frederick's embassy to the emperor had returned empty-handed. The Guelf had scoffed at his offer, deriding at him as the "pope's boy," conveniently forgetting that without the pope's support, he himself would never have become emperor. Meanwhile, the pope had enlisted the aid of the king of France. Otto of Brunswick was a nephew of England's King John. England and France had been at war over English claims in France, and Otto sided with his English uncle, who had supported him in his bid for the imperial crown.

Philip Augustus of France approached the anti-Guelf faction in Germany. The German princes, however, were not receptive. Although professing outrage at the emperor's treachery, many privately resented the pope's high-handed assumption of temporal powers, and thought with nostalgia of the good old days when the German emperors had told the popes what to do.

As soon as Otto crossed the Tuscan boundary, the pope excommunicated him publicly in Saint Peter's, making him an outcast. Letters were sent to the German bishops, to be read from the pulpits of every church, releasing the emperor's subjects from their fealty. Otto, however, continued undaunted on his path of conquest. One by one, the cities of Apulia surrendered to him: Trani, Barletta, and Bari fell one after the other. Only Brindisi held out. By the end of September even this last bastion of royalist loyalty had fallen to Otto's army.

FREDERICK PACED UP and down the chamber. Finally he came to a halt before his page. "Find the admiral and the archbishop, and be quick about it." The boy scurried away.

The messenger still remained kneeling on the floor. At last, as he almost tripped over the man, Frederick noticed him. Dismissing him, he resumed his pacing, then stopped. "That miserable son of a poxed German whore!" His fist crashed down on a lectern. The falcon on its perch in the corner shrieked in alarm, flapping its wings.

"What a disrespectful way of referring to the Holy Roman Emperor!" Frederick wheeled around.

Alaman was crossing the room with his swaggering seafarer's gait. "So, what has the barbarian done now?" he asked, flinging his cloak across a bench. "I understand your feelings, but his mother wasn't German, but English, sister of the Lionheart. That, of course, does not preclude her from having been a whore. I believe the whole family has peculiar sexual habits, including the heroic Richard, who favored fair boys. As for being poxed . . ."

Frederick, usually amused by Alaman's ribald humor, gave the older man a look that stopped him in mid-sentence. "Otto and his army are encamped across the straits of Messina."

The blood drained from Alaman's face. "It can't be."

"It is. I've just had a message from the garrison commander there. Otto is waiting for the Pisan fleet, to launch his invasion of the island."

"If they cross to the island, we can't stop them for long. You know that, don't you?"

Frederick nodded. He knew it, better than anyone else. He had lain awake at night for weeks, considering his options in the event that his counselors might be wrong. They had all assured him that Otto was unlikely to attempt a conquest of the island. They had all been wrong.

"Alaman, I want you to give orders for two fast galleys to be ready in Castellamare to carry myself and my family to Tunisia. We'll have to return to fight another day. This is one battle we are not going to win."

"Are you thinking of taking the queen and little Henry, too?"

"Can you imagine what would befall my son if he fell into the emperor's hands? His aim is to exterminate the Hohenstaufen."

Before Alaman could reply, an alarmed-looking Berard walked through the door. "Frederick, you sent for me?" he asked.

"Otto and his army are in Reggio Calabria and about to cross, on Pisan ships, to the island. I've instructed Alaman to have two galleys riding at anchor, ready to take myself and the court into exile."

Berard stared at him. No one had believed that Otto would go as far as attacking the island. It was assumed that once he had consolidated his hold on Apulia he'd return to Germany, satisfied with having reclaimed lands that the Empire had disputed for centuries. There was a certain tenuous justification in that, with which he could whitewash his treachery.

"For how long can we stop them?" Berard asked.

Frederick said: "If we trap them in the narrow passes leading out of Messina, for a while. But they may not land there. In that case, for a day or two at most."

Alaman nodded.

Frederick continued, "I want you to ensure that the treasury and the chancery archives are removed and put on board tonight, in the greatest secrecy. Take Mahmoud, with a few helpers." He gestured toward the Saracen who acted as his body servant and guard.

"Mahmoud, go with his lordship and make sure no one knows about this. You have men you can trust?"

The Saracen salaamed. "I can vouch for them, my sultan." With a shadow of a smile he added, "No German gold could buy them."

Turning to Alaman, Frederick said, "Make sure the galleys are well guarded, but in such a way as not to arouse suspicion."

The Genoese nodded.

Berard looked at Frederick. "Are you going to inform the council of this?"

"In good time. From now on, I make my own decisions." Frederick's voice was flat.

He looked toward Alaman. "See to it that Messina gets all the reinforcements we can afford."

"I'll do so immediately." The Genoese grabbed his cloak and left the room, with Mahmoud following.

"Berard," Frederick put his hand on the archbishop's arm, "I don't wish to impose this on you. I'll understand if you choose to remain here. Will you come with us if the need arises?"

Berard looked at him. "Need you even ask? Of course I'll come with you. One archbishop or another is much the same as far as a diocese is concerned. But if we are to reclaim Sicily, I can be of more use if I am with you."

Frederick smiled. "Thank you, dear friend." He put his arm around the burly archbishop. He often thought these days that Constance and Berard were all that he had left in a world that was collapsing beneath him.

FREDERICK STOOD BY the window and watched the long line of donkeys leave the outer bailey in the torchlight. The panniers and bales looked like provisions destined for a royal hunting lodge. Caged chickens cackled in annoyance at having their sleep interrupted. On others, baskets with cabbages and apples were wedged between closed panniers.

As he followed the donkey train with his eyes, Frederick thought how low the fortunes of Sicily had once again sunk. The contents of the chancery and the treasury, including the crown of Sicily, were wending their way to Castellamare amid hens and cabbages. He turned back to the room. There were heaps of clothing everywhere. In the midst of this disorder, Constance and Juana had been busy for hours, cutting open seams and hems, selecting jewels from an open casket and sewing the openings closed after concealing the gems inside.

Frederick sat down on a settle and poured himself a cup of wine. He felt hollow inside. Would it ever end, this cruel game that God had played with him since childhood? Every time, just as his luck seemed to turn, fate, with a malicious twist, called forth a new disaster. He ran his finger along the rim of his cup as he watched the two women. Constance's features were drawn, dark shadows under her eyes. Even those associated with him were sucked into the vortex of disaster that was his life.

At last, Constance and Juana packed the garments back into a chest, removing all evidence of their activity. Juana bade them a good night and left the room. Constance, already in her night shift, a cloak over her shoulders, came over to him. She sat down beside him and leaned her head against his shoulder. A deep sigh escaped her. "Frederick, can't we go to Aragon? At least there we would be safe."

He shook his head. "It's too dangerous to cross the open seas. Pisan ships will be on the prowl as soon as our flight is discovered. But they can't patrol forever, and then we can slip out of Tunis." He gestured to the chest that contained the dresses with the jewels. "Was that really necessary?"

"When I had to flee from my husband's brother in Hungary, the jewels I had sewn into my hems saved my life." With a sigh she added, "If we get taken by the Pisans, they'll certainly take my jewels, but there's a good chance they'd let me keep my clothes. One can bribe one's way out of confinement with enough jewels."

Frederick admired the calm with which she had taken the news of their impending flight and prepared for it. He got up and yawned. "Let's sleep. I'm exhausted and so must you be." He put his arm around her waist. He had chosen to sleep tonight in her bedchamber. On his way to bed he blew out the sputtering candles. They had nearly burned themselves out. Somewhere, a church bell chimed matins. It was two o'clock in the morning.

THE NEWS FROM the garrison in Messina, watching the enemy across the narrow straits, remained the same. Otto was still waiting for the Pisan fleet. As the days went by, the tension in the palace rose. Tempers became more and more frayed. All forts commanding the harbors where the enemy might land had been strengthened. Since Messina seemed the most likely target, its garrison had been reinforced with the best available men and an additional contingent of Saracen archers.

Constance spent her days in the nursery, surrounded by her women, cradling her baby son. She tried to stay away as much as possible from Frederick, who was beginning to show the strain too. On the fourth day the weather changed. Clouds began to drift across the blue skies, harbingers of colder weather.

THE MAN STANDING guard outside the loft looked up at the sky. Black clouds blanketed the heavens. He stepped back under the wooden shelter and pulled the cowl of his brown cloak over his head. A cold wind had begun to blow from the sea. It was turning into a gale.

"No birds will be flying in this weather, I promise you," he said to his companion, rubbing his callused hands together to keep them warm. They had several more dreary hours to go before their relief was due.

He had barely uttered the words when the pigeon whirled toward them. Flapping its wings to keep its balance in the blowing wind, the bird gripped the perch in front of the pigeonhouse, impatient to enter the safety of the loft.

The two sentries rushed forward. Stroking its feathers and murmuring reassuringly in Arabic, the older man relieved the pigeon of the message tied to its tail, while the younger one fed it a pellet of seeds and honey. Pulling on a rope, he opened the trap door to the loft. The pigeon fluttered eagerly into the warmth of the dovecote.

Holding the tiny brass cylinder in his raised hand like a trophy, his companion ran toward the guardroom.

"A message from Messina, for the king. Have it delivered immediately."

CONSTERNATION SHOWED ON the faces of those bending over the tiny scrap of parchment.

Straightening, Walter of Palear shook his head. "It's impossible. It must be a forgery."

The others nodded. Carrier pigeons were vulnerable to attack by trained falcons. Sometimes wind brought them down in enemy territory. If spotted, such birds could be sent on their way again after their message had been changed.

"I agree that it makes no sense at all," Berard stroked his black beard, "and yet, somehow, I don't think it is a forgery. What would they be achieving with it? In a day or two, at most, we'll know whether it's true or not."

Frederick, so tense that his knuckles were white where he gripped the edge of the table, turned to Mahmoud. "Ready an escort of fifty men. I'm riding for Messina."

"Frederick, don't do anything rash. This could—"

"Berard, don't argue with me," he cut him off. "I've been sitting here for weeks on your advice when I should have been in Messina."

Berard said, "That's utter nonsense. There's nothing you could have done there except endanger yourself. If this is a trap, the Germans will be waiting for you. Without you as a rallying point, Sicily is theirs."

Frederick gave him a hurt look. That was the last quarter from which he had expected attack.

Berard put a hand on his arm. "Please, Frederick, be reasonable. Wait for a day or two, for the messengers to arrive."

Frederick brushed his hand off. "I'm going to Messina. By a way no German spy would know." He strode out of the chamber, clattering down the stairs in his haste to be gone.

FREDERICK STOOD ON the ramparts and stared across the narrow straits of Messina at the mainland. To hide his trembling hands, he folded his arms across his chest. The sea lay calm and shimmering in the November sun. On the other side the plain of Calabria was arid and empty. It was true. They were gone!

Mahmoud stood by his side, beaming, as did the castellan and his officers, all of them filled with wonder. Frederick wanted to hug them. He contented himself with grinning at Mahmoud. "Well, Mahmoud, it seems we are saved, at least for the moment."

"Allah is great, my lord."

"What I'd like to know is, how did Allah arrange this?"

Frederick turned to the castellan. "Ranulf, tell me once more what your informers said."

The Norman knight bowed. "Your Grace, first they reported that the Germans were striking camp in frenzied haste, dismantling their tents and packing their equipment. Within hours, they were on their way. Afterward, we heard that the emperor, with the army, was marching north along the Adriatic toward Ravenna."

"And Otto has been seen, alive and well?" Frederick asked.

"Yes, Your Grace, there can be no doubt that the emperor is in the best of health."

"What, in the name of the Lord, can have made him abandon a certain prey and rush off like a madman?" Frederick raised his hand to shade his eyes from the sun and took a last look at the deserted plain across the sea where a few days ago an army of thousands had been encamped. Right there, before him in the blue waters, were Scylla and Charybdis. Monsters that rose from the inky blackness of the sea to devour sailors, whole ships that disappeared without a trace, sucked into the depths by infernal whirlpools . . . His head spun. He felt dizzy. Whole armies, German emperors, too, vanished? He made his way slowly down the spiral stone stairs.

In the great hall, he ungirded his sword, let it clatter to the floor. He sank onto a bench. Mahmoud knelt to pull off his mud-caked boots, calling for a basin of hot water for his feet. Frederick's body ached with fatigue. He had spent two days in the saddle, without sleep, halting only to change mounts at forts along the way, doubt and hope battling in his breast.

He buried his face in his hands. When all hope was lost, miraculously, he had been saved. Why? Was it possible that God's capricious games with him were over, or was this just another promise held out to him, only to be snatched away again? Was God testing him, testing his endurance, his faith, which He knew was shaky? A shiver ran through him. Despite his doubts, God had saved him.

PALERMO, JANUARY 1212

Frederick watched the great falcon circle in the sky, closer and closer to the flock of wild geese on the ground.

"Isn't she magnificent?" he whispered to Fakir.

The falconer inclined his head. They were sitting their horses at the edge of a marsh. The late afternoon held that crystalline clarity of a sunny day after plentiful rain. The sun was setting into a band of wispy clouds. The trees at the water's edge mirrored themselves, stark and black, in the burnished water.

Frederick breathed in the crisp air. He felt exhilarated. The ger was the king of falcons. Much larger than the saker or the peregrine, it could fly to great heights and was superbly powerful. It was found only in the icy reaches of the far north. Whole expeditions were launched to trap just one or two of these birds. This one had been a gift from the king of Aragon. It was the pride of Frederick's mews. Suddenly, the geese rose in a perfect, arrowlike formation. They were still out of reach of the falcon. She tried to swoop on them, but missed. With a loud rustling of wings, they flew into the setting sun.

Frederick cursed. What had startled them? He glanced at the hounds. They were still pointing, ears back, tails wagging, looking expectantly toward the houndsmen. Then he heard the drum of galloping hooves. He turned to see a lone rider coming toward them. The hunters parted to let him through. The man, a messenger from the palace, drew rein. He jumped from his horse.

"My lord, I beg your pardon. A message from the lord chancellor. An embassy from Germany has arrived, seeking an audience with Your Grace."

Frederick frowned. "How many?"

"Two, with a small escort."

Frederick hesitated. Then he said, "Tell the chancellor I'll see them on my return. And don't come rushing into a hunt like that again. You've spoiled those geese for us!"

"Yes, my lord." The man shuffled his feet and stared at the ground, but did not move.

"What are you waiting for?" Frederick grabbed his reins.

"My lord, I . . ." the messenger's voice faltered.

"Damnation, man, what is it?"

"The chancellor said I was to tell you to return to the palace without delay."

Frederick's eyes narrowed. "Tell the chancellor that I don't take orders from him."

"Very well, my lord." The messenger's face was a study in discomfiture.

Fakir blew his whistle, holding his flat bag out to the falcon. Germans or no Germans, he had to distract the bird from pursuing her quarry. That was how many falcons were lost. After a last desultory circle, she dropped and settled on the bag, devouring the morsel of meat Fakir held out to her.

Despite his tenseness, Frederick smiled. For a hunter, only a hungry falcon was a good falcon. "Come, Fakir, let's see if we can find those geese again."

The old falconer cast him a long look. "Yes, my lord."

He knows I'm not interested in those geese anymore, Frederick thought. He spurred his chestnut stallion forward. The dogs ran ahead, followed by the houndsmen. The rest of the party with their hawks cantered behind. An apprehensive silence had settled on what had been, moments before, a gay hunt.

Frederick felt cold with fear. All through the winter, ever since the Germans' disappearance, he had waited for an explanation. First, the only news that reached Palermo was that Otto was hurrying across Italy in a bid to pass the Alps before winter. News traveled slowly in winter. The roads turned to quagmires of mud, almost impassable to wheeled traffic. From November to March the Alpine passes were closed to all but the most intrepid travelers. A messenger who spared neither himself nor his mount could hope to average eighty miles a day in summer; in winter, he was lucky if he covered twenty.

When he'd finally learned that Otto and his army had crossed the Brenner Pass, even Frederick began to believe that he wouldn't turn back. He chewed his lip. What could the emperor's messengers possibly want? Was Otto suddenly so desperate that he wished to negotiate the return of Apulia? The conquered towns had been left well garrisoned by the departing Germans. Did he need money to quell a rebellion at home, or to fight an invasion from abroad? He had refused an offer of gold before, but maybe he had changed his mind.

His instincts for negotiation told him to take his time. Despite his anxiety, he continued with a hunt in which he had lost all interest. But negotiate what? Nothing good could be associated with Emperor Otto's name.

CONRAD VON URSBERG wiped his brow. How much longer were they to wait? He was hot in his thick furred cloak, made to ward off the numbing cold of northern winters. But here it wasn't even cold outside and inside one sweltered. The German was a towering figure of a man. He was broad-shouldered, with a thick, muscular neck, a graying blond beard, and blue eyes that missed little.

His younger companion glanced at him. Just as tall but lighter of build, Anselm von Justingen didn't feel the heat as much. His lanky brown hair was cut in a fringe across his forehead and curled inward just above his collar. Intelligent brown eyes looked out of a clean-shaven face. He, too, wore a fur-lined cloak. "Patience, Conrad, it won't be long now," he whispered.

Conrad nodded. This could go on for hours. There was no way he could take off this accursed cloak. He tried to distract himself from his discomfort by looking around the audience hall. A room of splendid proportions, its walls were covered in gold mosaics depicting exotic trees and animals. The vaulted ceiling was a star-studded firmament of brilliant blue. At the far end, on a dais under a fringed canopy, stood the throne. Of carved and gilded wood, it rested on two crouching porphyry lions. The floor, too, was inlaid with red and white porphyry. It was said that the young king and his country were impoverished. His Norman ancestors, however, must have been immensely wealthy to have built such a palace.

At last, fanfares sounded. The bronze doors swung open. The ranks of courtiers bowed. Conrad, who had been in Constantinople with the Fourth Crusade when they captured the city from the Byzantines, caught his breath. He felt himself transported back to the Bosporus.

Flanked by a ceremonial guard of Saracens in crimson turbans, scimitars held aloft, the king advanced toward the throne. He wore a dalmatic of white silk. From his shoulders fell a scarlet mantle, with gilt-embroidered palms, lions, and camels picked out in pearls. A large ruby flashed in the clasp that held the cloak. As the king passed, Conrad caught a whiff of an incenselike, flowery scent. At least, Conrad thought, making an effort not to wrinkle his nose, he has Barbarossa's hair and a good square chin.

The whole apparition glittered with exotic magnificence. Only the sea-green eyes weren't those of an oriental potentate. They belonged neither to his German heritage nor to the Eastern opulence around him, but were wholly his own.

After the king had been enthroned, a herald signaled them to step forward. "The ambassadors, Conrad von Ursberg and Anselm von Justingen," the herald announced.

Conrad and Anselm knelt.

"You may rise." The voice was deep for one so young. "Welcome to my court, my lords."

"Thank you, Your Grace." Conrad glanced at Walter of Palear beside the throne. "Your lord chancellor has overawed us with your hospitality."

"My lords, crossing the Alps in winter is an arduous enterprise. What is the nature of your errand?" The green eyes rested on him, cold and unblinking.

Conrad took a step forward. "Your Grace, we have come to bring you the news that the Emperor Otto has been deposed by the prince-electors of Germany."

A murmur of astonishment ran through the hall.

"He has been deposed, by his own people?"

Conrad nodded, "Yes, Your Grace."

A smile, greatly appealing, impish almost, softened the king's face. "This is welcome news indeed. We shall celebrate Otto's fall with a banquet, of which you shall be the guests of honor."

Conrad inclined his head. So he had also inherited Barbarossa's ability to charm at will. "We thank you, my lord." Conrad drew breath: "May I continue?"

The king nodded.

"At the same meeting in Nuremberg, the princes elected a new emperor. We have been sent to ask you, for the weal of Christendom and the peace of Germany, to accept the imperial crown." He went down on one knee. "Only you, as the last Hohenstaufen, will be able to command enough loyalty to unite the Empire, torn by conflict for so long."

Silence filled the hall. It was as if those present were holding their breath, waiting for the king to reply. After what seemed an eternity, Barbarossa's grandson spoke at last. "This is an unexpected honor. Tell me, has the pope been advised of this?"

"Yes, Your Grace. Before the election, he was approached by the bishops of Basle and Speyer. In principle, the Holy Father's reaction was favorable. We were to inform you first, before halting in Rome on our return."

"My lords, this is a most weighty matter. We will reconvene later, when you can explain all this more fully to me and my counselors." The king's smile was tight. He dismissed them.

Trying not to show his disappointment, Conrad rose to his feet. After months of exhausting travel, Frederick of Sicily's reaction to his incredible good fortune seemed like a terrible anticlimax.

FREDERICK STOOD WITH arms outstretched as Mahmoud removed first his cloak, then the dalmatic, gloves, and sandals. The Saracen laid the garments on the bed with infinite care. Later, they would be carried down to the treasury, to be put in their chests and protected from moths with peppercorns. Mahmoud alone had a key to the vault in which King Roger's garments were kept.

Mahmoud held Berard's fibula in his hand, about to place it in its leather box.

"Don't return it to the archbishop yet," Frederick said. "I'll wear it at the banquet for the Germans." He laughed. "I've always been the king of beggars, Mahmoud. Now I might even become their emperor."

Mahmoud lowered his eyes. "Aye. I have heard that the Germans want you for their emperor." He bent down and began to unroll Frederick's cream silk stocking. After a moment's silence, he added, unrolling the second stocking: "But how, oh lord, could you ever be sultan of those you have such reason to hate?"

"That, Mahmoud, is one of many questions I must answer to myself."

Frederick turned to the fire, warming his hands. Thoughts tumbled through his head like acrobats. Everyone would be clustering in turmoil in the privy hall, waiting for him, waiting to overwhelm him with questions, with advice.

One of the oil lamps in the room flickered brightly, then died. Even if Constance or Berard didn't appear soon, the servants would come to replenish the oil, trim the candlewicks, close the shutters. He needed to think, to be alone.

"Mahmoud, wait for me at the kitchen postern with two horses. Make sure no one sees you."

THE MOSQUE WAS empty. The evening prayers were over. The sweepers had gone, and the few old men who came to honor the last prayer of the night would not be here for a while. Frederick slipped off his hood. There was no one to recognize him.

From the bench along the north wall he could see the courtyard through the horseshoe arches. Clouds lit by a partly hidden moon scuttled across the sky. The orange trees cast black shadows over the pavement. From beyond the gate tower, a horse whinnied. It was Mahmoud with their horses.

Two tall bronze cressets lit the *mirhab*. Frederick leaned back and closed his eyes. In his head, voices whispered warnings, encouragement, doubt. Was this God's latest move in his cruel game of chess? Was God offering him his queen only to distract him so that he could snatch his king? Or was this a genuine truce, an end to his challenge? In his mind's eye he saw the German ambassadors, heard their strangely accented Latin: "We . . . ask you, for the weal of Christendom and the peace of Germany, to accept the imperial crown . . ." The crown of the Holy Roman Empire, Charlemagne's crown . . . it had not been offered to the Hauteville king of Sicily, but to the last of the Hohenstaufen. Who were they, so revered and so hated by so many? Becoming emperor would mean becoming a Hohenstaufen. It would mean becoming German . . .

Later, he would listen to Berard, to Constance, to Walter. But first he needed to fathom the answer for himself. He would find it here, in this deserted mosque of his childhood, the mosque of his years of penury and solitude. A sense of calm, of detachment almost, began to fill him.

"Frederick of Hohenstaufen!"

The words echoed through the mosque. Frederick leapt up, reaching for his dagger.

"Forgive me for startling you, oh king." A figure detached itself from the shadows and came toward him. The green turban bowed. "I was meditating when you entered . . ."

Frederick stared at Ibn el Gawazi. "How could you know . . . Why did you call me by that name?"

The scholar spread his hands. "Call you what, oh lord? I merely wished the peace of Allah upon you."

Frederick sheathed his dagger. "I am sorry, my friend. I heard a voice calling me by a name I have never used, a German name, my father's name." He looked at the scholar, "I have been elected emperor, in place of the deposed Emperor Otto. He still has much support. It is a grave decision, a decision that could make Sicily the heart of Christendom or destroy her."

"I see." Ibn el Gawazi showed no surprise. After a moment, he said, "And have you made your decision?"

"Yes."

"In that case, allow me to walk with you to the gate. It is not seemly that the emperor of the Franks should walk alone in the night, even if the blessing of Allah is upon him."

THE PARCHMENT CONFIRMING Frederick's election lay unrolled on the work table in his privy chamber. Weighted down by four bronze inkhorns, it was more than five feet long, and bore the signatures and seals of the German electors.

Berard had watched Frederick read it over and over again, staring for long moments at the signatures and glossy red seals on the creamy vellum. Frederick stood bent over it now. Raising his head, he frowned at Conrad. "Why king of the Romans?"

"My lord, when a new emperor is elected, his title is king of the Romans, which means king of Germany. He is crowned as such in Aachen. Although he is emperor in all but name, it is only after his coronation by the pope in Rome that he officially assumes the imperial title."

"Does that mean that the pope has the ultimate veto on the emperor's coronation?"

"Yes, Your Grace."

"Is there anything the pope will not try to control? What worldly ambition for one whose concern is supposed to be the spiritual welfare of mankind!"

Berard winced. Conrad and Anselm, however, nodded in agreement. The power of the papacy had never been popular with the German nobility, nor with their emperors.

Frederick walked around the table. Berard caught his breath. Frederick's shoulders were rigid; a nerve twitched above his left eyebrow. "My lords, as you know, I have spent the last two days with my counselors, considering your offer." He paused. "Against their advice and that of my queen, I have decided to accept the imperial crown."

The two German lords fell to their knees. They reached for Frederick's hem and raised the cloth to their lips. "My liege," Anselm, the younger, said, "we pledge ourselves to you. May you bring peace to our land."

The gray-bearded Conrad said, "As a young man, I served your grandfather, the Emperor Barbarossa. I was with him in the Holy Land. With God's help, you will bring back those happy days." His eyes were moist.

Frederick laid a hand on the old warrior's shoulder. "With the help of Germany's princes and her people, I promise to restore the Empire to its greatness."

Berard felt a stab of fierce pain. The boy he had nurtured was no more. The ambition to rule the world ran in his blood. Without knowing it, Frederick had been waiting for this moment all his life.

FREDERICK SAID, "COME, my lords. We need to plan." He took Berard's elbow, propelling him to settle beside the fire. For several hours they plotted Frederick's course of action. Although Innocent had given his tacit approval of Frederick's election during secret negotiations with the German ecclesiastical princes, the first step was to go to Rome and secure it in person. After that, Frederick would make his way to Germany, past Otto's remaining allies, to the duchy of Swabia, where he could count on support and reinforcements. From there, he must set out to win the Empire.

When Conrad and Anselm finally took their leave, Frederick and Berard remained alone in the small study. The light outside was fading. In the hearth, the fire had nearly burned out. A few glowing embers smoldered amid the ashes.

Frederick leaned forward, elbows on knees. He looked at Berard.

He knows, Berard thought, how I feel. For the last two days, every one of Frederick's counselors had advised him to refuse the imperial crown. They recited the pitfalls of this dangerous enterprise. They reminded him that being elected emperor was not the same as being in possession of the Empire. They pointed out the continuing presence of Otto, still with an army, and considerable remaining supporters, not the least of which was his uncle, King John of England. They warned him that Innocent would never consent to his remaining king of Sicily and emperor at the same time. Yes, it was true, he had given his consent to Frederick's election, influenced by the French king, in a desperate bid to destroy Otto of Brunswick, convinced that only the Hohenstaufen name could overcome Otto. But the price the pontiff was certain to exact would be the crown of Sicily. Frederick listened as if in a trance. His council's warnings had had as little effect as Berard's private entreaties and Constance's tears.

"Berard, I have to accept the Empire for Sicily. If I refuse, the disappointment would demoralize the German princes who have broken with Otto. One day, stronger than ever, he would be back to conquer Sicily."

Berard pursed his lips. There was some truth in this, but it was not the whole truth. He said nothing.

Frederick said, "I'll convince the pope when I am face to face with him."

Berard raised an eyebrow. "I know you can be very persuasive, but you'll need more to persuade the Holy Father. Innocent's goal is to make the Church an unassailable territorial power. I cannot see how he can allow the Empire and Sicily to be joined in your person. The papal state would be surrounded by one power."

"Berard, come with me to Rome, plead my cause with the pope, and then accompany me to Germany."

"You want me to come with you, despite the fact that you know I disapprove?"

"You know that there is no one whose advice I value more." With a smile, he added, "Even if I don't always act upon it."

Berard sighed. Frederick needed him now, perhaps more than ever before. He nodded. "I'll come with you."

Frederick contemplated his hands. "You're right, you know. I'm not accepting the imperial crown for the sake of Sicily alone, although Sicily will always come first. It's my fate. This is my Rubicon, and I, too, must cross it, regardless of the consequences." There was something like regret in his voice. "Berard," he asked, raising his eyes, "will you stand by me, no matter what happens?"

"Of course, Frederick, you know that."

"Even against the pope, if necessary?"

Berard looked at him. "I pray to God that I will never have to make such a choice."

* * *

CONSTANCE PACED UP and down Frederick's chamber. Since the appearance of the German emissaries, he'd lost every shred of his considerable common sense. "I implore you, Frederick, once more, don't do this! It'll never work. Do you really think Otto is just going to accept his deposition? Your Germans themselves admit that he still has a large part of his army and support in the north."

He was standing in a pool of sunshine, booted and spurred, his hunting cloak over his arm, staring at her, saying nothing. She'd arrived as he was about to go hawking, with the Germans. He, who had hated all things German! He had even begun learning German. It was preposterous. His refusal to argue, to react, added rage to her fear for him. "Do you really believe you'll be able to command enough German loyalties to defeat him? You, an unknown stranger? You're nobody, you have no gold with which to pay an army, you can't even speak their language. You're nothing but an immature boy dreaming childish dreams of glory!"

With one swift stride, he was at her side. He grabbed the front of her gown and shook her. "Don't you ever speak to me like this again, do you hear me?" As suddenly as he had pounced on her, he released her. "I'm sorry, Constance. I must follow my destiny." He picked up his cloak from the floor. "I know you don't understand, but I truly believe that it is possible to restore the Empire to its greatness. That is why I am going to Germany. I am leaving next week, from Messina."

Constance hung her head. There was nothing more she could say.

On the threshold, Frederick turned around. "If anything were to befall me, I am leaving Sicily in your hands. You'll be queen-regent, together with Berard, until our son comes of age. While Berard is away with me, Walter will act as co-regent."

Constance stared after him, dry-eyed, numb with pain. This time, she knew, she had lost him for good, to a new mistress more dangerous and more bewitching than any woman: the dream of a new Rome.

A COLD SPRING wind filled the sails as the royal galley made its way out of Messina harbor. The sky was gray with the threat of rain. Spray from the waves splashed across the deck as the oars dipped into the black water to the somber beat of the galley master's drum.

Frederick stood and watched the island slowly recede into the distance. Would he ever see Sicily again? In his mind he could hear Constance's voice, a voice he'd refused to heed. What lay ahead seemed suddenly as danger-filled as the churning waters around them. He glanced at the lookouts who were watching for Pisan galleys. Skirting the coast, both to avoid the Pisans and to be able to make a quick landfall, the ship followed the Sicilian mainland, heading toward Rome.

The icy wind stung his face. As he steadied himself on a rope, he thought of his escort in the cramped space below deck. Thirty knights, Berard, Alaman, the two Germans, and a handful of Saracens. Surely never before had a smaller group attempted a greater feat. In Rome Innocent would provide them with additional men and, God willing, funds as well. Once across the Alps, they would be in Swabia, where he could count on further reinforcements.

He pulled up the hood of his cloak to shield himself from the drizzle. With a last look at Sicily disappearing in the mist, he clambered down the slippery stairs.

ROME, APRIL 1212

FREDERICK REINED IN his horse on the summit of the ancient road. Before him lay Rome. He thought of the nights he had spent as a boy, reading and re-reading the writers of antiquity. How often had he imagined this city and the great men who had walked the shady arcades of her marble-paved Forum . . .

He turned to Berard. "What a sight!" He swept his arm across the horizon as if to embrace the city. "Look at the size of her, at the length of her walls!"

"When you get closer Rome loses much of its luster," Berard was slumped in the saddle with fatigue. "The stench and the flies are terrible, the sewers no longer work, the pavements are gone."

"Oh, Berard, it isn't that bad," Alaman grinned. "Rome has the most beautiful courtesans in Italy. Unfortunately, the rich cardinals have been driving up their cost. But at least, at the prices they charge, they aren't poxed!"

Frederick suppressed a smile. Alaman was baiting Berard. A churchman who practiced what he preached didn't fit in with the Genoese's opinions of the clergy. Although Alaman liked Berard, he'd once told Frederick that he found him to be an enigma. No mistresses, no pleasure boys, no hidden offspring; it was unnatural!

"We had better be on our way if we are to reach Rome before nightfall," Berard said, ignoring Alaman. "Even in Rome, the city gates close at dusk."

With a last look at the city of Caesar, Frederick headed his horse down the slope, followed by the others. In a cloud of dust, their cloaks billowing behind them, they cantered along the Via Appia toward Rome.

POPE INNOCENT STOOD at the window, looking out over his city. Tall and thin, he had a long face, an aquiline nose, and deep-set eyes whose piercing glance made most people feel uncomfortable. Innocent's moral principles, combined with a shrewd pragmatism and an iron will, had made him the most powerful pope since Gregory the Great.

The Lateran Palace, residence of the popes since the time of Constantine, commanded a magnificent view of Rome. In the distance, beneath a bank of clouds, the Colosseum towered over the city; symbol of her pagan past, it dwarfed the buildings around it. Everywhere were signs of Rome's vanished greatness: the baths of Caracalla, triumphal arches, remains of palaces and porticoes, even the aqueduct below the Lateran square, still carrying water in its clay pipes to the Palatine hill, as it had done for more than a millennium.

Cheek by jowl with the remains of antiquity grew the Christian city. Sometimes the new buildings were so entwined with the old that they shared a common wall. Many churches, public buildings, and the fortresslike towers of the nobility were built of Travertine marble pillaged from ancient buildings. Thus, Innocent thought, pagan Rome lives on in the Christian city, blended together with bricks and mortar. And perhaps in the hearts of men, too . . .

Innocent sighed. The bell towers of Rome's innumerable churches and monasteries proclaimed her dedication to Christ. For nearly seven hundred years, the popes had ruled Rome. They'd staved off barbarians and Saracens, maintained order, arbitrated between the perpetually feuding nobility, and kept the populace more or less under control. The power he wielded was based on faith. But how deep was this faith really?

This question was at the core of the imperial problem. Otto's breach of promise was a challenge to the doctrine of total obedience owed by all Christians to the pope. It was also a dangerous example. The papal lands had to be recovered; they had shrunk to less than half their previous size. Without sufficient land, he couldn't secure their borders, couldn't maintain an army worthy of the name, but had to depend on the unreliable protection of his vassals.

There was a knock on the door, followed by his secretary. "Your Holiness, the king of Sicily has arrived."

The pope glanced up. "I'm coming."

The secretary bowed and withdrew.

Innocent sighed. Frederick of Sicily. Now here was a tricky problem. What was he like, this young man? The lad had done well in Sicily since coming of age, despite setbacks. Seventeen years old, impecunious and inexperienced, his vassal. He, at least, would have to rely on the support of the Church. A welcome change from the towering Otto with his army, his English uncle, and his wealth. Every time Innocent thought of Otto's treachery, his ulcered stomach knotted in pain.

Young Frederick will have to do, Innocent thought. He gathered his purple mantle and went to meet his erstwhile ward for the first time.

FREDERICK KNELT AND kissed the papal slipper. Then he pressed his lips to the Fisherman's ring. The ceremony of homage over, Innocent rose and embraced him. They exchanged the kiss of peace. The pontiff held him at arm's length.

"We meet at last, my son." The voice was that of an accomplished preacher, smooth and sonorous.

"Your Holiness, this is indeed a joyful day for me," Frederick said, holding the pope's gaze.

Innocent's sharp eyes, accustomed to seeking out the failings of his fellows, carefully scrutinized the young man before him. Fearless, he thought. He smiled. "Well, Frederick, this is a great honor and a heavy burden you are about to assume."

"Holy Father, with God's help and your guidance I am confident of success."

Smiles of approval appeared on the faces of the prelates standing about the pope. Several nodded.

"We have much to discuss, Frederick." The Pope motioned to the two cardinals flanking him. "Ricciarelli and Orsini, come, let us go to my study."

Frederick followed, accompanied only by Berard and Cardinal Savelli, the papal legate to Sicily. The rest of his retinue waited outside in the antechamber.

They remained closeted for several hours. When they emerged at last, Frederick's face was stony. Their little group was standing in the Lateran square before the equestrian statue of Marcus Aurelius, waiting for their horses to be brought by the papal grooms.

"What happened?" Alaman da Costa asked, unable to contain himself any longer, as the horses appeared. "What conditions did he make?"

"Ask Berard," Frederick snapped, swinging himself into the saddle with a look of disgust.

FREDERICK PACED UP and down like a caged bear in the whitewashed chamber in the monastery where they were lodged.

". . . and that's not all. On Easter Sunday I must do homage to him for my kingdom, like any miserable vassal for a few acres of plowland! There's no end to this priest's ambition, is there? I'm surprised he hasn't tried to become emperor himself!"

Berard shook his head. To him, Innocent's conditions seemed more reasonable than he had dared hope for.

A knock at the door interrupted them. "A gift from the prior, my lords."

The cellarer, a rotund Benedictine in a black robe with a large bunch of keys at his belt, came in bearing a tray. He set down an embossed jug and two silver cups on the chest against the wall. "The best vintage, from our vineyards in Frascati," he beamed.

Frederick inclined his head. "Thank you. Tell the prior his gift is most welcome."

The monk waddled out. Berard poured two cups and handed one to Frederick. He took a sip. The wine was deliciously cool and crisp. "Let's look at this calmly, Frederick. Anger will get us nowhere."

Frederick sat on a stool opposite him. With the toe of his boot he cleared the rushes, then put his untouched cup on the floor. His anger had run its course. He was ready to listen.

Berard said, "So Innocent wants you to hand over Sicily to little Henry as soon as you are crowned king of Germany. I'm surprised he has not demanded that you sever all connections with Sicily. All in all, the Holy Father is being very reasonable."

Berard took another sip of wine and continued, "And as for his stipulation that you renew your mother's concordat, it makes sense to renew the bonds of vassalage that bind you to the papacy. The tighter they are, the less you will be able to renege on your promises, as Otto did."

"God's truth, Berard, and the condition that during Henry's minority the kingdom be administered by a regent of the pope's choosing? That effectively bars me from ruling my own country!" Frederick jumped up. He glared at Berard.

"But that's precisely what you're not supposed to be doing," Berard said. "You're supposed to rule the Empire instead."

Frederick sat down again. "And for good measure, I must pay an annual tribute, to be handed over every year in a public ceremony. Can you believe that?" He shook his head in disgust.

"The tribute is not very large; it's more symbolic than anything else."

"It's still an unspeakable humiliation. Can you imagine Caesar paying tribute?"

Berard leaned forward, resting his hands on his knees. "Look, Frederick, the best way to understand an adversary is to put yourself in his place," he said. "The pope is a very worried man. He made one mistake in backing Otto and he wants every possible reassurance that he's not making another, worse one, with you. After all, the Hohenstaufen emperors have all been at loggerheads with the papacy!"

"Only because the popes have meddled in the Empire's affairs. If they contented themselves with running the Church, there would be no conflict." Frederick paused, then sighed, "If only my mother hadn't signed that concordat with the pope. How could she have done anything so stupid?"

"She had no choice, just as you have no choice now. By making Sicily a papal fief, she was trying to protect your life, and your heritage from invasion. You know that you must accept the pope's conditions if you are to be emperor."

"Have no fear. I'll swear the oaths, I'll sign the agreements, I'll go down on my knees and grovel. But I promise you one thing," he said viciously, "one day I'll teach the papacy a lesson it will never forget."

"You can't do that." Berard's voice rose. "You're imperiling your immortal soul!"

"Ha! My immortal soul! What about *his* immortal soul? I should think that extorting promises under duress is worse than committing perjury to save my kingdom! My forefathers were kings and emperors long before this plebeian was in swaddling clothes. And in any case, is there really such a thing as a soul?"

"Frederick!" Berard rose. He was very calm. Putting a hand on Frederick's shoulder, he said, "I beg of you, do not do this. Let us find a compromise, let us reason with Innocent, but do not begin your reign as emperor with a falsehood. The wrath of heaven is a terrible thing."

Frederick shook his head, "Berard, there are some things that we will always see differently. I'm a king. You're a priest. God has appointed us to different tasks, and I must do what I consider necessary, whatever the price." He jumped to his feet. "I'm going to take a walk around the cloister, I need fresh air."

As he reached the door, he turned.

"Berard . . ."

"Yes?"

"Don't worry about my soul." It was said lightly, with a smile, but in his eyes there was sympathy for Berard's turmoil.

After he had gone, Berard sat looking for a long time at the crucifix on the wall. His eyes scrutinized the face of the Saviour as if seeking an answer.

In a way, Innocent and Frederick were both right. Each was protecting his God-given right. One his crown, the other the independence of the Church. Where was his own duty? He owed allegiance to the pope. But above Innocent stood a greater One. On whose side would He wish him to be? The carved, emaciated features of the crucified Christ looked down on him full of compassion.

In the distance, Berard could hear bells. They were ringing compline. The monastery bell, too, began to chime, calling the brothers to the day's last service. Since childhood, Berard's life had been ordered by the sound of church bells. Bells divided the day and night into the sections set aside for devotions by the monastic orders, but they also marked time for everyone else. Bells announced fire, death, war, as well as feasts, births, christenings, and weddings.

The strokes of the bells rose and fell, back and forth in a steady rhythm, a beautiful sound that brought peace to Berard's heart.

ON EASTER SUNDAY, before the Roman nobility and a glittering array of cardinals, archbishops, bishops, and officials of the curia packed inside the Lateran basilica, Frederick paid homage to Innocent as his vassal. He renewed the concordat of his mother, and took the oath the pope had demanded.

In a steady voice, his right hand on a jewel-encrusted book of the Gospels, Frederick swore that as soon as he was crowned emperor he would renounce the throne of Sicily in favor of his son Henry. His face was calm. He accepted the pope's embrace with a smile of gratitude and thanked him for his help and protection.

In the dim light of the basilica, amid the wafting incense and candle smoke, Pope Innocent looked at the serene young features of his vassal and was satisfied. This time, he thought, the papacy might be well served. Acolytes in white and gold surplices swung silver censers. Frederick knelt. The pontiff raised his right hand and made the sign of the cross above him.

"Go with God, my son, and may your reign be blessed!"

IN ADDITION TO his blessing and four thousand gold bezants, the pope gave Frederick a parting gift even more precious than gold: orders to the German bishops to assist him in every way, particularly with the supply of men and arms.

However, the curia's spies reported that Otto and his army were at Trent, guarding access to the Brenner Pass. North of Rome, the Italian cities friendly to the Guelfs were barring him from crossing the other Alpine passes.

"I can't believe this!" Frederick fumed. "Here I am, elected emperor by an overwhelming majority of the German princes, and I can't even get across Italy, past a few miserable city states ruled by dyers, cobblers, and coopers!"

"They're not that miserable, Frederick. Most Italian communes are as rich as Croesus. They can afford the best foreign mercenaries. As for the tradesmen you're sneering at, it is precisely their trade that has made them wealthy," Berard said.

Frederick glared at him. "You think that cities should rule themselves?"

"I'm just saying that they've succeeded remarkably well. They're a force to be reckoned with."

"I for one see only the havoc wreaked by these city-states. They continually harass their neighbors, and fight the pope or the emperor or both."

"The emperors who have ignored the power of the Italian communes have done so at their peril. Remember that."

Frederick decided to go by sea to Genoa. This would at least take them in a northeasterly direction. In addition, the Genoese might be induced to offer support, both financial and in the form of fighting men. But this plan too was delayed when they heard that the Pisans were patrolling outside the Roman ports. Furious, Frederick remained in Rome.

Finally, Alaman found a Genoese captain who smuggled Frederick and his escort, dressed as Saracens, on board his merchant galley amid a cargo of cloth, olive oil, and cheese. The Pisan spies in the port were hoodwinked. As the bay of Genoa came into sight, Frederick and his men unwound their turbans. The Genoese, bitter rivals of the Pisans, gave him a tumultuous welcome. A huge crowd brandishing boughs of greenery followed Frederick and his escort from the harbor through the winding streets to the Doria palace.

Niccolò Doria, head of a family who had supplied the republic of Genoa with statesmen for more than a century, was also leader of the Ghibelline faction in the city. An elderly man with impeccable manners, a bulbous nose, and the hands of an aristocrat, he had nevertheless, like most Genoese, the shrewd instincts of a merchant. His small black eyes appraised Frederick. "My lord, you do me and my family great honor in accepting our humble hospitality."

He is, thought Frederick, evaluating the benefits to be gained from ingratiating himself with the new emperor.

With a flourish of his wide-cut velvet sleeve, Niccolò introduced them
to his family, assembled in the atrium of their palace. His wife, a middle-
aged, tired-looking woman in a brocaded headdress, curtsied. The cause of
her pallor appeared in a large brood of children, ranging from an infant in
the arms of a wet nurse, to several plain daughters of marriageable age, and
two handsome, dark-haired sons, Percival and Barnabo.

Frederick took an immediate liking to the elder of the two, Percival,
about his own age. Percival and a chamberlain escorted them to their quarters, which occupied a whole wing of the palace. After the Doria servants
had left their baggage, Frederick looked around. Frescoes of country scenes
covered the walls. The bed hangings were of thick cendal, the beds massive, raised on platforms of carved oak. The mattresses were stuffed with
soft down, the first featherbeds Frederick had ever seen. Punching his fist
into a mattress, he grinned at Berard. "The Dorias enjoy showing off their
wealth, don't they? How did they acquire it, by piracy or fulling?"

"Shipping, my son. Most honorably."

They spent their days entertained by the rulers of Genoa. Jousts,
hunts, and gargantuan banquets followed one after another. Weeks
passed. Still, the friendly Italian towns urged caution. All routes over the
Alps were watched by his enemies. Frederick became more and more
impatient. His only distraction was his new friendship with the Doria
heir, Percival.

Although at first the young man had been a little reticent, he had soon
lost his reserve. He introduced Frederick to his friends. Together, they
read poetry until late at night, or debated Boethius, a Greek philosopher
recently rediscovered. Accustomed all his life to the company of people
much older than himself, Frederick revelled in the camaraderie of men
his own age. They would do the rounds of the better wineshops behind
the Ripa Maris, the arcaded seafront, where all Genoa's trade and most
of her public life took place. Alaman, a kinsman of the Dorias, often
joined them.

THE TAVERN, CUT deep into the rock, resounded with laughter. Men filled
the long unplaned tables, sweat glistening on faces flushed with revelry.
The lute player in the corner strummed his instrument, urging them to

join in. Song filled the vaulted room. Cups were raised and drained. Serving wenches staggered past carrying heavy earthenware flagons.

A barefooted girl, her unbound hair tumbling down her back in a tangle of yellow curls, jumped onto the wine-stained table at which Frederick and his friends were sitting. Alaman tossed her a coin. "Dance for us, Catalina!"

The lutenist strummed harder. The singing grew more raucous. Stamping her feet, the girl began to dance. Slowly at first, then gathering speed. Skirts flying, eyes closed, she turned into a blur of spinning hips and heaving breasts and long wild hair. Frederick stared at her, mesmerized by her feral vitality.

As suddenly as she had started, she came to a halt. The tavern erupted into wild applause. Coins flew through the air and landed at her feet. As she bent down to retrieve the coins, Frederick realized that he, like everyone else, was leering at the white flesh protruding from her low-cut bodice.

The girl jumped off the table in one lithe movement. Alaman slapped his thigh. "Come here, my dove." She threaded her way toward him, adroitly avoiding the hands that reached out from other tables, and sat on Alaman's lap. Lazily, with a gesture born of long practice, she removed his hand from her bodice whenever it got too close. Her eyes, green and slanted like a cat's, were fixed on Frederick.

"Here, drink this!" Alaman urged, handing her his wine cup. Over the rim of the cup her eyes smiled at Frederick.

Alaman, who could drink like no other man Frederick knew, emptied cup after cup, ordering more flagons. All the while he fondled the dancer, watching Frederick and her. Determined not to be outdone, Frederick downed the unwatered wine almost as fast as his friend. His legs began to feel heavy. Percival, beside him, was slurring his words. Glancing across the table, Frederick caught the critical look on Anselm von Justingen's face.

Two more girls joined them. One of them sidled up to Frederick and tried to sit on his lap. He pushed her aside.

"Come on, Frederick, don't be so surly, they're all juicy morsels."

He gave Alaman a withering look and drained his cup in one gulp, slamming it down on the table.

"Let's leave, I've had enough of this place."

* * *

OUTSIDE, FREDERICK GRATEFULLY inhaled the crisp sea air. The pungent odor of spilled wine and unwashed bodies in the tavern had been overpowering. His head felt heavy and his mouth was dry. He had drunk far too much spiced wine. As the longing in his loins subsided, he felt relief at having preserved his dignity.

Somewhere, the call of the night watch on their rounds echoed through the deserted streets. In the stillness, their footsteps rang out on the cobblestones as they made their way back to the palazzo Doria. As they rounded a corner, a small figure darted out of an alley. A scruffy urchin tugged at Frederick's cloak.

"*Messire! Messire!*"

"What . . . ?"

Another tug, motioning him to bend down. Frederick listened to the child. Bursting into laughter, he fished a coin from the purse at his belt and gave it to the boy. His resolution vanished. He turned to the others: "You go along. I've been sent an invitation by a beautiful lady."

"A lady she assuredly is not, but you'll enjoy her. A hot little wench, made for bedsport. Selective, too," Alaman said. "As soon as she clapped eyes on you, I could see that tonight it was neither my prowess nor my gold she was after."

Preceded by two Saracens carrying lanterns and tailed by Mahmoud, Frederick followed the boy through the dark, tortuous alleys. They went up a narrow, creaking outside staircase. The room was small and dingy. A single tallow lamp threw a circle of light onto the low whitewashed ceiling. Catalina came towards him.

"I knew you'd come. You want me, don't you?" When she smiled, her cheeks dimpled. She showed no sign of respect or awe, though she knew full well, as did everyone in Genoa, who he was. With a casual gesture, she began to unlace her bodice. Her breasts were large and white. Frederick's mouth went dry. He took one step across the room and tried to grab her. "Come here," he said, his voice thick.

With a little laugh she evaded him. "What an impatient young buck you are!"

The blood was pounding in his temples now, a mixture of headache and lust. He lunged forward and caught her by the wrist. "Don't taunt me, you little wildcat!" Bending her head back, he kissed her hard. They stood pressed together, tasting each other hungrily. Out of breath, he let go of her and wiped his aching mouth with the back of his hand.

With a deft movement, she bent down and undressed him. "By the milk of the Virgin!!" She ran her tongue over her lips as she stared down at him. Then, gently, reverently, she held him with one hand while she stroked him with the other.

Frederick closed his eyes. He opened them again. "I don't think that's a good idea . . ." She stopped. "Come," she whispered. She pulled him across the room. Leaning backward over the table, she raised her skirts. With half-closed eyes, her hair fanned out on the table, she offered herself up to him.

He sank into her with a groan. He hadn't had a woman for weeks. Every fiber in his body ached for the moment of release, yet he wanted to continue, to torment her twisting flesh by denying it what it craved. The power to enthrall her was as heady as the urge in his loins. Finally, unable to hold out any longer, he slumped forward. The girl screamed, a wild, triumphant scream, and fell back onto the table.

With his heart pounding, Frederick straightened his back. He took in the air in great gulps, feeling strength and breath flow back into him. After a moment, Catalina wrapped her legs and arms around him. "Take me to bed, like this," she whispered.

With their bodies still joined, he carried her over to the truckle bed in the corner. He began to move again, taking his time, feeling a new wave of excitement building up, rising in a slow, exquisite curve, higher and higher.

As HE CREPT down the creaking staircase in the first light of dawn, followed by Mahmoud, who avoided his eyes, and his companions, who had spent the night wrapped in their cloaks on the threshold outside, he felt sick. His temples pounded, his stomach heaved. With a mixture of disgust and dispassionate curiosity Frederick asked himself how he could have spent the night with a common harlot in a squalid hovel. And yet he knew that he would see her again. He had given her his whole purse, which was not very much, with an apology. Catalina had only laughed, a deep, guttural laugh, and curled up again on her pallet.

*　*　*

THE QUARTER WHERE Catalina's father was a tavernkeeper became as familiar to Frederick as the palaces of Genoa's aristocracy. Whenever he could, he sneaked away, with only Mahmoud as an escort. They coupled with a frenzy that left him drained and contented. Even his worries seemed to seep out of him.

On the day before he left Genoa, Frederick went to see Catalina for the last time. He untied a leather pouch from his belt. Taking her hand, he spilled the contents into her palm.

"This should buy you a dowry, Catalina. Take them to Percival Doria. He knows about you. Ask him to change them for you. He will see that no one cheats you."

Catalina stared at the coins. "Real gold?"

"Gold bezants, from Byzantium. Unclipped."

"But so many?"

Frederick smiled. "It's a prince's duty to reward those who give him pleasure."

Catalina wrapped her arms around him. She put her head on his chest. "One day, I'll tell my grandchildren that in my youth I loved the Emperor Frederick," she whispered.

THE MORNING WAS already hot. They left Genoa behind and climbed the steep road leading north across the Apennines. As they gained in altitude, the landscape became more solitary and forbidding. Vertical walls of rock rose before them. Bluish-gray outcrops of slate covered the land. Here and there, a few stunted trees clung to the sparse soil between the rocks. Bright patches of yellow gorse flowered along the dusty road. Behind them, the Gulf of Genoa shimmered under a cloudless sky.

Frederick, riding a splendid gray stallion, gift of the doge, thought with relief that Genoa was behind him. Not that he hadn't enjoyed his stay there. For a while, even the subtle haggling with Genoa's rulers had amused him. The deal had been a good one for both parties: The Genoese offered money as well as men in exchange for pledges to be fulfilled upon his accession. He promised to confirm the privileges granted by previous Hohenstaufen emperors, and added several new ones which would benefit Genoa to the detriment of Pisa and Venice. He had signed the deed in the grand hall of the dogal palace: *Fredericus Rex et Imperator.* It was the first time he had used his new title.

THEY ARRIVED IN Pavia a week later without incident, despite having been warned that the Guelf towns had posted scouts. In Pavia, Frederick was received as if he were already the reigning emperor. He rode through the town gate festooned with Hohenstaufen banners, a black eagle on a field of gold, to the Palazzo Pubblico, where he was was welcomed by the leaders of the city to the pealing of church bells. From there they escorted him in solemn procession to his lodgings at the bishop's palace, the purple canopy reserved for the emperor held above his head.

With a sigh of contentment, Frederick leaned back in the hot water. The wooden tub had been well lined with linen to protect him from splinters. He closed his eyes. A banging on the door roused him with a start.

Couldn't they ever leave him alone? "Who's there?" he bellowed. Mahmoud poked his head into the chamber.

"The archbishop. Says he's just received some urgent news."

"Well, if it's that urgent, let him in."

"In here?" The Saracen's eyes widened.

"Yes, in here!"

Berard, in a spotless tunic, his beard freshly barbered, sat down on a bench, betraying no surprise. He had been confronted with Frederick's passion for bathing before. Frederick suspected that Berard thought this Saracen custom of soaking in scented water odd, if not actually effeminate.

"Frederick," he leaned forward, "an envoy from Cremona has just arrived. The Milanese are leaving Milan to patrol the Lombard plains. We have to leave now."

"But we've just arrived."

"I know, but if we don't leave Pavia before nightfall we won't get through to Cremona."

Frederick stood up, splashing water all over the floor.

"Give me a towel, will you?"

Berard, averting his eyes, handed him one of the linen towels from the bench he was sitting on.

Rubbing himself dry, Frederick stepped out of the tub.

"I must admit that I would have liked to spend a night or two in a bed," he said. "Can we get enough fresh horses?"

Berard smiled. "I've already requested them."

THE MESSENGER FROM Cremona was waiting in the hall. He was young, remarkably handsome, and exhausted.

"Count Manfred Lancia, at your service, Your Grace." He removed his dusty hat with an elegant flourish.

"I see you have ridden hard. I wish I could offer you some rest, but I believe we must leave immediately?"

The other nodded. "There's no time to be lost. The Milanese know where you are heading, Your Grace, and are on their way to Cremona with a large force of archers. They're also patrolling along the Po, searching every barge."

Frederick smiled. "That's one place they won't find me. What route are we taking?"

Alaman, Anselm, and Berard crowded around.

"The Cremonese will meet you at the river Lambro, about half a day's ride from here. If we ride east through the night we should meet with them before mid-morning."

Berard said, "The count tells me that the Lancias have long been associated with your family. His grandfather was knighted by Barbarossa."

"I've never known much about my German side," Frederick said, picking up his sword belt. "The further north I travel, the more I realize how much loyalty to the Hohenstaufen there still is."

Manfred Lancia stared at his feet. Mahmoud came in, loaded with traveling gear.

Frederick said, "Mahmoud, you remain here with half the Saracens and the money chests till I reach Cremona safely. If I don't, return to Sicily immediately."

Mahmoud opened his mouth to protest and closed it again. He salaamed. "As you command, my lord. May Allah go with you."

"And with you, too."

Frederick saw Manfred Lancia's eyes widen in shock.

"You find it strange that the Emperor should wish on his servant the protection of Allah?"

Lancia crimsoned. "My lord, I . . . Well, it is surprising . . . I didn't mean . . ."

"You see, Manfred, in Sicily, Christians, Jews, and Muslims live in harmony, respecting one another's God."

"They do?" The young man looked interested.

"Well, most of the time. They are, after all, men. But think, if I could spread this idea . . ." Frederick stopped himself. He let Mahmoud drape his cloak over his shoulders, then snapped the clasp shut.

Manfred said, "My lord, shouldn't you—"

"Shouldn't I what?"

"I was thinking, for your safety, would it not be wiser to wear armor? There could be fighting."

Frederick gave him a broad smile. "The truth, my dear Manfred, is that I don't have any. What about yourself? I don't see much steel on you either."

"Chain mail is heavy, my lord, not suited to swift riding." Manfred grinned, "It is also very expensive."

"Well, there you are. Let's be on our way!"

It was already dark outside. In the flare of the torches the restless new horses threw dancing shadows on the walls of the sienna-colored buildings that lined the piazza. As he swung himself into the saddle Frederick noticed that Berard was wearing a large sword with an old-fashioned hilt. It was the first time he had ever seen him wear one.

A group of heavily armed Pavian knights, in hauberks of chain mail, were waiting beside the portal. As they cantered through the town gates, opened for them at this late hour, Frederick sensed gloom descending on the men around him. They rode in silence, each alone with his thoughts. Behind them, they could hear the grating of the winches as the drawbridge was raised again.

Hour after weary hour they rode on. For fear of detection, the men had doused their lanterns. Manfred, slumped in the saddle with fatigue, led the way. Around midnight, the cloud cover lifted. The moon was almost full. The fertile plain of Lombardy was hauntingly beautiful in the eerie silver light. Windbreaks of stately poplars stood in rows, casting dark shadows over the moonlit paddies filled with young rice. They encountered no one.

Their numbers, now well over a hundred, ensured that any brigands lurking in the woods remained out of sight.

As the fading moon gave way to the first rays of the sun, they came within sight of the river. The Lambro, a fast-flowing tributary of the Po, separated the territory of Milan from that of Cremona. Their guide halted on a ridge overlooking the valley. Below, a dense wood hugged the river bank. Beyond, the Lambro made a wide curve to the east.

Frederick drew rein beside the young count. Manfred pointed a gloved finger. "The ford is over there, to the right, just behind that glade. I suggest we cross the river as soon as possible and wait for the Cremonese on the other side."

Frederick nodded. He wheeled his horse around. The sooner they forded the river the better. He called to Berard and Alaman, who transmitted the order to the back. They set themselves in motion again, cantering downhill toward the trees. The scent of fallen pine needles and damp soil filled the wood. The leaves filtered the sunlight into dappled green.

Frederick could see the river ahead. What relief it would be to stretch his numb legs! At that moment, something hissed overhead. His horse whinnied and reared. It would have thrown him had he not clung to its mane.

"Ambush! We're ambushed!" The cry went up behind him. Arrows rained down on them. Frederick bent as low as he could, cursing. He dug his heels into the horse's flanks and raced across the glade toward the ford. The Pavian knights in their chain mail were riding neck to neck with him, trying to protect him. In front he saw Manfred Lancia's red cloak billow out behind him as he, too, galloped toward the river, his head level with that of his mount. Just as he reached the end of the clearing his horse stumbled and Manfred flew through the air.

In the split second before he, too, was thrown from his horse, Frederick saw the rope. Several of the Pavians and Saracens managed to clear it, while those behind crashed into each other trying to avoid it. Frederick leaped up, drawing his sword. Men were swarming out from behind the trees. A Milanese ran at him with a lance. With a sideways blow of his sword, he sent him sprawling. Frederick ducked as an arrow whined past him. He looked about. They were surrounded and heavily outnumbered. With a glance he measured the distance to the nearest riderless horse.

In the bobbing sea of helmets and men he could make out the bright turbans of his Saracens raining down blows on the Milanese pouring out of the forest. Swords clashed on swords. Bending so low he was almost crawling, he had nearly reached the horse when a Milanese pikeman rose before him, swinging his murderous weapon. As the bearded giant gave a shout of triumph and raised his arm to crash the pike down on him, Frederick ducked and lunged forward, plunging his sword deep into the man's belly.

The man crumbled and would have fallen on top of him if Frederick had not leaped to one side. As he came crashing down, blood gushing out of him, the pike struck Frederick's left arm. He felt a piercing pain as it cut through his flesh. Wrenching himself free, he ran on, doubled over, holding his left arm with his right to stanch the slippery wetness. He had caught sight of another riderless destrier, a huge warhorse, a few yards away.

As he reached the destrier he saw Manfred, who had managed to remount, his tunic stained with blood, wielding his sword savagely left, right and center, cutting men down as they came at him. He was protecting Berard, who, standing against a tree, was clumsily lashing out at his assailants with his sword.

Frederick grabbed the trailing bridle and leapt into the saddle. He wheeled the horse towards Berard. "Berard, quick, jump up!" Manfred covered their flank while Berard tried to heave himself onto the rearing horse.

"For Jesus' sake, hurry!" Frederick cried.

The horse shuddered under Berard's weight as the archbishop finally managed to pull himself up. The leader of the Pavians, a burly knight on a roan stallion, yelled, "Ride, my lord, we'll cover you!" before bending to strike a blow at a Milanese who was trying to unhorse him.

"Follow me! To the river!" Frederick shouted, waving his injured arm. He dug his spurs into the horse's flanks. Men were fighting everywhere. Dead and writhing bodies littered the ground. Frederick's horse trod on something soft. Lurching, they nearly fell. The beast regained its balance and raced forward, maddened by the reek of blood and the shrill clangor of steel on steel. Behind them, the Milanese were shouting: "The king, capture the king!"

They headed straight for the water. On the plain beyond the other bank, a cloud of dust appeared. Shields and helmets glinted in the sun. The Cremonese!

Jumping down, Frederick unclasped his heavy cloak and threw it off. He grabbed the bridle. As he was about to leap in, he caught sight of Berard staring panic-stricken at the water.

"I can't . . . I can't swim. Save yourself, Frederick!" he cried. "I'll stay here and distract them for as long as I can."

Frederick cursed. He glanced over his shoulder. Men were running after them, whether friend or foe he could not tell. They had no time to lose. He shoved Berard forward. "Hold onto the horse's tail!" Pushing the animal, with Berard clinging to it, toward the water, he gave it a resounding slap on the rump before leaping into the swirling current to safety.

IN THE LATE afternoon they reached the Lancias' country estate on the outskirts of Cremona.

The horsemen clattered through the gate of the fortified manor house, scattering chickens and farm animals. Servants and laborers dropped whatever they were doing and gaped openmouthed as the vast yard filled with armed men.

Designed like a Roman latifundium, the main building was a long double-story structure of red brick. On either side there were bake and brew houses, the kitchens, stables, and barns. The whole was enclosed by a fortified wall and stout double gates. In times of trouble the residents could seek refuge in the tall circular tower in the center of the main building.

Frederick grimaced with pain as he brought his horse to a halt before the loggia. His wounded arm, resting in a sling, was throbbing unbearably. He turned around, waiting for Manfred Lancia. The count suggested they halt here to take care of the injured. After the Milanese had beaten a hasty retreat at the sight of the Cremonese, Frederick's men crossed the river again and collected the wounded. They were now being carried into the yard on makeshift litters. Mercifully, they had lost only a few men. The main body of the Cremonese had left them here and was returning to Cremona. Frederick would follow with the remainder later.

Retainers ran toward them.

Manfred jumped off his horse. "Over here, for His Grace," he waved at two grooms carrying a mounting block. They helped Frederick dismount. As he leaped to the ground sharp pain shot through his arm. He swayed and held onto the groom. Manfred cast him a worried glance. He extended his hand. "Lean on me, my lord. Let me help you up the steps. My mother is skilled with herbs and salves. She'll clean and bandage it for you properly."

As he spoke, a tall woman came running out of the house. Although her raven hair was streaked with gray, her face was still that of a great beauty. Her eyes, lavender blue like her son's, widened in alarm as she took in the scene.

"Don't worry, Mother," Manfred smiled reassuringly. "We were ambushed by the Milanese, but as you can see, His Grace the emperor is safe."

She curtsied before Frederick. "Welcome to our humble manor. We are greatly honored."

Before Frederick could reply, she saw the blood-soaked bandage on his arm.

"You've been injured, my lord?"

"It is nothing, Countess. Just a superficial gash."

"All the same, please let me have a look at it."

A little girl of four or five shot out from behind Countess Selvaggia's skirts and wrapped her arms around Manfred's legs. "Pick me up, pick me up!" she begged, jumping up and down.

"Bianca, go inside immediately!"

Ignoring her mother, the child continued to cling to Manfred's legs.

"My youngest daughter is very attached to her brother," the Countess said. "Do forgive her."

Frederick smiled. A pretty little thing. Judging by the brother's age, she must have been a latecomer to the Lancia brood.

Manfred grinned at the little girl. "Off you go, Bianchina, if you don't want to get in the way of Maddalena's stick." Blue eyes looked up at him pleadingly. "Will you let me ride on your horse later?"

Manfred nodded. "I promise, but only if you're a good girl now."

She turned her small dark head, covered in a white linen cap fastened under her chin, toward Frederick. "Can I ride on his horse, too?"

"Run back to Maddalena. Now, Bianca." Manfred gave the child a gentle push.

She pointed a stubby finger at Frederick. "Is he really the emperor?"

Manfred nodded.

"But he doesn't look like one, he's so dirty!"

Frederick laughed. "She's quite right. If appearances were all, I wouldn't stand much of a chance right now, would I?"

A fat nurse came bustling out of the house. With a last look at the stranger, the child allowed herself to be dragged into the house. The countess led the way into the cool vestibule.

Frederick decided to spend the night at the Lancias' estate. Countess Selvaggia cleansed and bandaged his wound, pronouncing herself satisfied. Just as he had been drawn to her handsome son, he conceived a liking for the mother and her four children. Although the Lancias were of an ancient lineage, related to some of the greatest families in Italy, they were impoverished. The old count had died a few years ago. Manfred confided to Frederick that his father, a brave knight and accomplished poet, had been a bad manager of his affairs.

On an impulse, Frederick asked Manfred to accompany him to Germany. "I'll need loyal men to serve me. You'll be well rewarded. What do you think?"

Manfred agreed immediately. His mother gave her blessing. An old bearded uncle added his. Neither of them, Frederick thought, is voicing their misgivings. What if this last Hohenstaufen fails to become emperor?

THE FOLLOWING MORNING, Frederick was welcomed by the fiercely Ghibelline citizens of Cremona. The story of his escape across the Lambro was on everyone's lips. The streets were black with cheering people. "*Viva Federico! Viva Federico!*" they chanted, stamping their feet and throwing their caps into the air.

Frederick waved to the crowds as he rode bareheaded in the sunshine through the banner-hung streets. He remained in Cremona for more than a week. Despite their professions of loyalty, the city rulers, like the Genoese, were quick to secure promises of imperial favor for the future. Loyalty to the Empire, he began to realize, always had a price. It was not a divinely ordained duty, but a bargaining point for freedom from taxation, trading rights, permission to extend city walls, mint coins, and a multitude of other privileges.

When they left Cremona, Manfred Lancia rode behind Berard in Frederick's growing train. From a window of their city mansion, the countess waved at them. Frederick raised his hand in salute. His last image of Cremona was that of Manfred's handsome mother and a little dark-haired girl beside her.

FOR SEVERAL WEEKS they traveled north via Mantua and Verona up the valley of the Adige in southern Tyrol toward Trent. Although Otto had retreated to central Germany, the Brenner Pass was still held by the dukes of Meran and Bavaria, loyal to Otto. With the help of local guides Frederick and his men crossed the Alps on a little-known mule track of vertiginous steepness. Even in summer the path was under threat from avalanches. Once safely through the worst of it, even Frederick crossed himself. By the second week in August they had reached southern Germany and were approaching Chur, a strategic Hohenstaufen fief that controlled access to several Alpine passes.

They were riding above the tree line, making their way down toward the walled town lying in a broad, stony valley at the foot of the mountains. The air was crisp, with a hint of chill. Around them rose majestic snow-covered peaks. The Alpine pastures over which they rode were carpeted with wildflowers. Game abounded. Once, when they came across a magnificent bear, Frederick had to use all his powers of persuasion to stop his excited men from launching into a hunt.

Tension gripped Frederick as they drew closer to Chur. He had sent Anselm, the only one who spoke German, ahead to announce their arrival. While the ecclesiastical princes would be fluent in Latin, many secular German lords could not speak it with ease, and most were unlettered. In his mind, Frederick went over the German words and sentences Anselm continued to teach him around the campfire every evening. The likable young knight had become an invaluable source of information on all things German. Trying to get his tongue around the guttural words, Frederick cursed himself for never having learned what to him had always been the language of his oppressors.

Yet this was his country too, home of his forefathers. How would he be received by the people, he, a stranger who couldn't speak their tongue and was ignorant of their customs? Would his name alone suffice to elicit the loyalty he needed to succeed? They waited in a rocky clearing within sight of the walls. Below the town, a narrow river glittered in the midday sun— the young Rhine, flowing north toward Lake Konstanz.

A company of horsemen cantered toward them. At the head of the cavalcade rode a broad-shouldered man. That must be Arnold von Matsch, the bishop of Chur. A princely figure, Frederick thought. An impeccably cut cloak of brown velvet fell in rich folds to his knees. Across his chest he wore a heavy gold chain with a jeweled pendant.

Arnold von Matsch bowed from the waist, without dismounting from his destrier. "Your Grace, welcome to Chur. Praise be to God for having brought you here safely." Small brown eyes scrutinized him from under bristling black brows.

"My lord bishop, I thank you. I too, am grateful to have reached here safely." Frederick said. "So far, quite a few obstacles have been put in my way. What word of the Guelfs?"

"A messenger from the abbot of Saint Gall arrived yesterday with news that he is in Nuremberg, trying to buy support. You needn't fear, Your Grace, Otto von Brunswick would never dare lurk in these lands." He made a deprecating gesture, as if flicking away a fly. "I would make short shrift of him and his Saxons. Pray let us proceed into the town. You and your lords will lodge in my palace."

While the manner was irreproachably respectful, the tone was that of a man used to being obeyed. No Sicilian bishop would have dared address his overlord as his equal. But not only was Arnold von Matsch one of the most powerful German bishops, Frederick's had been one of the votes that had elected him. He inclined his head and smiled.

Arnold now dismounted. To Frederick's surprise, he took hold of his reins. "Your Grace, allow me to lead your horse in the time-honored way."

The bishop himself, holding Frederick's bridle, walked at the head of the procession through a massive guard tower, up a steep cobbled hill on which stood an imposing cathedral and the episcopal palace. Behind him followed the notables of Chur, who had ridden out with the bishop. The bishop's own horse, far more splendidly accoutred than Frederick's, was led by a groom walking a few paces behind. Frederick glanced down at the bishop's three-cornered fur hat. He could not help feeling that he was being led, with a great show of outward submission, like a docile pawn of the men who truly ruled Germany: her great feudal princes, both secular and ecclesiastical.

Nowhere had he been honored thus, yet the crowds that pressed against the steeply gabled wooden houses were far less exuberant than those of the Italian cities. There was something dour and wary about the people, even the children. Mostly dark of eye and hair, these descendants of Romans and barbarians scrutinized him with the suspiciousness of mountain dwellers. Their cheering was perfunctory.

How many of them, Frederick wondered, remembered his grandfather Barbarossa, so beloved by his people, or his father, the feared Emperor Henry? Certainly, the only Hohenstaufen the younger townspeople would have known by sight was his uncle Philip, who had recently been assassinated.

Did the people's loyalty still belong to the Hohenstaufen, or did they now only pay allegiance to their masterful ecclesiastical lord?

BISHOP ARNOLD STROKED his pockmarked nose. "The most I can let your Grace have are two hundred horsemen. The abbot of Saint Gall, together with the local barons, I am sure, will be able to provide you with several times that number."

Frederick suppressed a sneer. Two hundred men! That was many fewer than he had expected, a fraction of the army he needed to face Otto in battle. On Frederick's instructions, Anselm had, for the last two days, been indulging in friendly discussions of horseflesh with the bishop's head groom. Frederick knew that Arnold could have spared three times as many men. The good bishop was hedging his bets in case Frederick didn't gather enough support further north.

"That is far less than I expected," Frederick replied, steepling his fingers together. "I realise you cannot leave Chur unprotected, but it is my understanding that you have nearly eight hundred men within these walls, more than half of whom are mounted. Correct?"

Taken aback, the bishop nodded.

"My dear bishop," Frederick leaned across the table. He held the other's gaze, "I am sure that with an effort, you could manage at least another hundred, don't you think?"

Arnold ran his tongue over his lips. He was trapped. "At risk to the town, my lord, if you command me to do so, I will."

"I shall remember the risk you are taking when the time comes to share some of the benefices now held by Otto's prelates." Frederick smiled. "In fact, as soon as I have defeated Otto, I'll need some trustworthy men of proven ability." He clapped the bishop on the shoulder. "Your record is such that I might consider you for the post of chancellor."

Frederick caught Berard's look. He's thinking that such bizarre tactics won't fool a man as shrewd as Arnold, Frederick thought. Yet the bishop's small eyes glittered with greed.

"I shall give orders for your troops to be ready on the morrow, my lord. Word has been sent to Saint Gall. I myself will accompany you there."

THEY RODE THROUGH the gatehouse into the cobbled courtyard of the Benedictine Abbey of Saint Gall. Grooms came running to lead the horses to the stableyard. The gatekeeper sent a lay brother scurrying to announce their arrival to the abbot.

Frederick, dismounting, took in his impressive surroundings. Berard had been right. Saint Gall was one of the largest abbeys in Christendom, a major center of learning and education. Founded in the seventh century by Saint Gall, an Irish hermit, it had been endowed by Charlemagne with vast landholdings. Its abbot was a prince of the Empire and its library the envy of Europe.

Encircled by massive fortified walls, the abbey was a self-contained world. A physic garden and infirmary, bake and brewhouses, mills, workshops and threshing floors, kilns, stables, and pens supplied those within its walls with almost every necessity. Guest houses for the poor, the noble, and the ecclesiastical offered hospitality to travelers. In the scriptorium, scores of monks copied, bound, and illuminated devotional texts and books from the classical world. In its school, young boys destined for the Church acquired the learning that had been safeguarded here for centuries.

The abbot, erect and elderly, white hair circling his tonsure, came striding briskly down the arcaded walk, followed by the prior and subprior.

"Welcome, my lord of Hohenstaufen. Our house is at your disposal. The brother hospitaller here will show you to your quarters. I'm afraid they are simple, my lord, but I trust you will find them adequate nevertheless. Your men will be taken care of in the outbuildings."

"Thank you, father. How can I find fault with quarters that once offered shelter to Charlemagne?" Frederick smiled. "As you can see, we are weary and grateful to be here." They and their mounts were covered in a gray layer of dust, the flanks of their horses foaming.

"I would be pleased if Your Grace would do me the honor of dining with me tonight."

"The honor, Father Abbot, will be mine."

Abbot Ulrich von Sax smiled. Frederick saw him cast a discreet glance at Mahmoud, turbaned and scimitared. No doubt the first Saracen the abbot had ever seen.

"This is Brother Johannes, our hospitaller. He will take care of all your needs. I bid you a good rest, my lord." The abbot bowed.

They followed the friar across the courtyard and through the cloister to the guest wing reserved for high-ranking ecclesiastics and the nobility.

FREDERICK SAT BY the open window, clad only in his unlaced tunic and hose. The sun fell on the floor rushes. He had moved the table closer to the window in order to have more light. The chamber, although spacious, was dark and chilly, with only one small unglazed window, but in the sun it was pleasantly warm. The cloister, with its well-tended herb and flower beds, was peaceful. While it did rain a lot, these northern summers were not as dreary as he'd thought. The rivers and forests of Germany were beautiful, the fields lush without the need for waterwheels, and the sun surprisingly hot. There was also a frankness about the people, exemplified in the abbot, which he liked.

He picked up a parchment from the pile on the table. Among the dispatches and letters waiting for him at the abbey there had been one from Constance. Her voice echoed in his mind as he read her letter for the second time.

"My worshipful lord and beloved husband, I greet you and send you God's blessing. . . . All is well in your realm, thanks to God and the good men who are helping me. The burdens of state weigh heavily on me, beloved, and I wish you were here. . . . Our son is well and walking already. You would be proud to see him. . . . I am in constant fear for your safety. I am having prayers said for your success and speedy return every day in the chapel. . . . I call the blessing of the Virgin Mary and all the saints upon you. May they keep you safe and bring you back to me soon."

He dropped the letter and sighed. Well, at least she was praying for his success. That was an improvement on her previous attitude. He regretted the way they had parted and the things he had said in anger. For the first time, he realized how much he missed her. He'd make amends, send her a jewel perhaps, as soon as he could, as soon as he had gained a foothold in Germany. But when would that be?

Otto had strengthened his position in northern Germany. As soon as he heard of Frederick's approach, he marched south at the head of an army several thousand strong. Frederick's next objective was Konstanz. So far, no German city had acclaimed him. Chur, a family possession, did not count. If he wanted to rally those German princes who were still wavering, he had to secure the cities. Abbot Ulrich had called a meeting of Swabian barons in the abbey. With their aid, Frederick hoped to raise a force strong enough to defeat Otto in battle.

He reached across the table for some writing material. Constance was proving an able regent. Even Walter praised her in his dispatch! He sat thinking for a moment before dipping his quill into the inkhorn. He wrote rapidly. Endearments became entangled with advice on everything from placating the pope's new legate to collecting port tolls in Messina. Every now and then he paused to sharpen the goose quill absentmindedly with a small knife. As he thought of Palermo, a sharp longing gripped him. He longed for the sea, for the bells of San Giovanni and the calls of the muezzin . . .

Absorbed in his thoughts, he didn't hear the clatter of boots in the cloister. There was a knock on the door.

"What is it, Mahmoud?"

Mahmoud's tall form was blocking the view beyond the door-frame.

"A messenger. From the count of something-or-other. I can't understand him. The abbot sends him."

"Show him in."

"Your Grace," the messenger fell to his knees, his breath still coming fast. Sweat was pouring down his begrimed face.

"Here, drink this." Frederick handed him his own half-empty cup of watered wine. The man drank, then wiped his mouth with the back of his hand.

"I bear an urgent message from the Count of Kiburg. Otto of Brunswick and his army are encamped at Ueberlingen, on the northern shore of Lake Konstanz. Tomorrow, he will cross the lake and make his formal entry into Konstanz at vespers."

Frederick caught his breath. The Count of Kiburg was a loyal supporter of the Hohenstaufen. There could be no doubt about the truth of his warning.

"But that's impossible. A week ago Otto was still in Nuremberg. How do you know this is true?"

"The man who brought the message, one of our spies, came from Otto's camp on the lake last night."

Frederick let out an obscenity. The city of Konstanz was only twenty-six miles north of Saint Gall, half a day's ride at the most. He had no idea how much further Ueberlingen was, but it couldn't be far if Otto could reach the city in less than a day.

"How many men does he have?"

"Over four thousand, my lord."

Frederick blanched. "Mahmoud, my cloak and boots, quickly! Send Manfred to the abbot. Ask him to assemble all the lords who are already here in the chapter house within the hour. And call the archbishop. I want him here immediately."

In his haste, he nearly fell over the messenger.

"The brothers will lodge you overnight."

"Thank you, my lord. There is one more thing my lord bade me tell you." The man hesitated, clearly uncomfortable.

"Yes?"

"He said to tell you that if you remain here, your life will be in danger. Otto of Brunswick is capable of violating the abbey's sanctuary. My lord suggested that you take refuge in his castle of Kiburg. You and your party could get there before nightfall."

*   *   *

"THESE ARE UNWELCOME tidings indeed, my lords," Abbot Ulrich said. He looked at Frederick. "What, my lord Frederick, do you propose to do?"

Frederick glanced at the tense faces in the chapter house. In addition to Berard, Alaman, and Manfred, there were a number of ecclesiastical princes present, amongst them the powerful abbots of Pfaeffers and Reichenau, as well as several Swabian barons.

"I suggest we ride for Konstanz tomorrow morning at first light."

This was greeted by an uproar.

Frederick raised his right hand, commanding silence. They stared at him with open dismay.

"My lords, I know this may seem risky. But I must reach Konstanz before Otto does. I cannot allow him to take possession of such a strategically important city."

The abbot of Reichenau, a portly prelate with the shifty eyes of a weasel, rose from his seat. "But my lord, we don't have sufficient men. The bishop of Konstanz has declared for Otto. He won't change his mind at the sight of a paltry force such as ours. Would it not be better to wait till the other princes have arrived, and then march on Konstanz with a substantial army?"

"Then we'd have to engage in a long siege. If we get there before him, we will be able to ride into the city unopposed."

The abbot of Reichenau raised his thin eyebrows. "How, my lord Frederick?"

"By the powers of persuasion. I am the rightful emperor. I have both the Lord's and the pope's blessing." With sarcasm he added, "Surely even the bishop of Konstanz would not wish to offend two such formidable powers."

"But what if your plan doesn't work?" one of the barons objected. "We'll be trapped outside the gates, a certain prey for her bishop and possibly for Otto."

Heads nodded. He had voiced what they were all thinking. Frederick's plan was foolhardy. While they supported his cause for a number of reasons, none were prepared to risk their lives for it.

The abbot of Saint Gall stood up. He surveyed the gathering of prelates and princes before him with scarcely concealed irritation. "My lords," he said in a firm voice, "I myself will ride with the Emperor Frederick to Konstanz tomorrow."

A murmur of astonishment went up from the assembly.

Surprised, Frederick glanced at the frail, patrician figure of the abbot in his austere black habit. The least warlike of men, the old abbot was the last man he had expected to support him in this. He gave him a grateful smile.

The abbot of Reichenau was clearly annoyed. "Is it wise to subject your person to such danger?"

Abbot Ulrich gave him a withering look. "The Emperor Frederick's cause is a just one. I believe that his accession to the throne of Charlemagne will bring peace to Germany. There has been enough strife and bloodshed. The land and the people are exhausted. I, unlike some of us, have faith in the Lord."

The abbot of Reichenau sat down abruptly, red in the face.

A towering man with a vivid scar across his chin stepped forward. Count Rudolf of Hapsburg was head of a great family long associated with the Hohenstaufen.

"My lord Frederick, I too, with all my men, will join you."

The abbot of the great abbey of Pfaeffers rose too, slowly. "I also, my lord, will accompany you."

Seeing himself outnumbered, the abbot of Reichenau conceded defeat. "In that case, I, too, will join you tomorrow."

Within moments, every man in the chapter house had pledged himself to follow Frederick to Konstanz.

THEY FOLLOWED THE old Roman road along the southern shore of the lake in a northwesterly direction. By the time the sun stood at its zenith, the towering walls of Konstanz were visible in the distance. Straddling the infant Rhine as it left the lake on its long journey to the North Sea, the city, once a Roman station, was now a bishop's see. Konstanz had been granted her freedom charter by Frederick's grandfather Barbarossa. The capable rule of her bishops had made Konstanz one of the wealthiest free cities in the Empire.

They halted in a forest clearing by the roadside, not far from the city. Frederick dismounted and handed his reins to Mahmoud. He looked around uneasily. The memory of the last ambush was still vivid in his mind.

This time, he'd posted sentries all around. Nevertheless, they would do well not to tarry here any longer than necessary.

Beside him, the abbot of Saint Gall was being helped off his palfrey. The abbot looked tired. The long ride had been too much for a man of his age. "It grieves me, my lord abbot, to see you so wearied on my behalf. Perhaps you should remain here a while longer, while we press on?"

Abbot Ulrich smiled, his blue eyes sparkling in their web of leathery creases. "When you're as old as I am, which God grant you, you'll realize that a little fatigue more or less makes no difference. I've been used to aches and pains for a long time now."

Frederick nodded, touched. "Thank you, Father."

"I'm only doing what I consider my duty. There's no merit in that."

Frederick extended a helping hand as the abbot lowered himself onto a mossy boulder.

Abbot Ulrich smiled up at him. "Do not worry, these old bones may creak, but they're still fit to do the Lord's work for a little while longer!"

Frederick went over to Berard and drew him aside. "You have the documents in an accessible place?" he whispered.

Berard patted the left side of his tunic. "Right here, close to my heart."

"Good."

He turned to Manfred. "Tell Mahmoud to have the garments brought."

The other lords were standing about, many stamping their feet to loosen their stiff joints after the long ride. Stepping onto the root of an oak tree, Frederick raised his voice, "My lords, I suggest we all don our finery now. Please make haste."

The impact of their arrival before the city walls would certainly be enhanced by a show of splendor. Servants began scurrying back and forth from the packhorses with clothing draped over their arms, carrying leather coffers. Within minutes, the dust-covered riders in their dull traveling cloaks had been transformed into a splendid gathering. Jeweled miters shimmered in the dappled sunlight; cloaks in a rainbow of colors flashed with gold thread and gemmed clasps. Even the horses had been changed into elegant steeds by the addition of rich trappings.

Mahmoud was putting the finishing touches to Frederick's hair with a comb. He stood back to admire his handiwork. A fir-green camlet cloak trimmed in beaver was draped over his shoulders. At his throat sparkled

Berard's ruby clasp. He was girded with a sword encased in a scabbard of gold filigree. On his feet he wore scarlet boots of soft kid. Gloves of the same leather, worked with gold thread, covered his hands.

"How do I look?"

Mahmoud beamed. "Like the Prophet Mohammed himself."

"I hope not," Frederick smiled, "that wouldn't do at all for the good burghers of Konstanz."

Alaman and Manfred shook with laughter. Berard's brows rose in warning.

Frederick surveyed their group. They were an impressive sight. He swung himself into the saddle. The others followed suit.

At the head of the horsemen, with banners flying, cantered the heralds, resplendent in yellow tabards embroidered with the black Hohenstaufen eagle. Frederick and Berard rode side by side, followed by the abbots of Saint Gall and Reichenau. Behind them came some of the greatest temporal lords of Germany. Often at loggerheads, they were now joined by a common goal: the destruction of Otto of Brunswick.

THE TRAFFIC CONVERGING on Konstanz was dense. Frederick raised his hand. The men behind him slowed down. The heralds blew their trumpets. Carts and pedestrians, riders and flocks retreated into the fields to make way for them. Sentries began running on the ramparts, helmets flashing in the sun. Above the jingle of harnesses and the murmur of the crowd, a loud creaking noise could be heard. The huge iron-studded gates grated toward each other.

"They're closing the gates!" Frederick called to Berard. The gates clanged shut. They could hear the great bolt being rammed into place.

The crowd, angry at being locked out, pressed behind them. Frederick whispered to Berard, then turned and spoke to Manfred. The latter spurred his horse forward to transmit Frederick's instructions to the heralds. The chief herald, carrying Frederick's banner, moved his charger to the front and drew rein before the gate. The herald's voice rang out: "In the name of Frederick of Hohenstaufen, king of Sicily and German emperor, I command you to open the gates!"

"Go away, impostor! We have orders to admit no one but the rightful emperor," came the reply from above.

Frederick nodded imperceptibly. Berard threaded his horse forward. At the gate, he bellowed:

"I, Archbishop Berard of Palermo, and legate of Pope Innocent, demand, in the name of the Holy Father, to speak with your bishop!" The sergeant bowed and vanished.

The midday sun beat down. They waited. The sentinels in their helmets stared down, impassive as statues. Frederick wiped the perspiration off his face with the back of his hand. He felt sweat trickling down his ribs. They were trapped. If Otto were to appear now . . .

His horse, sensing his tension, pawed the ground. Behind him he could hear the others shifting in their saddles. He felt their eyes on his back. He had led them into this trap, trusting his luck. How could he have believed that his mere appearance would overcome all obstacles?

There was movement within the gate tower. A man of obvious authority, tall and fleshy, in a wine-colored gown, stepped out onto the parapet. He was flanked by archers in metal breastplates, bows at the ready.

"I am Conrad of Tegerfelden, bishop of Konstanz," he bellowed. "Who demands to speak to me?"

Berard raised his face. "Berard of Castacca, archbishop of Palermo. As envoy of his Holiness the pope, I request that you open the gates to the new emperor, Frederick of Hohenstaufen."

Leaning over the parapet, the bishop called down: "The Emperor Otto is expected here at any moment. He is the lawful emperor, crowned by the pope. I have no knowledge of a new emperor." As he stepped back, Berard stopped him.

"Otto of Brunswick has been deposed by the electors and excommunicated by the pope. If you refuse entry to the Emperor Frederick, I am empowered by Pope Innocent to lay the city of Konstanz and all her people under the ban of excommunication!"

A murmur of dread went up from the populace, which had clambered onto the battlements. An excommunicate was forbidden the sacraments and thus entry into paradise. Under pain of being excommunicated himself, no man was allowed to aid someone thus punished.

Conrad wheeled around. The shock on his face, Frederick thought, seemed genuine.

Conrad addressed the abbot of Saint Gall. "Lord Ulrich, is this true?"

The abbot nodded. "It most certainly is."

A frown appeared on Conrad's brow. "Have you any proof of this, my lord of Castacca?"

In reply, Berard drew a folded parchment from his tunic. He read out the papal bull of excommunication against Otto. When he'd finished, he moved his destrier a few paces forward. Unsheathing his dagger, he nailed the parchment to the gate with it. "There is your proof, citizens of Konstanz!" he thundered. "Beware, at the peril of eternal damnation, of joining Otto of Brunswick among the outcasts of God!"

For a moment, there was silence. Frederick tightened his grip on the reins. Then a roar of voices rose from the ramparts: "Open the gates! Open the gates!"

From behind the walls, the invisible crowds in the streets picked up the call. "Open the gates, open the gates!"

The bishop nodded to the captain of his guard.

The battle for Konstanz had been won.

COLOGNE, NOVEMBER 1212

Dusk was falling as a courier on a lathered horse clattered across the drawbridge of Cologne's castle. He slid off his mount and handed the guard a leather satchel.

"An urgent message for the Lord Chancellor!"

The man nodded and hurried along a covered walkway toward the chancery.

ICY COLD PERVADED the palace chapel. Six tall beeswax candles in silver candlesticks stood on the altar steps, illuminating the sanctuary. The words of the evening Mass rose toward the stone vaulting. Otto's eyes were closed as he listened. To shield himself from the cold, he slipped his hands under his fur cloak.

Conrad von Scharfenburg threaded his way toward the emperor. "A word with you, please, Your Grace," he whispered.

Startled, Otto opened his eyes. The faraway look in his eyes changed to one of wariness. He nodded.

He knows it's bad news, the chancellor thought. He watched the emperor, reluctantly, turn away from the comfort of the Mass. They walked to the back of the chapel, through a door that gave directly onto Otto's private apartments.

A fire blazed in the central hearth. Otto sat down on a settle. He looked at Conrad: "What news?"

"A message from Strassburg."

Otto sighed. "What's that pope's puppet doing now? Making gold from clay?"

"My lord, you'd do well to take him more seriously. He's more than just a youth cloaked in an illustrious name."

"And what, Conrad, has made *you* accord him such praise?"

Conrad von Scharfenburg hesitated. He looked at the emperor, whom he had served long and well. The years of struggle had left their mark on Otto. The dashing young Duke of Brunswick, in whose service Conrad had risen to become chancellor of Germany, was now a weary middle-aged man who drank too much and slept too little. He was also becoming uncharacteristically pious. Having retreated up the Rhine to Cologne, Otto's only hope now was English support. But John of England, notoriously shifty, had begun to doubt the wisdom of continuing to back his German nephew.

Conrad said slowly, "Philip of France has signed a treaty of alliance with Frederick."

"What?"

Conrad nodded.

Otto said, "Pour us some wine, will you?"

Conrad poured one cup and handed it to the emperor. He went over to the window. Through a gap in the shutters, left open to allow the smoke to escape, he looked at the fading day outside. A cold November wind was blowing the last leaves off the trees, whirling them around the courtyard in small brittle eddies. Beyond the moat, the Rhine glistened gray and steely under a heavy sky.

Conrad rubbed his forehead to ease the pressure he often felt these days. France and England had been at war for years over English claims to

French land. Since King John supported Otto, the French king had been Otto's foe from the start. But Conrad never thought he would risk putting a French army in the field to support Frederick of Hohenstaufen. He closed the shutter.

The emperor looked at him: "We're slowly being encircled, aren't we?"

Conrad pursed his lips. "It may not be as bad as it seems. It could actually be to our advantage."

"How so?"

Conrad suppressed a sigh of irritation. Subtlety had never been one of Otto's strong points. "If you can persuade your uncle of England to join us now, we'll destroy the French, and Frederick, too. The treaty calls for mutual aid in case of attack. Frederick and the south German lords will have to obey a call to arms by the French king."

"And why should my uncle risk war against the French now, when he's been avoiding it for years?"

"Because, my lord, you have to convince him that with your help and that of your allies, he must crush the French now. Otherwise Frederick, with French support, will gain control of the whole of Germany. Once that happens, Frederick and Philip will drive the English out of France forever."

"Hm." Otto stirred the floor rushes with the tip of his boot. "You may well be right, Conrad. But you know how indecisive John is. Do you really think he'll stop procrastinating and take action?"

"Yes, I do. King John has so much trouble at home with his rebellious barons, he can't afford to lose his French possessions. Faced with a threat of this magnitude, even John will go to war. You must persuade him. It is our only hope."

Otto sighed. "I agree with you. With God's and John's aid, we might be able to defeat both Frederick and the French, once and for all."

OUTSIDE, A VICIOUS wind was sweeping through the snow-covered forest, tearing at the shutters. Berard could hear the wolves howling. At night, the beasts, emboldened by hunger and attracted by the flames in the watchtowers of Haguenau's castle, crept right up to the moat.

A warm glow pervaded the small paneled chamber. Berard adjusted the fur rug that had slipped from his chest. He leaned back on his settle. The last months had been exhausting. As Frederick's following grew, the frequency with which they moved from city to city and castle to castle had increased too. They often spent days in the saddle.

He looked at Frederick, seated at his worktable. If the Lord hadn't made him a prince, he'd have been a scholar, stooped and myopic. In many ways, he had the temperament of one. Berard watched him frown over a German petition. Frederick pulled out a grammar specially compiled for him, consulted it, and returned to the document. He was learning the language with the same thoroughness with which he tackled ruling the country. Perhaps it was the outpourings of popular affection or his dormant German blood, or a mysterious linking of the two, but Frederick had begun to develop an empathy for Germany that astounded Berard.

Frederick had conquered southern Germany. The story of Konstanz preceded them up the Rhine valley. Tales of his success spread like wildfire as city after city acclaimed him. In castle, cloister, and village, he was hailed as the new Barbarossa, come to end years of lawlessness and strife. Villagers put down fir branches for him to ride over. In the cities, people kissed the hem of his cloak. Frederick was becoming a legend.

The bishop of Strassburg had met him at the gates of Basle and held his stirrup, adding five hundred archers to Frederick's forces. One after another, the vacillating lay lords followed the ecclesiastical princes and joined Frederick. All that remained now was his coronation in Aachen and after that as emperor in Rome. Aachen, however, was still held by Otto. The imperial insignia were also in Otto's possession. Having failed to halt Frederick's advance, Otto entrenched himself in Cologne.

Frederick had decided to spend the winter in Haguenau, in his grandfather's palace, where he could consolidate his forces for the coming spring campaign against Otto.

"God's teeth, these documents are a mess!"

Berard woke from his reverie. "What's a mess?"

"The whole administrative system." Exasperated, Frederick flung the scroll onto a pile of others already on the table. He looked at Berard, wrapped up to his bearded chin in a fur rug, a tankard of ale in his hands. "Are you sure you're comfortable, Berard? You're getting far too soft. Like a hibernating bear who doesn't leave his cave."

Berard laughed. "Very comfortable. And as for riding out for pleasure in this infernal climate, I leave that to you and your new German friends."

Frederick poured himself a cup of ale and sat down beside him. He rested his elbows on his knees and stared into the fire.

"You know that I sometimes feel I've lived here all my life?"

"Really?" After all the complaints Berard had at first heard about the scarcity of civilized amenities in Germany, he found this rather amusing.

"Maybe my grandfather wrestled with the same problems in this very room." Frederick waved his hand across the cozy chamber with its coffered blue and red ceiling. The stone fireplace had a bulging chimney. An exotic innovation, such fireplaces were rare in Germany.

Hagenau Castle was a palatial fortress situated on an island in the river Moder. It was the grandest of several imperial residences built by Barbarossa. In addition to fireplaces with chimneys, it possessed a main hall floored with red marble and a great library.

"What do you think?" Frederick asked, "Will the French honor their promises?"

Berard scratched his beard. "Philip Augustus is a man of honor; so is his son Louis. And France needs all the friends she can get at this moment. Yes, I think they will. I'd even think so if they hadn't pledged their faith with silver, silver you no longer have."

This was a sore point between them. The French king had sent Frederick twenty thousand silver marks as a token of friendship. Against Berard's advice, Frederick, at the Diet in Frankfurt, had distributed this vast sum among the leading German princes. Although this had gained him great popularity, the treasury was now so empty that Frederick had recently had to mortgage three of his towns in Swabia.

Frederick pretended not to hear. "I'll be riding to a place called Schoenburg tomorrow to see Matilde of Spoleto."

"She must be seventy," Berard said, "at least."

"It's said she is still very lucid. She's asked to see me. She was my mother's best friend. She was with her in Jesi when I was born."

". . . THEREFORE THE INHABITANTS have unanimously subjected their town of Moderheim, which they possess free of all lordship, to our power, on

these terms, namely that they and all their posterity will pay the Empire
twenty-five measures of wheat each year in order to be under the protection of our imperial highness."

Frederick nodded.

The secretary laid the charter before him. He glanced at it briefly before signing it. "The last one for today?"

"Yes, Your Grace."

Frederick stood up and stretched. Government matters had been neglected everywhere. He had yet to appoint a chancellor. The notaries and
clerks kept the chancery running, but only just. The *ministeriales*, officers of
state who administered the Empire, were as divided as the country: some
followed Otto, while others were loyal to Frederick. All of this placed a tremendous strain on an administrative machinery that, by Sicilian standards,
was cumbersome and inefficient.

The two black-garbed secretaries, voluminous leather folders wedged
under each arm, bowed themselves out. Although it was only early afternoon, the room was already darkening. Candles and torches burned everywhere from dawn until late at night. In winter, daylight penetrated the
interior only as a dim glow through the oiled parchment on the windows.
The air was stale with lamp smoke. Try as he might, he could not get the
servants to keep the windows open.

He stepped up into the window and opened the latch. Icicles in gorgeous shapes hung from the eaves. Beyond the ramparts, as far as the eye
could see, stretched endless forests of dark fir covered in powdery whiteness. How beautiful these northern winters were, despite their harshness.
In the town below, wisps of smoke rose from snow-covered roofs. The
streets and alleys were crowded. Pigs rooted in the gutters. On a frozen
canal, children skated. It always amazed him how they managed such a feat
on a piece of carved bone. He smiled as he watched for a moment, then
closed the window.

He went back to the draft of a bull he was to sign at Whitsuntide. The
pope's support doesn't come cheap, he thought, pursing his lips. The document had been written by the papal curia. It reconfirmed all the privileges
granted to the Church by Otto. This time, Innocent had demanded that
the bull be countersigned by the leading princes of the Empire.

In it, Frederick was to surrender all fiscal and judicial rights over the German ecclesiastics. The bull granted such autonomy to the German bishops as to create an almost independent ecclesiastical state. The papal title to the disputed territories in Italy would also be confirmed. The papacy would finally be a temporal power.

He stared with disgust at the fine creamy vellum. With his signature he would undo much of what his father and grandfather had achieved. He had no choice but to obey. This time . . .

Someone cleared his throat at the door. "My lord, it is nearly time for Mass."

Manfred stood in the doorway, cloaked and gloved, an elegant yellow cap with a pheasant feather on his dark head.

"Ah, Manfred. You look splendid. You'll turn all the ladies' heads tonight."

Manfred shook his head. He grinned: "Alas, they only have eyes for you."

"If only they weren't all married, or watched like Saracen virgins! Must I really attend Mass every evening? That chapel's freezing."

"Orders from the archbishop. I'm to look after your immortal soul while he entertains the bishop of Mainz."

Frederick sighed. "For Berard's sake, then."

"And for the sake of the Germans."

He gave Manfred a long look. Then he smiled. "You're right. As emperor I must set an example."

THE LOGS IN the two great fireplaces at opposite ends of the hall were being replenished for the fourth time. Observing the pages dragging yet another basket of firewood across the floor, Frederick yawned discreetly. Not, he thought, that anyone was likely to notice. The only ones still sober were the lords whose turn it was to serve at the high table. The ladies' voices had long become strident, their laughter overloud. Even Berard, whose drinking, unlike his eating, was usually moderate, was sinking deeper and deeper into his chair, his beard resting on his chest.

The overcooked stag had been devoured, the bowls of tasteless porridge emptied. The gravy-sodden trenchers had been taken away, to be given in the morning to the poor at the kitchen gate. Frederick suddenly felt an overwhelming craving for a fragrant juicy orange. No one here had ever seen such a fruit. He imagined the orange groves of Palermo, heavy with ripe fruit. As a boy, he used to sit in their shade, watching the oranges fall. There'd be a rustle in the dark leaves. Then a soft plop. The oranges lay dotted on the moist brown soil like golden orbs. For an instant, Frederick imagined the bittersweet aroma of orange and citron, the fishy smell of the waterfront, the tang of tar from the ships, the sea . . .

He shook himself out of his reverie. Thinking about Palermo always filled him with useless longing. There were other longings, however, more easily satisfied. He beckoned to Manfred, his cupbearer tonight.

"Yes, my lord?"

Frederick pulled him down and whispered.

Manfred nodded, a smile on his lips.

THE GIRL, A pretty, fair-haired wench with a saucy smile, was waiting in his bedchamber when he arrived. She curtsied clumsily.

Without giving her another glance, he began to strip off his clothes. Mahmoud caught each item as it was discarded, a reproachful look on his face.

"Has she taken a bath?" Frederick asked in Arabic.

"The water was as muddy as if a water buffalo had been washed in it." Mahmoud wrinkled his nose. "She smelled like one, too, when she arrived. They all do," he said, picking up Frederick's hose.

Frederick smiled. This was Mahmoud's subtle way of indicating disapproval. Mahmoud did not like Germany, or the Germans. Least of all did he like German women. This, Frederick suspected, was because they did not like him. They were terrified of Saracens.

"Leave us, Mahmoud. I'm not to be disturbed till the morning."

"Yes, my lord." The voice, too, was reproachful. A king did not remain alone, ever. His insistence on privacy when satisfying his manly needs was incomprehensible.

"Mahmoud!" Frederick bellowed.

"Yes, my lord?" he asked innocently.

"How many times must I tell you to open that window before I go to sleep?"

"I beg your forgiveness, O Sultan. I thought—"

"Don't think. Do as I say or I'll have your worthless head detached from its even more worthless trunk!"

Mahmoud shuffled to the window and undid the latched shutters. Before pushing them out, he turned around: "It is terribly cold tonight. Ice is falling from the skies."

Frederick glared at him.

Mahmoud salaamed and withdrew, casting a last disapproving look at the girl, who stood pressed against a pillar.

"Take off your clothes. All of them." Frederick commanded.

She stared at him with a mix of fear and surprise. "Everything, my lord?"

Frederick nodded. "I like my women naked, particularly if they're as pretty as you." He smiled at her. "Don't be afraid. The emperor is only a man like any other, a man with a need."

Her blue eyes flashed for a moment in rebellion. Then she did as she was bid. Frederick watched her undress. Her breasts were big, with large brown nipples. He could feel himself swell.

THE GIRL STIRRED beside him in her sleep. Somewhere, there was a soft, scraping noise like the gnawing of mice. Frederick pulled the fox rug higher over his shoulders. An icy cold pervaded the darkness. The oil lamp that always burned in the far corner must have gone out. The moonlight threw eerie patterns of light and shadow onto the black and white floor tiles.

Drowsily, Frederick stretched one arm across the girl's back and cupped her left breast in his hand. Torn between desire and sleep, he was just about to close his eyes again when something caught his eyes. He stiffened. A shadow on the floor had moved. Or had he imagined it? The girl's breath was deep and regular. Too regular, he thought, suddenly alert. Her heart under his fingers was racing.

Someone was in the room, very close. With one rapid movement, Frederick heaved the girl over himself. As the dagger struck her, she gave a gurgling groan. He threw her off and rolled onto the floor, reaching for his sword. Before he could do so, a heavy boot, padded with something, crushed his fingers. A dark hooded figure loomed over him, the dagger poised to strike again.

With his free hand he grabbed the man's ankles and threw him against the wall. Lunging forward, he reached for the sword. Breathlessly, he waited. A cloud passed over the moon, making the dark shape of the man disappear. He heard him wheel about. A heavy weight jumped on his back. Frederick fell sideways and knocked his head on the step of the bedstead. A searing pain shot through his head. His sword clattered to the floor.

Gasping for breath, they rolled on the floor, each trying to find a vulnerable spot on the other. Huge hands tightened around Frederick's neck, squeezing, squeezing tighter. In the darkness, the face came closer, white teeth bared in a diabolical grin. Frederick let himself go limp. Sensing victory, the murderer slackened his grip just long enough to catch his breath. It sufficed for Frederick. He lunged at the face. His teeth sank into the soft flesh till he tasted the salty, metallic flavor of blood. The man let loose a howl of pain.

Frederick grabbed him by his doublet. Behind loomed the open window through which the man had entered. With his last strength he catapulted the assassin out of the window, past the still dangling rope, into the abyss below.

Only then did he become aware of the sound of splintering wood and shouting voices. They were breaking down the door. For a fleeting, panic-filled moment, Frederick imagined a conspiracy. Then he realized that the assassin must have shot the bolt on the door.

"Halt! I'm drawing the bolt," he cried over the din.

The guards stared at him, drawn swords in midair, before rushing past, their torches held up to light the chamber. He realized only then that he was naked. He felt a warm trickle of blood running down his neck.

The girl lay dead, her mouth open in an unfinished scream. She stared at the ceiling with the chilly fixity of death.

In response to the captain's query, Frederick jerked his head toward the open window. "I threw him out the window. Have his body fished out of the moat. It may give us a clue about who sent him, although we don't really need it, do we?"

The man shook his head grimly. "No, my lord. This is the Guelfs' doing . . ."

"Sweet bleeding Christ!" Manfred, a nightshirt showing below his cloak, turned white as he walked into the chamber. "Did she try to kill you?"

Frederick grinned. "No, she was just the bait. Otto's assassin is floating in the moat."

Then he barked at the captain: "Find the accomplices inside the castle. Put them to the rack, then have them executed. Their heads are to remain on the bridge till they've rotted!"

ON THE DAY Frederick went to call on the old Duchess of Spoleto, he was accompanied by a large company of mounted men-at-arms. Normally, he would have protested at such a large escort. But after the attempt on his life, he had become more amenable to warnings. The road crossed the Alsatian hills, sloping down from the Vosges mountains in gentle folds toward the Rhine.

Anselm acted as Frederick's guide. He pointed out places of interest, explained local customs and supplied him with information and gossip about the local magnates. Anselm pointed, "Over there, my lord, on the right, Julius Caesar won a great victory over the Germanic tribes."

Frederick stared at the plain, still treeless after more than a thousand years. How far the Romans had come, and how much they had achieved. He sank his chin deeper into his cloak. Despite the sun that warmed his back, the cold air stung his lungs. With the muffled sound of the horses' hooves on the snow a backdrop to his thoughts, he pondered, as so often before, the question of how to recreate an empire such as that of Rome.

Central rule was the key. But how to achieve that when on every hilltop a different nobleman ruled as if he alone were king? When rebellion simmered in every hall? His thoughts turned to Otto. At the Diet in Frankfurt it had been decided to attack him when the season for war began in spring. Since then, a flurry of messengers had been coming and going between Otto's court and the English king. Although his spies had not been able to find out more, this activity gnawed at Frederick like an unresolved riddle.

His counselors assured him that Otto and his uncle and ally King John had always been close and that there was nothing new to worry about. Frederick would have preferred a surprise attack on Otto now, while he was still trapped behind the walls of Cologne, before he might receive reinforcements from his uncle. But the barons had just stared at him when he suggested it. Go to war in winter? In ice and snow, over roads mired in mud, impassable to transport carts, only to freeze and starve besieging a well-provided city like Cologne? Or ambush Otto with a small detachment of knights when he rode out to hunt? That would be both dangerous and dishonorable.

War to these lords, he had learned to his dismay, was a seasonal occupation to be pursued with a minimum of discomfort and for only just the length of time they owed their overlord as the price of their vassalage.

Frederick sighed. What he needed was a well-drilled Roman legion, ready to march with unquestioning obedience at the call of a horn . . .

"Over there, my lord. Schoenburg Castle." Anselm pointed to the towers of a hilltop castle against the horizon.

Frederick had almost forgotten the purpose of this outing.

THE SUN FLOODED the solar in which the dowager Duchess of Spoleto received him. She was wrapped in furs and propped up with cushions in a high-backed Italian chair beside a brazier. Her ladies sank into a low curtsy.

He had come alone, leaving his escort below. He took her veined hand and brought it to his lips. "My lady, I am honored to meet you."

The old blue eyes scrutinized him. "They say you resemble Barbarossa. I think you look just like your father, you know," she said. "Your mother was disappointed when she saw that you had his coloring." Although she was as thin and frail as a little sparrow, her smile was lively. "But you're far better looking than Henry ever was."

"You flatter me, my lady."

"No, I don't. I never flatter anyone, these days. At my age I don't need to any longer. Come and sit by me."

"Waltraut," she called, "bring the emperor a stool!"

She smiled. "Although she didn't want you to be emperor, I'm sure your mother would be proud of you. So young, and already a legend. You know," she chuckled, reaching out to take his hand, "my ladies talk of nothing else but you."

Frederick laughed.

Matilde looked up. "Ah, there you are, Adelaide!"

Frederick caught his breath. The young woman who had just entered had the cool crystalline beauty of a northern winter. Her flaxen hair was so fair it was almost white. She wore a gown of pale yellow wool, girded under her breasts with a brocaded girdle. She bent down to kiss Matilde.

"This is my niece Adelaide," Matilde said. "Since her husband's death she lives with me."

The old duchess patted Adelaide's hand. "Maybe the emperor will find you a suitable husband. I'm too old to haggle over land and dowries."

Adelaide lowered her eyes. As she lifted them again, their eyes met. Frederick mumbled something about a fortunate bridegroom.

For the next hour, Frederick listened as Matilde rambled on about the past, recalling events from her life and her friendship with his mother. As the sun lost its brightness, Matilde's chatter slowed down till it came to a halt. Gently, Frederick extricated his hand from hers. She had fallen asleep.

A glance outside told him that it was getting late. They would be returning in the dark. He still hadn't become accustomed to the short daylight of winter here. Rising to his feet, he walked softly across the room, taking care that his spurs did not clink as he walked.

Adelaide followed him. She was so close that he could smell a faint scent of violets. At the door, he took her hand. "Farewell, Adelaide. I don't often have the pleasure of encountering such beauty. I hope we'll meet again."

She curtsied. "That would please me, too, Your Grace."

On the ride back to Haguenau, Frederick found himself whistling a merry Sicilian tune. He would send her an invitation to court, chaperoned of course, as soon as was decently possible.

ON HIS RETURN, he found the outer bailey filled with men and horses. Grooms were scurrying about the torchlit courtyard, carrying leather buckets of water and oats for the horses. Frederick glanced at the surcoats of the men holding the reins. He looked at Anselm. "Do you recognize that coat of arms?"

Anselm nodded. "The bishop of Strassburg."

"At this time of day?" Frederick slid off his horse and strode up the stairs. In the hall he nearly collided with Berard.

"You've a most unexpected visitor waiting for you, Frederick."

Frederick grimaced. "I know. What does the bishop of Strassburg want at this hour, and unannounced, too? Bad news?" He was both hungry and tired.

Berard's eyes widened for a moment. "Bishop of Strassburg?" Then he nodded. "Come and see for yourself. I'm sure you'll find this very interesting."

The portly man in a beaver-trimmed hat warming his hands by the fire in the audience chamber bore no resemblance to the bishop of Strassburg, even from behind. He turned around slowly and removed his hat.

"My lord, you do not know me. I have presumed on my friendship with the good bishop to have me escorted here in secret. I am Conrad von Scharfenburg."

Frederick's heart missed a beat. Otto's chancellor! As coolly as he could, Frederick asked, "And what, my lord Conrad, might your business here be?"

"What I have to say is for your ears only. May we speak alone?"

Frederick hesitated.

"Don't, I pray you!" Anselm put a restraining hand on his arm.

Conrad laughed. "Do I look like an assassin? All my life I have wielded the pen to far greater effect than the sword."

Frederick jerked his head toward the door. "Leave us. I will hear what he has to say in private."

Frederick gestured to a bench. "Pray be seated. Just because we're enemies doesn't mean we can't observe the niceties of hospitality."

The chancellor shot him a surprised glance and sat down. Frederick went over to a credenza and filled two silver goblets with wine. He handed one to Conrad.

Frederick scrutinized his uninvited guest. So this was the man behind Otto's success. Was he also responsible for his errors? he wondered. The chancellor didn't look as his renown would have made one expect. He looked more like a mild-mannered priest than the formidable politician and prince of the Church that he was. Even his robe, although lined with costly fur, was of a dull slate blue that differed markedly from the brilliant colors normally worn by the great. Perhaps he cared more for power itself than for its trappings. An interesting thought, that. After taking a sip of his wine, Frederick asked: "Well, what is it you have come to negotiate?"

"I have come," Conrad said slowly, "to offer you my services."

Frederick managed to keep his face impassive. Otto's position must be much worse than they thought. It would not do, however, to show his elation. "God's truth," he said with indignation, "Why should I trust someone who is betraying his master?"

"Because you are a man of reason and not a sentimental fool. I have proven my worth in many years of service to Otto. He is doomed. Whether I leave him now or not will not change the course of his destiny. But it may well prove advantageous to both of us. You need a chancellor. And I wish to continue serving Germany."

"You want to be my chancellor?"

"Naturally. I'd be wasted in any other post. There is no man in Germany better qualified to help you rule the Empire than I."

Frederick stared at him. Then he began to laugh. Great guffaws of laughter shook him.

Conrad observed him impassively.

When he had calmed down, Conrad asked, "Well, what say you?"

"I could now, could I not," Frederick said, "feed you to my mastiffs?"

"Yes, you could. But I don't think you will. Feeding me to your dogs would be wasteful in the extreme."

Frederick looked at him, intrigued. "Why so?" Despite the distaste he felt for Conrad's betrayal of Otto, he admired his self-assurance and cool logic.

"Because I'm more useful to you alive. If you appoint me chancellor, you will not only gain an able and loyal administrator—"

At this, Frederick began to laugh again.

". . . a loyal administrator," Conrad went on unperturbed, "but also the allegiance of several great princes, including the bishop of Cologne."

"The bishop of Cologne?" Frederick asked with quickened interest.

Conrad nodded. "Otto behaves more irrationally with every day that goes by. The only reason all his allies have not yet abandoned him is because they trust in my stewardship. Once I am gone, most of them will follow."

"Mmm." Frederick rubbed his chin. "What makes you think that I'll succeed where he has failed?"

"Your Uncle Philip failed in his bid for the Empire because he was too weak to beat Otto's Guelf faction. Otto was deposed. In his case it was not weakness but foolishness. Against my advice he antagonized the pope. You, my lord, are neither foolish nor weak." Conrad smiled, "I see now that you couple that with another weapon."

"Which one?"

"A winning manner. That, too, is a great asset."

Frederick looked at the older man and shook his head. "Surely flattery is beneath you?"

"Not at all. And if it happens to be true, it suits me even better. But the proof that I speak the truth," Conrad said with sudden solemnity, "is my presence here."

Frederick twisted his seal around his finger. He had a deep aversion to turncoats. They reminded him of those who had dispossessed him as a child. Yet Conrad's defection would greatly strengthen his position. He did need a chancellor. As long as his luck lasted, Conrad would serve him well enough.

"Before I make up my mind," Frederick asked, "tell me: why have you decided to abandon Otto now?"

A shadow flicked across the chancellor's eyes. For an instant, he hesitated. Then he said, "An English rout of the French and their Hohenstaufen allies was Otto's last hope. John of England, after protracted negotiations, has finally decided not to go to war after all."

Frederick sucked in his breath. So much for the assurances that nothing untoward had been happening in Otto's camp. What danger he had escaped without knowing it! Frederick stretched his shoulders. He felt stiff from tension and too many hours in the saddle.

He had made up his mind. "I accept your offer, my lord von Scharfenburg. I'll call a council tomorrow. I must keep up appearances with the electors. As you know, they're a touchy lot and like to be consulted." He added, "My steward will see that you and your retinue are lodged discreetly."

FREDERICK HELD HIS Whitsun court that year at Eger, in Bohemia. After a week of hunts, tournaments, and festivities, during which young knights were dubbed, the court was to culminate in a great feast on Whitsunday. The event was attended by all the great nobles and their families. Frederick calculated that the cost of his Whitsun court would have sufficed to feed an army of five hundred men for two months. Although he groaned inwardly at the expense, he set out to charm his guests.

And they responded in kind. The older princes treated Frederick as fond fathers would. They cheered when the Duke of Lorraine, long a staunch supporter of Otto's, paid homage to him. Kneeling before the throne, the duke bent his grizzled head. He ungirded his sword and laid it at Frederick's feet. In a steady voice he took the oath of fealty. A roar of approval went up as Frederick raised his new vassal, kissing him on both cheeks. One of Frederick's last great opponents had been won over. The defection of Otto's chancellor had indeed been a boon.

VASSALAGE, FREDERICK THOUGHT, as he afterward sat in the hot sun under a purple awning and watched the new knights joust, was a peculiar institution. Unknown to the Romans, vassalage sprang up in the twilight of Rome, when men turned to each other for the security the state could no longer provide. All land was held in vassalage, in a downward pyramid starting with the king, who held his land in trust from God. The king distributed fiefs to the great nobles, in return for allegiance. These lords in turn had smaller vassals of their own, right down to the poorest knights with no following.

A great nobleman might owe his suzerain the services of an army, mounted and equipped, for several months a year, while a small landholding knight with only one squire performed a few weeks' service. The bonds of vassalage often transcended national boundaries. If a man held fiefs simultaneously from the French and English kings, say, on whose side would he be when both these liege lords demanded military service at the same time?

Frederick sighed. The system was fraught with danger. The Romans, as usual, had had a better one.

ON WHITSUNDAY FREDERICK signed the Golden Bull of Eger, so called because of its golden seal. His lips were pressed together as he stood back while the prince-electors filed past him in the great hall to countersign the document.

The charter confirmed the German ecclesiastics in their exemption from imperial taxes and jurisdiction and granted the papacy the disputed lands in central Italy in perpetuity. By virtually renouncing his sovereignty over the bishops' territories, he had laid the foundation for a state within a state. This would make the unification of Germany difficult if not impossible. And it was no use arguing that he had only confirmed an existing state of affairs.

Thirty pieces of silver, Frederick thought glumly. The price of an empire.

AT THE FEAST that followed, Frederick was irritable and restless. He leaned back, drumming his fingers on the tablecloth, and studied his guests. Laughter filled the hall, drowning out the lutes.

After the trestle tables had been cleared away to make room for the entertainment, the strict order in which the guests had been seated disintegrated. Bishops mingled with chaplains, dukes with counts, minor nobles with high court officials. Frederick gestured to his cupbearer to refill his goblet. He wanted to get drunk. Seriously drunk. He wanted to forget the document he had been forced to sign. To think of pleasant things. Such as Adelaide.

The minstrels in the gallery struck up a merry dance tune. Couples came forward. Frederick spotted Adelaide. He rose to join them. Like a sleepwalker he followed the music, his eyes on her. The chain of dancers swayed to and fro. Adelaide danced between a burly markgrave and Rudolf of Hapsburg. The long slashed sleeves of her ruby red gown fluttered with each step. From her forehead hung a gray drop pearl, secured to a headdress of red and gold brocade.

Although she had accepted his invitation, arriving with a large retinue and a half-blind elderly uncle, she had evaded him whenever possible during the festivities of the last days. Dancing opposite him now, she came tantalizingly close, close enough to touch, only to recede again with the next wave of music. Every time they approached each other, Adelaide smiled. Was she mocking him?

Yesterday, at the hunt, he had offered her a peregrine. Securing the bird to her wrist, his hand brushed the bare skin above her glove. She had thanked him with cool courtesy. Frederick felt weak with lust. He wanted to bury his head between the two mounds that rose and fell beneath her gown. He wanted to unpin her hair and spread it like molten gold on a pillow.

He nearly crushed the hand of a fat dowager on his right. The lady squealed coquettishly. He mumbled an apology, his eyes on Adelaide. He must have her. The wenches on whom he appeased his hunger only reminded him that Adelaide was everything they were not, even as she was toying with him. But she was in for a surprise. He'd teach her a lesson she was not likely to forget.

THE LOCK HAD been freshly oiled. The key turned soundlessly. The narrow side door swung on its hinges. Frederick bent his head and crossed into the bedchamber. An oil lamp burned on the little travel altar beside the bed.

Adelaide, kneeling before an image of the Virgin, whipped around. Her eyes widened.

"Ssh." Frederick raised a finger to his lips.

She drew herself up. Her shift of thin white linen, girded high in the waist, emphasized her breasts. "How dare you!" she hissed.

Frederick noticed with amusement that she had hissed in a whisper. One scream would have brought her maids running from the anteroom where they slept. "Adelaide, stop teasing me, it's quite useless." He opened his arms.

He was barely an ell away from her. She caught a faint whiff of something like frankincense. They said that he bathed every day, in perfumed water. Was it true? His eyes, those amazing eyes, held her gaze, compelling. Trifling with the emperor at a distance was one thing. Now that he stood before her, she suddenly felt a little afraid.

He smiled, a beguiling smile. "Come," he commanded.

Adelaide took a step forward. Frederick's arms enfolded her. His mouth came down on hers. All her careful pretense of indifference forgotten, she kissed him back, in way she had never kissed her uncaring dead husband. She had wanted the emperor. Now she wanted the man as well.

He raised her shift and buried his face between her breasts. "I've been dreaming of you for so long, you little vixen . . ." His voice was like a caress. She pressed herself against him.

* * *

VALLEY OF THE NECKAR, AUGUST 1213

Frederick's initial distrust of his new chancellor changed into growing respect as the months went by. He began to draw more and more on Conrad's vast experience. Under his direction, the imperial chancery was reorganized. New directives were issued to the highest officers of state. Chests of documents were sorted and their bulk reduced. This was essential, as the entire chancery traveled with Frederick every time he moved from one castle to another.

The dusty smell of parchment and ink, and the industrious scraping of the secretaries' pens filled Frederick with satisfaction whenever he was in the chancery.

"HOW MUCH WILL we be able to raise this year, Conrad?" Frederick, who had been bending over a scroll, straightened. He looked at his chancellor. "The treasury is desperately in need of funds."

Poll taxes, salt taxes, road tolls, bridge tolls, scutage, taxes on mills of every kind, all were in arrears. Many villages and vassals paid their dues in kind: so many bushels of wheat, so many sheep or barrels of wine. If the harvests were bad or a late frost killed half the lambs, taxes would be lower. Towns that had been granted the right to hold markets or fairs were the best sources of revenue. Their trading enabled them to pay their taxes in silver rather than in kind.

In the years when rival emperors had been preoccupied with warring rather than ruling, corruption became rampant. A new system of checks on bailiffs, with severe penalties for offenders, was beginning to show results.

"I know," Conrad nodded. "It's a perennial problem. Like weeds in a garden, it springs up every year." He pulled out a grubby ledger from under a pile and studied it. "Without the latest report from the bailiffs of Swabia, I cannot say for certain, but I think we should be able to raise—"

Conrad broke off as the door opened. A page bowed in the doorway.

"My lord, dispatches from Palermo."

Frederick turned the letters over, scanning the seals. He brightened as he saw the quartered arms of Aragon and Sicily. Constance wrote all her

THE FALCON OF PALERMO 141

personal letters to him herself, in a tall, even hand. Her Latin was almost faultless. He was lucky to have such a wife. Despite initial opposition from the regency council, who had balked at being headed by a woman, she had won their respect. And when it came to raising taxes from the recalcitrant Sicilian barons, she was very successful.

He smiled as he read. Dear Constance. He'd known she wouldn't disappoint him! The money he had asked for had been paid to a Florentine banker in Messina, whose representative in Basle would pay the funds. The harbor of Catania had been dredged. The town walls of Bari were being repaired, although the repairs were costing far more than expected. They could not be completed until next spring. And little Henry, who was nearly three, was playing with a wooden toy sword . . .

If only he could bring the boy and Constance to Germany. But the pope would see his old terror, the union of Sicily and the Empire, resurrected at the mere mention of his son's presence in Germany. Henry had been crowned king of Sicily and must remain there. He couldn't afford to antagonize the pope. Not yet.

He thought of Sicily and sighed. For how long would he be able to rule two countries? Although he worked long hours governing Germany, he spent almost as much time on Sicily. He often stayed up in his apartments till late at night, dictating letters for Palermo to wary secretaries trying to write as fast as he talked. He took pains not to flaunt his involvement in Sicilian affairs, yet of course many knew about it. What could be construed as divided loyalty might one day be used against him. Particularly when the barons awoke to the fact that once he had secured his position, he would brook no further interference from them . . . He returned to Constance's letter. He smiled at her endearments and the prayers for his welfare with which she ended all her letters.

As he put the parchment down, the chancellor cleared his throat. "My lord, a word with you before you go. I need to speak to you about those Jews accused of killing a Christian child."

Frederick's brows shot up. "Have they been found guilty?"

"No. The judges are unable to pass judgment. You stipulated that they ascertain whether the law of the Jews really incites them to murder Christians. No one can understand their laws. They're in Hebrew, in a book called the Talmud."

Frederick shrugged. "Then let them find a convert from Judaism who can translate that book."

"There are no such converts in Germany. There may be a few in England or Spain."

"Well, write to my brother of Aragon. Ask him to send two converts versed in Jewish scriptures. I've always wanted to know what their laws are really like."

Conrad shot him a surprised look. "That will take time. The townspeople are angry at the delay. They're clamoring for justice, the way it was always done. Their lord agrees with them." Conrad leaned forward. "Sire, let them burn the Jews and raze their quarter." Lowering his voice, he added, "Several princes grumbled when you established a special court to investigate this case. Don't jeopardize their new loyalty to you for the sake of a few old men."

Frederick gave him a steely look. "I won't hand them over to a bloodthirsty rabble till I'm sure of their guilt."

"But my lord, they're only Jews. Jews have always been tried by local courts. They've never had the right of appeal to the imperial justice."

"I don't care," Frederick snapped. "This custom that every town and every lord have their own court is a travesty of justice anyway. How often do you think their decisions are guided by prejudice, greed, or revenge? Don't you think that a reeve appointed by the local lord to sit in his court will favor his master's interests over those of the accused?"

"In many cases, I'm are sure you're right," Conrad agreed. "But it's still better than no justice. Our itinerant imperial judges could never cope with every suit about a stolen cow brought by one villein against another."

"Well, then we'll have to improve the system, won't we? I don't believe these Jews are guilty. When I think of the learned Jewish scholars of Palermo, I find it hard to believe that their holy book tells them to crucify Christian children to mock Our Lord. They deserve a fair trial. If they're found guilty, they'll burn. If not, I'll take them under my personal protection."

Mahmoud, who trailed Frederick like a shadow, gathered up the dispatches from Sicily and prepared to follow him.

In the doorway, Frederick paused. "I want you to issue a proclamation that from now on, every citizen of the Empire shall have the right to appeal to my courts, whether he be a villein, a Jew, or a prince."

Conrad stared at him, aghast. "The barons will resent such interference with their rights. They'll—"

Frederick silenced him with his hand. "The German lords are weary of disorder. I think for the sake of peace they may well be prepared to sacrifice a few privileges here and there."

"If you insist, Sire," Conrad said doubtfully.

Frederick had no doubts. Since Eger, he had been buoyed by a new confidence. For the first time, he felt totally certain of success. Even the recent flurry of activity in Otto's camp, which not long ago would have gnawed at him, didn't worry him. They were just the death throes of a lost cause . . . Within a short time, the whole of Germany would be his. He strode briskly out of the chancery, humming snatches from an Arabic song.

UPPER RHINE, JULY 1214

Unable to sleep, Frederick paced up and down in his tent. Although it was midsummer, the night air was damp and chilly. The army was encamped in a clearing close to the river. For the past few weeks they had been constantly on the move, harassing the enemy, waiting for news from the French.

For the hundredth time, he asked himself, pacing, how he could have been so stupid. It was no use telling himself that even Conrad, who knew Otto so well, hadn't thought it possible. The betrayal by his chancellor had jolted Otto out of his deranged lethargy. In a burst of energy reminiscent of the great feats of his youth, he crossed the sea to England. There, he persuaded King John to change his mind and go to war against France. King John and his army landed in Aquitaine. At the same time, in a concerted movement, Otto and the Duke of Brabant invaded France from the north.

Phillip of France called on Frederick for aid. At a hastily arranged Diet in Koblenz, he summoned the south German lords to war. Under his leadership, they attacked Otto's rear on the upper Rhine, thus relieving the pressure on the French. Siege warfare was a slow and tedious business. When the message from King Phillip had come three days ago, they had been laying siege to a particularly stubborn Rhineland lord. Holed up in the keep of his castle with his garrison, he refused to surrender even after they breached the outer walls. Leaving a small force to continue the siege, Frederick and his army set out with all speed to join the French for the decisive battle with Otto.

Frederick hugged himself. This coming confrontation would decide the future of three nations. If they lost now against the English, half of France would become part of England. Otto of Brunswick, backed by a victorious King John, would be emperor for good, while John of England would become the most powerful monarch in Europe. What an irony. "John Lackland" the greatest monarch in Europe! Once the landless youngest son of Henry II and Eleanor of Aquitaine, John had seen all his brothers die before him, finally becoming king.

Frederick glanced at the hour candle, burning with infuriating slowness. He longed to break camp and be on his way. By nightfall they would have joined the French. Outside, he could hear the men of the watch talking. From the next tent came Rudolf of Hapsburg's loud, uneven snoring. He flung himself onto his pallet and closed his eyes in another attempt at sleep. Thoughts kept on racing through his brain, wrestling with each other. Finally, after a long time, a welcome heaviness began to invade him. He turned on his side and drifted into sleep.

Somewhere, a dog barked. Horses neighed. Then came the thud of running footsteps. An agitated exchange of whispered words outside his tent. Frederick opened his eyes and sat up.

The sentry poked his head into the tent. "Messengers from the French king have arrived. They insist on seeing Your Grace."

Frederick grabbed his cloak and stepped out into the starlit night. His heart was racing. If Phillip's messengers wanted to see him at this hour, something dreadful must have occurred.

Torches driven into the ground threw some light between the dark rows of tents. Outside each tent hung its occupant's shield with his armorial bearings. The greatest lords were grouped around Frederick's own tent at the top of the hill. In decreasing order of importance the tents ran down toward the river. The poorest knights found themselves right at the water's edge, plagued by gnats. Their squires bedded down at their masters' feet, while the ordinary fighting men slept in the open.

A group of men was approaching, led by Frederick's herald. On the muddied surcoats over their chain mail Frederick recognized the arms of France: golden fleurs-de-lis on a field of powder blue.

Their leader, a tall figure with a neatly trimmed black beard, bent one knee on the trampled grass. "Sire, I am Josseran d'Aubrecicourt, herald of France. My lord King Phillip sends you greetings. He hopes Your Grace is in—"

"For sweet Jesus' sake, what news?" Frederick demanded.

"At dawn yesterday, battle was joined between us and the enemy at the town of Bouvines. King Phillip inflicted a crushing defeat on them. The English fled in disgrace. Some of the greatest lords in England, including the king's brother, were captured, and scores of noble knights and squires, too. Hundreds were slain. The rout was so great that even the men-at-arms and the archers were able to take prisoners, some three or four apiece."

By now the entire camp had been roused. Disheveled lords were emerging from their tents, fumbling with their clothing. A crowd had formed before Frederick's tent. His mouth was dry. "What of Otto?"

"Most of the Germans were killed or taken prisoner. The rest fled in disgrace. The Duke of Brunswick's men were decimated. His standard-bearer was killed beside him. He himself escaped on his marshal's horse after his own horse was killed under him."

Frederick swore. First the French had tackled Otto alone, depriving him of his revenge, and then they let him escape!

"Where is he?"

"No one knows."

The Frenchman beamed. "The imperial treasury was found in his camp. It will be sent to Your Grace, suitably escorted. In the meantime, the king bade me hand you this."

He turned around and gestured to a young knight.

The knight held out to Frederick a bundle wrapped in a length of blue velvet. As soon as he felt the parcel, Frederick knew what it contained. His disappointment receded somewhat. He untied the rope and raised up the smoke-blackened cloth for all to see. One wing of the embroidered eagle was missing, slashed out by a cut.

For a moment, silence reigned as the gathered lords stared at the tattered banner of the man who had once been their emperor. The old Duke of Lorraine, long a friend of Otto's, crossed himself, while his son Thibault looked away. Others shouted with joy, brandishing their swords. As the news spread, cheering swept through the camp.

In the east, above the mist that hung over the Rhine, the horizon turned from the first pearly gray of dawn to a deep orange. The sun was about to rise over the Hohenstaufen camp.

THE FORTRESS TOWERED on an outcrop of granite high above the town of Annweiler. Dense forests surrounded it, sloping down steeply to the town. From its square keep, the pennon of Brunswick fluttered in the cold wind under a gray sky. Looking up at Trifels Castle from his horse in the marketplace, Frederick caught his breath. No wonder the exchequer's reserves and the imperial insignia were kept there. It must be the safest stronghold in Germany.

The castle was the principal link in a chain of fortresses guarding the paved Roman road that led west from Speyer on the Rhine toward Alsace and the salt mines of Lorraine. Since time immemorial, heavily laden trains of sumpter mules had wound their way along that road with cargoes of salt and other commodities for the Rhenish towns.

By now, nearly all the imperial strongholds that were part of this defensive system were in Frederick's hands. Most had surrendered without a fight. A few had been taken by assault or siege. Trifels, however, would not be an easy conquest. Although Otto was virtually powerless now, the governor of this castle remained loyal to the Guelf.

Winter is coming, Frederick thought. He must take Trifels before the end of the campaigning season. Not only did he need Otto's gold, but he also wanted Charlemagne's crown. Trifels had become a symbol. The castellan's stubbornness only reinforced his determination to conquer it.

The jingle of a harness interrupted his brooding. Conrad was riding up to him.

"What a position!" Frederick exclaimed, gesturing to the castle.

"Aye, my lord. It has never been taken since your grandfather built it. Your father fortified it further. He imprisoned Richard the Lionheart here, while he waited for England to scrape together his ransom. The almost vertical glacis it's built on makes assault with siege engines impossible."

Frederick nodded. Moreover, one of Otto's ablest lieutenants, Diemar von Falkstein, was the governor of the castle. It was sure to be well garrisoned and provisioned.

"What is the south side like, Conrad?"

"Just as steep and even more densely wooded."

"And von Falkstein, what manner of man is he?" Frederick asked.

"Brave and honorable."

"You mean we can't buy him?"

The chancellor smiled. "Would you put a corruptible man in charge of the imperial treasure, Sire?"

Frederick shook his head. Then, looking at his chancellor, "You're a persuasive man, Conrad. You try and convince him to surrender. I'll be magnanimous. I'll offer him a safe-conduct to Cologne if he wishes to join his master. Go and parley with him in the morning."

"It won't be easy. He has some very old-fashioned notions," Conrad said. "However, I shall try to justify your growing faith in my abilities." There was a glint of amusement in the chancellor's eyes.

"Do that," Frederick said with a smile. "You'll save me a lot of bother. This place is as impregnable as I was told. Only slow starvation will batter down those walls. Or the force of reason . . ."

Frederick glanced up at the darkening clouds. "Let's ride up closer. I want to take a look at it from the other side before the rain."

FREDERICK PEELED OFF his sodden gloves as he listened with growing irritation to Conrad. Having spent the morning inspecting the encampment in the pouring rain, Frederick was in no mood for what he was hearing.

His new body servants removed his wet cloak and boots. He would have much preferred the familiar services of Mahmoud, but he had had to concede that on campaign, the Saracen and his men were too visible a reminder of his foreignness.

"We'll be here till next spring if this hardheaded idiot can't be made to see reason!" Frederick growled.

The chancellor spread his hands. "He won't hand over the fortress to anyone but Otto. He took an oath to that effect and nothing will make him change his mind."

"You read him the bull of Otto's excommunication?"

"He told me it's a forgery. But he said that even if it were genuine, he takes orders only from his lord, not from the pope in Rome."

"A man after my own heart," Frederick said.

"My lord, I was just thinking . . ." Anselm spoke up.

Frederick looked up. "Yes, Anselm?"

"Why don't you speak with von Falkstein yourself? He naturally sees Conrad as a traitor to the Guelf cause." Anselm sketched a bow toward the chancellor, as if to apologize. He went on, "Your presence, Sire, might sway him. By all accounts he's honorable. He won't betray a flag of truce."

"How can I be seen to negotiate the surrender of what is rightfully mine? We'll begin the siege at dawn."

THE HORSES' HOOVES skidded on the sloping ground, slippery with fallen leaves. A putrid smell of rotting vegetation hung in the air. It had been raining for days. Up on the rock, Frederick could hear the trumpets calling the besiegers in small groups for the noontime meal. Rain was dripping from the nosepiece of his steel helmet onto his chin. Ahead of him rode his standard-bearer, holding the dripping banner aloft. Behind him followed an escort of knights and men-at-arms, more a formality than a necessity. There was no danger.

The enemy was securely ensconced in the fortress, unyielding still, but at least safely contained. Slowly, very slowly, in weeks or even months, they might come to their senses as hunger began to gnaw at their insides. This was going to be a long, grim siege, Frederick thought as he rode on in the swirling mist. It might well last through the winter. And it wouldn't be easy to convince his vassals to remain here that long.

They crossed the bridge into Annweiler. The town itself was almost deserted. At the army's approach the townspeople had fled into the forests, taking with them whatever possessions and livestock they could, and abandoning the rest to the inevitable pillage. Only there had been no pillage. Frederick had issued warnings that no towns were to be looted, under pain of death.

Now, after the news that Annweiler had not been sacked had reached the townspeople, some were cautiously coming out of hiding. In the empty marketplace, a family of villeins were pushing a creaking handcart piled with belongings through the churned mud. One of their children was leading a black pig on a rope, probably their most valued possession. Cold and tired as he was, Frederick smiled. It would not be long now before a delegation of leading burghers arrived, imploring his mercy and swearing allegiance, as had happened elsewhere.

He and his lords were lodged in the town hall, a two-storied wooden building across the marketplace. Soon, he thought, I'll be in a hot bath. He had been up since daybreak. As they crossed the square, a woman's scream rang out. Frederick reined his horse in and listened. All was silent. He jerked his head toward the left. "Quickly! Up there, behind the church." Two abreast, he and his men clattered through the narrow lane in the direction from where the scream had come.

THE MAN'S SMALL shifty eyes darted with fear. A burly foot soldier whose red face bespoke a fondness for ale, fell on his knees before Frederick's horse. "My lord," he stammered, "they were robbing yonder house, the one with the open door. When I came upon them she struck me with that wooden pole."

The woman was lying face downward in the mud, where the soldier had been dragging her when they came upon him. Sobs racked her thin form. An old man with a long white beard, who had been cowering in terror against the wall, bent over her. Against the peeling plaster of the tenement stood a donkey as old as its owner. On its back was an array of household possessions carefully wrapped in bits of cloth and strapped together. Thieves did not waste time packing their loot in this way, Frederick thought. The two must be returning to their abandoned home.

"Old man," Frederick commanded, "help her up."

The girl was but a child, a thin, waiflike creature with stringy yellow hair. Thirteen or fourteen at the most. She stared up at Frederick with brown eyes huge with fear. One glance at her confirmed what he had suspected. Her dress of patched gray homespun had been ripped open down the front. On the white skin of her left breast was an angry red weal.

The soldier flung himself forward until he was on all fours. He raised his hands. "Have mercy, my lord. I didn't touch her, by the milk of the Holy Virgin, I swear it, I was only—"

A murderous rage rose in Frederick. "I gave orders that no woman was to be raped! For attempting to violate this child, you should hang!" he yelled. "But I'll teach you myself what you get for lying to the emperor!" He grabbed his ax. The blade hissed through the air. With one stroke, he severed the man's head. The head thudded to the ground, rolling a few paces before coming to a halt. The sightless eyeballs stared up at the gray sky in a glaucous haze. Blood gushed from the trunk. Frederick threw the bloodied ax on the ground. His face was red. Above his left eye a nerve twitched.

He took his reins. Just as he was about to turn his mount, he remembered the girl and the old man. In his anger, he had forgotten them. They stood huddled together, the graybeard's arm around the girl's shoulders. Tears streaked down her grimy cheeks.

Frederick raised his hand. "Go in peace, both of you," he said. "And know that from now on, there is justice in Germany."

THE CHAMBER WAS in an uproar. Saddles, bags, chests of all sizes were everywhere. Servants dragged chests and panniers to the waiting baggage carts. Four guards staggered past, carrying a money chest on two wooden poles.

Frederick raised his arms above his head. His page slipped his mail hauberk over his padded undertunic. Within the hour he would be leaving for Speyer while his officers continued the siege.

"Frederick!" Manfred strode into the chamber, out of breath.

"What's the matter?"

"There's a villein outside who's making a great stir. He wants to see you. I passed just as the guards were dragging him away."

"What does he want?"

"Says he can help us take the fortress. He won't speak to anyone but yourself. A madman, no doubt, but I thought you'd want to hear him out."

"Bring him here."

The bent figure of an old man in tattered homespun was shoved into the chamber by two burly guards.

Frederick's eyes flickered with recognition. "Leave us," he commanded, waving his attendants out. "You, Manfred, stay!"

Frederick saw Manfred finger his dagger, as if to reassure himself.

With great difficulty, the newcomer knelt.

"Speak!" Frederick said

"I would have come earlier, my lord." His long white beard quivered on his chest. "Your men wouldn't let me. They chased me away twice." He glanced about vacantly, as if he had forgotten the purpose of his presence.

"What did you want to tell me? About the fortress."

"Oh, yes. The fortress." The old man nodded. "You saved my life and the honor of my granddaughter. She's all I have left in this world. In my youth, long before you were born, I was a man-at-arms of the bishop of Speyer. The Emperor Henry, afraid the English might liberate Richard of England, brought him here in great secret and imprisoned him in the castle."

"Go on."

"We brought the king during the night from Speyer to the hunting lodge in the forest beneath the castle. From there, the same night, we took him blindfolded through the underground passage that connects it to the castle."

"Gesùmmaria! And that passage still exists?"

"I think so. Few knew about it. We were sworn to secrecy. We kept the secret." The old man stroked his beard. "I think, my lord, that the new castellan does not know about the passage."

Frederick nodded, eyes shining. "Obviously, or he and the treasure would long have disappeared toward Cologne."

He turned to Manfred. "Quickly, call Conrad and the duke!"

Manfred shot him a worried glance. "My lord, this could be a trap."

Frederick shook his head. He was helping the old man up. "If this works, old man, you shall never want for anything again."

THE CHESTS STOOD in rows along one wall of the treasury. Their lids had been flung open. Some contained ceremonial vestments, stiff with gold thread and precious stones. From the glittering silks and damasks rose the faint aroma of the peppercorns that protected them from moths. Others were filled with gem-studded vessels of gold and silver plate. On the far end, in rows of money chests, gleamed crude silver ingots for the imperial mints.

"Open the confounded thing!" Frederick bellowed, standing before yet another coffer.

The elderly monk in charge of the treasury flinched. With trembling hands he unlocked another beautifully wrought lock.

"Damnation!" Frederick stared at the open casket before him. Empty. Empty just like the other two reserved for the crown jewels. On the lining at the bottom, the spot where the imperial crown had rested was marked by a perfect octagon where its weight had crushed the blue silk. Next to it was a rounded depression where the orb had lain. The sword of Saint Mauritius, said to convey invincibility on the emperor, was also missing, as was the Imperial Cross, a reliquary containing a nail from the True Cross.

Frederick glanced about him. Only one door led into the treasury from the chapel below. This had been barred with three huge padlocks. The keys in the monk's hands had been taken from the governor himself when they had burst in on him. There had been no time for him to spirit the insignia away—unless von Falkstein had hidden them when the army first appeared in Annweiler. That was a possibility. "Bring the governor!" Frederick bellowed.

While he waited, Frederick's mind wandered from the missing regalia to the stroke of luck that had delivered this fortress into his hands. Manfred and his men had easily found the passage in the disused hunting lodge. The narrow tunnel issued into a well shaft with steps hewn into its sides. They forced the iron grid covering the top of the well and clambered out into a courtyard. The entrance to the keep was just a few paces away. They overpowered the two guards lounging at the keep door and reached the hall, while a few handpicked men crept to the gates. Holding a dagger to his wife's throat, they forced the governor to order the garrison to lay down arms.

It had all been over in minutes. Frederick drew his mantle close. A bone-chilling cold filled the chamber. In a corner, the monk was praying, moving his lips and fingering the beads of his chaplet. The officers at the door were restlessly shifting from one foot to another.

Strange, Frederick thought as he glanced at the bare whitewashed walls, how redolent with meaning this room was. It was here that the vast ransom paid by England for the Lionheart had been stored. And it was to this room that the Norman treasure, stolen by his father, had been brought from Palermo. He had been a rapacious man, his father. Greedy and harsh, but able. Perhaps even brilliant. But for his untimely death, he would have succeeded in his planned annexation of Byzantium, which would have accomplished the fusion of the Eastern and Western empires.

His tutor William had often told him as a child the story of the black day when King Roger's treasure was taken from the palace in Palermo. Loaded onto oxcarts, heavily guarded by German soldiers, the wealth of the Normans made its long journey over the Alps to this room. Frederick, with his Norman soul, understood his mother's seething anger at the callous way his father used Sicily's resources for his own ends. From that day on, William told him, the empress had dressed herself in mourning.

But as emperor, Frederick also understood the extent of his father's vision. What could have been nobler than the reunification of the two empires into the old Roman one, providing peace and prosperity to its citizens? Was it not justifiable to use Sicilian gold to accomplish such a goal?

His thoughts were interrupted by von Falkstein's arrival. Surrounded by guards, hands tied behind his back, the governor was pushed through the doorway.

"You wished to see me?" The voice was cold but not insolent.

The governor, tall and well made, looked at him without fear, openly assessing him. A pointed dark beard accentuated his long face. His brown eyes were slightly melancholy, the eyes of a scholar, not a warrior, Frederick thought. Intuition told him that threatening the count would be fruitless. He changed his planned speech.

"It is not my way to inflict the agonies of torture on anyone unnecessarily. And I wouldn't relish doing so to this old brother here." He indicated the monk, who had shrunk against the wall. "I therefore ask you, rather than him: where are the crown jewels?"

"My lord of Hohenstaufen, the imperial insignia are safely with the emperor in Cologne. There's no need for torture. I personally transferred them to their traveling cases with the help of the good monks in whose care they are. In yonder cupboard you will find the receipt, signed by the emperor himself." He turned to the monk and commanded, "Adalbert, get the receipt."

Frederick noticed with amusement that von Falkstein still gave orders. The monk shuffled over to the large oaken wall cupboard on the other side of the room. Rolls of sealed parchments were neatly stacked inside. The monk took the topmost one and handed it to Frederick. It was dated more than two years ago. Neither the wax nor the ink looked fresh. Otto's scrawl was illegible. He remembered hearing that whenever the crown jewels were transferred, a receipt had to be signed by the new custodian. With a curt nod he returned the parchment into the monk's trembling hands.

The regalia had eluded him in the simplest manner imaginable—Otto had removed them in good time. And he, idiot that he was, had hoped to find them here! He threw his head back and laughed "What a fool I've been!" he exclaimed. He grinned at the governor. "Well, at least I enjoyed myself, entering your impregnable castle. Not, if truth be told, that I deserve credit for that."

Von Falkstein struggled unsuccessfully to suppress a smile. For a brief instant, captor and prisoner, each having savored his partial victory, smiled at each other. Then von Falkstein's face set itself back into its lines.

Frederick threw up his hands. "What shall I do with you?"

The governor stared at him. "Why, my lord, surely you must do to me what I would have done to you, had our positions been reversed." A garrison that refused to surrender was always put to death.

Frederick nodded. "You would have beheaded me on the morrow. I, however, am not sure I wish to do that to you. You're a good man. Loyalty is a rare quality. Will you take an oath of allegiance to me if I pardon you and spare the lives of your men?"

Von Falkstein swallowed. "My lord, I . . ." He took a deep breath. "Your Christian magnanimity is worthy of loyalty. I shall be proud to become your liegeman, on one condition."

Frederick was amused by the man's audacity. "And what would that be?"

"That while I will in every respect be loyal to you as my liege, I shall never be called upon, either directly or indirectly, to cause harm to Otto of Brunswick."

"Good God, man, do you know what you're asking?"

"I do, my lord." Slowly, as if each word pained him, he continued, "But I can't buy my life at the price of becoming a traitor."

"I'll grant you your wish. I won't call on you to drive a dagger into Otto. Not," Frederick added. "that I need to stoop so low."

Von Falkstein fell to his knees. "My lord of Hohenstaufen, you are worthy of Charlemagne's crown."

ADELAIDE CROSSED INTO the gallery and was about to descend the stairs when the sound of Frederick's voice stopped her. She went over to the parapet.

Frederick stood in the center of the vast hall gloomy with blackened oak beams. A group of craftsmen clustered around him.

Adelaide couldn't understand why he had taken such a liking to this isolated fortress. She much preferred the comforts and gaiety of Haguenau to the austerity of Trifels. Frederick, however, wanted to spend the winter here, and was enthusiastically making plans for embellishing the place.

His hands were sketching a row of columns in the air. The hands were a mirror of the man himself, of his changeable, contradictory personality. Strange that she'd never noticed it before. Well formed—almost too well formed for a man's—with long, flexible fingers, they could switch from force to tenderness in an instant.

"Pink marble, veined with gray." He nodded, more to himself than to the others. "The marble's color and opulence will contrast beautifully with the rugged exterior of this aerie. For the flooring, checkered gray and white."

The master stonemason, a short, wiry man with close-cropped, curly grizzled hair, said, "My lord, pink marble may be impossible to get."

"Nonsense, Norbert, nothing's impossible. See me when you've got the samples." Norbert was one of the best craftsmen in Germany. He had recently carved a magnificent window for the palace chapel in Haguenau.

The stonemason and his assistants took their leave, escorted by a thin-lipped steward.

"Adelaide!" Frederick smiled, swinging her off the last step as she came down. The feel of his hands on her made her blood course faster.

"Let me show you what I'm going to do to this gloomy hall. It will be light, and cheerful. I'll replace those dark oak posts that support the gallery with rose-colored marble columns. The windows will be enlarged down to the ground." He pushed the floor rushes away with his foot to reveal wooden boards stained dark with age. "This henhouse flooring will be replaced with marble squares. No more rushes. A hall fit for an emperor!" He smiled. "What do you think?"

"I'm sure it'll be splendid, like everything you do." Adelaide gnawed her lip, "but don't you think all this expense could be put to better use elsewhere? Trifels is far too small for the court."

"That's one of its attractions. I'll have some peace. The hunting is excellent. And the views alone are worth the journey. Come." He put his arm around her waist and pulled her with him.

"Isn't it glorious?"

Perched on its cliff, the castle seemed to float above the treetops. A vista of endless forests of green and gold stretched to the horizon, interrupted here and there by a distant hilltop fort.

Adelaide dutifully admired the scenery. She had seen it before, and found it monotonous. His enthusiasm for nature was another strange quirk of this strange man. He wanted to know all about trees, animals, even crops. It reminded her of the villeins who worked her estates. They, too, showed the same intense interest in the soil and all that grew on it. Once, during a hunt, he had actually reined in his horse and questioned a crofter working his field about his plowshare and whether he used the two-field or three-field system. The other lords had waited on their horses, stony expressions on their faces, while they watched the emperor chat to a peasant about growing peas.

But what did it matter? He pleased her in other ways. And he was emperor and would remain emperor, of that she was certain, despite the whisperings of some.

She pressed herself against him. In a low, husky voice she said, "The view's lovely, but I'd rather see that marble pillar in the bedchamber."

"You realize that sooner or later I'll have to find you a husband?" Frederick stroked her cheek.

She wrenched herself free and sat bolt upright in bed. "I'm not marrying a hairy old beast just because you say so!"

"Why an old beast? I'll find you a young beast. What about the Duke of Limburg? He's very handsome and rumored to prefer boys!"

She cuddled up to him. Nibbling the nape of his neck, she whispered, "The only man I want to marry is you. Why don't you persuade the pope to annul your marriage to that old woman?"

Frederick stiffened. "Don't speak about my wife like that!" he snapped.

Cold hatred washed over her. She stared at him, resisting the impulse to pick up the candlestick on the nightstand and fling it at him. He was just using her after all. Despite his youth, he was as hard and selfish as any other man. She'd thought he was besotted with her. When he began taking her everywhere . . .

Frederick studied her dispassionately, a sardonic smile on his lips. "Come here," he stretched out his hand. "Only one thing calms that temper of yours."

Let him think that. Let him think that she was his slave. A show of submission, an inner voice told her, would serve her aims better. She smiled and wrapped her arms about his neck. One day she'd have her revenge. On the steps of the altar at which she became empress.

THE BREATH OF the two men clouded the morning air. They parried and thrust at each other on the dirty snow of the tiltyard, strewn with pebbles to give them better footing.

Steel ground on steel. Frederick's sword pressed against Manfred's, immobilizing his arm. With clenched teeth Manfred held the pressure for as long as he could. Then his sword clattered to the ground. He conceded defeat with a grin. "This time you win. But I'll have my revenge in the lists!"

Frederick laughed. It was true. There was no one to equal Manfred with a lance. Whether in the gaiety of a court tournament, bent on pleasing a lady whose colors were pinned to his sleeve, or in the frenzy of a battle charge, Manfred excelled in the art of unseating his opponent with a swift powerful thrust of his lance.

Frederick clapped Manfred on the back. "Half a capon, some hot ale, and a chunk of bread is what I need now," Frederick removed his helmet. He was pushing back the woolen cowl underneath when a movement caught his eye. On the terrace above, against the gray sky stood a burly figure in a traveling cloak.

"Berard!"

Frederick ran up the steps. They embraced. Berard held him at arm's length. "You look well, Frederick. This dreadful climate agrees with you." He glanced at the snow that still lay thickly on the battlements of Trifels. "In Rome, the sun was shining when I left. The first almond blossoms were out. I almost wanted to remain there."

Frederick laughed. "I'm glad to see that I rate higher in your estimation than the Eternal City. How was your journey?"

Berard smiled. "The last leg by barge up the Rhine wasn't too bad. The Alps, however, and the roads . . ."

"Come, join me in breaking my fast. I never eat before practice," Frederick linked his arm through Berard's. "I'm marching next week against the Duke of Brabant. His Flemish mercenaries are supposed to be even better fighters than our Saracens."

"The ferocious Henry of Brabant?" Berard asked.

"The same. Otto's last ally of importance. His daughter is Otto's wife. Though he's not quite so ferocious anymore. His army was decimated at Bouvines."

". . . THE GREATEST CHURCH council in history," Berard was saying.

Frederick cut himself another chunk of bread and dipped it into the duck's gravy. He stared at it for a moment. "You know, Berard, the fasting rules of the Church don't make sense. Duck, frog, beaver, eggs, unborn rabbits, all are classified as 'not meat.' What penance is there in eating duck on a fast day, as opposed to the flesh of a stag?" He shrugged. "Well, I suppose with over two hundred fast days a year the Church has to be lenient. But go on, tell me more about this council."

Berard spooned honey onto his frumenty. "Hmm, this honey is excellent." He savored another spoonful. "Peach blossoms, I think."

Frederick smiled. Berard's dedication to good food and fussy taste in culinary matters always amused him. He traveled with his Apulian cook, and exchanged recipes with other prelates. "I'm glad the honey's to your taste, but tell me about the council."

Berard looked up, "You're sure you want to hear about it?"

Frederick shook his head. He smiled. "No, but I need to know what's happening in Rome."

Berard leaned across the table. "Imagine, Frederick. Four hundred bishops, seventy archbishops, eight hundred abbots, the patriarchs of Jerusalem and Constantinople, representatives of countless princes and towns, as well as envoys of every Western king will be present in Rome in November. The whole of Christendom will be represented at this council. Perhaps even united."

Frederick grimaced. "And what's the reason for this grandiose undertaking?"

"Mostly to settle important matters of law and dogma for the universal Church. But it's also to decide on the imperial succession."

Frederick's eyes widened.

Berard nodded. "I know, but that was a private pact between the pope and you. He wishes to ratify this officially. You need not fear. Innocent was very pleased with the Bull of Eger. He refers to you as his 'most beloved son.' The council will endorse Innocent's will and confirm Otto's deposition."

"Hmm. And since when has a church council had the authority to depose an emperor? Innocent is arrogating to himself rights no pope has ever had before."

"Now, Frederick," Berard leaned back and smiled, "you can't have it both ways. You owe the imperial crown to Innocent's support. I grant you that the German princes elected you, but without the support of the papacy their rebellion against Otto wouldn't have gone far."

Frederick's face flushed. "That itself is proof of the papacy's unacceptable power!"

Berard said quickly, "The other matter close to the pontiff's heart is the new crusade."

"Another one?" Frederick groaned. Innocent's pontificate had so far been filled with them. The crusade against the Albigensian heretics in France. The fourth crusade to recapture Jerusalem. The crusade against John of England. The tragic "children's crusade" in which thousands of French and German children had perished.

Frederick said, "Under Innocent's rule 'crusade' has become a convenient term for stifling resistance to his authority."

"Innocent is a great pope," Berard said. "You are too harsh on him. He's going to lead the next crusade himself, despite his age, to revive the crusading spirit."

Frederick put down his tankard with a jolt. "What can a brittle old pope, steeped in incense, possibly know about fighting Saracens? Surely not even Innocent can delude himself that he'll succeed where great warriors such as Barbarossa and the Lionheart failed!"

"The pontiff has had a lifelong desire to secure the Holy Places for Christendom. He reasons that if he heads the crusade, great princes will follow, supplying men and gold."

Frederick looked down at his hands. Jerusalem! How evocative of glory that name was. Since the first crusade had established the Christian Kingdom of Jerusalem a little over a hundred years ago, the city itself had been lost and won several times. Jerusalem had been in the hands of the infidels now for nearly thirty years.

Crusading had become widespread, fashionable almost. If the hardships and dangers were many, so were the rewards. Crusading offered a remission of sins in the next world and a deferment of debts and taxes in this one, with the added prospect of travel, bounty, and excitement.

Frederick shuddered as he thought of the immense prestige that would be attached to the papacy if Innocent succeeded in recovering Jerusalem. He had lost his appetite. Signaling to the page for a handbasin, he rinsed his fingers. "If you're not too tired, come with me to the mews. I want to see if my new Ger falcon is getting used to her lodgings."

Berard glanced up from his unfinished food. "Frederick, there's something else I wish to talk to you about. Will you spare me a moment?"

"Of course." He sat down again and poured some more ale into his tankard. Taking a mouthful, he put it down, wrinkling his nose. "I don't know how you, who are so discerning, can drink this."

"Come now, Frederick. When you're in a bad mood, you criticize everything. When things go your way, Germany is the land of your hero Charlemagne, her people are more loyal than your Sicilians, and her snowy winter landscapes magnificent. And as for the German wenches that pass through your bedchamber . . ."

Frederick shot Berard a surprised glance. So the palace gossip reached him, too. Casually, he said, "What do you mean? Before you can bed them, you've got to order them to have a bath. Bad for their health, it seems!"

"Frederick, it's not your wenches that worry me, it's Adelaide I must talk to you about."

Here it comes, Frederick thought. It was bound to happen sooner or later. Better get it over with quickly. "What about her?" he asked.

Berard looked at him. "By flaunting your adulterous liaison with this woman, you're playing into the hands of your enemies. And you are antagonizing the pope. Adelaide is dangerous. Because of her family connections many of those who matter listen to her. Her own serving women are spreading the rumor that she'll become your wife. I'm certain that Adelaide herself makes sure they do."

"That's absurd." Frederick shook his head in disbelief.

"I don't think, Frederick," Berard said, "that you realize how ambitious Adelaide is. She wants to be empress. Before I left for Rome, someone I trust overheard her saying to a group of barons that you should have a German wife. She argued that your wife, in addition to being foreign, is away governing Sicily instead of being at your side. And the lords, aware of who that new wife would be, heartily agreed with her."

"Oh, she's just jealous of Constance," Frederick said. He suspected that Berard was about to suggest that he give her up. He added, "Why I can't imagine, since she's here and Constance is in Sicily, but that's typically female."

Berard leaned forward and lowered his voice. "Frederick, listen to me. Adelaide is stirring up resentment against you with her talk. You're too foreign for the German princes anyway. They're bound to resent many of your reforms. Unless you tread carefully, they'll soon be disappointed by your lack of docility as well."

Berard went on, "The poor fellows thought they'd elected a malleable youngster who would be grateful to them for elevating him to the purple, only to find themselves confronted with an emperor who has the instincts of a despot."

Frederick laughed. "I like that, Berard. Hm, the instincts of a despot. Not bad at all. In fact, that's exactly what these scoundrels need. A tyrant to keep them in line!"

"Listen to me," Berard said, serious again. "I'm not trying to save you from a minor sin. On that, you'll have to argue your case with the Almighty yourself. Your goal, as you yourself have said so often, is to give the Empire peace and unity, and I am trying to help you achieve that. Banish her from your court, marry her to a great lord, send her to a nunnery, anything to get her out of the position she now occupies. And do so quickly, before she stirs the winds of discontent any further."

Frederick looked down at his hands. "I've tried to marry her off. She won't hear of it."

"Maybe the husband you suggested wasn't rich and powerful enough?"

Frederick sighed. As much as he hated to admit it, Berard was probably right. She had been dropping hints for months that kings had been known to divorce their wives, citing the divorce of Louis of France and Eleanor of Aquitaine. But he couldn't lock her up in a convent simply because she was scheming to marry him.

"I can't just banish her, Berard. She's done nothing to justify it. Gossiping about me with her kinsmen is not a crime, you know. Nor, for that matter, is falling in love with me."

Berard twisted his mouth, "Is she in love with you, or with your throne?"

"Oh, come now, Berard. Isn't it possible to love a man, as well as the power he wields? Why should the luster of a crown appeal only to men? Any woman in her position would want to marry me. Adelaide's not a common serving wench, but the great heiress of a noble name. She'd make a perfect empress," he added with a smile, half to bait Berard and half because it was true . . .

Berard blinked in alarm. "I sometimes think that that woman is in league with Satan. Perhaps she's cast a spell on you. They say her old nurse has great knowledge of herbs and philters. Maybe maid and mistress brew them together on moonlit nights . . ."

"You can't possibly believe such nonsense."

Berard pursed his lips. "She's trouble, one way or another. Think about what I've said. Promise me you'll keep her more in the background. Don't flaunt her at official functions. Don't take her with you on every progress." He leaned across the table: "Do you know that the common people call her the 'Uncrowned Empress'? Imagine the pain this will cause Constance when she, as she must, hears about it."

Frederick lowered his eyes. Berard's last words had hit their mark deeper than all his previous reasonings. "I'll be more discreet, I promise you."

AACHEN, JULY 1215

On a hot cloudy July afternoon Frederick made his entry into Aachen. He was escorted by the clergy and princes who had welcomed him outside the gates. A sea of townspeople lined the route of the procession and filled the narrow side streets. The starched wimples of matrons stood out like white sails in the bobbing crowd. On the city walls, the ramparts were black with spectators. The streets had been swept and watered to settle the dust. Tapestries hung from the half-timbered houses of prosperous burghers along the main thoroughfare. Here, as in Alsace, storks' nests dotted the roofs.

At the head of the procession rode the portly archbishop of Mainz on a gray palfrey with a crimson saddlecloth. Behind him came the princes of the Church in a glittering array of jeweled miters, processional crosses, and brocaded banners.

Frederick, mounted on a white stallion with sky-blue trappings, glanced at the sky. In the evening, there'd be a thunderstorm. Behind him followed the temporal princes and the highest dignitaries of the Empire, including the newly loyal Duke of Brabant. He'd been amused earlier to note that Henry of Brabant's saddlery was far more splendid than his own, with a golden bit and spurs to match. Henry's way of soothing his bruised ego? The duke, whose ferocity and love of splendor were bywords, had submitted to Frederick with good grace. A rational man, and a civilized one to boot . . .

Here and there the crowd pushed forward in their enthusiasm, trying to touch Frederick's horse or his mantle. At a junction, a ragged beggar threw himself forward, crying "Mercy, Mercy!" Frederick had to rein in his horse sharply to avoid the man.

The beggar gripped Frederick's stirrup, his face uplifted in supplication. Silence descended on the crowd. For a moment, Frederick was baffled.

Then he realized what the man wanted. A sovereign's touch was believed to have miraculous healing powers. Frederick peeled off his right glove. Trying not to show his revulsion at the festering sores that covered the man's face, he leaned down and laid his hand briefly upon the matted grizzled hair.

A roar of approval went up. Frederick, a wave of nausea rising in his throat, pulled off his ring. Some decent food would do the poor wretch more good than any touching. He handed him the ring. The disfigured face transformed by a toothless smile, the old man sank to his knees. "May God bless you, my lord." He rose unsteadily to his feet and melted into the crowd.

The procession moved forward. The cheering reached a frenzy when the mounted heralds began casting largesse to the people, who scrambled over each other in their eagerness to grab the silver coins as they rolled into the dust.

Frederick was still thinking of the beggar. The royal laying on of hands, widely practiced by the kings of England and France and sanctioned there even by the Church, had always filled him with unease. Perhaps distortions of the mind could be overcome like that, but rotten lungs or festering flesh made whole? Should a king stoop to . . .

Frederick suppressed a gasp as he caught sight of Charlemagne's palace. It was the most splendid building he had seen in Germany. A double-storied complex of reddish stone with gilded roof tiles, it had none of the forbidding austerity of the fortified castles elsewhere in Germany. This was palatial in the true sense of the word: not defense, but magnificence was its primary purpose.

At one end stood the Royal Hall. At the other, connected to it by a wing of the palace, rose the octagonal church that was the glory of Germany. The church was surmounted by a dome, the only one north of the Alps. In front of the church, in the manner of a Byzantine basilica, was an enclosed atrium. Frederick now understood why they called Aachen "the Rome of Germany." Charlemagne had made the old Roman spa of Aquisgranum his capital, embellishing it until, at least in the minds of his people, it rivaled the Eternal City.

Frederick, calm, almost detached until now, felt his heart pound as he looked at the church. Tomorrow he would be crowned there, the fourteenth emperor to be consecrated in it since Charlemagne resurrected the Western Empire just over four centuries earlier.

FREDERICK KNELT ON the cold marble floor before the altar. His eyes were closed. His mind felt empty, cleansed. All emotion had drained out of him. Never before had he felt such a deep sense of peace.

He opened his eyes. The little side chapel was shrouded in almost total darkness. A single oil lamp flickered on the altar. How long had he been kneeling like this? He glanced up at the stained glass window. No glimmer of daylight shone through it yet. It must still be the small hours of the morning, an hour or two before they came to bathe and dress him.

In the stillness, he sensed the presence of his predecessors, who, too, had kept vigil alone in this chapel during the night before their coronations. He bent his head. For a moment he stared at his hands. Unlike Berard, he had no experience in talking to God, yet he felt a need to speak to him, to ask his blessing. He closed his eyes. "Oh God," he said into the silence, "Give me the strength to carry this burden. Help me to make the Empire strong and enduring. Aid me in giving my people justice and order. And protect Sicily, oh Lord, I beg of you."

Tears stung his eyes. He raised them to the emaciated Christ above the altar. In the flickering shadows the carved lips of the Saviour on the cross seemed to be moving in silent benediction.

He blinked, shaking his head. He must be overtired, overwrought with emotion. Like the mystics, after spending hours on his knees, he too was beginning to imagine things.

THAT MORNING, AFTER a ritual bath, his fast unbroken, Frederick emerged from the palace into the atrium that connected it to the Palatine chapel. Before him in the sunshine walked the clergy in solemn procession, bearing Aachen's sacred relics.

The princes awaited him in the courtyard. They raised their shields, clanging their swords against them. "Long live the Emperor Frederick, long live the Hohenstaufen!" Again and again, the chorus of voices rose above the din. Once, long ago, before the anointing and crowning of kings, the

Germanic rulers had been confirmed in their dignity by being raised upon the shields of their warriors.

After the last man had sheathed his sword, they escorted him to the church. Fanfares sounded. The bronze doors, silver-green with the patina of centuries, swung open.

Charlemagne's double-storied church was a magisterial blend of two cultures. Its octagonal splendor was Greek, the solid simplicity of its construction Germanic. The sanctuary was separated from the outer octagon by eight massive arches of horizontally striped black and white marble. On these rested the upper gallery, with arches of the same design. The cupola was covered in gold mosaics depicting biblical scenes. On the eastern side, facing Jerusalem, Christ the King sat enthroned, lifelike in the glow of hundreds of candles. What, Frederick wondered, had Charlemagne's rough barbarian lords thought as they gazed upon what to them must have seemed like a miracle of the builder's art?

Above the altar, suspended from the dome, hung the famed Barbarossa chandelier. The crown-shaped luster spanned half the octagon and illuminated the entire sanctuary. Frederick felt a surge of elation as he gazed at his grandfather's gift. He'd give Germany back her ancient pride, her glory. At the same time . . .

"Sire . . ." The archbishop of Mainz touched his sleeve. Together they walked to the altar. On it lay the royal insignia: the crown, the purple mantle, the orb and the scepter, and the state sword.

In a blur of hallowed words and gestures, he was girded with the sword, anointed on chest, back, shoulders, and forehead, cloaked with the coronation mantle, and crowned. The orb and scepter were handed to him. The clergy then escorted him to the upper gallery to be enthroned on Charlemagne's throne, a simple seat of four slabs of white Parian marble, yellowed with age.

After Mass, as the choir intoned the Te Deum, Frederick made his way down again. The assembly sank to their knees. From their throats rose an ancient hymn to Christ's victory, "*Christus Vincit, Christus Reignat, Christus Imperat,*" with which the German people paid homage to their newly crowned kings.

The coronation was over. He was now expected to leave the church, to be acclaimed by the populace waiting outside. Instead, he turned back to the altar. The prelates, glancing at each other in surprise, followed. He raised his hand. The murmurs died down.

"Princes and people of Germany," he said, "With God's help, I will bring you justice, peace, and prosperity. I shall work to unite the Empire and make it once again as great as in the days of Rome."

This was greeted by loud cheering. He went on: "Like my grandfather Frederick Barbarossa, I, too, wish to show my gratitude to Him who has raised me to the throne of Charlemagne." He raised his right hand. "I swear, before God and every man here today, to lead a crusade to Jerusalem, for the glory of Christ and the Holy Roman Empire. To Jerusalem!"

The congregation erupted into uproar. The name of Christ's city echoed through the great church like a battle cry. "Jerusalem! Jerusalem! Jerusalem!" they chanted, shaking their clenched fists skyward.

Frederick, watching, let a smile pass over his lips. Not the pope but the emperor would now be the leader of the next crusade.

EARLY THE FOLLOWING morning, despite the festivities that had lasted till the small hours, he was back in the church. Crowned and cloaked in the coronation mantle, he sat beside the altar, applauding the crusading preachers.

Berard, too, applauded, but with far less enthusiasm. These peripatetic priests were common all over Europe. Roaming from town to town, they kept the zeal to liberate Jerusalem alive. In years when an official crusade was declared, their number and the fervor of their preaching increased greatly.

Still, three in one town, the day after Frederick's announcement . . . Berard, whose head ached from too much wine drunk in annoyance, and too little sleep, told himself that at the first opportunity he'd get the truth from Frederick. This sudden crusading fervor was too well organized to be spontaneous. He must have planned it all beforehand. Perhaps with Siegfried's connivance? The archbishop of Mainz was known to be at loggerheads with Rome. He would welcome any opportunity to enhance German prestige at the expense of the papacy, particularly if it was made to look like the emperor's spontaneous idea.

Excitement ran high. It was only natural, Berard thought. Not since Barbarossa had an emperor summoned the German people to a crusade, promising to lead them to victory himself. To many, it must seem as if the dignity of Germany was about to be renewed. And the symbol of that renewal was a young emperor, sweeping away the woes of decades like so many cobwebs. But did Frederick fully realize the immense responsibility he had so insouciantly shouldered? There were only two ways of redeeming a crusading vow: fulfillment or death.

At midday, as the bells rang sext, Frederick himself mounted the gem-studded pulpit. He had thought of everything. On his mantle was stitched a red cross on a white background, the crusader's emblem. He would have made an excellent preacher, Berard thought as he listened. Frederick was eloquently painting a harrowing picture, sadly all too true, of the state of Jerusalem and the beleaguered Christian principalities in the Holy Land. At the end, he got so carried away that he thundered, "No Saracen shall ever again stable his horse in the tomb of Christ!"

Berard lowered his eyes. No one familiar with the Muslim respect for "people of the book," least of all Frederick, could believe this. Years ago Berard had been astonished to learn, after his arrival in Palermo, that the Muslims, too, venerated Abraham and respected Jesus as a prophet. They even accorded the Virgin Mary a special respect as Jesus' mother.

Jerusalem was on everyone's lips. Berard alone was filled with misgivings. Despite the sun outside and the press of bodies within the church, he felt cold. He drew his cloak closer around him.

THE FADING SUMMER light fell in soft beams onto the gray marble floor of what had once been the anteroom to Charlemagne's bedchamber.

"I'll deliver the Holy Places to Christendom," Frederick said. "That doesn't mean I've become a fanatical crusader." He spread his hands. "Look at it this way, Berard. Religion is the bulwark of civilization. A people who believe nothing and therefore fear nothing will create anarchy, for themselves and others. The holy places are fundamental for the dignity of Christendom. I, as emperor, must therefore recover them." Leaning back against the settle, he smiled. "From a ruler's point of view Christianity's a splendid religion. That's why Constantine adopted it as Rome's religion. A religion that preaches morality, hard work, and obedience to God and government is the answer to every sovereign's prayers, don't you think?"

Berard's dark eyes widened. "Frederick," he asked with trepidation, "do you then not believe in God?"

"Of course I believe in God! I'm just not sure that it is the exclusive God of the pope I believe in. If God made the world and everything in it, he also made those who don't believe in Christ, didn't he?"

Berard was appalled. "Frederick, you know that all those who don't embrace Christ will be consigned to eternal damnation."

"I don't know," Frederick shook his head. "I sometimes think that the Church invented it all to increase her power. There are people in distant countries such as Cathay who *can't* embrace Christ because they've never heard of him. How can they be condemned to hellfire because the Lord forgot to send them an apostle?"

Berard crossed himself. This was heresy. Men were burned at the stake for far less. "Frederick," he said, anguish on his face, "I know you don't mean what you're saying, that your inquisitive mind is only exploring ideas. But I beseech you, be careful. You're on very dangerous ground. If this ever got out . . . there's no telling what the consequences might be."

"I'll be careful. And I'm sure the Lord understands."

Berard sighed. "I'll age before my time in your service. As for your heathens in Cathay, if the Lord didn't send them an apostle, they probably didn't deserve one. Perhaps they're so steeped in depravity that they're beyond redemption." Drily, he added, "In any case, this fabled Cathay may not even exist. Perhaps the Venetians invented it to enhance the value of their exotic wares."

"Of course it exists! There're two large vases in my palace in Palermo from there. They're pale green, like the first leaves of an apple tree. On their bottom they bear strange writing, a little like Kufic, but different, which no one can read."

Against his will, Berard smiled. How like Frederick to look on the underside of a vase!

Frederick had picked up a bunch of grapes, and was plucking them off one by one, chewing with gusto. He grinned: "You realize that you'll be the most important delegate at the Lateran Council? You'll be representing not only the emperor but also the future conqueror of Jerusalem. The envoys will all be bilious with envy."

Berard folded his hands over the jeweled crucifix on his stomach. What would God make of such an opportunistic crusader? And what if he failed and, like his grandfather Barbarossa, perished in the attempt? After a long silence, he said, "And how do I explain your crusade to the Holy Father?"

"Explain? You don't have to explain anything. By the time you reach Rome, he'll know already. I sent him a letter this morning, informing him of my decision and asking very humbly for his blessing."

So Frederick was writing to the pontiff on his own, Berard thought, just as he had conceived this dangerous idea of becoming a crusader without his knowledge. Until now, Frederick had always asked his advice when dealing with Innocent. Berard forced a smile. "You're becoming an expert at spreading your views."

"Absolutely. Conrad is running the chancery very efficiently. It would've taken my Palermitans three times as long to produce the epistle I'm sending to the princes of Europe. I want them to hear it from me first, before those masters of distortion in the papal chancery twist the facts! In any case, the pope has been preaching the recovery of Jerusalem for years; he can't be seen to condemn me for carrying out his wishes, can he?" he asked sweetly. "Except that it'll be my prestige, and not his, that will be enhanced when I take Jerusalem."

Berard nodded wearily. The pontiff was in a tight spot. But so was Frederick.

FREDERICK REMAINED in Aachen for the rest of the summer, spending long hours in the palace library or hunting in the royal forests. Though he had planned an expedition to take Cologne, he stayed his hand when secret negotiations with the archbishop there began to look promising.

With the first mists of autumn came the news that Otto had left Cologne. The Guelf was a sick, broken man, so short of funds that he agreed to leave in return for the discharge of his debts. Disguised as a merchant, he slipped out of a postern gate one morning with his wife and a few remaining retainers, and made his way to Brunswick. When some of

Frederick's counselors urged him to pursue the fugitive, he shook his head. "Let him be. He's ill in mind and body. Why should I interfere with a war God is waging on my behalf?"

He went instead on a progress up the Rhine, culminating in his triumphal entry into Cologne. The citizens awaited his arrival with trepidation. Although they had obtained assurances of his pardon, it wouldn't be the first time that a victor put a city to the sword for supporting a rival. Frederick, however, wasn't interested in vengeance, only in consolidating his hold on the major trading centers such as Cologne. He demanded only a fine of five thousand silver marks. This the relieved bishop and the leading citizens handed over without demur.

Frederick, walking past the money chests while the silver was being counted, commented drily that salt herring and English cloth must be very profitable, judging by the ease with which Cologne had raised this hefty fine.

There followed three weeks of lavish banquets and tournaments in Frederick's honor. When he finally left to spend the winter in Haguenau, the people of Cologne breathed a second sigh of relief. A town favored by an imperial visit had to foot the bill for the upkeep of the emperor and his vast retinue.

Like his predecessors, Frederick traveled constantly from one part of Germany to another. The German system of governing was very different from the Sicilian one, where the Normans ruled almost entirely from their palace in Palermo. This was made possible by the efficient centralized government, based on the Byzantine model, that they had created.

The rulers of western Europe had only the scant beginnings of such a system. They were constantly on the move in order to govern their territories and administer justice, as well as to keep their great vassals in check by their presence. Frederick, who hated this peripatetic life, nevertheless had to acknowledge that at least it saved the treasury a considerable sum of money.

IN NOVEMBER, THE eyes of Christendom turned to Rome, where Pope Innocent presided over the greatest church council ever held. Berard, conscientious as always, dictated a report about it the morning after the final session and dispatched it to Frederick over the snow-covered Alps by swift imperial couriers.

Frederick read the report three weeks later in the chancery at Haguenau and burst out laughing.

He turned to Conrad, who was sitting opposite him, going over a petition. "Listen to this," he chuckled. "Over two thousand two hundred delegates. Imagine! The crush was so great that the poor archbishop of Amalfi was killed. When it came to the question of the imperial succession, our delegation became involved in a brawl with Otto's representative. Rising to defend Otto's claim, a group of envoys with Guelf sympathies began clamoring for Otto's rights. Our side leaped up from their seats as well and the venerable hall began to echo with insults. Otto's ambassador then resuscitated the old Guelf slander about my being the bastard son of the butcher of Jesi. At this, Manfred Lancia grabbed him by the collar and called him a godless liar. Otto's emissary then punched Manfred, who felled him with a blow! The Holy Father rose in indignation and left the council chamber, followed by the rest of the clergy."

With a smug grin, Frederick added, "After a recess, during which order was restored, the council reconvened and confirmed my title to the Empire almost unanimously."

Conrad studied his hands in silence. That had been a foregone conclusion. What interested him far more was Innocent's reaction to Frederick's intention of leading the next crusade.

"As expected, the pope officially called for a new crusade to liberate Jerusalem. All the ambassadors were already aware of my vow to lead this crusade, so Innocent's call was a little belated," Frederick added gleefully.

"And what did His Holiness say about your taking the leadership out of his hands?"

"Berard, prudent as usual, hasn't committed this to parchment. But we'll soon hear. Berard was to set out shortly after the courier, and should be here in another month or so. Not that it matters, Conrad," Frederick said. "There's nothing the pope *can* say, except give me his blessing."

Conrad nodded. "You're quite right. Outwardly, Innocent will be forced to agree. But having dealt with him for years, I know how he must resent your action. He chose you because he wanted a submissive emperor."

There was a glint of malice in Conrad's usually impassive eyes: "Poor Innocent!"

Frederick grinned at his chancellor, then continued reading. There followed an account of the council's main ecclesiastical decisions, which included the adoption of transubstantiation as dogma. Long a point of dispute, this was the teaching that affirmed the miraculous conversion of the bread and wine into the actual body and blood of Christ during the Eucharist.

The amused expression on Frederick's face turned to boredom. He flung the parchment onto the table. The niceties of religion interested him not at all.

WHEN CONRAD LEFT the chancery that evening, he heaved a sigh of relief. It had been a long day.

The chancellor, despite his advancing age, worked long hours, often making his officials and secretaries labor well into the night. His energy and dedication to hard work were characteristics he shared with Frederick. Frequently, the two men sat together until late, going over state documents in silence interrupted now and then by a brief question or comment. The speed with which Frederick absorbed a complicated problem, often finding a startlingly simple solution, still impressed Conrad, particularly when he thought back to Otto's lumbering thought processes.

The Hohenstaufen were undeniably a talented breed. Quick-witted, cunning, mercurial, and handsome, all except Frederick's father had also possessed an easy, winning manner that was hard to resist. Sometimes, as he watched what was perhaps the most exceptional member of this outstanding family, Conrad was filled with unease. Greatness did not normally run in a male line. On the contrary, great men tended to produce sons who were but pale shadows of their fathers. The Hohenstaufen had been blessed with spectacular success, but had their luck not lasted too long already? Frederick's uncle Philip, almost as gifted as his nephew, had met an untimely death at the hands of an assassin. Had that been the turning point? And this crusade, how would it end? Conrad usually tried to dismiss these visions of gloom as the thoughts of an old skeptic, but they kept recurring. Today, with the resurgence of the crusade question, they had assailed him again.

Behind him now he could hear the official in charge locking the iron-studded doors of the chancery. The pitch torches along the walls had already been lit and were throwing pools of light onto the floorboards. As he walked along the open gallery in the rapidly falling dusk, the guards on duty saluted him by raising their halberds.

The air was bracing, a relief from the chancery, filled with wood and lamp smoke. Soon the first snow would fall. Conrad pulled his cowl lower over his head, hugging his arms around his portly frame beneath his cloak. He peered down into the uncommon calm of the courtyard. Everyone would be eating by now, he thought, suddenly feeling a pang of hunger himself. In order to reach his private chambers, he had to descend the wooden stairs and cross the cobbled yard to the west wing of the palace.

Conrad crossed the courtyard, deserted except for the heavily muffled guards standing at attention. A horse neighed in the stables behind the bailey. In the stillness he could hear laughter and voices coming from the great hall. Just as he was about to climb the outer staircase that led to the upper floor of the west wing, a cloaked figure shot from a doorway and nearly collided with him.

"My lord, I beg your pardon!" Conrad cried.

Frederick was white with rage, his lips pressed together. The nerve above his left eyebrow was twitching.

Conrad took an involuntary step back. "Is something amiss, your Grace?"

"She can rot in hell," Frederick hissed between clenched teeth, more to himself than to Conrad. "If it weren't for the child, I'd have her head!" Conrad had no need to ask whom Frederick was referring to. So Adelaide had finally overreached herself? It didn't come as a surprise to him. Neither did he blink at the news that she was carrying a bastard. What surprised him was the violence of Frederick's reaction.

Frederick, mumbling something about ramparts and fresh air, turned and stalked off.

Conrad climbed the stairs to his chambers, where his servants would have a hot dinner and a glowing fire ready for him. It was probably a good thing that Adelaide had fallen from grace. Her hold on Frederick had begun to spread dangerously beyond the bedposts, which was where a mistress's influence should stop. Conrad himself, although an ordained bishop, had for years enjoyed a discreet relationship with a comely widow. He had recently moved her to a pleasant three-story house in Haguenau, where he visited her when the inclination moved him. This, he thought with mild regret, was unfortunately not as often any more as in his younger days.

As he pushed open the door to his lodging, he thought with idle curiosity that it would be interesting to see who would replace Adelaide in Frederick's favor.

ON A GRAY afternoon in January, a messenger rode into the bailey of Haguenau to announce that Archbishop Berard was within a few miles of the town. He would reach the castle before vespers. Frederick decided to ride out and meet him.

Despite the icy air that bit into his lungs, he felt exhilarated as he cantered out under the massive portcullis of the main gate. Once past the town, the country became solitary and still. The woods on either side of the road were black and somber under a light dusting of white. Large snowflakes began to fall. He spurred his horse into a gallop. The stallion, as pleased as his master at his freedom, raced ahead, hooves thundering over the frozen ground. His escort, weighed down by armor and mounted on sturdier horses, struggled to keep up with them.

At the summit of a hill, Frederick reined his mount in abruptly. In the valley below, he could see a line of horsemen, followed in the distance by a lumbering baggage train. Patting the shuddering animal, he waited for the convoy to approach. As he recognized Berard, he had to smile. Even at this distance, Berard's bulk and slumping seat were unmistakable.

Wrapped up to his nose in a furred cloak, a fur hat pulled down almost over his eyes, he was a picture of misery. Absurdly, Berard, who was at best an indifferent horseman, always rode the most splendid destriers, the only kind capable of carrying his weight. The column, having recognized the imperial standard, came to a halt. Berard, too, reined in his mount. Cautiously, like a tortoise, he raised his head just far enough to see what the disturbance was. At the sight of Frederick he broke into a smile.

"Frederick!" Suddenly infused with life, he leapt down with astonishing agility and clasped Frederick, who had also dismounted, in a great hug. Then he held him at arm's length, "Is something wrong?"

Frederick laughed. "Nothing, Berard. I just felt like welcoming my brawling ambassadors back from Rome!" He looked around. "Where's our hero?"

"Manfred had to remain in Italy. His mother's very ill. He'll follow as soon as he can."

Frederick remembered, as if in another life, the beautiful countess who had bandaged his arm on the morning after the ambush at the Lambro. "Have a Mass said for her every day till we get word that she's well. She brought me luck."

Berard gave him a searching look. "Such faith in the efficacy of prayer is something new, Frederick."

"I've appointed a new chaplain," Frederick said, "a truly saintly man. He prays in my place if I can't or don't feel like attending Mass. I'm sure his prayers will be heard." With a grin, he added, "That must've been a tremendous punch Manfred packed!"

Berard laughed. "He certainly lost his temper. In his defense I've got to say that that envoy was insufferable."

Still beaming with pleasure at the honor Frederick had shown him, Berard turned and indicated a tall stranger who had been riding beside him. Cloaked in a white mantle with a black cross on his left shoulder, he was waiting to be introduced.

Even from a distance, Frederick had noticed the man's excellent horsemanship. He also noticed that despite their large escort, he had kept his hand on his sword hilt until the riders on the road were identified.

"Frederick, this is Hermann von Salza, Grand Master of the Teutonic Order. An old friend of mine. We met at the council. We were both bound for Germany and decided to travel together."

Von Salza stood well over six feet tall. Although well past middle age, he had the muscular leanness of a young warrior. The tanned, leathery web of wrinkles on his face bespoke years spent under the relentless sun of the East. He knelt in the swirling snow.

"Sire, I am honored to meet you."

Frederick extended his hand. "Rise, my lord. Let's leave before we're covered in snow. You will, naturally, be my guest."

Von Salza inclined his head. "I thank you, Your Grace." Steel blue eyes looked at him levelly from under bushy gray eyebrows.

Frederick smiled. He had heard much about this man and his order. Newer than the other two orders of militant knights, the Hospitallers and the Templars, the Teutonic Knights too were dedicated to the protection of pilgrims and the nursing of the sick in the Holy Land. Called Teutonic because only Germans of noble birth were admitted, they were the strictest and most elitist of the three. Von Salza might be very useful to him in the coming crusade.

Turning to Berard, who was stamping his sodden boots on the ground, Frederick said, "You should travel in a covered wagon, you know." He took his elbow. "Come. You look as though you could do with a roaring fire and some mulled wine!"

Berard added, "And a seat that doesn't wobble!"

THE PAGE REFILLED Frederick's cup, an expression of grave concentration on his features as he carefully ladled the hot wine into the tankard. Frederick ruffled his fair hair. He was Anselm's nephew. The child, for he was little more than that, had overcome his initial fear, and now followed him everywhere. He somehow felt sorry for these young boys, sent to learn the manners of knighthood at his court. Although it was a great honor that would stand them in good stead later, they must long for their families, their mothers, if they had any . . .

Frederick took a mouthful, savoring the wine's aroma. Beside the spices and honey, there was another taste, slightly metallic, a taste of gravelly sun-baked earth. Sicilian earth. Berard had brought several casks of this garnet-colored wine from Sicily.

A slow-burning fire crackled in the hearth. Berard, Frederick, and his cousin, the Landgrave of Thuringia, were seated around the fire listening to the grand master. Von Salza was explaining the difficulties of campaigning in the Holy Land. "One of the principal problems of each crusade has been the absence of a central command. Every prince wants to do it his way. The Germans don't see eye to eye with the French, the Genoese can't stand the Venetians, and the Christian princes in the Levant claim superior knowledge and try to overrule everyone. During the third crusade the Lionheart and the French king never stopped arguing, countermanding each other's orders at every turn. Saladin was delighted.

"You, too, my lord," von Salza said to Frederick, "will face this problem. A crusade never is, and cannot be, the effort of a single nation. Even if you establish yourself as supreme commander, you'll still have to deal with contingents from different lands, having divergent loyalties, interests, and fighting methods."

"Yes, but I won't have any fellow sovereigns to contend with," Frederick put in. "No one with the standing to dispute my leadership. It will be *my* crusade."

He got up. Resting his palms on the table, he faced the others. "The first and second crusades were called by the papacy; the third was conceived jointly by the kings of France, Germany, and England. The disgraceful fourth crusade ended at Constantinople. The next crusade will be led by me. Crusaders from elsewhere will be welcome, provided they obey my orders."

Von Salza stroked his beard. In a respectful tone he said, "I wouldn't be so sure, my lord. The Hungarian envoy hinted that his king might join. I've heard that the Duke of Austria is going to take the cross. Once a crusading movement gathers momentum, it acquires a life of its own. From all over Europe, princes and paupers, knights, nuns and monks, whores, mountebanks and swindlers, those seeking salvation as well as those seeking escape from wives, debts, or boredom, will follow you. Men, seeking forgiveness or glory, will pawn their wives' jewels and mortgage their lands to finance armor and horses. Entire families will waive their right to an inheritance so that one member may fight for Jerusalem, the glory accruing to all. You can't control it. The advantage is that the more great lords join, the less your financial burden will be. But it'll still be enormous," the grand master warned.

Frederick said, "I thought the Church raises a special tax for this purpose."

"Yes, the Church declares a crusading tithe, but it's never enough. Crusaders like the Duke of Austria, who fight under their own banner, pay for their equipment and that of their men. But the cost of feeding, transporting, and housing the men who fight under you will be yours. The price of a crusade is huge, my lord, both in lives and gold."

"I understand that," Frederick said. It almost seemed as if the grand master, whose interest surely lay in the recovery of Jerusalem, was trying to dissuade him. "But tell me, which route is best? How long will it take to get from Sicily to Jerusalem?"

"The traditional route has always been by land, east via Greece across Asia Minor. Then along the Mediterranean seaboard to Palestine. However, this is dangerous. The Bulgars, for example, have been known to attack even large groups of crusaders. Once you reach Constantinople, you're supposedly traveling in friendly Byzantine territory. But, after what happened with the last crusade, the Byzantines look askance at Christian armies passing through their territories. Moreover, Byzantium herself is threatened by the Seljuk Turks. They'll harass you mercilessly all the way to Jerusalem."

"But that's far longer than crossing by sea!" Frederick exclaimed.

"Obtaining enough ships for so many men and horses is almost impossible. It might be done with Genoese or Venetian ships, but the Maritime Republics aren't keen to antagonize the Saracens. When they do, their charges are exorbitant! If you add to this the dangers of sea travel, and the far greater cost, you'll see why crusaders have mostly preferred the land route."

"How long will the whole thing take?" Frederick asked.

Von Salza threw his palms up, "Two years, perhaps three. I can't tell you. No one can."

Frederick frowned. "There must be a faster way. What we need is ships, lots of them." He felt a surge of excitement. "I'll build them in Sicily. They wouldn't be wasted. Later they'll become the navy Sicily so desperately needs." Too late, he realized what he had said. The landgrave, thoughtfully staring into his tankard, hadn't noticed, but the grand master flashed him a searching glance. Von Salza was close to the papal court. Although Frederick instinctively trusted him, he couldn't be sure.

Berard, catching Frederick's look, said quickly, "What about supplies? If the hinterland is held by the Saracens, where do we get supplies?"

"By sea. Ideally from Cyprus. Provided her king is prepared to help."

Frederick said, "But he's a vassal of the Empire. Surely that won't be a problem?"

Von Salza smiled. "Yes and no, Your Grace. The Christian princes in the Levant are very concerned with their prosperity. They may pay lip service to the idea of a crusade, but they don't necessarily want a new one. It would interfere with their Saracen trade."

"God's teeth! The whole of Christendom wants Jerusalem freed, and the Franks of the Levant are trading with the Saracens instead of fighting them!"

"I know, Your Grace," Von Salza said. "Alas, trading has always been more profitable than fighting for a cause. The Christian rulers in the East have been arranging truces with the Saracens for years. This suits both sides. Trade is flourishing. Remember that Venice, Genoa, and Pisa are firmly entrenched in Palestine. The quays of Acre and Tyre are overflowing with Saracen merchandise. Ties of vassalage don't count for much when the distance separating overlord and vassal is too great."

"This kingdom of Cyprus," Frederick said. "As I recollect, the Lionheart conquered the island and then sold it to the de Lusignan family. The island's small, producing little besides wine and oil, isn't that so?"

Von Salza shook his head. "Not at all. Cyprus is almost as large and as fertile as Sicily. It produces virtually everything a crusading army needs." He smiled, a smile that transformed his austere features. "You've given me hope, my lord. Hope for Germany and hope for the Holy Land. Our order possesses estates on Cyprus and our knights are well versed in Saracen warfare. I shall do what I can to aid you."

Frederick returned the smile. "Thank you. Your help will be most valuable."

Von Salza leaned forward and stirred the fire. Frederick, observing him, thought what unlikely allies they made. He himself, young and skeptical, who dreamed of reviving the age of Augustus and breaking the power of the papacy, and a blunt, devout warrior past middle age, leader of a great religious and military order, who had devoted his life to the protection of pilgrims. Yet a feeling of empathy had sprung up almost instantly between them. What a man to have on his side, if he could wean him away from Rome!

Frederick stared into the flames. While he couldn't admit it even to Berard, the idea of recovering Jerusalem and humiliating the pope, which had so appealed to him only a short while ago, had already lost much of its luster. The time, the cost and the effort were enormous. Who needed Jerusalem, anyway? Looked at dispassionately, it was just a barren city atop a rocky plateau in the middle of nowhere, a bone of contention that throughout its history had caused fearful bloodshed in return for—what? Jews, Romans, Saracens, and Christians had all fought bitterly over a city that was holy to three religions and yet had produced nothing but misery.

For a moment, Frederick was taken aback by his own audacity. To think of the holiest city in Christendom in such terms was heresy. But if one reflected calmly on the matter, it *was* true. God himself couldn't deny the facts. Yet he was trapped. Carried away by dreams of glory and revenge and made giddy by the heroic atmosphere of Aachen, he himself had snapped shut the snare from which there was no escape. He had to conquer Jerusalem, whether he liked it or not.

THE BELL OF Schoenburg's chapel had just finished ringing sext. Adelaide, lying in the great bed, stared listlessly at the leaping flames of the fire. It was only noon and but the room was as dark as night. A candlestand cast tenuous circles of light onto the wall hangings without relieving the gloom. Through the gap where the shutters met came a faint glimmer of daylight.

Light and air, Adelaide thought. She picked up the bell beside her and rang it.

"Yes, my lady?"

"Open the shutter. I'm sick of lying in a dark room."

Her maid Irmgard stared at her in horror. "But it's snowing. The physician said—"

"Do as I say!"

Irmgard pursed her lips, ready to do battle. "Only after I've covered you with another rug."

Irmgard returned carrying a heavy bearskin rug, which she spread on the bed and tucked around Adelaide. "There, my lady. Now don't fret." She could not resist adding bitterly, "It's too late for that, anyway." Still grumbling under her breath, the stocky old woman who had been her nurse went to unlatch the shutters.

Adelaide stared through the open window at the white flakes falling against the grey sky. The sight was strangely soothing. Slowly, as she lay in the cold silence, the bitterness of the last few months began to drain from her like poison from a wound. She moved her hands under the covers, hesitantly at first, and laid them on her belly. The child moved.

For the first time she was able to touch its hidden form without resentment. Tears welled in her eyes. "Forgive me," she whispered, "forgive me." Since the first wave of nausea she had hated it. She'd done everything to destroy it. She'd always known that a pregnancy would put an end to her dream. While a discreet liaison was tolerated at court, as soon as it showed signs of its natural consequences a woman was branded as fallen. No one could marry her, certainly not the emperor.

Adelaide bit her lip. She'd been so careful. She'd always managed to insert the herb compresses Irmgard procured for her. For a long time her luck held. Then, one morning, she woke up retching.

With a shudder she thought of the old crone Irmgard had brought to her, at whose filthy hands she had risked not only eternal damnation but also painful death. Many women died in the attempt to rid themselves of unwanted offspring. Poor peasants, drained by innumerable childbeds, were as affected as noblewomen, victims of a passing weakness during their husband's absence at war or crusade, who risked death at the stake if their adultery was discovered.

She had hated not only the child but its father as well. And yet how she longed for him now. She hadn't seen Frederick for five long months, since that dreadful day when she told him that she was with child.

His initial delight had turned to stony silence when she demanded that he divorce Constance. She tried to reason with him. She'd long suspected that he nursed the old ambition of turning the Empire into a hereditary monarchy. She told him that since Henry was king of Sicily, he needed another heir to inherit the Empire. She'd give him the sons Constance was too old to have.

He stared at her for a moment, taken aback. Then he said coldly, "There's nothing wrong with Constance. She's my wife and will always remain my wife. When she comes here she'll give me all the sons I need."

He had never before mentioned bringing her to Germany. Adelaide had assumed that her presence in Sicily was indispensable. If Constance were to come to Germany . . . Panic washed over her. In despair she threw herself at his feet. "Marry me, Frederick, I beseech you! I'll be ruined if you don't!"

Frederick looked down at her, "I offered you a husband to safeguard your reputation. You didn't want one. Now you'll have to live with the consequences of your thwarted ambition."

"I'll kill you," she screamed, "I'll have you assassinated!"

"Do that if you can, my dear. In the meantime, I have pressing matters to attend to." He turned.

It was then that reason deserted her. Blinded by tears and rage, she screamed, "I'll rouse the German princes against you! They'll chase you away like the butcher's bastard you really are!"

That afternoon she had been banished from court. She left under armed escort. Even in enmity, though, Frederick had remained generous. The fief of Marienheim, with its extensive lands, was to be hers in perpetuity. She had written him letter after letter, begging his forgiveness. The commander of her guard assured her that her letters had been delivered. Yet no reply ever came.

The chamber was getting colder and colder. Outside the snow continued to fall. Adelaide burrowed deeper into the covers. She felt tired. Her pregnancy had been difficult from the start. Her legs had become so swollen that for the last few weeks she had been confined to bed. And the child would not be born for another month at least. Maybe, like so many women, she'd die in childbirth. The thought didn't seem so frightening any more. It was oddly comforting to think of death, of deliverance . . .

She closed her eyes and drifted into sleep.

When she awoke, the shutters were closed and the room was once again in semidarkness. Fresh wood had been laid on the fire. Irmgard was sitting by the fire, carding wool into a basket.

Suddenly, a sharp, stabbing pain shot through Adelaide's lower back. The bedsheets felt wet. She slid a hand under her back. They *were* wet.

"Irmgard, quickly," she cried, "I'm bleeding!"

The old nurse jumped up. Flinging the covers to one side, she pushed up Adelaide's shift. Her face relaxed. "It's only water, my lady."

"Water?" Adelaide blushed. Surely she couldn't have . . .

"Your waters have broken. It happens to all women at the onset of labor."

Adelaide's eyes widened. "Onset of labor? But the child isn't due for at least another moon!" A dreadful, cold fear gripped her.

Irmgard shook her head helplessly. "We had better call the midwife."

She went over to the door and called to the women spinning in the adjoining chamber to send to the village for the midwife.

"WALTER, COME AND see how well this one's eating!" Frederick stroked the bird's head again, before offering it, with a thickly gloved hand, another piece of raw fowl, which it snapped up hungrily.

Walter von der Vogelweide smiled. "She's getting used to her new surroundings. And to you, Your Grace."

After their capture in the wild, young birds were kept in darkness for several days in a separate loft in the falcon mews. Then, gradually, they were exposed to their new habitat, every day a little longer, until they lost their fear of humans. It was essential, however, to get them to eat quickly.

This one was a particularly easy hawk. Or perhaps just a very greedy one. Frederick stroked her head, whispering blandishments as he fed her. "There, my beauty, there. Don't be afraid. We'll have much fun together." Despite his lulling tone, the peregrine, tied to his wrist, fluttered her wings. She refused the next morsel. Frederick glanced at Walter. "Do you think she's had enough?"

Walter nodded. He undid the jesses and took the bird, smiling. "You certainly have a way with birds of all feathers, if I may make so bold." He handed her to a waiting falconer, to be returned to her perch in the darkness.

Walter, whom he had recently appointed to the prestigious post of chief imperial falconer, was known for his irreverent wit. The most celebrated of Germany's minnesingers had a long, melancholy face and veiled green-brown eyes. He was still youthful despite being in his forties. Although not really handsome, he had a way with women. It was rumored that his famous love lyrics were inspired by the great ladies who, during their husband's absences, had succumbed to the charm of their court poet. This explained, malicious tongues said, his frequent and precipitate changes of patron.

A more probable explanation for his wanderings was his outspokenness. Scathing criticism of the great was often woven into his verses. He spared nobody: The barons, the clergy, the moneylenders, and particularly the pope all came under his scrutiny. He felt strongly about German unity, and argued against papal interference in German affairs. He was, without doubt, Germany's greatest poet. He was also one of the first German bards to write in the vernacular. Now everyone, not just the educated who were versed in Latin, could understand his songs.

Frederick had taken an instant liking to this unlikely courtier. His lyrics spread Frederick's views far more effectively than any imperial decree. And his erudition and outstanding knowledge of falconry were a source of delight to him.

A falconer entered, doffing his moss-green hunter's hat. "I beg your pardon, but the lord von Seebach is below. He requests to see Your Grace."

Frederick frowned. "Von Seebach himself?"

"Yes, my lord."

Frederick groaned. Not another tearful plea from Adelaide—he'd thought she'd given up writing those. But why would her castellan come in person? He peeled off the thick falconer's gloves.

RUPERT VON SEEBACH, cloaked and gloved, twirling his beaver hat in his hands, stood waiting in the snow. He looked ill at ease.

"Your Grace, the lady Adelaide's pains began more than a month early. After a long labor, in the early hours of yesterday, she gave birth to a son. The child is fine." He stared at the dirty snow.

"And the mother?"

Rupert shifted his feet. "She begs you to come. She has bidden me tell you that this is the last request she'll ever make of you. Your Grace, I do believe that it may go ill with her. Her women say she's lost a lot of blood and is very weak. It would . . ." Rupert bit his lip. "I'm sorry, Your Grace. I . . ."

So she'd bewitched even the man he set to guard her. To think that for a moment, he'd felt himself weaken, felt a flicker of remorse, had even feared for her . . . "Tell her," Frederick said, "that the boy is to be christened Enzio." With that, he turned on his heels.

HAGUENAU, APRIL 1216

Frederick, sitting in a window seat of the library, watched the clouds drift westward across a serene April sky. He had an uninterrupted view across

Haguenau's thatched rooftops. On many could be seen large nests, still empty. Soon, the storks would return from the south. The snow had begun to melt in large patches, revealing the straw-colored grass underneath. The last vestiges of an exceptionally harsh winter would soon be gone.

Storks were considered harbingers of good luck. Shortly after his arrival in Haguenau, Frederick, irritated by the clattering noise they made with their long red beaks, had ordered a nest in a tower near his apartments to be removed. The servants had been aghast. The nest was particularly auspicious: it appeared just before his arrival. Rumor held that as long as the nest remained, the Hohenstaufen luck would hold. Although he scoffed at such superstition, he had nevertheless allowed the nest to remain.

At the approach of spring, he'd catch himself glancing up at the tower. Once, when the storks seemed to be taking overlong, he had casually asked one of his pages: "Are the storks back in town yet?" The youth, aware of the question's reason, answered, "Not yet, my lord." Within days there was a furious clattering of beaks outside his bedchamber. Frederick relaxed.

Although the day had been warm and bright, the sun was setting into a hazy horizon. During the night it would rain. He was beginning to know the local climate. He was, it was true, becoming Germanized. Recently, he had been amused to hear one bishop in his cups lean over and tell another equally inebriated prelate that the emperor was becoming less foreign every day.

He often spent time in the library, reading or, more often, grappling with a problem. It was one of the few places where he could escape his courtiers and think undisturbed. The marvelous collection of manuscripts in Barbarossa's library had been started by Charlemagne. Frederick's awe of his great predecessor had faded somewhat. He'd been disconcerted to discover that his hero had never learned to write, despite keeping stylus and wax tablet under his pillow to practice his letters. Frederick had begun to suspect that perhaps Charlemagne had just been a gifted Frankish chieftain, and not the great universal Caesar of popular myth. He put down the book he had been holding. It was a new edition of Boethius, sent to him recently by the abbot of Saint Gall, where it had been copied. The abbot's friendship had never wavered. Every now and then he'd send him a beautifully illuminated volume, accompanied by his blessings. Today, however, he lacked the calm mind reading demanded. Problems seemed to be multiplying. The Lombard cities were restless. The crusade loomed closer and closer on the horizon. And Sicily . . .

Leaning forward, he rested his chin on his hands. With every dispatch, the news of Sicily grew more ominous. The Sicilian barons were falling back into their old ways. Taxes remained unpaid and tolls collected by them were not handed to the crown. Travelers were increasingly waylaid by bandits, often in league with the local lords. In certain areas, the royal demesne lands were again being encroached upon.

Berard had said bluntly the other day that this was only to be expected. A country with an absent king, ruled by a woman and an old bishop, must sink into chaos. There was only one thing to be done. He would have to go to Sicily. He had been away for nearly four years. But could he leave Germany, trusting in the newfound loyalty of her princes to safeguard his throne during his absence?

He first needed Henry here, to consolidate his hold. But how could he bring his son to Germany without awakening the pope's old fear that he was planning to join Sicily to the Empire?

He brightened suddenly. How stupid of him. The solution had been there all along, and he had failed to see it. The crusade! That was the key. He needed talk to Berard immediately.

HE BURST INTO Berard's apartments, only to discover that the archbishop wasn't there.

"In the privy kitchen! What in heaven's name is he doing there?"

Gregory, Berard's chaplain, whom advancing age had rendered increasingly obtuse, continued to thread the broken rosary he was mending, peering at it shortsightedly. Frederick would not have tolerated such disrespect from anyone else, but he had a soft spot for old Gregory.

Without raising his head from his work, Gregory replied, "Cooking, Your Grace."

"Cooking?" Frederick stared at him.

"His lordship likes to spend time stirring pots and pottering about in the kitchens, to the annoyance of the cooks." The old man tied the last knot into the rosary of amber beads, then bit the string off with an evident sense of satisfaction. "Shall I send for him, Your Grace?"

"No, don't trouble yourself. I'll go myself. I want to see this with my own eyes."

Guided by a frail old chamberlain, Frederick descended a spiral stone staircase into the privy kitchen.

So called because it served only the emperor and his immediate entourage, the privy kitchen was a relatively recent innovation, and a great improvement on the older system, where everyone had been fed by the great kitchen. The much smaller privy kitchen, conveniently situated near the imperial apartments, provided greater flexibility as well as improved quality. It also offered better protection against the hazards of poisoning.

Frederick, who in his childhood had roamed the palace kitchens in Palermo, looked about with interest.

"This, my lord, is the wine cellar." Behind an iron grille were rows of stacked barrels. "That's a double lock. The keys are held by two officials, the chief butler and the chief pantler, to avoid pilferage."

Frederick glanced at the complicated lock. On either side was a keyhole, divided by a wrought-iron maiden holding a jug of wine.

"Is there a lot of it?"

"Oh, yes, Your Grace," the chamberlain beamed. "Every year we select the choicest wines delivered by your vassals. There are several hundred casks in there, and many more in the great kitchen's cellar."

Frederick smiled. "I was asking about theft."

The chamberlain's face fell. "Despite all precautions, thieves are everywhere." He sighed, "They're a plague of the times. In the old days, no one would have dared to steal from the emperor. But today . . ."

"What do they steal?"

The old man shook his head. "Oh, everything. At night they even fish carp out of the moat. We are now chaining the ladders, so many disappeared in the years after your uncle Philip, blessed be his memory, died." The chamberlain crossed himself before adding, "Perhaps now, with Your Grace here, things will change for the better."

"I hope so." Servants had been stealing from their masters since the dawn of the world, and would no doubt continue to do so until its end.

Frederick sniffed the air. An appetizing aroma was coming from the pastry room behind one of the arches. A baker was shoving pasties on a long-handled wooden peel into an oven, while his helper, muttering a Paternoster, was sealing the door of another oven with wet mud.

Frederick jerked his head toward the helper. "Why's he praying?" he asked the chamberlain.

"A good pastry cook knows exactly how many Aves or Paters a particular pastry needs for baking, Your Grace."

In the next room, rows of geese hung upside down. At a table, a buxom kitchen maid was plucking a swan, carefully laying the feathers in piles according to their size so that after the bird had been roasted it could be reassembled before being served.

The central area had a huge open fireplace with a spit large enough to roast a whole stag on. Cooks peeled and chopped at long wooden tables warped with age.

At the end was the smaller and much cleaner saucery. Here stood Berard, his back to the entrance, a white apron tied around his ample middle. He was bending over a mortar, critically tasting the contents from a wooden spoon. "A little more ginger, I think," he said to his Apulian cook Luca, who was vigorously pounding something with a pestle, "and perhaps a bit more cinnamon. Add a little salt, too."

"Gesùmmaria, Gregory was right!" Frederick exclaimed.

Berard whipped around. A scullion carrying a pail of hot water almost dropped it as he recognized Frederick. Regaining his wits, he fell to his knees, as did everyone else.

Berard grinned. "Old Gregory's a mule. He should have sent for me instead of telling you where I was. Now I'll never hear the end of this. But since you're here, try this cameline sauce I'm experimenting with. It's wonderful for venison. By putting in less cinnamon and more ginger, it acquires a sharper taste. I got the recipe from Cardinal Colonna's cook in Rome." He dipped a long-handled wooden spoon into the yellow mixture and held it out to Frederick.

"No thanks," Frederick laughed, "my midday meal is still heavy in my stomach. Winter fare!"

"As you wish, but promise to dine with me tonight." Berard leaned closer: "I can offer you an additional inducement. I've got six jars of candied oranges. Just arrived from Palermo." He kissed his bunched fingers. "They're sublime!"

Berard's apartments, Frederick knew, were like a hamster's warren. Chests and cupboards and jars contained all sorts of Italian delicacies, which Luca transformed into nostalgic Italian dishes that Berard shared from time to time with Frederick and a small circle of friends. Although Frederick contented himself with whatever the local kitchen offered, Berard knew that he had a weakness for Sicilian sweetmeats, candied citrons and oranges in particular.

Berard waved his arm at the paralyzed kitchen staff. "Get on with it, all of you."

He untied his spotless apron. "Keep on pounding till it's perfectly smooth, Luca. Only then add the bread. Mind you, squeeze all the vinegar out."

Turning to Frederick, Berard asked, "And what brings the mighty into the bowels of the earth?"

"I'll tell you presently." Frederick took Berard's elbow. "Let's go up."

"IT MIGHT WORK," Berard said a little later, seated in Frederick's privy chamber. "Innocent will have his suspicions, but as you say, in the eyes of the world, he has to give you the benefit of the doubt."

Frederick's eyes gleamed. "It's perfect. Even the poorest knight puts his house in order before going on crusade. He can't expect me to leave without seeing my son and wife. Once Henry is here, I'll have him elected as my successor. There's nothing Innocent can do afterward. With Henry installed as king of Germany, the Empire will be secure, and I can go to Sicily to put order into that nest of vipers."

Berard scratched his beard. "You, too, were elected king of Germany as a child. And yet it came to naught . . ."

"Yes, but I was in Sicily and my father was dead. I'll be alive and liable to reappear at any moment at the head of an army. Henry'll be here, visible to the people and protected by a regency council of loyal bishops who'll rule Germany in my absence. The ecclesiastical lords are all on my side."

It was true, Berard thought. By heaping privileges and lands on them, Frederick had succeeded in turning the princes of the German Church into his keenest supporters. They might even support him against Rome. But at what a price . . . The more imperial lands and rights, such as mints and tolls, Frederick gave away, the more he eroded the crown's power. On the other hand, as Frederick had often pointed out to him, the princes of the Church could not threaten his throne the way secular lords might if they became too powerful. They had no dynastic ambitions.

"I grant you that's true," Berard allowed, "but how are you going to convince the lay princes to elect Henry in the first place? They have always balked at the creation of a hereditary empire. An imperial dynasty would seriously curtail their power."

Frederick smiled thinly. "Henry will be the sixth Hohenstaufen king of Germany. Wouldn't you call that a dynasty? The princes seem to have missed this obvious fact, perhaps because they're clinging to the delusion that they'll remain kingmakers forever. As for convincing them, leave that to me. I'll offer them inducements they cannot resist: gold and land."

He picked up a walnut from a pewter bowl on the table. "Afterward, if they get too big for their boots, I'll take it away from them. That's what my grandfather did with Henry of Brunswick when his power went to his head."

"That's also what started the feud between the Guelfs and Ghibellines that led to civil war," Berard said. "Would you bring renewed bloodshed to a country you've just brought peace to?"

"There'll be no more feuds. With a pacified Empire and a prosperous Sicily behind me, I'll crush anyone who opposes me as swiftly as this nut." Frederick put the nut between his teeth and cracked it in half.

ADELAIDE, CONTRARY TO her expectations, hadn't died, but recovered from her confinement with astonishing speed. More than half a year passed before Frederick saw his little son Enzio for the first time. As the imperial standard appeared in the courtyard of the castle in which she was still a prisoner, Adelaide, watching from a window in the solar, willed her heart to stop pounding.

She must be calm. This could be the most important moment of her life. Despite the May sunshine outside, a fire blazed in the fireplace, making the chamber warm and welcoming. A large earthenware vase of peach blossoms stood on a chest. She seated herself on the carved Italian chair that had belonged to her aunt Matilde. She had chosen a spot where the light from the window would highlight her face. Her ladies helped her drape the folds of her gown and then scurried away. Only the nurse holding the baby remained.

Adelaide stared at the door. She clasped her hands in her lap to stop them from trembling. Any moment now, Frederick would step across the threshold. Just like the day I first met him, she thought bitterly.

Then he entered. She watched, torn between fury and hope as he took the child from his wet nurse. He held him at arm's length, cooing and smiling. "You're a beautiful little boy, aren't you? And you look just like me, don't you?"

It was true, Adelaide thought. Her son had the same blue-green eyes and auburn hair. Watching him now, holding the infant, making faces for the child's benefit, she could almost not believe that this was the same man who had treated her so cruelly.

The baby stared at him with huge eyes. Frederick tickled him under the chin. "Come, give your father a smile, seeing that your mother won't give him one," he coaxed.

The child, reassured now, smiled. Frederick deposited a kiss on the silky little head and handed the swaddled bundle to the waiting nurse, to be taken back to the nursery.

He turned to Adelaide. "I see that you're well, despite all your protests to the contrary. You're looking more beautiful than ever." He smiled, "I should have known not to believe a word."

Her beauty had indeed mellowed, he thought, marveling once again at its perfection. The chiseled features had filled out, softening the sharp line of chin and cheekbone. Dressed in a gown of mustard yellow, with a thick necklace of amber beads and pearls falling to her waist, she looked like a queen.

"If you're going to insult me, you had better go," she said.

"Oh, but I thought, from your last performance, that insults were your preferred form of conversation."

Adelaide jumped to her feet. "Get out of here! Leave me alone to rot in this boring, godforsaken castle, as you've done for the last year! Leave me in peace!" Tears of rage trickled down her rouged cheeks.

"Come, Adelaide, that's not the way to speak to me. You must learn not to give orders."

Adelaide gave a cry. She swayed, clutching the chair for support. Frederick crossed his arms and observed her, his lips twisted in a sardonic smile.

Adelaide straightened herself. "I've been getting these dizzy spells since Enzio's birth. I'm fine now," she smiled at him. Stretching out both hands, she came towards him. "Please, Frederick, for the sake of our son, forgive me my past errors. I was blinded by jealousy, hurt, confused . . ."

She slumped against him. "Oh, Frederick, I've been so lonely. And so bored." She looked up at him. "Will you forgive me?"

Her eyes were luminous and pleading. He had been determined to see the child and leave immediately. But now, so close to her, he felt his resolve weaken. She was only a woman after all; a wily one, to be sure, but need he really hold her insults against her still? And she had given him a beautiful son. He was certain that if he gave her her freedom, she would now do as he said, marry a convenient nobleman . . .

"I'll forgive you, Adelaide, but only once. Next time you'll lose that lovely head of yours." He bent down and kissed her on lips already parted.

She wrapped her arms around his neck and pressed herself against him. "I've longed for you so," she whispered, her breath caressing his ear, sending shivers through him. "It's been so long since you've held me." It was true, she thought, amazed. She suddenly wanted him.

He grabbed her head with both hands, bending her backward. He kissed her roughly. Although the way he was bending her back hurt, all she felt was triumph. Her hands wandered down his chest, slid under his tunic, lower, till they found what they were searching for.

He stopped devouring her, his eyes dark with hunger. "Where?" he asked.

Without a word, she led him through a little anteroom into her adjoining bedchamber.

A single, tall candle burned on a stand in a corner of the darkened room. The bed, with its hangings drawn back, stood against the wall. From the rushes on the floor emanated the summery scents of rosemary and lavender.

As he sat down on the bedstead to remove his boots, he noticed that the fire had been lit in the hearth. The trap, he thought, has been well baited. Then he looked up. His mouth went dry as he watched her undress.

Adelaide was opening button after button of her gown with slow, deliberate movements. First one firm, rounded breast appeared, then the other. As the last layer of clothing fell from her shoulders, her slender body, unmarred by childbirth, glowed like the marble statue of a Roman goddess. She stepped out of the circle of stiff brocade and white linen and stood before him, gloriously naked.

With the solemnity of a pagan sacrificing to a deity, he slid off the bed onto his knees and buried his face in the triangle of soft tawny hair, inhaling the scent of seashells that rose from her hidden parts. As he began to explore her with his tongue, at first with feathery movements, then slowly increasing the pressure, she started to moan, her hands caressing his head.

As he felt her desire mount, his own became unbearable. He jerked his head away. There was no time now for anything but swift gratification. Later, he would linger. He let himself fall onto the bed and pulled her onto him.

A wave of pleasure engulfed him, thundering in his ears and sweeping him away.

I still can't sign this," Frederick said with disgust. "It's a complete renunciation of my rights. By the Host, Conrad, find another way of wording it!" Booted and cloaked, about to go hunting, Frederick tossed the document onto the table.

Conrad looked at the offending parchment with rising anger. It was the fifth draft of a letter to Pope Innocent that Frederick had rejected in as many days. What he demanded was impossible, in Latin or any other language known to man.

After a moment's silence, Conrad raised his head. With pursed lips, he fixed on Frederick. "Your Grace," he said, "it is beyond my powers to couch this letter in the terms you desire. It is not possible to both renounce a throne and retain it in a written document. It may be possible to do so in reality, although you know my views on the dangers of misleading the pope, but I cannot draft this letter the way you wish. Miracles are wrought by saints, not chancellors. I suggest that you get another to do your bidding in this matter, as I am unable to satisfy your wish." Conrad inclined his balding head. "May I have your leave to go?"

Frederick stared at him. A furrow appeared between his brows. About to make an angry retort, he changed his mind. He picked the letter up and began to read it once more.

"Well," he said after he'd finished, "it is, after all, only a letter. I'll sign it if I must." The corners of his mouth rose a little. "You're quite right, I was being unreasonable."

Conrad, without so much as a flicker of surprise, motioned to the secretary to hand Frederick a quill. The secretary threw some sand on the ink and after a moment rolled the document up, to be folded and sealed in the chancery.

"You have my leave to withdraw now," Frederick said.

As the two men left, Frederick stared after them. Tomorrow, the letter to Innocent, phrased in the most respectful and reassuring terms, would be on its way to the Lateran. In it, Frederick informed Innocent that he was making arrangements to bring his wife and son to Germany so that he might see them before his departure on crusade. He assured the pontiff that after his imperial coronation in Rome, on his way to Palestine, he would renounce the kingdom of Sicily in favor of prince Henry.

The way was clear for Henry and Constance to come to Germany.

BERARD WAS SURPRISED to see Frederick stride through the press of people in the inner bailey who had come to see the grand master off. Hermann von Salza was about to swing himself onto his horse. He halted and looked up.

"Your Grace?" Hermann's bushy gray eyebrows shot up.

Frederick smiled. "No change of plans, Hermann. I just came to bid you farewell. I was held up in a council meeting and feared I might have missed you. May God go with you, Hermann."

"Thank you, my lord. You needn't worry. Lombards or not, the empress and Prince Henry will be safe." He patted his sword hilt. His craggy face was softened by a smile.

Frederick smiled. "I know. That's why I'm entrusting them to you."

Von Salza swung himself into the saddle. He raised his hand. "Farewell, Your Grace. May the Lord keep you. With his blessing we'll be back before winter." With a last wave he wheeled his horse around and cantered out over the drawbridge, followed by his knights. A contingent of imperial troops that had been waiting in the outer bailey fell in behind them.

They traveled lightly, these knights, Berard thought as he watched the last banner disappear under the raised portcullis. Not a single packhorse in the cavalcade. Whatever they needed was strapped to each man's horse. There, he thought, goes another whose loyalties must at times be difficult to reconcile. Just like him, the grand master now owed fealty to Frederick as well as to the pope. Frederick had become the order's most important patron, granting it extensive lands in Germany. He had entrusted von Salza already with several important diplomatic missions.

Frederick had remained where he was, following the riders with his eyes. Berard crossed over to him. Around them the courtyard began to empty.

"Let's walk over to the ramparts," Frederick suggested. They stood together, looking down. Beneath them, the bare rock fell away with dizzying steepness for hundreds of feet. In the distance, the Rhine flowed broad and majestic in the sun. There was no sign yet of the horsemen on the narrow road below.

"If only I could have gone in his stead!" Frederick stared down at the road, lips pressed together.

Constance and Sicily, Berard thought, the two things he loves most . . . In the last year, Frederick had consolidated his hold on Germany. His position was now unassailable. The ecclesiastical princes were all on his side. The lay lords had been either won over or defeated. What, Berard asked himself, did Frederick feel as he stood here, above Germany's greatest river, her heartland at his feet? How much of himself had he given to this land that had welcomed him with such enthusiasm? Sicily would always be closer to Frederick's heart, yet it was undeniable that he felt a deep empathy with the country and its people.

His German son had an Italian name, Enzio. Frederick had recently conferred a Sicilian county on the not yet two-year-old. Frederick doted on the child. Even Berard, whose dislike of the mother had only increased with the passing of time, had to admit that he was an engaging little fellow. The boy was often to be found romping in Frederick's chambers, climbing all over his father. How was he going to explain that to Constance? Royal bastards, provided for but out of sight, were a fact of life, but Frederick's domestic arrangements were altogether different. At least he had come to his senses sufficiently about Adelaide to oblige her to marry one of his vassals, who seemed content to share his wife with the emperor.

On the road below, the horsemen had appeared. The cross of Jerusalem and the Hohenstaufen eagle streamed in the wind. Berard could make out Hermann's broad figure. With luck, he'd be back before the year was out, bringing Constance and Henry with them. After that there'd be the coronation in Rome, then Sicily, and then the crusade.

PERUGIA, JULY 1217

Perugia, high above the Umbrian plain, was quiet and empty in the July heat. Behind the thick walls of the bishop's palace, Pope Innocent lay dying.

The sickly sweetish scent of lilies wilting in the heat filled the papal chamber. In the canopied bed hung with mulberry-colored silk, Innocent opened his eyes. Two young Franciscans knelt at the small altar beside the bedstead, praying in silence. At the lower end of the chamber clustered a group of prelates. They talked in whispers punctuated every now and then by the dry cough of a frail elderly bishop.

The pope, watching the praying friars, read the words of the Miserere on their lips. He groped at the rosary entwined in his fingers. Clasping the cool ivory beads, he too began to pray to the Queen of Heaven. He felt at peace. The burning fever and racking pain of the last few days had subsided after he had received the last rites. Satan, cheated of his prize, had ceased tormenting him.

With an effort, he turned his head toward the window. Although the shutters were closed, in his mind's eye he saw the plain of Umbria, Lake Trasimeno glittering in its center, neat fields of green and gold divided by rows of graceful poplars. Terraced hills silvery with olives ringed the plain, their summits crowned by castellated fortresses. Through this landscape of rich earthy hues the Tiber flowed on its way to Rome.

On the other side, on the flank of Mount Subasio, lay Assisi. How strange that in that belligerent imperial city had sprung up one as pure as Francis. In the years since he had taken Francis and his small band of mendicant friars under his protection, their movement had steadily grown. If only there were more like him and if I had time, he thought, more time . . . He closed his eyes. Even the little sunlight entering through the gap where the shutters met was too bright a reminder of the world he would soon leave.

A rustle made his eyelids flutter open again. A group of cardinals from Rome approached. Kneeling on the steps of the bedstead, they took leave of him one by one, kissing for the last time the amethyst on his hand. Innocent, with great effort, blessed each of them.

He motioned the white-haired Cardinal Savelli to come closer. The cardinal, his mild blue eyes wet, bent down. "Holy Father, it is too soon," he said, his voice choking. "I've been praying for your recovery. I'm sure—"

"You're talking nonsense, Cencio. The Lord has called me and I, like all of us, must obey. Cencio," the pontiff whispered, "if you follow me on the throne of Saint Peter, promise me that you won't abandon my reforms." He tried to raise himself on one elbow. "If the Church isn't purged of the evils that corrupt her she'll destroy herself."

"Your Holiness, I . . ." Cardinal Savelli stammered, also in a whisper, aware of dozens of straining ears behind him, "I'm not worthy. Surely the Spirit will bypass a humble man like me and choose one of the great sons of the Church. One who . . ."

Innocent fixed the Cardinal with a steely look. "Promise me," he commanded.

Savelli sighed. "I promise to rule according to your precepts, should I become pontiff."

Innocent's eyes softened. "You're a good man, Cencio, without guile and ambition. The cardinals will elect you for that very reason, because they can't bear to see one of their powerful rivals on Peter's throne."

Savelli pressed Innocent's hand to his face, brushing the Fisherman's ring with his lips. The violet stone was as cold as Innocent's hand, with the glassy chill of death. Tears ran down the cardinal's rosy cheeks. They had been friends since childhood.

As Savelli was about to rise, Innocent beckoned him down again. Exhausted from the effort of speaking, the pope attempted to say something, then sank back onto the pillows. He took a deep breath, as if to rouse his faltering voice for a last effort. In an almost inaudible whisper he said, "Beware of the emperor, Cencio. Frederick . . . of all the Hohenstaufen . . . ruthless ambition . . . too able . . . a danger for the papacy."

His head fell to one side, dark eyes staring unseeing at the splendid coffered ceiling.

SWABIA, OCTOBER 1217

Constance watched the golden fringes on the purple silk curtains tremble with each step of the men who carried her.

The litter was an elaborate affair in yellow wood, with the imperial arms painted on its back and front. About a mile before the encampment she and Henry had been moved from the hide-covered wagon in which they had been traveling to a litter sent by Frederick.

After the excitement of the last few months she suddenly felt apprehensive. For five long years she had dreamed of nothing else but seeing Frederick again. Against opposition and mistrust she had governed Sicily to the best of her ability. A constant flood of orders and instructions, often in minutest detail, had been her only contact with her husband in all this time. Sometimes a personal note penned himself had been attached to his letters, almost as an afterthought. Although they were brought to her by a network of imperial couriers riding across Germany and Italy at breakneck speed, his letters were frequently outdated by the time she received them. Often she'd been forced to make a decision alone, at times against the regency council's recommendation. Mostly, Frederick approved her decisions. He rarely praised her, but when he remembered to do so, she was filled with pride.

And now, within the hour, she'd see him, hear his voice, feel his arms around her. Why, then, was she so ill at ease? Her head ached. Riding in the litter at least brought relief from the rattling wagon wheels. At times during the past few months she had fancied that she would hear the creaking of that wagon for the rest of her life.

She glanced down at the small fair head against her shoulder. Poor little Henry. He, too, had hated the boredom of endless days spent in the dusty semidarkness of the traveling wagon. She'd suggested that he ride instead, but he seemed to prefer the wagon. Henry, though a handsome boy, was sensitive and small for his age. Horses, sensing his insecurity, tended to bolt under him.

Constance pressed him against her. She sighed. Soon, he'd leave the women's quarters and have his own household. Male tutors to teach him, young lords as playmates, and older ones to school him in hawking, hunting, and the practice of arms.

Henry, her only child. In a recent letter, Frederick had mentioned more sons. He needed another son to wear the crown of Sicily, now that he was planning to make Henry heir to the empire. Was that why he had called her to him? Trying to brush aside the thought, she parted the curtain and peered out. They were skirting a forest, russet and gold in its autumn colors. The road was carpeted by fallen leaves, damp with last night's rain, providing relief from the clouds of dust that had choked her for most of the journey.

Constance let the curtain drop. She leaned her head back. The rhythmic swaying of the litter was pleasantly soothing. Her head felt a little better. At least, she thought, Innocent was no longer alive to stir up trouble about Henry's coming to Germany. Poor Innocent, to die so suddenly, before his time . . . Frederick, with his dislike of his erstwhile guardian, must have been pleased by his death. She, however, had prayed for him. Innocent had been a great pope. His successor, Honorius III, was a very different man, gentle and erudite. As Cardinal Savelli he had for years been papal legate in Palermo, frequently mediating between Frederick and his master in Rome. A friend of Berard's, his election must have pleased Frederick.

Shouts rang out. Harnesses jingled as the riders reined in their mounts. The litter-bearers slowed their steps. Hermann von Salza's deep voice boomed above the others. They were within sight of the imperial camp!

Constance touched her headdress, suddenly self-conscious. At their last halt, Juana had dressed her in the garments she had selected in Palermo for this moment. Over a bliaud of turquoise cendal, with pointed sleeves that reached to the floor, she wore a mantle of violet camlet edged in miniver. She had daringly decided to wear the latest Sicilian fashion on her feet: brodequins of gold-embroidered velvet with three-inch-high soles. They suited her, making her look taller and slimmer.

Would her appearance please Frederick? How much had he changed? Was he still her golden boy, or had the struggle for the Empire and the power he now wielded transformed him into a remote stranger?

The litter was set down with a jolt.

"We're here, my heart," she whispered to the dozing Henry, brushing a strand of hair from his forehead. He looked up, wide-eyed: "Is the emperor here?" Constance smiled, trying to hide her own nervousness: "The emperor's your father, silly. You needn't be afraid of him."

Emerging from the litter, Constance stared. In a large meadow rose a city of brilliantly colored tents like giant flowers put there by a magician's wand. She clutched Henry's hand. Before the largest tent, a splendid affair of crimson and azure silk, the imperial pennon flying from its central pole, stood Frederick. Around him clustered burly German lords, bowing deeply.

Was it truly him? He seemed taller, broader. Still clean-shaven, his face was unchanged except for the jutting angle at which he held his chin. The green eyes danced, echoing his smile.

Her heart pounded. She could hardly breathe. Then his arms were around her, hugging her with the old disregard for ceremony.

"Constance!" Kisses covered her face. He held her at arm's length. "You're even more beautiful than I remembered!"

After kissing her again, he bent down. "And you're Henry?" he asked.

The boy nodded, gravely appraising the smiling stranger before him. "Yes, my lord." He edged closer to Constance.

"You don't have to call me that. I'm your father. I've missed you so very much." Frederick stretched out his arms.

For an instant, Henry's lips puckered rebelliously. Then he allowed himself to be picked up. Frederick hugged the stiff little body. He set him down again, ruffling the fair head. "In time, we'll get to know each other, my son. I've got a lovely black pony waiting for you, with a red saddle especially made for you!"

Henry stared at the ground. "Yes, my lord," he said in a small voice.

CONSTANCE RAISED THE mirror and scrutinized herself. Large gray eyes looked back at her from the polished silver with veiled melancholy. Her pale skin was still smooth, except for two lines that ran along the sides of her mouth, and a web of fine creases around her eyes. She pulled the skin taut with two fingers. For an instant, the lines disappeared. She let go and smiled at herself.

Her brave smile died, chased away by a thought far more oppressive than the fear of growing old. Old age, at least, was approaching her at a pace that was mercifully slow. But the problem confronting her wouldn't wait. She put the mirror back into the inlaid coffer on the table and sighed. What, oh Lord, must she do? For months she had wrestled with this question. She could ask advice from no one. In any event, it was not the answer that eluded her, but the courage to face its consequences.

Frederick, with a regularity that must have the entire court gossiping, had appeared in her apartments every night since her arrival six months ago. And while he never questioned her, she sensed his disappointment as month after month went by.

The image of his mistress rose before her. She had seen her only once, yet till her dying day she would remember every feature of that perfect oval face, every elegant fold of the crimson velvet gown, laced under her breasts in a style that emphasized her condition. They had glared at each other across the packed hall at the Christmas court in Nuremberg. Adelaide's handsome limp-wristed husband strutted like a coxcomb with his beautiful pregnant wife on his arm. The Margrave appeared content to share the wife that had been provided for him. Everyone knew that in her swollen belly Adelaide carried the emperor's bastard.

Pregnant mistress and barren wife! After the initial pain subsided, Constance, in her lighter moods, was able to savor the irony. She derived a bitter satisfaction from imagining Frederick's feelings when, as he must do, he contemplated such injustice. Did he, she wondered, ever see it as retribution for his sins?

Constance closed her eyes and buried her face in her hands. She had to tell him. At the next opportunity, when he was in a good mood, she'd tell him. The longer she delayed, the greater his anger would be. What, Merciful Mother of God, would his reaction be? There was only one course of action open to Frederick. He must divorce her and marry a young princess who could give him the heirs he needed. Frederick's reasons for wanting more children were more pressing than those of other rulers. He had no brothers or uncles who could provide for the Empire or Sicily. She had to make it as easy as possible for him. She'd take the veil, retire to a convent. Honorius would grant him an annulment. Unlike Innocent, who had frowned on the dissolution of marriage for purposes of expediency, the new pope would be more sympathetic to Frederick's plight.

Her eyes filled with tears. She loved God, but she loved Frederick, too. Was it her fault that she had been left in Sicily while her remaining child-bearing years ran out like sand in an hourglass? Last year still, she would have been able to bear him another son. Now it was too late . . .

"My lady, what is it?"

Constance had been too absorbed in her grief to hear Juana enter. She raised her tear-streaked face. "It's nothing." She wiped her cheeks with the back of her hand and attempted a smile. "It's nothing," she repeated.

Juana gave her a doubtful look. "Worry is gnawing at you, my lady. Soon there'll be nothing left of you." She pointed a stubby finger at Constance. "Look how thin you are getting. There's nary any flesh on your hips, nor anywhere else." In a lowered voice, she added, "And then the emperor will turn from you. Men don't like women like wattle sticks."

Constance shook her head with resignation. "It's no use, Juana. No matter how seductively rounded I should become again, he'll still turn from me. It's God's will." She began to cry again.

"Hen's folly!" When Juana got agitated, she tended to relapse into the language of the paternal farmyard. She laid a hand on her mistress's shoulder. "Just because your belly won't quicken any more isn't a reason to lose courage, my queen. He'll get used to it in time. You've proven twice that you aren't a barren vine. No one can point an accusing finger at you. Just don't say a word to anyone, and all will be well. His Grace dotes on you, everyone knows that. So much so that he's even married off that she-devil!"

Constance looked up at her, flabbergasted. "But how . . . how did you know?"

Juana's brown eyes looked at her kindly. She shrugged. "A woman notices these things. I take your washing down to the privy laundry. You needn't worry, my lady, no one else will ever know. Your secret's safe with me."

For an instant, Constance allowed herself to feel a surge of hope. Perhaps it was really as simple as this shrewd peasant was making it out to be. Perhaps she could keep it a secret and just continue living as before. She

frowned, struck by something Juana had said. "What about the laun-
dresses? Surely they'll notice. Perhaps they're talking about it already?"

Color shot into Juana's rounded face. She stared at the floor rushes. "I
hope my lady won't mind, but I've been taking care of that. What with His
Grace's other ladies, paying the servants to discover things about you, I
thought it prudent to do so."

Constance looked at her with new respect. "I never realized what a resourceful girl you are."

Strange, how the reference to Frederick's dalliances didn't hurt any
more. In Sicily, she would have slapped Juana for daring to mention such
a thing. But since arriving in Germany she had discovered so much about
her husband's amorous exploits—mostly from Juana, who was a font of
gossip, but also from her new German ladies-in-waiting, some of whom she
suspected of having themselves on occasion shared Frederick's bed—that
nothing seemed to touch her any longer. The soul, she thought, is like the
body. When pain becomes too great to be borne, it loses its sharpness. And
despite it all, she loved him still, perhaps more than ever before.

The young king whose smile had first melted her heart, who had survived disaster after disaster by his nimble wits alone, who had sought solace in her arms, was gone forever. But the emperor who had taken his
place, although less appealing, was far more compelling. During the last
few months, Constance had watched Frederick negotiate the ocean of
rocks and whirlpools that was the Holy Roman Empire, and her admiration
for him had gradually grown into something resembling awe.

She took a deep breath and straightened herself against the hard
wooden back of the chair. The small flutter of hope died within her. It was
useless. For too long already had she kept a despicable silence.

"I can't deceive him any longer. It's a sin to do so. Tomorrow I will tell
him."

Juana shook her head in incomprehension at such folly.

THE ROAN STALLION raced across the turf. Frederick, his cloak flying, the
breeze cooling his face, was letting the horse have its way. Just before horse
and rider reached the lake, he drew rein, bringing the horse to a sudden
halt.

He leaned down and patted the sweaty neck. Nestor, who had a will of his own, pawed the ground, snorting. "Easy now, you brute, or we'll lose the lady."

He turned and waved to Constance. She was carefully guiding her white palfrey down the grassy slope of a knoll. Drawing rein beside him, she smiled. "This is a lovely spot."

The small lake lay in a shallow bowl of land ringed by trees. Spring flowers dotted the young grass. The oaks and beeches were unfurling their new leaves. Birds flitted about the branches, ferrying twigs and greenery to their new nests.

Frederick laid his reins across the horse's neck and jumped to the ground. He swung Constance out of her saddle. "Ah, what joy, to be a poor woodsman who can do as he pleases!"

He undid his cloak and spread it on the grass. Flinging himself on it, he patted the place beside him. "Come and lie by your woodsman in the Elysian fields." He plucked a few yellow primroses and scattered them on the cloak. "See, I've strewn your bed with blossoms!" He grinned up at her, hands folded behind his head. Constance remembered dimly that the fields Frederick was referring to were somehow connected with death. Not a good omen . . . She sat down beside him, tucking her legs beneath her.

Frederick sighed. "If only I could come here more often. It's a curse. They never leave me alone. Since that pea-brained Otto tried to have me assassinated, I can't even sleep alone any more."

Constance smiled down at him. "But Frederick, *nobody* sleeps alone." She shook her head. "I don't understand this need of yours to be alone. Surely a few loyal attendants sleeping at the foot of your bed cannot give you reason to complain? I, for one, am glad of it. That way I needn't worry about your safety."

Frederick sat up. "God's teeth! If I bothered so much about my safety I'd long be dead from worry! This, for instance," his arm swept the clearing, "is a perfect place to murder me." He grinned at her. "Not only do I come here regularly, but I come alone or with just one or two friends, such as Berard or Walter von der Vogelweide. Neither could put up much resistance." To tease her, he added, "My men, waiting in the glade, wouldn't even hear our screams."

Constance looked at him, eyes wide.

He leant across and kissed her on the tip of the nose. "I love that look of a wise frightened doe you have when you think I'm being foolhardy again." His eyes twinkled: "Like when I got it into my head to become emperor! That was a very angry queen I left behind in Sicily."

Constance steeled herself. Now was the moment, quickly, before her courage deserted her. "Frederick," she said, leaning forward, "while your success has been astounding, all is not won yet."

"Yes, I know." Constance had always had a tendency to lecture him, even if she did so in a tactful manner.

"You need more sons."

As if he didn't know it! Sons he had aplenty, but all born on the wrong side of the coverlet. And Adelaide was sure to produce another any day now. But what was she saying? Was she finally . . . ?

Constance, with a sinking heart, saw his eyes light up. Before he could say anything else, she quickly added, "I have something to tell you, but it isn't good news."

"Well, what is it?"

She stared into her lap, smoothing her tunic. "Frederick, I can't have children any more."

"It can't be! Why, what's wrong? Tell me!" He grabbed her arm, shaking it.

"My monthly courses have stopped. Once that happens, a woman can't conceive any longer."

"You mean they just halt and then . . ." He stared at her.

She nodded, blinking back tears. "It happens to all women when their childbearing years come to an end, somewhere after the age of thirty."

"And it has now happened to you?"

Again, she nodded.

"Can't anything be done?"

She lifted her head and looked into his eyes. "No, Frederick, there is nothing that can remedy this. Divorce me. I'll not stand in your way. I'll take the veil. Honorius will annul our marriage and you can marry again." She gave a dry laugh. "This time you can choose your bride, so you won't have to marry an old woman like me."

For a long time Frederick stared ahead, saying nothing. The little lake lying in the sun dissolved into nebulous gray before his eyes. It couldn't be!

God, who had bestowed so many favors on him, could not deny him now. His eyes stung. What was a man without enough sons to carry on his life's work?

As Constance had said, he could divorce her. It might be possible. He had never considered it. He glanced at her profile. She was sitting very straight and still, her dove gray riding tunic spread about her like a fan. He noticed that her long, slender neck had become even thinner, resembling a graceful swan's. She, too, was staring at the lake, avoiding his eyes. Her hands, lying in her lap, clutched the fabric of her tunic.

Constance was his queen, the mother of his heir. Could he discard her now for a failing that wasn't of her making? On the other hand, what would become of Sicily and the Empire? He cursed the Christian habit of allowing a man only one wife. No sultan had ever been faced with such a problem. While his loyalty to Constance was genuine, another consideration weighed equally on his mind: as emperor, he couldn't be seen to divorce his wife. The princes of Europe, always attempting to rid themselves of inconvenient wives with the aid of complacent popes, would exploit this. The common people, too, would lose respect. The sacrament of marriage was indissoluble. This was a cornerstone of the Church's teaching. Ordained by God, only God, through death, could sever its holy bonds.

True, for those wealthy and well-connected enough, there existed an escape, based on another fundamental teaching of the Church: the doctrine that forbade marriage within certain degrees of kinship. Since most great families were distantly related to each other, it was often possible, if one searched diligently enough, to find real or spurious proof of a forbidden degree of consanguinity. However, Constance had overlooked the fact that if their marriage were annulled, Henry's legitimacy might become questionable. Sometimes, this problem had been overcome with the pope's aid.

A heron flew across the lake, skimming the water. The two horses, one white, one brown, were grazing a few feet away, nibbling at the young grass. What a tranquil scene, so unlike the churning thoughts and emotions within him.

His silence seemed interminable. She felt like one condemned to death. Thus, she told herself, must those wretches feel whom she had seen awaiting execution in many a market square. They cowered in chains, eyes wild with fear, taunted and jeered at by the populace come to watch the executioner's ax fall.

"Constance," he said finally, "look at me."

She turned her head. The ax was about to descend. She could almost feel its cold blade. "Yes?"

"You're my wife, and you'll be my wife forever. I'll never part with you."

For a moment she stared at him, incredulous. Tears shot into her eyes. "But you can't . . . you have to safeguard the succession. The Empire and Sicily are two separate realms, needing two rulers. Will you then give up your dream of a Hohenstaufen dynasty on the imperial throne?"

He took both her hands. "Have no fear, Constance, I'm giving up nothing." The light of a vision, nurtured over many years, shone in his eyes. "With God's will, Henry will one day rule over a new Rome. The whole of central Europe, from the Baltic to Malta, will be a Hohenstaufen dominion."

"And the pope?"

"The pope will once again become what Christ meant him to be: a respected servant of the state, ministering to the faithful."

They rode back a little later in silence. Fortunately, Frederick thought as he guided Nestor around a boulder, Henry had passed the most dangerous stage of childhood, those first few years of infancy when one child in every three succumbed to disease. Soon he could be betrothed to a foreign princess. By the time he was fifteen he'd marry and father children. In the meantime, the Lord would have to safeguard Henry.

SOMEWHERE OUTSIDE THE ramparts, a cock crowed. In the ancient castle above the Neckar the torches still burned in guard towers and passages, their light now dimmed by the breaking dawn.

Manfred handed his reins to a groom whose hair still bore bits of the straw he had been sleeping on. To the guard he said, "Take me to the emperor!"

"At this hour?" The man, a huge Swabian in steel helmet and cuirass, frowned at Manfred and his small escort.

"Now! I've come from Haguenau with urgent news!"

"I'll fetch the captain." He ran off to wake his superior.

Manfred followed the captain, who was lighting their way with a lantern. The hall lay in darkness, except for a glow of dying embers in the fireplace. Snoring filled the hall. They stepped around sleeping forms that lay in rows on foldable pallets. Not only the servants, but knights too—everyone, in fact, except the most exalted personages—slept communally in the hall. The two guards at the foot of the stairs let them pass.

FREDERICK STARED AT Manfred. He sat up in the canopied bed, naked except for the sheet that covered his lower body.

"Otto's dead?"

Manfred nodded. "Dead, and buried by now."

Frederick grinned. "Didn't I say the Lord was on my side?"

"They say he had himself scourged to death by monks as he felt the end approaching, to atone for his sins."

"Ugh!" Frederick shook himself, as if to ward off the horrible image. "What an undignified way for a prince to die."

"A dreadful death, but no doubt what he deserved. After all, he was an outcast."

Manfred yawned.

"Sit down, Manfred. You look terrible. I'll have some wine brought."

Manfred sat down on the bedstead. His bones ached. He leaned his head against the bedpost. Wearily, he let his eyes wander across the room. Eastern rugs covered the rush-free floor, there were bright cushions and a lectern with an open book. In a corner stood Frederick's bath, a huge tub of oak staves especially made for him, which took four servants to fill and traveled everywhere with him. Frederick bathed in it every day, sometimes twice. Manfred's eyes closed.

Frederick's voice jolted him back to wakefulness. "You'd better bed down somewhere before you fall over." He smiled. "Thank you for coming. But there was no need to kill yourself. You could've sent a courier!"

Manfred laughed. "I wanted to see your face. Oh, I forgot. His brother will hand over the regalia after twenty weeks."

"Twenty weeks?"

"According to Otto's testament, if the German princes don't elect another emperor in that time, the crown jewels are to be handed to you."

Frederick laughed. "Why, even in death he still hoped to defeat me!"

A page entered bearing a tray with wine, bread, and cheese. He set it down on the bedboard, bowed, and withdrew.

"At least I can halt work on the replicas. That'll save me a tidy sum," Frederick said. He poured some wine, handing a goblet to Manfred. He stared into his own cup for a moment. "I'll be crowned by the pope. Always the pope. This tradition that the emperor has to be crowned by the pope is absurd. Who does he think he is?"

"Why, Frederick, he's the Vicar of Christ, invested with his powers by God himself!"

"So he says. A convenient doctrine, don't you think?"

Manfred looked at him with consternation.

Frederick, snapping out of his black mood, raised his cup. "To Otto. May he have a pleasant sojourn in Satan's abode!"

THE HALL OF Nuremberg castle echoed with animated voices. All the great dignitaries of the Empire were present. From the upper Rhine to the Adriatic Marches and the lower Rhône they had come to attend Henry's investiture as Duke of Swabia.

Frederick, to general applause, had dispatched a boar single-handedly with his javelin at a great hunt that morning. He much preferred hawking, but his lords considered boar hunting the ultimate feat of venery. An unequal contest in favor of a fiercely dangerous animal, it was an opportunity to show off one's bravery. It was also brutal and inelegant. The hounds, rewarded with bones and entrails, were still gnawing at the remains in their kennels. Their snarls as they defended a well-chewed bone could be heard through the open windows. Unlike the dogs, Frederick thought with a wry smile, the princes were at peace with each other today. For the first time in a quarter century . . .

The heralds blew their trumpets. Frederick, in a purple mantle, the crown of Germany on his head, raised his hand. "Welcome, my lords and princes! We are here to pay homage to the new Duke of Swabia." He gave his son a gentle push forward.

Henry, in a small cloak identical to Frederick's, a golden coronet on his head, stood very straight and still, his father's hand on his shoulder.

One by one, the princes filed past the dais and knelt before the boy. Each laid down his sword and murmured the oath of allegiance before placing his hands between the child's palms. Frederick studied their faces. There could be no doubt in their minds that he was preparing the way for Henry to succeed him. Making him Duke of Swabia was innocuous in itself. As his heir, he'd naturally succeed to the family duchy upon his father's death. However, investing him with the duchy during Frederick's lifetime was a step of obvious significance. Every Duke of Swabia, for more than a hundred years now, had become emperor.

On the other hand, paying homage to his son as Duke of Swabia wasn't the same as electing him king of the Romans, which would give him the right to succeed to the Empire. He had raised the matter discreetly with some of the princes and found their reactions encouraging. He'd also discussed a new charter with the ecclesiastical princes, which would grant them the right to coin money and the testamentary freedom to dispose of their personal property.

The price he'd have to pay for the loyalty of the German Church was high. But then Germany could never be like Sicily: the autonomy of her princely territories was too great. By granting the ecclesiastical princes, who posed no threat to the throne, privileges and powers on a par with the lay lords, he'd be righting the balance in his favor, but he'd also be relinquishing even more authority. Still . . .

Looking down at his son, feeling his small shoulder under his hand, Frederick felt a tug of pride. His eyes sought Constance, seated on the dais. She, too, was watching Henry, a proud smile on her lips. Erect and golden-haired, in a miniature royal mantle edged in miniver, Henry was a perfect prince.

The princes completed their homage. They raised their swords and chorused: "Hail to Duke Henry, hail to Henry of Hohenstaufen! Long live Duke Henry!"

The child flinched. Frederick pressed his shoulder. "Don't worry," he whispered, "they're just showing how much they like us."

It was true. The princes had once again demonstrated their solidarity with the Hohenstaufen. But did their loyalty run deep enough to elect Henry king? It would take time, and time was what he didn't have. Sicily needed him.

* * *

THE JEW SELECTED another bolt of silk. He flipped the heavy roll forward with a flick of his wrists. The material cascaded to the ground in shimmering folds and eddies of cobalt blue.

Frederick held his chin, admiring the fabrics, colored with the costliest dyes of the East. Gorgeous Byzantine silks and brocades in saffron, magenta, vermilion, and azure, some worked with gold or silver threads, others plain, covered the floor like a rainbow. He turned as the door opened behind him. "Ah, Manfred, come and help me select New Year's gifts. I'm having difficulty making up my mind between all the marvels that Yehuda has spread out to tempt me." He winked at Manfred: "No doubt he'd like me to buy them all."

The merchant, whose name was Yehuda ben Solomon, bowed. "You should, my lord. Never again will you be able to acquire silks and baubles of this quality at these prices. With the cost of skilled slaves rising to the stars in Byzantium, next time I go to Constantinople, I'll have to pay double what I paid for this shipment. And silk, as you know, keeps forever. So do jewels."

Frederick burst out laughing. "You're an old rascal, Yehuda. That's exactly what you told me last year."

The Jew, a tall, dignified-looking man with a short graying beard, raised his beringed hand to his heart. "So I did, my lord, and I was right. Those bolts of vermilion samite you purchased last year have nearly doubled in value."

"That may be so, Yehuda, but I bet you a hundred gold bezants that once my Sicilian silk works resume production, the price of first-grade samite will fall by half. I'm having five hundred mulberry trees planted in Palermo this year, and another five hundred next year."

The merchant's eyes widened. Truly, the wonders of the Lord were many when emperors began talking like silk traders! This young emperor bargained like a bazaar merchant and worked an abacus as swiftly as Yehuda himself. In stark contradiction to this was his love of beautiful things. He fingered the facets of a gem or stroked a length of silk as if he were caressing a woman.

Frederick pointed to the cobalt-blue silk. "I'll take that for the empress, it's a color that suits her."

Yehuda's two assistants removed the bolt, expertly rolling it up between them. They placed it on a pile near the window, where the merchant's scribe was noting each purchase on a wax tablet with a stylus.

"That should appeal to the chancellor," Frederick said, indicating a length of russet Estanfort. "Conrad likes rich fabrics in dull colors. His taste in clothing is like his mind, very subtle." To Yehuda he said, "Add the necessary marten skins to fashion it into a furred gown."

One by one he went through the list a secretary handed him, of friends and courtiers who'd be honored with a New Year gift. For Berard he selected a curved Byzantine eating dagger in a gold sheath studded with flame-colored carnelians. He grinned at Manfred: "It'll be useful. He's always eating, and hereabouts everyone carries his own eating-knife."

He picked up a gold fibula set with pearls and a single deep red garnet. He held it to Manfred's throat and leaned back. "Hm, what do you think, would it suit you?"

Manfred blinked. "Frederick, it's magnificent. But it's far too costly. I can't—"

"Of course you can! You can wear it on your wedding day and dazzle that lovely girl completely! As for your betrothed, I think I'll take that green silk over there. It's exactly the shade of her eyes." He motioned to Yehuda to add the cloth to the other purchases.

Manfred shook his head. Frederick, despite being perennially short of funds, was incredibly generous. And observant, he thought with a little sting. Frederick had seen Manfred's German bride-to-be only once, and yet he had remembered the color of her eyes.

"Now, Yehuda, that pearl circlet for the empress. Did you get the matched pearls you promised me?"

"Of course, Your Grace." Yehuda handed him a small leather pouch.

Just then children's laughter rose from the gardens outside. Frederick, holding a pearl, went over to the window. In the garden on the ramparts below, Enzio and Henry were running on the leaf-strewn gravel paths between the flower beds, followed by their nurses. The smaller child was trying to catch the older boy in the maze of pear trees.

At least he's kindhearted, Frederick thought as he watched Henry run away, but at a pace that would allow the little one to reach him. Kindhearted, but spoiled and willful, and wary of his father. After more than a year, the boy still shied away from him, although he had learned to do so surreptitiously. Surely a boy of eight ought not to have a nurse any more and shouldn't be playing with a three-year-old? Although Constance, to his amazement and relief, had accepted Enzio's presence, he was too young to be a suitable companion for Henry.

It was high time Henry had his own household of male tutors and companions. Constance pleaded for more time for their son to adjust to his new life. Henry was suffering from nightmares since leaving Sicily. Although he was in good health, he was a picky eater. He refused dishes he was not used to and clamored for unobtainable oranges. He hated the cold and spent most winter days by the fire in the nursery.

How different was Enzio, at three a veritable little terror, falling into the half-frozen pond, throwing snowballs at the guards, constantly scuffing his knees and elbows bloody. Always cheerful, a mischievous grin on his angelic features, Enzio romped through Haguenau Castle endearing himself to everyone from scullery maids to chancery clerks. Whenever he spotted his father, Enzio would throw himself at him with shouts of delight.

Watching them now, their heads close together, Henry's golden hair against Enzio's dark curls, plotting some mischief out of the nurses' earshot, Frederick sighed with regret. If only Henry could be like Enzio . . . But Henry was still young. In time, with the right guidance, he'd change.

Fearful for Henry's health, Frederick, against his better judgment, had agreed to Constance's request. But now he resolved to act. Someone of suitable temperament and learning was needed to be his tutor. Henry must be removed from the circle of doting women in the nursery. He'd never grow out of his whining ways otherwise. The time had come to make Henry into a man.

THE YEAR OF Otto's death ended in a joyful Christmas court at Haguenau, during which Manfred's marriage to the daughter of a German margrave was celebrated. The following June Frederick received Henry of Brunswick in Barbarossa's palace at Goslar. The imperial crown and the regalia were handed over. The last Guelf thawed under Frederick's conciliatory manner. To demonstrate his faith in his new vassal, Frederick named him to a prestigious but mainly ceremonial post. The pacification of Germany was complete.

In the meantime, the crusading movement was in disarray. Just before Innocent's death, and at his instigation, a number of Frankish princes, led by Jean de Brienne, who ruled the kingdom of Jerusalem, had decided to embark on their own crusade. They were tired, they said, of waiting for the dilatory emperor. Their plan was to start their attack in lower Egypt, and from there sweep north along the Sultan's territory to liberate Jerusalem. Honorius, upon his accession, gave cautious sanction to their enterprise and urged Frederick to support them with men, ships, and money until such time as he could join them.

Frederick, unable to make up his mind whether he was peeved or relieved, and in no hurry to pour silver into a campaign he had no control over, did nothing. Soon he would turn his attention eastward, but not just yet. He still had unfinished business in Germany, the most important of which was his son's election.

WIMPFEN CASTLE, VALLEY OF THE NECKAR, MARCH 1220

Winter was reluctant that year to relinquish its dominion over the land. The countryside was blanketed in snow. Rivers and lakes were frozen. Navigation on the Neckar and the Mosel became perilous because of thick ice floes. Even the oldest peasants in the villages along the rivers could not remember the last time this had occurred. Only the Rhine continued to surge toward the sea.

Roads became impassable. A Diet at Speyer had to be called off. Day after day, black clouds hung in the sky above Wimpfen, unleashing fierce storms that filled the castle's courtyards with snow.

Frederick was bent over a parchment scroll, writing. The chamber was silent, except for the crackling of the fire. He halted and blew on his numb fingers. Despite the shuttered windows and the burning logs, he could see his own breath. The walls gave off a stinging chill despite the tapestries with which they were hung to ward off the cold.

Constance entered, stepping silently on the bearskins that covered the floor. "What a winter!" she grimaced, removing the hood of her fur-lined mantle. "What are you working on?"

The table was scattered with scrolls and sheets of parchment. Some were ink drawings. One represented a double-sided tower with an arched gate in the middle. Constance picked it up and studied it. "It's gorgeous. But where are you going to build it? Your grandfather's castles are splendid already. You don't want to make the princes jealous, do you?"

Constance was right. There was already a large difference between the elegant Italianate palaces built by his grandfather, such as Haguenau, Goslar and Wimpfen, and the squat castles of the German magnates. It wouldn't do to exacerbate them. But that wasn't his intention.

He adjusted the fur rug on his knees so as to cover the heated bricks his feet were resting on. "Come and sit," he patted the settle. "I'll show you some of these."

Her eyes widened as he passed her parchment after parchment with sketches of marble statues, friezes, architraves, buttresses, and a classical portico. Some were of gargoyles, others of charming, realistic animals such as bears, lions, and squirrels to be hewn in stone. There was one in particular, an eagle in flight holding a hare in its talons, that was astonishingly lifelike. "Are they Norbert's work?"

"The tower is. The others are mine, like this eagle."

"You drew this? It seems alive!"

"I've learned much from Norbert. The little fellow has a magical way with a piece of charcoal. With a few strokes he can create a work of art. And his proportions are almost always right the first time. I find it relaxing to sit during the long winter nights and draw."

She smiled. While no doubt not all his nights were spent in such innocent pastimes, the image of Frederick alone in this tower room, drawing in the deep of night, was endearing in its absurdity. The design of buildings and decorative elements was the domain of lowly craftsmen. Frederick had many interests that would have raised eyebrows among his subjects had they but known about them.

Constance, having lost her way one day in the gardens at Haguenau, and recognizing Frederick's voice, had found him in the stonemason's dusty workrooms beside the stables, leaning over Norbert's shoulder. The bald little man was holding a chisel in one hand, while with the other he was showing Frederick a particular angle of setting the chisel to the stone. Both had been covered in white dust, their hair and eyebrows looking as if they had been coated in flour.

Her glance swept the table. The heading of the long scroll he had been working on caught her eye. She began to read in growing surprise.

A new Sicilian edict, the draft dealt with ordinances for the creation and maintenance of a fleet. Some fief holders and towns were to supply timber or money for the building of ships and their maintenance. Others would furnish regular quotas of sailors.

There followed a list of towns and vassals by name, with annotations in Frederick's hand, indicating whether the dues might be paid peaceably, or how much resistance was to be expected. Beside some could be read the remark: "Requires my presence."

So this was what he did when he locked himself away with his secretaries of an evening! Since the early days in Germany there had always been what amounted to a separate, unobtrusive chancery that dealt with Sicilian matters, headed by Berard and supervised by Frederick, but she hadn't known to what meticulous extent he was planning Sicily's future.

"When are you going to return to Sicily?" The question had been in her mind since the day he had embarked from Messina. Now, after seven years, she asked it.

"Why, after the coronation."

"That's not what I meant. I know you're going there before embarking for Palestine. What I meant is, will you ever again reside in Sicily? It's impossible to rule Sicily and the Empire from here, even with the best officers of state. The distances are too great."

Frederick linked his hands behind his back. "Augustus ruled a far larger Empire from Rome."

"And where will your Rome be?"

He reached for the drawing of the gate tower. Tapping it, he said, "This gateway will one day rise in the heart of the Empire."

"But where?"

He smiled up at her. "I don't know yet. When I decide, I promise you shall be the first to know."

Frederick could be maddeningly secretive. Constance stared into the dancing flames. There were eight months left before the coronation in

Rome set for November. Eight months in which to have Henry elected
king of Germany.

VITERBO, AUGUST 1220

Pope Honorius' normally serene features turned crimson. "How dare he!"
He rummaged among the parchments on the table for a letter. With a stubby
finger he followed the lines till he found the paragraph he was looking for:

"Here's what the emperor wrote in February: 'As our son might die
without leaving a brother or child, we reserve the right to succeed him in
the realm of Sicily, not by imperial claim, but by the title of legitimate
succession, whereby a father takes the inheritance of his son, always recognizing that we hold the realm from the Church.'"

The pontiff dropped it and picked up another parchment, waving it
before von Salza. "And now, three months later, he sends you with this!"

In his raspy old voice, Honorius began to read: "'. . . our son was elected
German king without our knowledge. The princes' sole motivation was to
ensure a peaceful succession should we perish doing God's work. . . . Had
we ourselves not been away at the time, we would have restrained them
. . . However, our Mother the Church should have no fear on the subject of
a possible union of the realm and the Empire, because we ourselves desire
the separation . . .'" Honorius rolled his eyes to heaven. "I ask you . . ."

"Holy Father," Hermann said, "I can vouch for the fact that the emperor
wasn't present when Henry was elected. His father goes on crusade next
year. In the event of his death in the Holy Land, Germany would again be
menaced with civil war. Surely you wouldn't wish renewed bloodshed on
a country that has only just begun to recover from decades of devastation?"

Honorius felt trapped. The princes of the German Church had all taken
part in the election. He could hardly excommunicate every German
bishop. And discord was one thing Christendom couldn't afford right now,
with the crusaders in Egypt besieging Damietta while they waited for the
emperor. If he refused to crown Frederick in November, he couldn't afterward give him his blessing to go on crusade.

The Pope scrutinized Hermann. "Can you really tell me that Henry's
election was contrary to his father's wishes?"

"No, Your Holiness, I cannot." Hermann held the pontiff's gaze. "But I'm persuaded that his undeniable joy is founded more on his concern for the Empire than on pride of race. Frederick truly wants to ensure a lasting peace for his people."

The pontiff sighed. The August heat, although less terrible here than in Rome, was oppressive. How this towering German remained looking so cool in his thick cloak and heavy leather boots was beyond him. If only the emperor's boundless ambition, which his cardinals were always warning him about, could be proven to exist only in the minds of Guelf loyalists . . . He had known Frederick as a boy and then as a youth. He'd found him to be a likable young man. Wasn't it possible for the two heads of Christendom to stop sparring and join forces?

Conscious suddenly of a lapse in his manners, Honorius gestured to the loggia outside. "Please, my lord von Salza, let us take some refreshment outside, where it is a little cooler." He had been acquainted with von Salza for many years and regretted the harsh words that had passed between them today. The grand master and his order had always been loyal to the papacy.

They stepped out of the dimly lit study into the bright shade outside. Honorius sat down beside Hermann on a long stone bench. Shaded by vines heavy with nearly ripe purple fruit, the loggia of the papal summer residence was a pleasant spot. It overlooked terraced gardens planted with pomegranate, orange, and lemon trees. Through the foliage, he could see Viterbo's marketplace, paved with blocks of black lava. A monk brought cool well water, wine, and a platter of figs.

The bells of San Lorenzo rang the sixth hour. Honorius, with an apology to his visitor, folded his hands over his ample stomach and recited the office of compline. At the end he added a silent prayer: "May the Emperor keep faith with the Church, for the sake of Christendom and that of his soul, Amen."

AUGSBURG, AUGUST 1220

On the last day of August, Frederick and Constance led the imperial cavalcade from the Lechfeld, a vast field below Augsburg, from which the emperors traditionally departed for their coronations in Rome.

Behind them came a lumbering procession of riders and oxcarts containing the imperial household. Part of their escort of princes, prelates, and
officials would leave them at Innsbruck. The remainder would accompany
them to Rome and thence to Sicily. In the center of the convoy, surrounded by a detachment of Teutonic knights, rumbled the wagon containing the crown of Charlemagne.

Constance was grateful for the veil that protected her from the stares
of the townsfolk. In an effort to control her tears, she gripped her reins
so tightly that the silver embroidery on her gloves cut into her hands.
Would she ever see Henry again? She'd never forget the look of mutinous
rage on his tear-stained little face as he stood beside the archbishop of
Cologne. When the archbishop, who was a kindly man, put his arm
around him, he had precipitated another flood of tears. Frederick muttered that at nine a boy should behave with more dignity and rode away
without another glance at his son. How could he, himself bereft of par-
ents as a child, be so heartless?

Frederick glanced at Constance, saw the tightness of her bearing. He
would have liked to comfort her, but she couldn't have heard him anyway
in the din. When he had told her that Henry must remain in Germany, she
called him a monster. He patiently explained that it could take several
years before their return. Henry was now king of Germany. The loyalty of
princes and people needed a focus. But even Constance, far more intelligent than most women, had the typical female failing of being unable to
separate the wider issues from the narrow field of her private emotions. If
she refused to understand that the duties of an empress differed from
those of a cobbler's wife, he couldn't help it.

They left behind the farms and dwellings that sheltered beneath the
city walls. Open, rolling country stretched on all sides. The morning was
overcast but warm. Frederick inhaled the scent of freshly cut hay, spread
to dry on the fields. An invigorating sense of freedom filled him. The road
began to climb, skirting the river. They were on their way south, to Rome,
and to Sicily.

SILENCE FILLED THE basilica of Saint Peter's. For a moment, held in the
pontiff's hands, the ancient octagonal crown, adorned with gems and

enamel, seemed to float above the altar. Then Honorius placed it on Frederick's bowed head.

The years receded in Berard's mind. Instead of the emperor in his coronation regalia, he saw an eleven-year-old boy in a short grubby tunic, assessing him with wary eyes in a bazaar . . . I'm getting fanciful in middle age, he thought, blinking, and maudlin as well.

Unlike him, Frederick was calm and detached. No mystic fervor gripped him today as it had in Aachen. After receiving the orb and scepter, he stepped aside so that the pope could crown the kneeling Constance.

His grandfather's mantle fitted him today as if it had been made for him. Berard remembered the first time Frederick had worn it, at his wedding. It had been too wide at the shoulders then. Frederick had it brought especially from Palermo. True, it was grander than the German coronation cloak. But it was also a link with the past, with Sicily. Its splendid hem, silver-embroidered with Kufic characters, swirled over the steps above the tomb of Saint Peter in an image filled with symbolism. Like the mantle, Frederick too was half of the East and half of the West, half heathen and half Christian, half doubting heretic and half faithful believer.

Berard's eyes wandered over the congregation. The most illustrious guests stood close to the altar, under Constantine's mosaic-covered arch. The Germans were calm and dignified in their furred cloaks. Representatives of the Lombard League, voluble and gorgeously arrayed, stood side by side with stern, hawk-eyed governors of the imperial cities in Italy, each group ignoring the other. The Sicilians, gleaming with jewels, smiled obsequiously. With every league that Frederick got closer to the realm, the Sicilians' nervousness no doubt increased; the liberties of the past had come to an end.

After Frederick and Constance received communion and exchanged the kiss of peace with the pontiff, silver trumpets sounded. The choir burst into plainsong. Frederick, with Honorius and Constance, left the basilica erected over a thousand years before by Constantine. They stepped into the afternoon sunshine. The colonnaded atrium was crowded with those who hadn't been able to get into the church. In the square beyond thronged the Roman populace. Mercifully there was no sign of the riots that had broken out during previous coronations. Frederick had been generous.

Preceding their cavalcade all the way from the Monte Mario, heralds had distributed largesse to the crowd.

The square was black with people. Every balcony, every rooftop was filled with spectators. Frederick raised his hand. The roar of the crowd rose in a crescendo: "*Viva l'imperatore! Viva l'imperatore Federico! Viva! Viva! Viva!*"

"Bread and circuses. Nothing's changed," Frederick whispered to Berard. He said something to Constance but she didn't hear him. Her eyes were far away. She's thinking of Henry, Berard thought.

The papal chamberlain led the pope's white mule forward for the ceremony that had caused such bitterness in the past between emperors and popes. Frederick held the silver stirrup for Honorius with a smile, even lending his other hand in support as the aged pontiff mounted the richly caparisoned animal. How humble Frederick could be, Berard thought, when it served his purpose! It was the substance of power that interested him, not the symbols by which other men laid such store.

Frederick mounted his black stallion. With the pope in the lead, the cavalcade set off toward the Tiber. Surging, cheering crowds pressed in on them from all sides. At the Church of Santa Maria in Transpontina the procession halted. Honorius and Frederick exchanged a last embrace. "Go with God, my son," the pope said, kissing Frederick on both cheeks.

"May God be with you, too, Holy Father, and rest assured that I shall defend the Church from all peril."

The Pontiff raised his hand in a last salute. Amid flying church banners, he crossed the Tiber and rode back to the Lateran palace on the other side of Rome.

The imperial party rode up the ancient Via Triumphalis, toward their camp on the Monte Mario. At its summit, Frederick drew rein. Turning in his saddle, he stared for a long moment at the great city fading into amber dusk. Then, abruptly, he spurred his horse into a canter.

BARI, SICILIAN MAINLAND, APRIL 1222

Outside the walls of Bari, on the Apulian plain bordered by the Adriatic, a city of tents and makeshift hovels had sprung up for those who couldn't find lodging in the crowded city. An air of newfound prosperity filled the town. Carts rumbled through the streets, filled with produce or piled with building materials for the houses and palaces being repaired or the new buildings springing up everywhere. Half-veiled women walked in the dust, balancing bundles of firewood or jars of water on their heads. Little herd boys drove fat black swine to market, while Bari's fishermen gave thanks to their patron, Saint Nicholas.

Since the emperor had decided to spend part of each year here, a bushel of sardines fetched four times what it had two years ago. Couriers on lathered horses from as far afield as Lombardy or Germany were a common sight in the streets, jostling the well-groomed mounts of German and Sicilian lords. Haughty, black-garbed imperial notaries traveled on foot, preceded by stick-wielding servants to clear their way. Troubadours, craftsmen, sailors, whores, and mountebanks from all over Europe flocked to Bari.

BERARD MADE HIS way down the vaulted passage amid chiseling and hammering, sidestepping piles of masonry. Frederick was rebuilding this Norman castle, ripping open walls for lead piping to fill the baths by which he laid such store, and the flushing privies he said were the foundation of civilized life.

He sat down on a bench that ran along one side of the otherwise bare council chamber. The emperor, a page assured him, wouldn't be long. The room smelled of damp plaster. Weary from a long morning in the chancery, he leaned his head back. Despite the chill of early spring, the shutters stood wide open to allow the walls to dry. From his bench, he could see the sea, blue and calm, stretch to the horizon. He sighed with contentment. It was pleasant to be back in the town where long ago he had received his bishop's pallium.

Time in Frederick's service passed swiftly. Nearly two years had gone by since the coronation in Rome. Frederick hadn't lingered to savor his triumph. The next morning he left at dawn with a small escort that included Berard, leaving the court to follow. They covered a distance of more than sixty miles in a single day of exhausting riding. Berard saw tears in Frederick's eyes as that same evening, exhausted and saddle-sore, they crossed the boundary between the Papal States and Sicily.

In Palermo, Frederick was received with jubilation by the townspeople. They prostrated themselves before his throne, set in the old Norman manner under an ancient palm tree in the palace square. Frederick established his court there for the winter, and set to work at once. Before the astonished eyes of a much aged Walter of Palear he drew forth from his traveling chests scroll after scroll of new laws for the kingdom, ready for promulgation.

The edicts covered a wide range of issues. Roads were to be made safe for travelers. Tolls and other fiscal matters were dealt with, increasing the crown's revenues. The precarious land tenure of peasants was to be improved. Even Berard hadn't realized to what extent Frederick had planned every detail of Sicily's revival during his years in Germany.

One ordinance decreed that all castles built without royal permission since the death of Frederick's mother must be handed over to the crown. Hundreds of fortresses fell into this category. The lesser ones were demolished, the major ones retained. The barons who had resisted royal authority during Frederick's absence were declared outlaws. Offenses such as nonpayment of taxes, appropriation of crown lands, brigandage, even failure to maintain roads and bridges all fell under this.

The majority complied. A number of outraged barons appealed in vain to the pope. Some, headed by the powerful Count of Molise, rebelled. Frederick himself led the campaign that ended with the surrender or capture of every one of the rebels. Frederick didn't, as was customary, hand them to other, more trustworthy vassals. Instead, he did something unheard of: he made the castles crown properties. They were manned by soldiers paid by the treasury. Frederick was now the only Christian monarch, other than the Byzantine emperor, to possess a standing army as well as a string of royal fortresses throughout his realm. "Never again," he told Berard with a thin smile, "will the barons rise against me."

The following summer, Frederick moved the court to Bari. August, the date on which he had sworn in Rome to lead the crusade, had come and gone. Fortunately, just then the mountain Saracens on the island rose in revolt. Frederick wrote to the pope, and obtained a postponement of his departure to deal with the rebellion. He placated Honorius by sending much-needed aid in ships and gold to the crusaders floundering in Egypt, while occupying himself mainly with the restoration of Sicily and her navy.

Teams of shipwrights, recruited from as far afield as Greece and Byzantium by Frederick's agents, worked day and night in the newly dredged port of Bari to build a Sicilian navy under the supervision of Alaman da Costa, appointed admiral of the infant fleet. The republic of Genoa viewed this with concern. Genoa sent an embassage asserting her exclusive rights to the transport of merchandise to and from Sicily. Frederick, who had been waiting for just such a pretext, replied by canceling the treaty with Genoa. When the Genoese vehemently protested, reminding him how they had backed him in uncertain times, Frederick answered coolly that while his personal gratitude was undiminished, the prosperity of his kingdom took precedence over his private inclinations.

Berard was jolted out of his reverie by the opening of the door. Frederick emerged from the adjoining study listening to a wiry little man with a long face, a maroon cap pulled low above his beetling black brows. The older man was talking rapidly, his soft voice magnified by the bare walls.

Berard knew him well: Roffredo of Benevento. Frederick had met him in Bologna, where he was professor of canon law. Always on the lookout for talented men, Frederick offered him the challenge of unifying the welter of often conflicting oral and written laws of Sicily into a single code. Roffredo accepted immediately, undeterred by the fact that it would take him and a team of jurists, notaries, and scribes years to accomplish their task. The last such undertaking had been Justinian's code in the sixth century.

Frederick waved to the scholar. He turned to Berard: "What brings you into this builder's warren?"

"A man, just arrived from Palestine, whom I think you should meet. He's a famous friar. Some say a holy man. I thought you might find a first-hand account of conditions in the Holy Land valuable."

"Holy men, phew! They smell and are deranged by too many visions and too little food. I can't imagine that this fellow will have much of practical value to tell me!"

"He's no ordinary friar. He's a most remarkable man. My friend Elias of Cortona, who accompanied him to the East, tells me that he actually attempted to convert the Sultan of Egypt during an audience!"

Frederick smiled, "Such temerity appeals to me. What's his name?"

"Francis. Francis of Assisi."

"The one who had a dream about the tottering edifice of the Church? Whom Innocent helped found an order of mendicant friars?"

"The very same. They, say, too, that he speaks to the birds."

FREDERICK SLOWLY CUT a slice off his apple with an ivory-handled knife while he studied his guests. Elias of Cortona, the taller and broader of the two, was helping himself to another large ladleful of deer stew from the serving dish. Elias was a tall, muscular man in his forties, of noble birth, who had been drawn in his youth to join Francis' little band. Francis, unwilling to deal with the administration of the growing order, had entrusted this to the robust, more practical Elias.

Francis, of the same age but slighter than his deputy, ate almost nothing, turning the food over with slender elegant fingers. Although only in his late thirties, the penances and deprivations he'd inflicted on his body left him prematurely gray, with sunken cheeks and hollow eyes. He refused the wine and drank water sparingly out of his silver goblet. Although he was clothed in a ragged tunic of brown homespun, with a cord in place of a belt, his manners were gracious.

Berard had told Frederick that Francis had once been a fashionable young man. But after hearing God's voice, he gave away all his possessions. When his wealthy father, fearing for his sanity, cited him before the local bishop, Francis stripped himself to his loincloth and returned his clothes to his father. Poverty, he said was a virtue. The bishop, instead of censuring Francis, gave him his own cloak and sent him on his way. Preaching poverty and love, Francis, befriended by Pope Innocent, went on to found the Franciscan order.

In deference to the austere habits of the friar but also because Frederick wanted to keep any information about the East to himself, they were gathered not in the great hall, but in his privy chambers, around a table spread with the simple Apulian dishes he himself preferred.

He had warmed instantly to the Umbrian friar despite the latter's ascetic ways. Far from being the otherworldly fanatic he had expected, Francis had the serene, uncluttered intelligence of one who has done away with all unnecessary mental baggage, keeping in sight only his goal. His large hazel eyes were gentle but compelling. But the most outstanding thing about Francis was his voice. A voice of extraordinary beauty, rich, melodious and deep, it enthralled and filled his listeners with a sense of peace. With a voice such as this, perhaps he really did speak to the birds. Frederick said, "Tell me about your meeting with the sultan, Francis."

"Al-Kamil received us most graciously. He listened when I explained the benefits of Christianity, declining, however, to embrace it. In parting the sultan gave me and my companions a safe-conduct for our pilgrimage to Jerusalem."

"What manner of man is he?" Frederick asked.

Francis looked thoughtful for a moment, crumbling his bread. "A friar from Acre, who interpreted for us, told me it is said that he would rather have been a scholar than a sultan. Yet he rules as well, though not as harshly, as his predecessors." Francis leaned forward, his face suddenly animated: "I was astounded, Your Grace, to discover that Muslims, too, believe in the retribution of evil and the reward of goodness. When I exhorted him to save his soul by embracing Christianity, the sultan responded that good and pious Muslims went to heaven anyway."

Frederick smiled. "I've always told Berard that they aren't half as bad as Christians think they are."

"You are right, Your Grace," Francis said. "They, too, are God's children."

Elias glanced up sharply. Like a watchdog scenting danger, Frederick thought. If it were reported that Francis had actually said such a thing, it might be used against him. Because of his denunciation of the Church's abuses, Francis had many enemies. Leaning back in his chair, still toying with his knife, Frederick asked, "Tell me, Francis, do you really think it is possible to purge the Church of her evil ways? To stop her prelates from stealing and fornicating and selling indulgences to the credulous?"

Berard, who had just taken a mouthful of wine, nearly choked. Coughing, he sought refuge behind his napkin.

Francis raised his eyes, unperturbed. "Alas, Your Grace, I don't think so. The Church is made of men, and men are weak. I can't rebuild her the way Christ would wish her to be. But by our example we can inspire many to abandon their evil ways and love one another. Thus, we will at least buttress our mother the Church and stop her from falling, mayhap even righting her edifice a little."

"I too, would wish the Church to return to what Christ wanted her to be. I however, have less faith in mankind than you."

Holding Frederick's gaze, Francis said, "It would greatly benefit the cause of Christ if the princes of this world would abandon their sinful ways and set an example to the simple and the poor."

Frederick's eyes narrowed for an instant. "There are different ways of serving God, Francis." He rose, indicating that the audience was over. "You and brother Elias will of course be my guests for as long as you are in Bari." To the steward who was attending them, he said, "See to it that the friars lack for nothing."

Then, to Berard's utter astonishment, Frederick said, "Will you bless me, Francis?"

"How could I refuse, Your Grace?"

Frederick's eyes twinkled. "I think you quite capable of it, if you so wished."

Francis raised his hand and made the sign of the cross above Frederick's bowed head.

NORBERT, HIS SET square wedged under one arm, lead the way, kicking chunks of rubble out of their path. He pointed out the new windows to Frederick.

"Well done. I see much progress." Frederick, shading his eyes with his hand, admired the well-made walkways of plaited osier that covered the facade of Bari's castle. Secured into putlogs, they were far easier to work on than wooden scaffolding. Men with basketfuls of fresh mortar on their shoulders climbed ladders made of the same material.

Norbert rubbed his callused hands together. "It's marvelous to be able to build all year round, Your Grace. No snow and ice to freeze fingers and mortar. At this rate we'll soon be able to start on the one in Trani."

Frederick smiled at the Rhinelander's enthusiasm. Norbert had followed him, abandoning his homeland, without hesitation. Taking to Sicily as if he had been born here, he'd even found a local wife. "There's a great deal to be done, Norbert. Even you may yet get weary. For thirty years nothing's been built or repaired in Sicily. We need fortresses to defend the coast and—"

"Your Grace!" Norbert grabbed his arm, swinging him violently to one side. Together they fell into a pile of sand. A tremendous crash was followed by a cloud of dust. On the spot where they had been standing lay a huge block of dressed sandstone, still held in the giant steel pincers in which it was being raised. Above, halfway to the top of the central tower, dangled the broken end of the rope to which it had been attached. The three men who had been turning the windlass stared down in mute horror.

Workmen rushed forward. Frederick scrambled to his feet. His mouth was full of grit. He extended a hand to Norbert, sprawled on the ground, coughing.

"Was that an accident, do you think, or is one of my vassals trying to rid himself of me?" Frederick asked.

Norbert's hands trembled. "I don't know. As I glanced up, I saw the rope splitting." He glanced at the block of stone and shuddered. "It would have killed us, no doubt about it."

"God didn't raise me this far only to crush me like a grain of corn under a grindstone." Frederick smiled at the mason: "You've saved my life, Norbert. A lesser man would have leaped aside, thinking only of himself. Ask anything you wish as a reward."

Norbert shook his head. "You've been overgenerous already, my lord. I lack for nothing. It's enough that one day, men will marvel at your castles and say that Norbert of Cologne built them. The great just build cathedrals, nothing but cathedrals, while they live elsewhere in wooden barns like royal sheep!"

Frederick laughed. "That's noble but foolish, Norbert. I'll see that you're rewarded anyway." He glanced up to see riders crossing the drawbridge, escorting a long hide-covered traveling wagon. Beside it, on a chestnut with white socks, he recognized Manfred, a jaunty yellow feather in his cap.

Manfred slid off his mount. They embraced. Frederick pointed his chin at the wagon. "And that? What is it, your traveling harem?"

"Almost. Since you've given me permission, I've brought my family. I must introduce them to you. My sisters have talked of nothing but you for days."

He crossed to the wagon and called into the interior. Wooden steps were lowered. One by one, four ladies, their veils thrown back, clambered out. One of them was visibly pregnant.

"Your Grace." Manfred's mother sank into a curtsy, smiling at him. The passing years had been kind to her. While the dark hair that showed under her starched white wimple was touched with gray, the lines on her skin were few and fine. Frederick kissed her hand.

Manfred's German wife Beatrice, blond and rosy-cheeked, was far gone with child. Frederick greeted her in German and raised her quickly from her uncomfortable position. Manfred's two sisters made their obeisance together. The elder was fair-haired, buxom, and uncommonly pretty. The younger one, little more than a child, resembled her mother and brother. Thin and dark-haired, with delicate black eyebrows, she had the awkwardness of a young colt. She stared at Frederick, forgetting to rise.

"Bianca!" The girl, as if in a trance, slowly turned her head toward her mother.

"You may rise, my girl," Frederick inclined his head.

She crimsoned and did as she was bid. Manfred and the countess admired the castle's new facade. Frederick explained what it would look like at its completion. The countess pointed at the heraldic emblem carved above the main gate, an eagle holding a hare in its talons. "What does it signify?"

"My new emblem. It reminds me of myself and the pope," Frederick chuckled.

"Does the pope hold you captive, or you the pope?"

Frederick whipped around. Manfred's little sister fixed him with huge dark eyes. "That's what you meant, isn't it, my lord?"

Frederick laughed. "Why, that's extraordinary. The same thought occurred to me, only the other day." He scrutinized her. "You're an outspoken girl, aren't you? I remember now. Last time I saw you, you told me I was dirty!"

The color rose again in her cheeks. This time, however, she stuck her chin out. "You *were* dirty. I was speaking the truth. And I was only a small child!"

Frederick smiled. "But I'm not blaming you at all. I can see you now as if it were yesterday, with your white cap." He went on, "It was the day we were ambushed at the Lambro; that's why I remember it. That day, too," he said, more to himself than to the girl, "like today, I escaped death by a hair's breadth."

Manfred's eyes widened. "What?"

Frederick waved the question aside. "I'll tell you later. I think your lady wife should rest." He took Beatrice by the arm and steered her into the half-finished courtyard. "I'm afraid you'll find living here a little chaotic for a while, my dear, with all this building. But the west wing has been completed. I trust you'll find your apartments comfortable. I've installed water pipes on every floor, so you can take a bath every day." He whispered something into her ear that made her giggle. She smiled up at him, eyes shining.

Manfred, following behind, grinned. In a low voice, he said to his mother, "It's disgusting. He could charm snakes if he tried."

The countess bit her lip. The warning she was about to utter died, unspoken. Her two daughters had caught up with them.

AMALFI, JULY 1222

The herald overtook them, enveloping the riders in a cloud of red dust. He drew up beside Frederick. "Your Grace," he gasped, "Archbishop Berard bids you wait. He's following with urgent news."

Frederick reined in, annoyed. He'd already been delayed in Amalfi that morning by a messenger from the governor of Naples. Now they'd have to travel through the midday heat to reach Salerno before dark. However, if Berard was braving the road himself, it must be of the utmost importance. Had Honorius changed his mind about granting him a delay for the crusade?

Berard's burly outline appeared on a roan charger from behind a rocky outcrop. His escort was as dust-covered as he. Out of breath, he reined in his lathered horse.

One look at his face told Frederick that something was terribly wrong. "What is it, Berard?"

"Frederick, I . . ." Berard's voice faltered. He swallowed. "Constance is dead."

Frederick stared at him. "Dead?" He gripped the reins, his knuckles white.

"She died a week ago in Catania."

"How?"

"A fever." Berard laid a hand on his arm. "Her final thoughts were for you. With her last breath she called your name."

Frederick sat motionless on his horse. The narrow road ran high above the sea, hugging the coastline that fell in steep cliffs to the water's edge. He could hear the distant crashing of the waves against the rocks. Slowly, as in a nightmare, he turned his head and looked out across the sea, toward Catania.

I sent you to Catania to do my bidding, he thought. And now you are gone, gone forever. Never again will I hear your voice or see you smile. A terrible pain spread across his chest, choking the breath within him. He tried to recall her face, but the more he stared at the misty line where sea and sky fused on the horizon, the more blurred his vision became.

Silence descended on those around him. Even the horses were unusually still. The sun, approaching its zenith, burned down. Behind a dusty bush a lone cicada began to chirp.

At last he turned to Berard, his face expressionless. "We'll take ship this afternoon from Amalfi. I want her to be buried in Palermo, beside my mother and father."

He turned his horse. Berard fell in beside him. Frederick stared at the road, mechanically controlling his mount, his shoulders slumped. Not a word passed between them till they reached Amalfi.

THE BELLS OF Palermo tolled for Sicily's dead queen. In the blinding light of a July morning, under a sky of joyous blue that seemed to Frederick like a mockery of heaven, Constance's funeral cortège moved slowly through the crowded streets.

He rode behind her bier, keeping step with the beat of the drums. The coffin in its crimson pall seemed to float above a sea of black. Black-garbed mourners, black-muffled drums, horses caparisoned in black. On the coffin lay a life-sized wax effigy of Constance, crowned and dressed in the sky-blue mantle she had worn for their wedding. He stared ahead, numb with pain.

As the bier passed, carried on the shoulders of twelve black-hooded monks, the crowd fell to their knees. The women, both Christians and

Saracens, tore their hair, strewing dust on their heads as they rocked back and forth on their heels, keening.

The coffin rested in the choir of the cathedral during the funerary mass. The wax effigy had been removed. Only Constance' s crown, his mother's crown, remained on a cushion of blue damask.

In the crypt, as the pallbearers were about to close the sarcophagus, Frederick suddenly raised his hand. "Halt! Open the coffin!" His face, which throughout had been impassive, not even his lips moved during the service, was contorted.

Berard, about to bless the sarcophagus with holy water, touched his arm. "Don't," he whispered. "It won't be a sight you'd wish to remember. She's been embalmed by the best Saracen embalmers, but in this heat . . ."

"Let me be!" He shook off Berard's hand. "I want to see her for a last time. I don't care if she's vile with putrefaction! Raise the lid!" he commanded.

The mourners backed away. Only Berard and the abbot of Monreale remained in their place.

Frederick gazed down at Constance. There was no sign of decomposition. In a crimson robe embroidered with pearls, she resembled a statue. Her skin, stretched tight over sunken cheeks, was the color of old parchment. In the candlelight her golden hair, plaited into two long tresses, shone as it had in life.

Tenderly, he brushed a strand of hair from her forehead. His eyes, which had remained dry since her death, filled with tears. He took two steps back. Unable to speak, with a gesture he signaled to the monks to close the sarcophagus.

FREDERICK SPENT THE winter in Palermo. He grieved in an intensely private manner, withdrawing from all but the most urgent business. Only after Berard's repeated urging did he write to tell his eleven-year-old son that his mother was dead. His protracted mourning became the talk of Sicily. How odd, the gossips whispered, that the emperor should mourn his wife with such an excess of grief after he had publicly flaunted his mistresses with such disregard for her feelings during her lifetime.

At the end of November, Frederick finally roused himself from his apathy. When Manfred sent word that the hideout of Ibn Abbas had been discovered and the Muslim rebel leader taken, Frederick called for his sword and cloak. Riding all day, he arrived at the traitor's mountain fastness just before sunset.

"Bring him here," he growled.

The rebel, his hands and feet shackled, was led in. A tall, wide-shouldered man with an unkempt black beard and a large ruby on his right hand, Ibn Abbas threw himself at Frederick's feet.

He raised his chained hands: "Oh great sultan of Christendom, have mercy on me!"

"Like the mercy you showed the countless travelers you robbed and killed?" Frederick thundered in Arabic. "Did you show pity to my bailiffs, whom you hanged in village squares? Was compassion your motive for pillaging churches and convents and raping and murdering nuns?"

"My sultan, we were misled. The emir of Tunis told us that now that you are leader of the Christians' crusade, you were going to force us to convert to your religion. Pardon me, and my people and I will keep faith with you forever."

Frederick's face contorted. "You've promised me that once before, when I was but a youth. I have a good memory, Ibn Abbas. You're a traitorous son of a dog and you shall die as one!" He lunged forward. With a vicious kick of his spurred boot he ripped open one side of the rebel's body. Ibn Abbas screamed, curling up. Blood seeped out of the wound in a dark viscous pool.

"Take him away. Make sure he stays alive. I want him hanged, drawn and quartered. His head and limbs are to be displayed in the main cities of the island!"

Manfred swallowed. Never had he seen Frederick like this. Even the officers in the tent were visibly shocked. It was almost as if the Saracen had been made responsible for Constance's death.

PALERMO, SEPTEMBER 1224

A magical garden of gold mosaics covered the walls of what had once been King Roger's study. As a child, Frederick had been enthralled by the plumed birds, leaping gazelles, and prowling tigers brought to life when the sun flooded the chamber in the late afternoon. But now, pacing restlessly up and down the splendid room, he had no eyes for their beauty.

His mind was on the Saracen rebellion. The rebel strongholds had nearly all been destroyed. But would this solve his problem in the long run? Ever since the Norman conquest, there had been pockets of Muslim discontent. The Saracens of the countryside were more prone to rebellion than those in the towns, whose prosperity depended on Christian trade. One solution was to kill them all. While Christendom would applaud such an action, it would rouse the urban Muslims against him. Sicily might be plunged into civil war. It would also be wasteful. They were good farmers and herdsmen, the rural Saracens.

He came to a halt, staring at a particular mosaic on the wall. Palm groves, heavy with ripe dates. Fields of emerald corn, irrigated by channels of brilliant blue . . . Of course, that was it! The rich, mostly uncultivated soil of Apulia on the mainland was the perfect place to settle thousands of farmers. Once there, contained in a single walled city far from any Muslim aid, they'd contribute to Apulia's prosperity by cultivating the land. They might even enjoy it. The summers were cooler. There was abundant water. He'd allow them complete freedom to live in their own way. They could have as many mosques to pray in and as many steamy *hammams* to bathe in as they wished.

Children's laughter rose from the gardens. He turned to see a group of little girls dancing in a circle beyond a pond with water lilies. They had made themselves garlands of blossoms, which they wore in their hair like miniature crowns. An older girl was leading the little ones in play. Nearby, under a large fig tree, sat their nurses.

If only Henry and Enzio could be here. Little Catherine, the last child Adelaide had given him, was nearly four. Henry, as king of Germany, must of course remain there. But perhaps he could bring Enzio and Catherine here. Their mother had never shown much interest in them.

He recognized Bianca, Manfred's younger sister, the one who always looked at him in a strange, puzzled manner. He smiled at the earnestness with which she was shepherding the little ones to their stations for some game she was teaching them. Then the youngest said something. Bianca laughed, a rippling laughter full of innocence. Bending down, she hugged the little girl.

For a moment he hesitated, about to go down into the gardens, then changed his mind. The unfolding evening scent of jasmine reminded him of how he'd wandered here as a boy in the late afternoons, talking to the gardeners, watching them tend the flowers and sweep the paths with their great gorse brooms . . .

He drew back. The smile faded on his lips. With a last glance at the children he turned back. Although his days were crowded with the business of government and the needs of his nights fulfilled by Saracen girls whose faces he didn't remember, there were times, like now, when he felt a terrible gnawing emptiness.

Oh Constance, he thought, why did you leave me? What will I do with the new wife Hermann and Honorius have picked for me? I don't want another wife, but if I must marry, I suppose the child queen of Jerusalem is as good as any. Yolanda can remain in the women's quarters, eating sweetmeats and bearing the sons we both need. Honorius hopes we'll produce the male heirs the kingdom of Jerusalem hasn't had for so long.

He's a good man, Honorius. You always said he was . . . So taken was he with my consent to marry her that he agreed once more to postpone my crusade. He understands the reasons, particularly now that he's seen what a shambles the papal legate Pelagius, an incompetent fool of a cardinal who fancies himself a general, and Yolanda's father, Jean de Brienne, made of their assault on Damietta. Instead of waiting for the forces I sent them, these hotheads surged ahead, only to flounder in a morass of Nile mud, dissension, and Saracen arrows. . . . Honorius, just in case, made me swear to accept my excommunication if I failed to depart on the agreed date. No matter, I've got another three years in which to build ships and raise money . . .

He glanced up at the sky. You, my beloved, would have enjoyed being queen of the Holy Land, but how suitable a king of Jerusalem will I make? The Almighty must have a sense of humor after all . . . The Frankish barons of the East are all enthusiastic about my marrying Yolanda. They imagine the Saracens fleeing into the desert at the mere rumor of my coming to claim my new kingdom. I'm not so sure. They're brave and determined, the Saracens . . . And wait till the barons get a closer look at their new king, they might not like what they see! He threw back his head and laughed.

Berard, coming along the gallery, thought it a harsh, mirthless laughter. "May I ask what the source of this solitary amusement is?"

Frederick looked up and shook his head. "Nothing, my friend, nothing at all. I laugh so that I don't weep. It's more becoming."

Berard nodded. He knew these moods of Frederick's. They came and went. Sometimes months went by without them. Then he would suddenly lapse into melancholy again. Although two years had passed since Constance's death, he continued to cling to her memory as to a living thing.

Frederick said, "I was thinking that Constance probably approves of the Jerusalem marriage."

"I'm sure she'd be pleased. It is a title of immense prestige, second only to that of the Empire."

Frederick shot him a surprised glance. Had Berard, who had been against this match all along, changed his mind? Or was he beginning to humor him, too, like everyone else? He stared at him, "Do you believe the dead can hear us? If they can, why don't they ever answer?"

Berard spread his hands. "I don't know. I wish I knew, but I don't. All I know is that you must let the dead rest."

AFTER THAT, FREDERICK often walked in the gardens. Sometimes he would stop to watch the gardeners. At first, they had been struck with terror whenever he appeared, prostrating themselves, their ragged turbans touching the dust, too awed to rise. After a while, they became used to him, going about their work and answering his questions.

One day he observed an old gardener taking a cutting from a gnarled lemon tree. The tree bore only a few small stunted lemons.

"Why are you taking a slip from this old thing?"

"My lord, in its youth this tree gave lemons that were juicier than the best oranges. Their rind, boiled with sugar and fennel, made sweetmeats for your grandfather's table. In this way, the best trees never die."

The old man sealed the wound with pitch, tenderly depositing the slip in an earthenware pot filled with wet sand. He salaamed and moved down the path, to the next old tree.

Frederick remained on his bench under an ancient palm. He contemplated the little green lizards darting across the path. Rebirth . . . It wasn't only lemon trees that could be rejuvenated. Countries and empires, too, could be restored.

Tomorrow, if the wind held, he'd take ship for Naples. There, scholars summoned from all over the Empire were awaiting him to present their proposals for the school he was founding in Naples on Saint John's day. A lay university. Administered solely by royal officials and funded by the crown. Soon he'd be the only Christian sovereign who didn't have to rely on the Church for the men he needed to govern his realm. When he'd explained this to Berard, the archbishop had taken his pectoral cross in his hand, weighing it, for a moment. Then he said, "You've been planning this for a long time, haven't you?" That had been his only comment.

The Sicilian bishops were in a ferment over this lay university. A papal protest wouldn't be long in arriving. The Church, with the obstinate bigotry and cunning of an illiterate village priest, clung to her power, terrified that knowledge untrammelled by dogma might set alight the bonfires of heresy.

A shadow fell across the path. Manfred's little sister stood before him, a half-finished posy of daisies in her hand. She couldn't have come up the path or he would have seen her. She must have crept through the flower beds. Was she spying on him? He felt amused rather than annoyed.

"Good day, my Lord." She curtsied with the grace of a great lady. Yet there was a hint of mockery, an exaggeration that rendered the reverence comical, as if with those intense blue eyes of hers she had seen through the often self-serving humility of those who bent their knees before him.

"You surprised me, Bianca. You walk like a cat, on padded paws."

She blushed. Instinctively, she looked down. Frederick, following her eyes, burst out laughing. That was the reason for her soundless walk! From under a long, high-necked tunic of rose-colored wool peered muddy bare toes.

"What would your lady mother say if she saw you wandering alone, and barefoot to boot?"

She tilted her head and smiled. "I'm not alone. I've left Peppa, my nurse, dozing under a tree over there. As for my lady mother, she's far too busy with my sister Violante's wedding. Seven days of banquets, jousts, and I don't know what. All this fuss and expense for a marriage to an old man twice her age! Manfred's even mortgaged the lands in Apulia you gave him. All to impress you, so you don't think we're paupers! As if Your Grace didn't know!"

Frederick, about to smile, stopped himself. He looked at the girl with new interest. The young were not supposed to see through the foibles of their elders with such clarity. Manfred's greatest weakness was indeed his pride.

He patted the lichen-covered seat next to him. "Sit down. I won't remind you that this time you're the one who's dirty." He glanced at her bare feet.

A renewed rush of crimson rose to her face. She lowered herself onto the furthest edge of the bench, her back straight, her feet under her tunic. Her hands clutched the posy of daisies.

"As for the old man Violante is marrying, he's only a year or two older than I, so you had better mind that sharp little tongue of yours," Frederick said. "He's also very rich, heir to one of Sicily's oldest Norman names. I chose him myself and I have a mind to find a husband for you, too. We can't have you wandering around like this."

They sat in silence. It was odd, he thought, how contented he was to sit here, listening to the cooing of the pigeons, side by side with this strange girl half his age.

Was it true, Bianca wondered as she waited for him to speak, that he never prayed? Peppa had told her that no one had ever seen him pray, not even when his wife died. Not a single church had ever been built by him. It must be lonely, she thought, glancing at his profile, not to be able to pray to God. Maybe that was why at times, in unguarded moments, he seemed so sad. She watched him often, in the gardens, at a feast or a tournament.

"How old are you?" he asked, turning to look at her. In the soft shadows of the afternoon, her fine-boned face with its arched black brows had the serenity of a Byzantine madonna. A few stray tendrils of ebony hair had escaped from her mauve cap, curling against her translucent skin. Her eyes were dark, their pupils large. They held his gaze. "Fifteen, my lord."

He rose. "Come," he said with a smile. "It's unseemly for you to be sitting with any man, let alone one with my reputation! Let's go and find your nurse."

BRINDISI, NOVEMBER 1225

In the center of the city, commanding the harbor, stood a soaring column of gray granite that since antiquity had marked the end of the Via Appia.

From the upper stories of the new castle on the western side of the harbor, the column was clearly visible. Manfred, pacing up and down outside the door to Frederick's antechamber, glanced apprehensively at the sun. It was already nearing its zenith. Although the sea and sky were still blue, black clouds were gathering in the northwest. Rain would really dampen the wedding. A breeze had sprung up, blowing through the gallery. If the wind turned, rain would follow.

Manfred inhaled the cold salty air. It dispelled some of the queasiness in his stomach. His head throbbed after the feast last night. It wouldn't do, today of all days, to look tired. He glanced at the silver casket in his hands. It contained Frederick's wedding gift to his new empress, a specially wrought crown made by a famed Rhenish goldsmith. While the gesture seemed considerate, he knew better. "No other woman is going to wear Constance's jewels," Frederick snapped when it was suggested that they be brought from the vaults in Palermo.

And that was before he had even set eyes on Yolanda of Jerusalem! As the convoy of galleys from Palestine sailed into port yesterday, excitement ran high among those on the quay. The legendary Frankish East was materializing before their eyes. For the first time, even he had felt a yearning to embark for the Holy Land.

The Frankish lords who escorted the queen of Jerusalem disembarked first. After that came the veiled queen herself, flanked by the archbishop of Tyre, Simon de Maugastel, her chancellor, and her cousin Balian of Sidon, once lord of the great city near Beirut that was now held by the sultan. The bride, upon setting foot on land, threw herself weeping, whether from joy or chagrin Manfred didn't know, into the arms of her father, who stood beside Frederick on the quay. A queer fellow, this Jean de Brienne. Although king only in right of his dead wife, acting as regent for his daughter, he'd strutted about Brindisi for the past week, annoying those in charge of the festivities with constant changes. He was an uncommonly handsome man in his late forties, golden-haired and copper-bearded.

As soon as his daughter raised her veil, it became apparent that she had inherited none of her sire's good looks. A slight, timid girl of fourteen, with lanky brown hair and a blotched complexion, Yolanda's best feature were her large hazel eyes, which she kept mostly lowered toward the curling points of her embroidered slippers. Frederick assessed his bride with one indifferent glance, kissed her hand and turned to greet her chancellor.

At the banquet that evening, Frederick, leaning across to Simon de Maugastel, launched into a long discussion about the defenses of Jerusalem, ignoring both the girl and her father. Frederick's eyes often wandered to one of the lower tables, lingering on a girl with auburn hair and milk-white skin, a cousin of Yolanda's, who tossed her head back with vivacious laughter. How could they have been so foolish as to include her in the queen's retinue? Her mere presence emphasized all of Yolanda's shortcomings. The future empress had eaten little and said less, crumbling the bread between her slender fingers.

What most puzzled Manfred was the absence of disappointment Frederick had shown. Even if one married a woman for her crown, it was surely not unreasonable to hope that she might be comely, particularly for a man of Frederick's tastes? The doors of the privy chamber opened. Manfred adjusted his cloak and went into the antechamber.

Frederick, flanked by two Saracens in gleaming breastplates, stood in the doorway. He glanced at the casket. "You've remembered my gift!"

Manfred positioned himself at the head of the Sicilian notables. As vicar general of Apulia, it was his duty to escort Frederick to the cathedral, where the archbishop of Brindisi was to celebrate the marriage jointly with the bishop of Tyre. An uncharacteristically quiet Berard fell in beside Manfred. Berard seemed glad he wasn't officiating. Berard had been against the Jerusalem marriage from the start. The objections he had raised in the council chamber had so far proved only too true. The girl, he had said, was too young to make an empress, even if fourteen was an acceptable age to be wedded. And her father, widely known to be both incompetent and ambitious, was likely to cause trouble.

Frederick, girded with Charlemagne's sword, the imperial crown on his head, was walking briskly ahead of them, his crimson cloak swirling over the flagstones. His mind was certainly not on his bride, more likely on his new kingdom. The ease with which he had slipped into the role of crusader king had surprised even Manfred.

*   *   *

FREDERICK REACHED FOR his cup and drained its contents. Greek wine of Samos, sweetened with honey. He had lost count of how many cups he had emptied. I'm getting drunk, he thought matter-of-factly, very drunk. He slumped back into his seat. The throne beside him was empty. A little crumpled white handkerchief was tucked into one corner.

Yolanda, trailing her train of cloth-of-gold, had long ago been escorted upstairs by her swaying father and giggling ladies. The nuptial bed, strewn with herbs and petals, would have been blessed by two archbishops with holy water. His new wife, her head bare of her diadem, clad only in a shift of virginal white, would be waiting for him. Starting at every sound, she'd be straining for the ribald laughter of the noblemen escorting her husband.

Husband? Wife? Thinking of those wide brown eyes staring at him like a cornered deer, he felt distaste rise in his throat like bile. Why couldn't it wait? He held his empty goblet out to be refilled. Then he beckoned to Manfred.

"Yes, Frederick?"

He pulled him down. "Go and tell Yolanda I don't wish to impose on her weariness tonight."

Manfred stared at him.

"Tell her anything you want. Tell her I'm too drunk, which is almost true." Frederick raised his cup.

Manfred opened his mouth, and closed it again. Frederick never got drunk. He always watered his wine and despised those who couldn't control their drinking. What was wrong with him tonight? How, oh Merciful Mother of God, did one tell a bride that she was being spurned on her wedding night?

Frederick scanned the hall. His mind was pleasantly numbed but still clear. The hierarchy of the feast had disintegrated. Many guests were strolling about; others had changed places. The tables were littered with overturned goblets, the white cloths stained with blood-red spills of wine, like the aftermath of a pagan sacrifice.

Berard was absorbed in conversation with Piero della Vigna, the new chancellor who had replaced Walter. Frederick had finally rid himself of the old man. In a histrionic speech, he'd publicly blamed him for failing to persuade the crusaders to wait for the Sicilian navy, thus precipitating the loss of Damietta. The new chancellor, although young, possessed as formidable a mind as Walter, but a far more adaptable temperament.

Henry of Brabant was sharing a joke with the patriarch of Jerusalem. The preceptor of the Templars and the grand master of the Hospitallers were seated at a safe distance from each other. Hermann was still in Germany, from where he would accompany Henry at Easter to the Diet in Lombardy. After six long years, Frederick thought, at last I'll see my son again.

Along the walls, on tiers draped in crimson, the wedding gifts were displayed. The torches reflected themselves in jeweled saltcellars, bowls and vases of Venetian glass and translucent agate, drinking cups rimmed in gemstones, gold and silver platters, basins and chalices. At the end of the display sat Manfred's mother, wife, and sisters. Next to them were the members of the loyal Aquinas clan. And then there was a cluster of what Manfred called "his sages": Michael Scot, the Scottish scientist and astrologer; Leonardo Fibonacci, the mathematician; Roffredo of Benevento, the jurist.

Because of the smoke, several windows had been thrown open. Outside, rain was falling in the darkness. A gust of wind swept the hall, blowing out some of the candles, and bringing with it the pristine smell of wet earth. Fresh air, that's what I need. Fresh air and a woman, a real woman . . . Frederick's eyes fell on Yolanda's cousin. As if she sensed his look, Alberia turned her auburn head and smiled at him. He got to his feet a little unsteadily and made his way through the press of people. Brushing past Alberia, he whispered to her. For an instant, she stiffened. Then, almost imperceptibly, she lowered her lashes in agreement.

As he crossed the hall, he saw Bianca Lancia watching him. Was it his imagination, or did he read disapproval in her eyes? Annoyed, Frederick parted the leather curtain and went out.

WHEN JEAN DE BRIENNE arrived the following morning at the meeting where Frederick and the princes of Outremer had gathered to discuss the coming crusade, he marched straight up to Frederick.

"How dare you!" de Brienne slammed his fist on the council table. "First you insult my daughter, and now me. The town criers proclaim you king of Jerusalem even as I speak! But I won't stand by idly. I'll report this to the Holy Father. We'll see whether you'll be allowed to steal my title!"

Silence descended on the hall. The Frankish princes stared. Yesterday, after the wedding, they had all taken the oath of allegiance to Frederick as their new king, in this same hall.

Frederick leaned back in his chair, swinging one arm over its back. "I am appalled, my lord, that you consider this a suitable place to discuss the affairs of your daughter's bedchamber. However, since you have raised the issue before these lords, I will tell you why I did not consummate the marriage." He fixed de Brienne with a steely look. "I do not violate children. You deceived me as to her maturity. She's not fit to be bedded, and I have no intention of doing so until she is."

Jean de Brienne blanched. "Yolanda is fourteen. Everyone here can attest to that," he cried. "She's had her monthly courses for almost a year, and is perfectly fit to be a wife and mother. It's your duty to consummate the marriage!"

"And who will force me to do so? You, perchance?" Frederick asked. "That child should be in a nursery, not in my bed. I prefer my women mature."

"So I have heard! There is a rumor that you spent your wedding night with my daughter's own cousin. What say you to that?" De Brienne, whose handsome face was turning crimson, glared at Frederick.

Gasps rose from around the table. Frederick smiled coldly. "My lord de Brienne, you sound like a slighted washerwoman. I find it hard to believe that even you would blacken the reputation of a virtuous young noblewoman out of spite." He laughed harshly. "And as for assuming the title of king of Jerusalem, why else would I have married a dowerless slip of a girl, queen of an impoverished kingdom half occupied by infidels?"

A murmur of agreement ran through the chamber. Heads nodded. Except for one or two staunch friends of de Brienne, the rest of the Frankish lords concurred.

Frederick rose. "Remove yourself from my court and my realm before my forbearance runs out!"

"You wouldn't dare!" De Brienne hissed. "I'm the empress's father!"

"Try me!" Frederick said.

Jean de Brienne straightened his broad shoulders. With a last venomous glance at Frederick, he turned on his heels and stalked out of the council chamber, trailing his peacock-blue mantle behind him.

BY THE END of the week, the court was ready to move north to Bari. On the eve of their departure, there was a commotion outside Frederick's privy chamber, where he was gathered with some of the Frankish lords who would be sailing back to Palestine in the morning.

Yolanda, in a hooded mulberry-colored cloak, entered the chamber. The Frankish princes rose and bowed. One by one, they kissed her hand. Taking their cue from the tense look on her face and the surprised scowl on Frederick's, they quickly took their leave.

Frederick glared at her. "And what do you think you're doing here?"

"I am your wife. It is my right to be with my husband." She drew herself up to her full height, at which she reached just below his shoulders. "I am coming to sleep in your bed tonight, since you do not seem to have any wish to come and sleep in mine."

Frederick laughed. "Are you now? And which one of your scheming uncles has put you up to this, I wonder?" He took two steps toward her. "I think, madam, it is best that we make one thing very clear. You, a dowerless girl, married me to become empress. I married you, Heaven only knows why, to add the kingdom of Jerusalem to my domains. We've both obtained what we wanted, although I fancy that you've got the better part of the bargain. As for bedding you, I will do so when and if I feel like it. In the meantime, go back to your apartments and leave me alone!"

Yolanda's naturally sallow complexion turned the color of wax. "That means that I'll never be your wife, that whenever it suits you, you can have our marriage annulled!" she whined. "That's exactly what Uncle Hugh said you were planning!"

There was such genuine distress in her eyes that Frederick felt a stab of pity. He put an arm around her. "Come now, Yolanda. I couldn't rid myself of you if I wanted to. There's too much at stake. Go back to your waiting-women and your embroidery, and be a good girl." He took her to the doorway and heaved a sigh of relief when, with a timid smile, she closed the door behind her.

BARI, MAY 1226

The hounds had just pointed a covey of partridges. The party spurred their mounts forward. Frederick, glancing about, noticed that Manfred's sister hadn't followed. He wheeled his horse around. Bianca was trying to free her hat, which had become entangled in the branches of a tree, while keeping her falcon steady on her wrist.

"Here, let me." He handed her the little green felt hat. "You should avoid low branches. They can knock you off your horse!"

She inclined her head. "Thank you, Your Grace."

"I love rescuing distressed maidens." He glanced at her bird. "That's a lovely peregrine. What's her name?"

"Guinevere, Your Grace."

"Why, I, too, once had a falcon called Guinevere, in Germany. An exceptional bird."

They heard the whooshing of wings above them. A cloud of birds was flying east. "I'm afraid they've been flushed." He laid his reins across his saddle. "Let's wait for the others." After a moment's silence he asked, "Well, little one, are you content with the bridegroom I've selected for you? I tried to find a man younger than your sister's husband, mindful of your dislike of old men!"

"Your Grace was very kind to trouble yourself. How can I not be content with what God and you ordain for me?" The dark blue eyes fixed him evenly.

Was she mocking him? Manfred's little sister, who always cheered him, was stiff and formal today, without trace of the impish fun he so liked about her. She was only two years older than Yolanda, yet in her company he always felt at ease. At times, he found himself speaking to her as an equal, a friend almost. At other times, he wondered what it would be like to kiss her.

"Ah, God." He smiled, "Do you believe that God exists, Bianca?"

Without flinching, she said, "Of course I do, everyone does!"

"But why? How can you be sure?"

"Because the Church tells us so."

"Just because someone tells you something doesn't necessarily mean that it's true, does it?"

She nodded, "Yes, I know, but the world is too beautiful for there to be no God. Do you think the devil made these?" she picked up a little bunch of spring flowers tucked into her saddle and held them up.

"No, although my friend Francis might tell you that he did, just to beguile you. But the devil certainly makes many other evil things. God and the devil must have much the same relationship with each other as I have with the pope, each trying unsuccessfully to vanquish the other."

Her eyes widened. She leaned forward, touching his arm. "My lord," she whispered, "you must never, never speak of this. People are burned for less. It's dangerous. Now that your relations with the new pope are troubled, it is even more so!"

Frederick stared at her. Then he smiled. "Why," he said, "you're flapping your wings more anxiously than Berard, who's always dreading my next misdemeanor!"

She drew back her hand. "I'm sorry if I've offended Your Grace. Please forgive me."

Frederick nodded, afraid of himself, afraid of how deeply her naïve concern had touched him. A shaft of sun had pierced the clouds, gilding her dark head. A torn leaf was entangled in the hair behind her ear. He wanted to stretch out his hand to remove the leaf. Instead, he said, "Let's find the hunters. They must have followed the quarry."

FREDERICK BEGAN TO avoid Bianca Lancia whenever he could. He scolded himself for his foolishness. And yet he couldn't get her out of his mind. Sometimes, if he caught a fleeting glimpse of her, hair demurely covered by a net of silver filigree, passing at the other end of a staircase or a courtyard, he felt a catch in his heart. Furious with himself, he'd summon a girl to his quarters and make love to her.

Mahmoud, who at times caught the direction of his master's eye, furrowed his brow. One day, as he was assisting him with his bath, the Saracen, with a familiarity born of years of intimacy, broached the subject.

Frederick was indignant. "By the beard of the Prophet, I can't bed the girl! She's Manfred's sister, and she's betrothed to one of the greatest lords in Sicily. Imagine how the scandalmongers all over the Empire would enjoy this."

Mahmoud handed him a sponge. "It will be worse if you continue to fret. No one need know about it. Once you have had her, the itch that steals your peace will leave you."

"And what about the bridegroom on the wedding night? He'll run straight to her brother and return her!"

"That is easy." Mahmoud permitted himself a smile. "There are ways and means of making a man believe he is deflowering a girl who is no longer a virgin."

Frederick raised an inquisitive eyebrow. "Really? How interesting." He leaned back against the wooden tub, lined with linen towels to protect him from splinters.

The Saracen nodded, "And most efficacious they are, too. Many a bride-groom has been hoodwinked thus."

Frederick grinned. "I have no doubt, you rascal. But I couldn't subject Mistress Lancia to such an indignity. Hand me the towel, this water's getting cold."

Mahmoud opened a large linen bath sheet. As the Saracen dried him, Frederick said, more to himself than to Mahmoud, "I couldn't do it to her, or to Manfred. Let her be wedded as soon as possible."

The Saracen gave Frederick a startled, almost pitying look. He feels sorry for me, Frederick thought. The greatest ruler in Christendom, and here I am yearning for a sixteen-year-old like a moonstruck stable hand! He saw Mahmoud shake his graying head in perplexity as he reached for the perfumed massage oil.

"*SALAAM ALEIKUM.*" THE ambassador bowed his turbaned head.

"Peace be with you," his interpreter translated.

"*Aleikum es salaam.*" And peace be with you, too, Frederick replied in Arabic.

A smile spread across the ambassador's bearded visage. "We had heard that the emperor of the Franks can speak our tongue, but did not give credence to such rumours. Now I see that Your Majesty verily speaks the language of Allah. I am Emir Fakhr-ed-Din, envoy of my lord Al-Kamil, sultan of Egypt. If Your Majesty will permit, I wish to present a few small and unworthy gifts, which my lord begs you to accept as tokens of his friendship."

Frederick inclined his head. "Any gift that comes in the name of friend-ship will be valued by me." The emir waved his hand. He stood back as two towering black Nubians stepped forward. Back and forth the two slaves went, unrolling Eastern rugs that shimmered like silk, splendid saddles, and gem-studded ewers wrought of silver, which they arranged at the foot of the dais.

The ambassador was tall, with a close-cropped black beard and sharp, aquiline features softened by well-formed lips. He wore a yellow tunic over baggy cream breeches, a golden turban with a large yellow diamond, and a curved dagger with a jeweled hilt. His dark eyes were large, without the cruel gaze often found in sharp-featured men. He was the first Muslim prince Frederick had ever met. He liked what he saw.

But what was the reason for this embassy? Tokens of friendship, from the sultan of Egypt to the emperor of the Franks, on the eve of a crusade? Frederick's regent in Palestine, Thomas of Acerra, had reported in a recent letter that the sultan of Egypt was in trouble. But just how serious was that trouble? Saladin's empire had been divided among three brothers of the Ayyubid family. One, Al-Ashraf, was sultan of Babylon, another, Al-Mu'azzam, sultan of Damascus. They had recently fallen out with the third, Al-Kamil, sultan of Egypt. Could it be, Frederick asked himself as he stroked the falcon beside him while the two black giants carried in more gifts, that Al-Kamil was desperate enough to enlist the aid of the Christian emperor against his brothers?

Of the three, it was Al-Kamil who held Jerusalem.

THEY HALTED IN an olive grove at the edge of the sea. While Frederick waited on his mount, Fakhr-ed-Din and his retinue prostrated themselves in prayer, facing east.

The emir had been at Frederick's court for almost two months. He had discovered that he had much in common with the emperor. Of an evening, they would often sit together, playing chess or debating. The emir's pas-sion were horses and falcons. He was also well versed in the arts of dialec-tic, astronomy, and poetry. Like the emperor, he enjoyed a game of chess with a worthy adversary.

The emir, rising from his prayer mat, reflected that it must have been these very characteristics that made Al-Kamil select him as his ambassador. Informed about the Frankish emperor's tastes, he had chosen the man most likely to find favour with him. The sultan, like the emperor, was himself a cultivated man of unconventional habits.

As soon as his guests had completed their devotions, Frederick gave the order to remount.

The emir glanced at Frederick. They were riding along the flat coast of Apulia, where land and sea were almost level with each other, toward Barletta. Although he had halted the whole company twice, so that his Muslim guests could say their prayers at the appointed time, the pace at which he rode was punishing. Fakhr-ed-Din, watching him for signs of fatigue, saw none.

For the last few weeks, they had been playing a game of mental chess with each other. To his surprise, Frederick hadn't shown much interest in the proposition he had made him. Was he so sure of success that he preferred armed conflict to a treaty that might deliver Jerusalem to him? The more he knew him, the less he thought this likely. Frederick, unlike his barons, was not a man to rush into battle for the sake of glory. It wasn't reluctance to be seen concluding a treaty with the sultan either, of that he was certain. Frederick had an admirable disregard for the opinion of others. Like his own master, the emperor was a skeptic. And, like Al-Kamil, Frederick, too, had fallen foul—and was likely to continue doing so—of the powers of orthodoxy in his realm.

Frederick's reluctance to commit himself to an alliance with Al-Kamil could only be mistrust. As he adjusted his aching buttocks to a different position in the saddle, the emir reflected that his caution was commendable. He was an impressive man, this Christian emperor. And unlike most awe-inspiring men, he was also likable.

"WHAT ARE YOU going to do?" Hermann von Salza asked.

Frederick passed his hand over his chin. "Nothing."

"But this could be a unique opportunity to drive a wedge into the enemy camp," Manfred said. "With the sultan of Egypt neutralized by a treaty, you can concentrate on fighting his brothers."

"Is it betrayal that's worrying you?" Berard asked.

"I'm sure the sultan's offer is genuine," Frederick said. "What worries me is time. We aren't ready to leave for another year. Much can change in that time. Should Al-Kamil defeat his brothers in the meantime, he'll no longer have any need of me and my army."

"Although I, too, was hopeful when this embassy arrived, I think you are right to reject their offer, Frederick," Hermann said. "You can't rely on Saracens. Their ways are as shifty as the sands of the desert."

"Fakhr-ed-Din leaves next week. I'll tell him that I wish to consult the princes of the Empire before committing myself to a treaty. And that I will send an ambassador to Egypt to continue negotiations with the sultan before the onset of winter."

Sensing the unasked question, Frederick smiled: "Berard will first go to the sultan's court in Cairo. After that, he will travel to Damascus, to see what the other brother might be induced to offer."

Piero della Vigna leaned forward, a frown on his high scholar's forehead. "With all respect to the archbishop, is it wise to send a churchman to the infidels? Might it not offend them and predispose them against you?"

Piero della Vigna epitomized the new type of official Frederick was encouraging. Unlike the men who had been administering chanceries in the West since the fall of Rome, Piero neither was of noble birth nor had he taken holy orders. He was the son of a bishop's steward, who by dint of his brilliant mind and hard work had managed to study at Bologna. Frederick, recognizing his abilities, had made him chancellor of Sicily. Like most men of humble birth who rise above their station, his burning ambition was fueled by a sense of inadequacy.

Frederick smiled. "The archbishop is no ordinary churchman. I have no doubt that he will carry out his mission with consummate tact."

The chancellor dropped his eyes. He toyed with the dagger at his belt.

Frederick, glancing at the hour candle, rose. It had burned past the third hour of the afternoon. "The embassy will leave before winter. In the meantime, my falconers await me. I've received two arctic Ger falcons, procured for me by the bishop of Lübeck, yesterday. I'm off to watch their first training session with live cranes."

Seeing the long faces around the table, he said. "Raise your spirits. The conquest of Jerusalem is not an easy task, and not one to be undertaken hurriedly, but in the end, we will prevail."

A WEEK LATER, Frederick himself accompanied Fakhr-ed-Din and his retinue to the harbor. Frederick embraced him and kissed him on both cheeks.

The emir said, "Farewell, my lord. May Allah grant that we meet again, and as friends."

Frederick raised his hand in a last farewell to Fakhr-ed-Din, who waved back from the deck. The galley slowly turned and made its way out into the open sea.

THE MINSTRELS STRUCK up a merry dance tune. In the great hall of Bari's newly completed castle feet began to tap. Soon, a number of young people formed a large circle.

Frederick hadn't seen Bianca for several months while he had been away. She's grown even lovelier, he thought as his eyes followed her among the dancers. Her future husband was a lucky man. She had spirit and understanding far beyond her years, in fact beyond that of most women.

As she swirled past the dais, Bianca glanced up. He inclined his head and smiled. Her heart began to pound. She felt the color rise in her cheeks. The tempo of the dance increased. She closed her eyes, letting the music carry her, not wanting to look up again. Why had he been avoiding her? He couldn't possibly know her secret. She would take it with her to her marriage bed and to her grave. At the thought of the man she had to wed, she felt her chest tighten. How often would she come to court once she was married, how often would she still be able to see him?

Tonight, as so often before, Yolanda wasn't present. It was said that after more than six months, he still hadn't taken her to his bed. The empress was rarely seen, whether of her own volition or because he kept her sequestered in her quarters no one knew, although he took her with him whenever the court moved, perhaps, as some said, afraid that her father would abduct her to get his kingdom back. He had finally sent that redheaded Alberia home to her husband. To deposit a cuckoo's egg in the marital nest, it was bruited. Perhaps . . .

A woman screamed, "Fire!" Within seconds the hall was in chaos. Benches and tables were overturned. People shouted, pushing and shoving, frantic to escape the flames. Bianca found herself cut off, pressed against a wall by a surging stampede of people. The fire swept across the floor rushes, fanned by a breeze from the open windows. The tapestries on the walls were burning now, too, flames devouring stags and knights. She was trapped by a sea of burning rushes. Everyone was gone. Terrified, she looked around for a way out. The windows were too far away. She screamed.

Smoke enveloped her, making her cough. She could hardly breathe. She raised her skirt and pressed it over her nose. With the tip of her shoe she kicked the rushes around her away, trying to make a clearing for herself.

A figure in a blue cloak appeared in the doorway, one end of his cloak pressed over his nose and mouth. He glanced at her and disappeared. The figure in blue reappeared with another man. Both carried wet cloaks in their hands. They began to beat a path toward her. Tapestries were crashing off the walls, falling to the ground in flaming heaps. The heat was unbearable. Bianca coughed, gasping for air. The smoke stung her eyes. The man in the blue cloak reached her. Glancing at the ceiling, he yelled a warning to his companion, slung her over his shoulder, and ran toward the door. An instant later the great bronze luster on the ceiling came crashing down.

Outside, in the torchlight, men were running about like ants, filling buckets on ropes with water or sand, making barriers to stop the fire from spreading to the rest of the castle. Her rescuer put her down and whipped the cloak off his head. "Now I know what hell must be like." In his blackened face, streaked with sweat, his teeth gleamed white as he smiled down at her. Behind him, Mahmoud, too, divested himself of his cover.

Bianca stared at him. "Your Grace, is it you?" she stammered. She began to cry.

Frederick put his arms around her. He could feel the sobs racking her. "Bianca, Bianchina, don't cry," he whispered into her hair, holding her, stroking her back.

Gradually, as she felt the warmth of his body, her sobs stopped. She raised her face, eyes brimming with tears. Then she smiled. Their lips met halfway, in a kiss that made them forget all else.

Thus entwined, they stood in the darkness on the ramparts above the sea, outlined against the orange glare of the flames devouring the castle. Above them, the dark canopy of heaven was strewn with stars.

THE ACRID SMELL of smoke hung in the night air. The fire that had gutted the whole upper floor of the castle's eastern wing had finally been put out. An eerie stillness filled the castle. Everyone, courtiers and grooms alike, lay asleep, exhausted. Soon the stars would begin to pale.

Frederick stretched out his hand. He stroked her cheek. Her unbound hair spilled over her shoulders and onto the sheet. He had brought her here after the fire was under control. The cushions from the divan still lay where they had fallen upon the floor. Swept away by a torrent of longing, they had tumbled to the floor and sated their need there before seeking refuge in the great bed. The night had passed like a dream, a dream pre-ordained by fate.

Bianca turned her head and looked at him. In the soft light of the guttering candles there was a feverish brilliance in her eyes that made his heart beat faster.

"I love you," she whispered. "I love you with all my heart. I don't care if I've committed a mortal sin. I've loved you since the first time I saw you, as a child. You rode into our courtyard on a mud-covered horse."

Looking at the way she upheld her chin, like a warrior throwing down a gauntlet, he was torn between laughter and bliss. She means it, he thought, she means every word of it. He put his arms around her and kissed the top of her head. Her hair, too, smelled of smoke. The smell of calamity, he thought, of calamity and of happiness.

"You're right. I'd forgotten it, but my horse too, was splattered in mud that day. You told me I was dirty."

He took her hand. One by one, he kissed the tip of each finger. He turned her hand over and began to kiss the inside of her palm. Slowly he removed the upper part of the sheet. Bending his head, he whispered between her breasts, "I want to see you, every beautiful part of you. I want to taste you, feel you, pleasure you."

He sank into her with the utmost gentleness, afraid to hurt her again. He was filled with a profound sense of happiness, and patience, endless patience. He buried his face in the softness of her hair. He could hear the surf beating against the rocks. She's like the sea, he thought, soft and yielding and all-engulfing, like the sea.

IN THE FIRST gray light of dawn Frederick gently shook the sleeping form in his arms. "Bianchina, it's late. You must go back quickly with Peppa." The old nurse had spent the night in the anteroom where Frederick had ordered her to wait.

Bianca sat up, tousled hair tumbling about her, eyes dim with sleep. "Must I?" she asked dreamily.

"Yes, my love, for your sake and that of your family." He brushed a strand of hair from her face. Softly, in wonder almost, he said, "Bianca, you know that I think I love you?"

She raised her eyes. "I know," she said.

BARI, JUNE 1227

Frederick was a different man. He walked the passages of Bari's castle whistling snatches of Sicilian songs, showing an affability not often seen any more since Constance's death. Although out of concern for Bianca, he behaved with uncharacteristic discretion, it was not long before the court discovered the cause of his newfound cheerfulness.

Gossip about the lovers began to circulate. When the empress discovered this new insult to her dignity, she made a fearful scene during a hunt, after which Frederick sent her under guard to the castle of Terracina, which, he announced, would henceforth be reserved for her and her court.

When Manfred, too, at last discovered the truth, he threatened to confine his sister in a nunnery. After much persuasion, Manfred bowed to the inevitable. His only consolation, he said, was that at least this had been spared their mother, who had died after a short illness on All Saints' Day the previous year.

Rumor of the empress's sequestration soon reached the papal curia in Rome. The new pope lost no time in putting it to good use.

FREDERICK AND BERARD walked along the ramparts in the fading light of late afternoon. Behind them, the setting sun cast a last glow onto the darkening waters.

Berard said, "You must stem these slanders, Frederick, the more so because there is truth in them."

Frederick frowned. His relations with the papacy were at an all-time low. Honorius had died unexpectedly in March. His successor, Gregory IX, was a man of Innocent's mold, a fanatical proponent of papal supremacy. Frederick's hopes of seeing his son Henry had been dashed. The Diet of Cremona never took place. The Lombard cities, banded into a new defensive league, refused Henry and the German princes passage over the Brenner Pass, unless Frederick agreed to their demands for more autonomy. The new pope, in an attempt to strengthen the papacy, supported the Lombards. In a series of letters to the bishops of Europe, to be read from the pulpits of every cathedral, Gregory attacked Frederick's morals, citing his treatment of the empress, as well as his Muslim sympathies. Gregory must be out of his mind to heap such invective on him just before his departure on crusade . . .

Berard's mission to the East last winter had proven fruitless. Al-Kamil had by then lost Jerusalem to his brother. Although Berard had been graciously received by Al-Kamil in Cairo, his brother in Damascus had sneered that he, unlike his brother, was not a woman who groveled at the feet of Christians. Frederick's crusaders were due to assemble in Brindisi next month. The date for the departure was set for August 15, the feast of the Assumption.

The news from Germany was also worrying. There were rumblings of discontent over Henry, who had come of age last year. Conrad of Scharfenburg, the chancellor, had been assassinated the previous year. The murderer had never been found. The new chancellor complained that Henry countermanded his orders, even if they came from Frederick himself. He sighed.

Perhaps it was just the way young men, like young falcons, tested their courage. . . . He, too, had resented being told what to do at that age, even by Berard. In fact, he still did, at times.

He glanced fondly at the archbishop. Berard was still in excellent health, his appetite for life undiminished. His superb teeth and his cheer remained intact. Only his thinning hair and grizzled beard showed signs of his age.

"You're right, Berard." Frederick said finally. "My lady wife will have to be dusted off and paraded, with a prominent belly if possible. We shall present an enchanting tableau of domestic felicity, an example to the rest of Christendom."

Berard came to a halt. He glared at Frederick. "You married her of your own volition. Marriage, whether you like it or not, is a sacrament. And Yolanda, whatever her shortcomings, is a girl of ancient lineage whom you have used ignobly."

Frederick glared at him. "She, too, married me for the sake of a title. We've both got our share of the bargain, so why can't she just leave me alone? Why must that nuisance of her father stir up the pope against me? His daughter is empress, she lacks for nothing, and I'm about to reconquer her realm for her while she amuses herself with her birdbrained ladies who are as silly as she is!"

"Because, Frederick, in your foolishness, you have provided them with a perfect weapon in the person of Bianca Lancia! Everyone knows about her. The whole of Christendom has heard about the intimate dinners where only a blind Saracen harpist attends you."

Frederick's face clouded. "I won't hide her more than I already do! If I could, I'd make her my empress!"

THE AUGUST SUN burned down into the marble courtyard of Melfi Castle. Although the court had moved to Melfi at the beginning of June, when the heat of the Apulian plain began to rise, this summer the old Norman hill town seemed as scorched and airless as the lowlands.

Men shifted from one foot to the other. Some had been standing for hours, waiting to present their cases. The shady arcades that surrounded the courtyard were crowded with noblemen, accompanied by their bailiffs or stewards carrying armfuls of scrolls in support of their claims.

Frederick, under a fringed cloth of estate, seemed oblivious to the heat. He had been here since early morning. His justice was open to all, the last resort of those who felt themselves wronged in a feudal court or by the royal justiciaries who administered the law in Sicily.

Bianca leaned her cheek against the cool marble pillar beside her. She watched him listen to an old serf in a ragged tunic. Frederick was leaning forward in an effort to understand the toothless old man. He asked a few short questions. Then he called for the old man's witnesses, after which he heard the steward of the serf's lord. The steward was accused of raping the old man's daughter and perjuring himself in the manor court. The serf was demanding three cows in compensation for his daughter's maidenhead.

Frederick had explained to her that dispensing justice equally to all his subjects was a king's foremost duty. "Where there is peace and justice, prosperity will follow by itself," he had said. She'd never given it a thought before, but now, watching him listen to this poor old peasant as patiently as he had dealt with the bejeweled lord before him, she began to understand what he meant. Her heart overflowed with pride.

Like a treasure, Bianca hugged to herself the knowledge of their love. It was not often that she was able to watch him as now, drinking in his appearance unobserved, to be stored in her mind for those endless days and weeks when he was gone or too occupied with affairs of state to see her. Sometimes a trusted messenger would bring her a short letter, penned in a distant castle in his tall, nervous writing. In rare moments of leisure he wrote poems for her, not in the customary Latin but in Italian, a new idea of his that his courtiers already imitated.

In between there were hasty embraces, furtive hours of love snatched from his relentless schedule. A kiss at dawn, a heavy veil, and she would be back in her own cold bed, filled with the essence of his body. And already the longing to be with him would be gnawing at her like a bittersweet ache. Alone in the curtained darkness of her bed, she'd go over every moment of the night before, every word and every gesture, each instance to be savored separately, like the countless seeds of a pomegranate . . .

Peppa pulled her sleeve. All heads turned toward the open gate. A tall, bearded stranger stood in its shadow. Behind him clustered others, their helmets in the crooks of their arms. The travel-stained stranger made his way through the crowd. Frederick leaped to his feet. He embraced the man, who

towered above him and everyone else in the courtyard. He must be a German, Bianca thought, narrowing her eyes against the glare. His hair glowed
like copper in the sun, just like Frederick's. He must be Frederick's cousin,
Lewis of Thuringia, who was to be joint leader of the crusade. Frederick had
told her that Hermann von Salza, the landgrave and nearly a thousand German knights, his contribution to the crusade, were about to arrive in Melfi.

They were here! Anguish constricted her throat. Thousands of others
would be arriving soon from all over Europe to gather in Brindisi, the port
of embarkation. The crusade had begun.

CRUSADERS SWARMED OVER the mountains, down the pilgrim roads and
along the coastal plains of Apulia toward Brindisi. In vast encampments
outside the city they waited in the merciless heat of August for embarkation to the Holy Land, which Frederick was providing free of charge.

The port was filled with vessels of every size and description, hired from
Venice and Genoa for the crossing, as well as the ships of the new Sicilian
navy. Yolanda had been escorted from Melfi to Otranto, on the tip of Italy,
there to await his return. Not only had she been provided with a garrison
of handpicked men, but a squadron of galleys was anchored beneath the
great seawalls of Otranto.

Frederick's concern was not so much for his wife as for the child she
carried. Finally, after seventeen years, he was going to have another heir!
He had been unable to contain his excitement when a shyly smiling
Yolanda confided that she was in the early stages of pregnancy. Michael
Scot, Frederick's physician, examined her urine, the lines of her palms, and
her eyeballs and pronounced that she was indeed with child. After consulting the stars, the famed astrologer and physician from Scotland confirmed
that she carried a son. In his gratitude, Frederick clasped the bewildered
Yolanda to him. She wasn't much to look at, and their lovemaking was a
grim business, but, as he had remarked to Master Scot, like a fallow field
she had proved very fertile, conceiving on their first night together.

Piero della Vigna, in the chancery, composed a triumphant letter advising Pope Gregory in Rome of this happy circumstance. Similar letters
were dispatched to the imperial vicars general, to Germany, and to the
Holy Land, informing the barons there, who had all been subjected to

Jean de Brienne's invective against the emperor, that their queen was with child.

That, alas, had been the only good news of this unbearably hot summer, Frederick thought as he passed a hand over his aching forehead. The writing of the dispatch he was trying to read was blurring before his eyes. He felt tired, immensely tired. No wonder his head felt as if it were about to spring apart. The numbers of crusaders had far exceeded everyone's expectations. This tatterdemalion crowd was hard to discipline. Each day, provided the wind held, different contingents embarked under their leaders, but embarkation was slow and cumbersome. There were constant arguments among crusaders of different rank. Lords and knights expected to be given preference. There weren't enough vessels to transport the great number of horses. Fights erupted between the different nationalities. Food was running short. Worst of all, a fever had broken out in the fly-infested encampments. Hundreds had died already. Many had fled, carrying the contagion to the surrounding villages.

Frederick and his immediate entourage had taken refuge on the little island of Sant'Andrea, at the other end of the port, to escape the disease. The thick walls of the old Byzantine watchtower where they had taken up makeshift quarters should have preserved the coolness, but instead seemed to be giving off the accumulated rays of the sun. Even now, at dusk, the heavy air didn't stir. The vessels that should have been loaded today lay becalmed in the port, their sails hanging limp and listless. When the wind finally rose again, at this time of year it would be the hot sirocco from Africa, which made men short-tempered and beasts of burden intractable.

The creaking door of what had been the tower's armory opened. Frederick's cousin entered. Lewis of Thuringia sat down heavily on a chest bench. He stretched his pillarlike legs on the rough gray flagstones and wiped his face. "The grain has arrived. It's been stored under guard."

Frederick nodded. "Good." He sat back and scrutinized his cousin. "Lewis, you're as red as a boiled crab. You must treat our Sicilian sun with more respect."

"The sun wouldn't be too bad on its own, but together with the throbbing in my head, I do feel like a boiled crab!" Lewis fanned himself with

a parchment from the table. His reddish hair was wet and dark, plastered
to his scalp.

"Your head's aching, too?" Frederick rose and walked around the table.
He laid a hand on the landgrave's forehead. Lewis was burning with
fever.

AFTER MASTER SCOT had examined them both and left Frederick's
bedchamber to prepare the tincture and cordials he had prescribed, ordering Frederick to remain in bed and the landgrave to take to his straight-
away, Lewis asked: "What are you going to do?" He was sitting slumped
against Frederick's bedpost, holding a wet cloth to his head.

"Wait for a day or two. If I don't get worse, I'll leave as planned. When
you've recovered, you'll follow with your men."

"But Frederick, you heard Master Scot. It takes several weeks for this
fever to run its course. That is, if it doesn't kill you."

"Lewis, I have no option. I've deposited fifty thousand gold bezants as
surety for Gregory. And I have taken an oath agreeing to my own excommunication if I don't leave on the appointed date."

The landgrave shook his head. "You're being absurd, Frederick. I know
the pope is no friend of yours, but not even Gregory could find fault with
you for postponing your departure under such circumstances."

"You don't understand, Lewis," Frederick sat up so abruptly that the
wet cloth on his head fell off. "Gregory's aim is to discredit me." The effort of talking was making Frederick's head throb even more, yet he
needed to speak. "He'll clutch at any pretext. He fears that I'll deprive the
Church of her temporal power. You only need to read his fulminations
against my university in Naples and the lay administrators it is producing.
This is all about power, Lewis, not faith. Like Innocent, Gregory believes
that the papacy should rule Christendom—"

"Frederick! What in Blessed Mary's name . . ." At the sound of Berard's
voice, Frederick turned his head. "The good doctor is treating us like
women in childbed!"

Berard, Hermann, and Manfred crowded around the bed. Their faces
were so gloomy that Frederick laughed: "Don't look like that. I'm not dead

yet. The thought of the pleasure my death would give old Gregory is enough to keep me alive!"

"You're not still thinking of leaving at the end of the week, are you?" Hermann asked, alarmed.

"Unless I can't stand on my feet, I'll sail as planned!"

BY THE END of the week Frederick felt somewhat better. With a still aching head he prepared to board the imperial galley. The landgrave, who despite his fever had insisted on sailing, too, refused to be carried in a litter and was walking up the gangplank, leaning on Michael Scot and one of his knights. The ship had been blessed and sprinkled with holy water. It was ready to sail. Those who had accompanied them to the port took their leave.

The last one to do so was Manfred. Frederick had appointed him regent during his absence. There were tears in Manfred's eyes. "May God grant you success," he said, "and bring you back safely."

Frederick kissed him on both cheeks. He gripped his shoulders. "I leave my kingdom and my heart in your hands. Take good care of both, and send me frequent tidings." He felt a sharp pain as he looked into Manfred's dark blue eyes, those same eyes. Would he ever see her again?

"MY LORD, A word with you, please." Michael Scot, who was as tall and thin as a reed, stooped in the doorway of Frederick's cabin. He entered, avoiding the lantern that swung to and fro from the low ceiling.

Frederick raised his aching head from the bolster. He felt giddy. "Yes, what is it?" He, too, had been running a fever again since last night.

The physician shook his head. "It's the landgrave. I've just examined him. His chest is full of the red spots that indicate the disease has progressed to its most dangerous stage. It is my opinion," he said, "that your cousin is near death. I have called for his chaplain."

"It can't be. He was better yesterday. He's as strong as a bear. I'll go and see him." Frederick swung his legs over the edge of his berth. His chest glistened with sweat. "Mahmoud, my tunic." He stood up unsteadily to allow the Saracen to slip the garment over his head. Suddenly he clutched his belly with one hand and the cabin wall with the other. "Quick, the privy chair," he gasped. The page ran to fetch it while Mahmoud and Michael supported him. Before the boy could drag the pierced chair across the floor, a flood of brown liquid ran down Frederick's legs. A foul smell filled the airless cabin.

"I think, Master Scot," Frederick said when the spasm had passed, "the landgrave may have company on his way to purgatory." Shaking, he sank onto the berth.

THE FOLLOWING MORNING, the twelve galleys of the imperial squadron were instructed to sail back to Sicily, just two days after leaving Brindisi. Aided by good winds, with every man straining at the oars, they put into the harbour of Otranto as dusk was falling. Within hours, every church in the city was ringing its bells, calling the citizens to pray for the lives of the emperor and his cousin.

"*Ave Maria, gratia plena . . . benedicta tu in mulieribus et benedictus fructus ventris tui . . . Ora pro nobis pecatoribus nunc et in hora mortis nostrae . . .*" Oh Holy Mother of God, grant me his life. I vow to forgive all his sins against me. Never again will I think of him in anger, if you, oh queen of Heaven, will save his life. I beseech you, for the sake of the child within me and my beleaguered kingdom, do not let him die . . .

Yolanda's head was bent. Over and over again she recited the prayer to the Virgin, twisting her rosary. Kneeling in the cool semidarkness of the chapel, she had lost all sense of time. Outside, the bells continued to ring, but something was different. Her lips stopped moving. She raised her head and listened. The pealing had changed from the urgency of a summons to a deep, somber tolling.

With a hasty genuflection toward the altar, she gathered her skirts and ran out into the castle's courtyard. Outside all was confusion. Men ran to and fro. Flying up the stairs toward the imperial apartments, she caught sight of Gerold of Lausanne, the patriarch of Jerusalem. He was wearing ecclesiastical vestments. Behind him two acolytes carried a gilt casket such as were used for administering the last rites.

"My lord Gerold!" she cried. The elderly patriarch halted. He came toward her.

Yolanda's eyes widened. In a whisper, she asked: "Is it . . . is it the emperor?"

Gerold shook his head. "No, Your Grace," he replied. "But his cousin, the landgrave of Thuringia, is no more."

Yolanda felt tears of relief sting her eyes. He was still alive! Since she was with child, he had sent her gifts, and inquired after her health. Once she gave him the son he so wanted, he might change, there'd be other children . . . She must go to him, even if he still doted on that whore and her upstart brother.

She touched the patriarch's gold-embroidered cope. "I want to see my husband. Please attend me."

THE CANDLELIT CHAMBER was filled with people. Despite the heat, the shutters were closed, to safeguard the patient from the sea air. Berard, Hermann, and the Duke of Limburg clustered around the bed. As Yolanda entered, followed by the patriarch, they bowed and made way for her slight figure.

Frederick's eyes were closed. His face was bathed in perspiration. "Storks, the storks are all leaving . . ." He began thrashing about with his arms. "Mustn't fly away, halt them, halt them . . . bad luck, the end . . ."

Berard cast a worried look at Michael Scot, who threw up his hands. Frederick had been delirious since yesterday. Nothing had been able to bring him back to consciousness. Like the landgrave, he was deteriorating rapidly.

Yolanda looked down at the figure flailing about in the large bed. He didn't look at all like the emperor, or the husband who had treated her so cruelly. He just looked sweaty and terribly sick. Was it possible that his life was to end now, like this? Compassion filled her. She bent down, whispering his name. Perhaps she could rouse him from whatever was tormenting him. His eyes remained shut. He groaned. His fists opened and closed in unconscious rage. Again, a little louder, she repeated, "Frederick, Frederick, it is I."

Frederick's eyelids twitched. He opened bloodshot eyes and looked at her, blinking, slowly focusing. Then he smiled, that marvelous smile that could melt the heart of a stone. He's recognized me, Yolanda thought, filled with sudden joy.

"Bianca," he whispered hoarsely, "Bianchina, you're here." He closed his eyes. There was a beatific look on his face now.

Yolanda drew back as if she had been stung. The blood drained from her face. With eyes lowered in burning shame, she walked out of the chamber.

IN THE EARLY hours of the morning, Berard awoke with a start in the chair in which he had passed the night. He reached out to touch Frederick. His forehead felt cool. He was sleeping peacefully. The fever had broken. Berard closed his eyes. He buried his face in his hands. "Thank you, thank you, oh Lord," he whispered.

The chamber was in silence, except for the wheezing breath of Master Scot who dozed on a truckle bed, and the occasional stirring of Mahmoud who slept on the floor. In a corner, a dim oil light burned on a chest. Through the chinks in the shutters appeared the first glimmers of light, the dawn of a new day.

NAPLES, NOVEMBER 1227

The gulf of Naples lay calm and blue in the sun of a winter morning. During the night it had rained, and now the air seemed clearer, the outline of islands and mountains sharper. The large fortified villa, put at Frederick's disposal by the Frangipani family, stood above a rocky promontory overlooking the sea at Pozzuoli.

Frederick pulled his fur rug around his neck. Against his physician's advice he insisted on being brought to this little terrace below the villa every day if the weather was clement. In the silence of the terraced gardens, bare now of flowers, he would lie on a truckle bed in the dappled shade of a gnarled pomegranate and look at the sea.

Twice a day his Saracen attendants carried him in a litter down to the thermal springs that had made Pozzuoli famous since Roman times. A special area had been cleared for him, away from the throngs of the sick and crippled that flocked to the baths even in winter. Sitting in a bathing chair, he was immersed in the hot bubbling water that rose from the earth amid clouds of sulfurous steam.

Back at the villa, under the stern eye of Michael Scot, he was made to drink beakers of the foul-tasting water several times a day. Its effects were miraculous. Within days of disembarking from Otranto the red spots that covered his chest and abdomen disappeared. His bowels stopped bleeding. Gulping down the sulfurous liquid one day, he remarked to the archbishop of Reggio that it must be like supping with the devil. The archbishop hadn't been amused. Although he was still so weak that he couldn't stand unaided, he was now able to eat some tasteless barley gruel, the only nourishment his body didn't reject.

Frederick took his eyes off the sea and resumed writing. A board across his knees served as a writing table. A bundle of sharpened quills and an inkhorn were balanced on the fox skins. The muse of poetry seemed to favor him here; perhaps because Virgil had once lived in Naples. He wrote for a while, making frequent erasures, then stopped and read the lines aloud to get a feel for their sound:

> *Secondo mia credenza*
> *non e donna che sia*
> *alta, si bella, pare.*
> *ne c'agia insegnamento*
> *'nver voi, donna sovrana.*
> *La vostra ciera umana*
> *mi da conforto e facemi alegrare;*
> *s'eo pregiare—vi posso, donna mia,*
> *piu conto me ne tengo tuttavia.*

He ran his hand over the feathery edge of the quill. ". . . unmatched in beauty, courtesy or worth . . . Your lovely face gives me comfort and cheer . . . Unworthy as I am, with each passing day, I value you more, O lady mine . . ."

It was passable, for a man whose main occupation was ruling. He imagined Bianca reading it in the light of a window or loggia in Bari, perhaps biting her lip, as she often did when concentrating. She *would* give him comfort and cheer, if only she were here. Then why didn't he send for her? Because he wanted to shield Bianca, or poor Yolanda, or both?

Yolanda's child would be born in April or May. Michael assured him it would be a son. He remembered the day he had explained to Bianca that he must consummate his marriage; that the act of love could be reduced to a mechanical coupling, that men and women, too, did so for practical reasons. Her eyes had remained steady. She didn't cry. At the end, she had said in a quiet voice: "I see. You, too, have done so before, I suppose?"

He yearned for her, her smile, the feel of her cheek against his. Yet he drowned his longing in ink. Bianca liked his vernacular poems—she'd once told him that they represented his real voice, the voice of the man, not the emperor. How right she was. Bianca, despite her youth, had an uncanny understanding of his different selves, those hidden layers of his soul he bared to no one.

What, he wondered, would Virgil have made of his writing in Italian? He would probably have approved. After all, Latin had been the vernacular of Virgil's day, as Italian was today's. The rigidity of Latin meters didn't lend itself to the light poetry he enjoyed writing. He laid the quill down, suddenly tired, and looked down at Pozzuoli.

It was now an insignificant little town, but in Roman times Pozzuoli and the neighboring village of Baia had been one of the most coveted strips of land in the Empire. Men who ruled entire provinces vied with each other for a single acre here. Marius, Sulla, Pompey, Julius Caesar, Nero, Cicero, and Lucullus all owned summer villas here. Frederick smiled to himself, imagining poached flamingo tongues being served to the greatest men in Rome, reclining on gilt couches at a dinner party in Lucullus' villa.

Riders came up the narrow road to the villa. He recognized the Duke of Spoleto's standard. The sentries let them pass. He sank back into the pillows. Had this embassy fared better than the first?

In Otranto, Hermann had pleaded with him to let him go to Rome and explain the circumstances to the pope. Frederick decided that he couldn't spare Hermann. The facts, after all, spoke for themselves. He appointed the Duke of Limburg temporary leader of the crusade, with Hermann as his deputy, and ordered them to sail immediately and begin preparing the defenses in Palestine. He'd follow with the remainder of the army in the spring.

A delegation headed by Piero della Vigna was dispatched to Rome. Gregory refused to receive them, thundering that this was merely the emperor's latest ruse to avoid fulfilling his crusading vow. By then, the whole of Rome knew about Frederick's grave illness. It was said that the pope's intransigence astounded even his cardinals. Frederick had sent a second embassy made up of the Duke of Spoleto, the archbishop of Reggio Calabria, and Berard.

Boots crunched on the gravel path that led down from the villa.

"My lord," Rainald of Spoleto bowed, "I trust you are much improved."

The white-bearded archbishop of Reggio looked tired as he made his reverence. Berard stood behind the others. Frederick sought his eyes. What he read in them didn't bode well.

"Well, my lords," Frederick said into the silence, "you're like tongue-tied maidens! What did Gregory say?"

"Your Grace, he refused to see us, too," the duke of Spoleto looked at his feet. "We were received by Cardinal Orsini. He told us that as we represented a traitor to the cause of Christ, the Holy Father couldn't receive us."

The Archbishop of Reggio, twirling the cross on his chest, added, "The following day, the pope elevated three Lombard bishops to the rank of cardinal."

Frederick looked at Berard. "Come, old friend. Out with the truth. It won't kill me, I promise."

"Frederick, my son . . ."

It *really* was bad news. Whenever Berard sought refuge in the language of the pulpit, he bore unwelcome tidings. Frederick asked, "Well, what is it? Does he want another five thousand ounces of gold?"

"Frederick," Berard looked at him, "the day after the consistory, Gregory excommunicated you."

The Duke of Spoleto studied his dusty boots while the archbishop of Reggio continued to twist his gold chain. Only Berard looked at Frederick.

"I see." He rubbed his chin. This didn't worry him unduly. The excommunication of tardy crusaders was fairly common. He was more concerned with what Gregory hoped to gain by his severity. "He's entitled to do so." He paused, "even if it's rather vindictive under the circumstances. But then Gregory is a vindictive old trout. Well, what humiliating penance does he demand? Bread and water, a hair shirt, or a pilgrimage?"

Berard sat down on the end of the wicker couch, which sagged alarmingly. He laid a hand on Frederick's arm. "I don't think I've made myself clear, Frederick," he said. "Gregory refuses to accept any penance whatsoever."

"That's absurd." Frederick sat bolt upright. "That would mean that I won't be able to resume the crusade in the spring. He can't be serious!"

Berard took a deep breath. "That's precisely what Gregory intends. He wants to thwart your crusade and discredit you. He's already issued an encyclical in which he lays the blame on you for every setback suffered by the crusaders. He even blames you for your cousin's death. He accuses you of having brought on the epidemic by not providing sufficient food."

"What! I never undertook to feed anyone." Frederick exploded. "In fact, I bought extra grain and distributed it free of charge to those inept fools who hadn't organized their supplies properly."

Berard nodded. "We know that, but others don't. His real aim is to destroy you, unless you accept the papacy's full overlordship over Sicily. Among other trumped-up charges, Gregory charges you with despoiling the Sicilian Church of her tithes. But read it for yourself. Here's a copy of the encyclical." Berard pulled a piece of parchment out of his cloak pocket.

As he read, Frederick's frown grew deeper and deeper. When he had finished, he threw the scroll across the terrace. He narrowed his eyes. "We'll see who destroys whom in this dangerous game that this upstart priest is playing with me! The first thing I'll do is warn the rulers of Europe that this wolf in sheep's clothing on the throne of Saint Peter is threatening the institution of kingship. And in the spring, I'll conquer Jerusalem, pope or no pope!"

"But as an excommunicate you can't lead a crusade!" the duke exclaimed. "No one will dare follow you. You must find a way to accommodate the pope."

Frederick glared at him. "We'll see about that. Naturally I prefer the matter to be settled. But if Gregory continues in his scheming, I'll depart on crusade regardless. God set me on my throne, not the pope. I don't need his permission!"

He flung his rug aside. "Help me up. I am going to dictate letters. The first is going to Henry of England. He, more than any other, has cause to be weary of the pope!"

Leaning on Berard and the duke, Frederick dragged himself up the path to the villa.

FOGGIA, APULIA, MAY 1228

All throughout the winter and spring of the following year, the battle between the Pope and Frederick raged on. With a public forbearance that even Berard hadn't thought him capable of, Frederick reiterated his acceptance of the Pope's right to excommunicate him, urging Gregory to state the penalty he would accept in order to lift his ban. He repeated his willingness to depart on crusade at the end of spring, knowing full well that that was just what Gregory wished to avoid at all costs.

Copies of Frederick's conciliatory letters to the pope were sent to the German and Italian princes and prelates, to the senate of Rome, and to the kings of Europe. In his private letters to Louis of France and Henry of England, however, Frederick dropped all pretense, unmasking the pope's true aim, which was to obtain total suzerainty over Sicily. If the papacy's rampant ambitions were not curbed, he warned, they would be the next victims of its territorial aims. The popes, he said, had abandoned Christ's teachings and reveled in the power, wealth, and usury they outwardly condemned.

Meanwhile, Frederick proceeded with preparations for his departure. When Gregory began to suspect that Frederick might actually go on crusade without his permission, he forbade the Sicilian Church to pay its crusading tithes. Despite his outrage, Frederick couldn't help being amused by the irony of this ludicrous action: here was the pope, trying to prevent the emperor from leading a crusade to recover the holy places for Christendom! The imperial chancery made sure that the news of this latest act of papal spite was swiftly spread across Europe.

Public sentiment was on Frederick's side. When Gregory attempted to preach a sermon against the emperor on Easter day in Saint Peter's, he was chased out of the Basilica by the citizens of Rome. Fearing for his life, the pope fled to Viterbo. Germany, too, remained loyal to the emperor. Frederick's generosity to the German ecclesiastical princes during his years in Germany had not been misplaced: to a man, they stood by him.

At the beginning of May, Yolanda gave birth to a son in the half-completed winter palace at Foggia. The future king of Sicily and Jerusalem was named Conrad. Frederick was so overjoyed that he danced up and down Yolanda's lying-in chamber with his new son cradled in his arms. The sight brought a weak smile to the bloodless lips of his wife, whose confinement had been long and arduous. Frederick ordered a week of festivities, dancing, and jousting, with free wine and meat distributed in the city. On the fifth day, Yolanda died of puerperal fever. She was barely sixteen.

After assisting at her funeral in the cathedral of Andria, Frederick retired to his apartments. He refused to see anyone.

FREDERICK WAS SITTING at a parchment-littered desk, working, when there was a soft knock at the door. He ignored it. The knock was repeated, this time with more insistence.

"Go away!" he growled. He had given orders to let no one in. Who in the devil's name . . .

The door opened. Bianca entered. She was dressed in black, a black veil on her dark hair. The harsh color made her skin look even paler than it was. She looked drawn. In her arms she carried a swaddled baby.

Frederick stared at her. "What are you doing here, and what—"

"I've brought you your son. He needs you, Frederick, he has no one else but you." She held the child out to him.

Frederick remained seated. He looked at the sleeping infant but didn't take him from her. Like his mother, Conrad had brown hair.

Bianca sat down on the bench opposite him, careful not to disturb the child in her arms. She glanced from the flagon of wine to the half-empty cup and the week-old stubble on Frederick's chin. She took a deep breath. Someone had to jolt him out of his gloom. No one else seemed to have the courage.

"Frederick," she said, "to wed at a tender age for reasons of state is the lot of most women of royal birth. And death from childbirth is common among women of all ages. Stop tormenting yourself. No one is to blame for her death. It is God's will. And if you are responsible for Yolanda's unhappiness while she lived, then so am I."

Frederick stared at her. The words had been spoken gently, but with unmistakable firmness. He had noticed before that she possessed a quiet authority obeyed by dogs, children and servants.

After a moment he sighed. "You are right. I've always thought that you are wise beyond your years, wiser by far than I am."

The child awoke with a gurgle. Bianca ran her finger over its cheek, her face softening into a smile.

If only, he thought, it were her child. He stretched out his arms: "Give me my son, beloved."

BRINDISI, JUNE 1228

On a windy morning in June, almost exactly thirteen years after the fateful day in Aachen when he had vowed to take the cross, Frederick departed from Brindisi for the second time.

Staring at the choppy waters of the Adriatic, Frederick thought how different this second departure was from the first. Then, he had been the blessed son of the Church. Now, he was the pope's archenemy, the first excommunicated crusader in history. For the second time in his life he was staking all on the outcome of a perilous enterprise. Like his ride to Germany to conquer the Empire, this crusade, too, was a desperate gamble. Unlike other royal crusaders before him, he could not afford the magnificent failure of a glorious dream. He had to conquer Jerusalem or risk the Empire and perhaps even his kingdom.

His spies had reported that Gregory was recruiting unusual numbers of mercenaries. While it seemed unimaginable that Gregory would actually attack Sicily during his absence, Frederick had taken all possible precautions, including that of appointing an outstanding general, the Duke of Spoleto, as regent of the realm. Yet, despite the enormous odds, he felt lighthearted, almost exhilarated, as he felt the wind in his face on this clear, sunny morning.

All had expected him to bow to the pope's demands under the terrible blow of the excommunication. No one had thought it possible that he would depart without having obtained absolution. The very idea was inconceivable.

His counselors, with the exception of Berard, all implored him to make his peace with the pope first, by whatever means. Berard alone had understood that the only way for Frederick to free himself forever from the threat of papal overlordship was to strike a final, crippling blow at the papacy's prestige. And the means to that end was the conquest of Jerusalem.

He turned to Berard. There was a glint in his eyes. "Can you imagine Gregory's face when he hears that I, as an excommunicate, have recovered Jerusalem? He'll be the laughingstock of Christendom!"

"I can," Berard said. "Only too well."

ACRE, SEPTEMBER 1228

The imperial flotilla of sixty galleys and transport vessels slipped into the bay of Acre in the gray light of early dawn. Berard and Balian of Sidon stood beside Frederick on the forecastle as the dim outline of the shore took shape under the fading stars. Before them the crusader city of Acre rose out of the waters, protected by her massive sea walls.

Since Jerusalem's fall, Acre had been the capital of the kingdom of Jerusalem and its principal port. Situated on an ancient caravan route that linked Egypt, Palestine, and Syria, the city was also a great trading center. Long before the time of Christ, camel caravans had plodded along her sandy highways. The rich produce of Palestine—olive oil, sugar, honey, dried figs, grapes, and dates—was exported from here to Europe. Silks, spices, and dyestuffs from Syria and Mesopotamia were shipped to the West by the great Italian trading entrepôts. Genoa, Venice, and Pisa each had its own quarter in the city, with houses, warehouses, and wharves.

"There, to the right, is Mount Carmel," Balian pointed at a mountain looming above the sea. "Straight ahead are the foothills of Galilee. Beyond lie the Sea of Galilee and the Jordan valley. Further south rise the hills of Judaea. Beyond Jerusalem they tumble down in a series of barren, bandit-infested ridges toward the wasteland of the Dead Sea."

Frederick, feet planted apart to balance himself on the heaving deck, nodded. He stared ahead, at the beaches on either side of the city, where a multitude of tents were becoming visible under the black silhouettes of palm trees. Some eleven thousand men were already encamped there.

Somewhere in the distance, on a plateau in the arid mountains of Judaea, lay Jerusalem. And the key to Jerusalem was Al-Kamil.

His first move would be to send an embassy to the sultan in Cairo, advising him of his arrival. Al-Kamil's situation had changed greatly since his first embassy to Frederick several years ago when, engaged in battle with his two brothers, he had sought Frederick's aid. Then, Al-Kamil had possessed much of the lands Frederick wished to recover. His brother Al-Mu'azzam had since wrested most of them from him, including Jerusalem.

For several years now, he had exchanged embassies, gifts, and personal letters with the learned sultan of Egypt. Together, they would rout the sultan of Damascus and recover the Christians' land. In return, Frederick would protect Al-Kamil's flank from the third brother, the sultan of Babylon, while Al-Kamil marched on to conquer Damascus.

ALERTED BY THE soldiers on the sentry walks, the city of Acre awoke in a tumult of joy. As the sun began to gild the dark rooftops and shadowy domes, people streamed out to the waterfront, carrying palm branches. The clergy, both Latin and Greek, appeared in procession, bearing jeweled reliquaries and golden crosses. Even the Jews, led by the chief rabbi, came to pay their respects to the new king of Jerusalem. The princes of Outremer, the leaders of the Templars, the Hospitallers, and the Teutonic Knights waited in serried ranks before the imperial galley.

Belowdecks, Mahmoud adjusted the crown on Frederick's head. He smoothed the emerald cloak edged in miniver on Frederick's shoulders.

"You have chosen the color of Islam for your cloak today," the Saracen said.

"I know, Mahmoud, may it bring me luck!"

A SMELL OF seaweed, frankincense, and rotten fish assailed him as he stepped on deck. Before him towered Acre's famed sea walls, built by the Lionheart after he captured the city from Saladin. The ramparts were black with townspeople.

His eyes fell on the clergy assembled on the quay. He recognized the patriarch of Jerusalem in a magenta cope. Beside him stood a stout, bald-

ing prelate in white and gold brocade. That must be the archbishop of
Caesarea, after the patriarch the second most powerful churchman in Palestine. He breathed a sigh of relief. Hermann had been right. He'd assured
him in his letters that the Christians in Palestine would welcome him
despite the pope's ban.

Seagulls wheeled above the waterfront, undeterred by the crowds and
the noise. The sky was clear and intensely blue. The color of the Virgin's
mantle . . . He glanced at Berard, and smiled. I, too, Frederick thought, am
getting caught up in this stirring medley of faith, humbug, and glory that
is the Holy Land.

The crowd caught sight of him. "Long live the Emperor Frederick!
Long live the king of Jerusalem!" they chanted, waving a forest of palm
branches. For more than forty years, ever since Barbarossa had died on
his way to Palestine, the Frankish East had awaited the coming of
an emperor. Waving to the crowd, Frederick stepped onto the soil of
Palestine.

The first to greet him was Hermann von Salza. Frederick embraced the
grand master. He held him at arm's length. "It is good to see you,
Hermann." He smiled. "I wasn't sure I'd ever set eyes on you again."

"My lord, you are come! I thank God for having spared your life and
brought you here safely."

One by one, the princes of Outremer, the prelates and leaders of the
military orders knelt on the thick Eastern rugs spread on the cobbles. Last
came Frederick's Sicilian and German lords, who had been there for nearly
a year now.

Like the barons in Cyprus, everyone in Acre was aware of the excommunication but seemed unconcerned by it. This was an excellent omen, although he sensed a slight coolness in the manner in which the patriarch
Gerold greeted him.

Berard, riding behind Frederick in the cavalcade, looked in wonder at
this crowded city that was a blend of East and West. Tortuous streets, dark
and scabrous with age, gave way here and there to sun-drenched squares
fronted by graceful mansions with elegant Saracenic fretwork screens.
Through vaulted lanes, Berard caught glimpses of huge warehouses, bales
of goods piled in their courtyards. A city of dark eyes and deep, dank cel-
lars, of veiled women, rich merchants, and innumerable churches. Pilgrims,

friars, knights, slaves, Jews, Muslims, and Christians from every nation
thronged the streets, staring at the emperor who had come to deliver
Jerusalem. And over it all loomed the great stone citadel of the crusaders,
reminder of the ever-present threat of attack.

Observing the joy on the crowd's faces, Berard thought what a welcome
change this was from the unpleasantness in Cyprus. There, Frederick had
behaved with uncharacteristic heavy-handedness toward the Ibelins. The
kingdom of Cyprus was an imperial fief. But its links with the Empire had
grown tenuous over the years. Upon his arrival, Frederick demanded recognition of himself as suzerain, and payment of the requisite taxes. John of
Ibelin, lord of Beirut, was the wealthiest and most powerful prince of Outremer. He possessed lands both in Cyprus and on the mainland. He was an
uncle of the dead Yolanda and regent of Cyprus during its king's minority.

Frederick decided to make an example of the Ibelins to establish his
authority over the equally independent-minded princes of Outremer. In
order to force John to relinquish Beirut and recognize Frederick as overlord
of Cyprus, he ordered his men to threaten John and his sons with drawn
swords at a banquet to which he had invited them in the castle of
Limmasol.

Berard had been aghast. However, the other lords of Outremer, including Balian of Sidon, himself a cousin of Yolanda, Bohemund of Antioch, and
Guy Embriaco backed him against the Ibelin faction. This, Berard thought,
was a sign of the rivalries that bedeviled the Christian principalities in the
Holy Land. The boy king of Cyprus had been taken along by Frederick as
hostage for his uncle's good behavior. A grim-faced John of Ibelin now followed in the emperor's retinue as proof of his submission. While the prospect of recovering his lands from the Saracens probably outweighed John's
hatred, Frederick was playing a dangerous game.

Berard prayed that Frederick would be able to curb his temper here. To
lead to success an army as disparate and rent by dissension as this one
would require all the diplomatic skills that had stood the young Frederick
in such good stead in Germany.

WITHIN HOURS OF his arrival Frederick met with Hermann and Thomas of
Acerra, his regent in Palestine. The only other man present was Berard.

The news couldn't have been worse: the sultan of Damascus had recently died, leaving an infant son. Al-Kamil had already reconquered Jerusalem and most of the Christian lands in his brother's possession, and was now encamped in Nablus, poised to attack Damascus itself. Even worse, Al-Kamil had concluded a treaty with his other brother, the sultan of Babylon. Together, they planned to divide the empire of Saladin between them. He had no further need of Frederick.

Frederick stared at the sea. The forces he had brought with him were far smaller than expected. Many had recanted for fear of serving under an excommunicate. Even with the men already in Acre, he could hardly take on the combined forces of Al-Kamil and the sultan of Babylon.

At length, he turned. "We must keep quiet about this. Since the other crusaders don't know of my arrangements with Al-Kamil, I'll suggest we negotiate before attacking. They won't like it, of course."

"But what will it avail you to negotiate with Al-Kamil now?" Hermann asked.

"Al-Kamil may have no need of me any longer, but my presence here with a large host is a constant threat to him while he turns north. Time is on my side. I may still be able to induce him to hand over Jerusalem."

"And if you fail?" Berard raised his black brows.

"Then we'll have to fight. I can't return without having recovered Jerusalem. If I fail, I must perish in the attempt."

THE AIR WAS cool and moldy in the cavernous underground hall of the great crusader fortress. Huge squat pillars of tawny stone, roughly carved with the cross of Jerusalem, upheld the vaulted ceiling. The castle of Acre had been erected with no thought for fine craftsmanship or comfort by Godfrey of Bouillon, first crusader king of Jerusalem, nearly two hundred years ago. The vast hall served both as refectory and council chamber.

Everyone clustered around a long unplaned table of cedarwood, dark with age, on which was spread a crude map of Palestine and Syria, drawn in red ink on a cow's hide.

All the leaders of the different contingents were present: the French and their squires, two English bishops who led the English forces, Hermann, representing the Germans, as well as the great princes of Outremer and the

278 MARIA R. BORDIHN

leaders of the Templars and Hospitallers. The Duke of Limburg, Berard, and other Germans and Sicilians were grouped around Frederick. The church was represented by Gerold, patriarch of Jerusalem, by the patriarch of Antioch, the archbishop of Caesarea, and several bishops.

Frederick, who had summoned them, was looking at the map, resting his chin in his hand. He had been doing this for a while, in absorbed silence.

A tall, distinguished-looking, young knight, unable to stand the suspense any longer, asked in French-accented Latin: "Well, my lord, where do we attack?"

Frederick glanced at his white mantle with its red cross. A Templar. The most belligerent of the military orders, they were always stirring up trouble. "We don't attack," he said, "we talk first. I believe that Al-Kamil may be amenable to negotiations. In the meantime, we'll drill our forces till they march with the precision of a Roman legion." He looked around the table, waiting for the outburst.

Everyone began to speak at once. The Duke of Limburg's booming voice overrode the others. "But Your Grace," the duke cried, "that's what my men have been doing for nearly a year. They're restless and bored, lusting for a chance to kill Saracens."

"Give them something to do. Make them build walls, roads, wells, anything to tire them and make them useful."

The duke glared at Frederick: "I've not taken the cross to supervise a building site."

Gerold of Lausanne raised his wheezy voice: "We've been negotiating with the Saracens for decades without result."

Frederick smiled. "That's true, but now we're negotiating from strength. When the first gambit proves inconclusive, as it will, we'll march along here," he moved his finger south along the red line that marked the Mediterranean, "to Jaffa, in a display of strength. The Saracen scouts will report it to the sultan. As you know, he's in Nablus, hoping to capture Damascus. Why should he risk a long and bloody war for an arid city in the hills of Judaea when the rich prize of Damascus beckons?"

Some nodded, though not many. This was not the way they had envisaged the crusade. After dealing with the distribution of arms and provisions and the storage of the Sicilian grain, soon to arrive to tide the army over the winter, the secular lords filed out of the hall.

After they had left, Gerold and the archbishop of Caesarea approached Frederick. Richard Filangeri, Frederick's marshal, had meanwhile unrolled another map, this one brought from Sicily. It, too, was a map of Palestine, except that it included Syria and Asia Minor. Drawn on fine vellum, it had been made by a Saracen cartographer in Palermo.

"But this map's a marvel!" Hermann cried. "It's far more accurate than ours!"

The archbishop of Caesarea, a small rotund man with darting eyes, on whose balding gray head sat a crimson cap, cleared his throat. "My lord," he began, "we wish to discuss a delicate matter with you, if you will graciously give us of your time." He folded his plump white hands over his silk-robed stomach.

Frederick inclined his head. It was vital that he maintain his friendly relations with the local clergy. He sat down on the chair that had been placed under a cloth of estate, and smiled. He'd been expecting this. He'd begun to wonder why it had taken them nearly two days to raise the issue.

"As Your Grace is aware," the archbishop said, "we are in a difficult position. We should, strictly speaking, show no obedience to you. Among other things, your presence at church services is, to say the least, irregular."

Frederick nodded. "I do understand, my lords. What remedy do you propose?"

"We have had word of the circumstances of your unfortunate disagreement with the Holy Father, my lord," Gerold said. "I myself, having been present, can attest to the facts that forced you to return after the first departure. The Holy Father's, ehh . . ." Gerold searched for the most tactful word, "intransigence was undoubtedly due to his fervent desire to see the crusade begin. We are convinced that now that you have fulfilled your vow, His Holiness will gladly lift the ban that so unfortunately still lies on your person."

Frederick smiled. "That is my opinion, too, Gerold. Who better to act as my envoy then than one of your bishops, who can bear witness to my presence here? I suggest that one of them and one of my Sicilian bishops leave for Rome without delay."

Frederick rose. "We will sup together tonight. And before long, I am certain we'll receive tidings from Rome that this regrettable misunderstanding is over."

As the two prelates bowed themselves out, Frederick wondered how long it would take Gregory to relent and lift the ban. It was almost impossible for him not to do so now.

Either way, he would gain precious time to conduct his negotiations with Al-Kamil.

FREDERICK, FINDING LIFE uncongenial in Acre's castle, surrounded by the stench and noise of the overcrowded city, went to live in a nearby fortress by the sea belonging to the Teutonic Knights. Here, at least, the air was clean, and it was possible to sleep at night. Here, also, fewer eyes observed his movements. The less his Frankish barons knew about his actions, the better. His falcons, hounds, book chests, hangings, and silver plate were loaded onto a long file of camels.

The money chests containing his treasury were escorted by a detachment of Saracen troops from Lucera, while he himself was flanked by his Saracen bodyguard. The presence of so many Muslims in his retinue had caused grumbling among the Franks, particularly as he permitted them to openly say their prayers. Frederick's explanation that it was useful to have troops who were familiar with Saracen fighting methods hadn't entirely convinced the barons, and even less so the clergy. No matter, they'd impress Al-Kamil with his Muslim sympathies.

Once installed in the fortress, he settled down to wait. Thomas of Acerra, bearing gifts, was dispatched to Al-Kamil at Nablus, to inform him of Frederick's arrival and formally request that he surrender Jerusalem to her rightful owner. Meanwhile, an embassy of churchmen had left for Rome. They weren't expected back for several months.

As the heat of September gave way to the balmy days of October, a stream of messengers, noblemen, prelates, and petitioners came and went through the gates of the fort. The administration and high court of the kingdom remained in Acre, but all major decisions had to be ratified by Frederick. Occasionally, he himself would dispense justice, enthroned under two palms in the courtyard. The lords of Outremer, accustomed to the supremacy of their high court, frowned on this assumption of royal privilege. To keep the army occupied, massive earthworks were thrown up around Acre. The fortifications of all nearby castles were strengthened, roads were leveled, wells dug.

The envoys to the sultan returned at the end of October. Jerusalem, however, was not among the rich gifts the sultan sent to his friend the emperor. Al-Kamil was as fulsome in his protestations of friendship as he was evasive. Soon, he would be sending an embassy to further deliberate the issue.

Unlike his fellow crusaders, Frederick was unperturbed by the result of the embassy. No follower of Mohammed would rush such a matter. Frederick smiled and went hawking with his falconers.

FREDERICK, IN A window seat above the sea, was immersed in Eusebius's *Life of Constantine.* He raised his head and listened. A great noise of rolling drums and vociferous voices was coming from the land side of the castle. Saracen drums . . . ?

Frederick leapt up. He collided with the Duke of Limburg, who burst into the chamber. "My lord," he cried, eyes shining, "I think you would wish to see this!"

Reassured, Frederick followed him. Leaning over the parapet of the gallery, he stared in wonder. The courtyard held a scene from Haroun Al-Rashid's Arabian Tales. A train of camels with cages on their back waited to be relieved of their burdens. In one of the cages, Frederick saw a leopard. Others contained furry creatures with long tails he had never seen before, with humanlike faces, gripping the bars of their prisons with what looked like hands. A file of six gray Arab mares with scarlet saddlecloths stood roped together near the gate.

The cause of all the noise, however, was an immense animal that seemed stuck in the gateway and refused to move forward. The drummers drummed. The turbaned keeper shouted and screamed, brandishing an iron prod. Others behind pushed and shoved, yelling and coaxing, all to no avail. Finally, a groom returned from the stables with a load of hay. Tempted by the fodder, the behemoth suddenly lumbered forward with surprising grace and began to pick up tufts of hay with its long and agile proboscis.

Frederick couldn't take his eyes of the animal. It wasn't possible . . . An elephant. He had read about the war-elephants with which Hannibal had crossed the Alps and nearly defeated Rome. He was so absorbed in the elephant that he failed to notice a group of Saracen noblemen in jeweled turbans and vivid robes, who stood waiting at the foot of the stairs. In their center was an exceptionally tall man who seemed familiar. As he turned his head to say something to the man beside him, Frederick recognized him.

He turned to the duke. "Why wasn't I informed the moment they arrived? How can you keep a great prince of Islam waiting like a villein!"

Frederick clattered down the stairs. At their foot he encountered John of Ibelin. The golden-bearded lord of Beirut fixed his sharp brown eyes on Frederick.

"It seems the sultan is reciprocating your generosity, my lord. What else is he going to part with, apart from exotic animals of no use to anyone?"

Frederick gave him a withering look. "My lands, and yours too, if you can curb your temper long enough," he snapped, brushing past him.

Under the incredulous eyes of Franks and Saracens alike, Frederick strode forward with outstretched arms and embraced Fakhr-ed-Din. The emir kissed him on both cheeks.

"Praise be to Allah. He has brought us together once more."

Frederick smiled. "In friendship, I hope?"

Fakhr-ed-Din inclined his head. "In friendship, my lord."

THE PERFUMED WATER cascaded from the ewer held by the slave girl over Frederick's outstretched hands into the silver basin. He dried his hands on the proffered linen towel, then handed it to his guest.

They were seated, in Muslim fashion, cross-legged on the thick carpets in Frederick's privy chamber.

Frederick waited for the veiled slave to leave before asking casually, "Well, my friend, what tidings do you bring?" He reclined, toying with the tassel of his silk bolster as if the matter were of no consequence. The meal they had just eaten lay heavy in his stomach. His mouth felt as dry as desert sand.

The emir looked at him. He saw through the inscrutable mask. He knew how much was at stake for the emperor. His difficulties with the pope were known to Al-Kamil. Despite his loyalty to the sultan, Fakhr-ed-Din found himself wishing that he had a different message to deliver, that somehow a compromise between these two men might still be possible.

"The sultan bids me tell you that his heart is heavy because he cannot accede to your request." The emir studied the pattern on the carpet. "If he were to surrender Jerusalem to you, he would bring down the wrath of Islam on himself. Jerusalem, as you know, is holy not only to Jews and Christians, but to Muslims as well. The prophet Mohammed ascended to heaven from there." He looked up. "The Dome of the Rock is, after Mecca and Medina, the holiest shrine in Islam."

Frederick leaned forward. His eyes were hard. "Tell the sultan that I, too, cannot lose face with my people by leaving without having recovered Jerusalem. But my need is greater than his. If he won't cede the capital of my kingdom to me by treaty, I'll wrest it from him with my sword. The hills of Judaea," he said, "will run with rivers of Saracen blood, and the blame will be his."

He added, "Tell him that, and tell him, too, that my patience and that of my men is running out!"

"I will, my lord," Fakhr-ed-Din said.

Frederick rose. With a smile, he said, "Tomorrow, we'll go hunting together, as we used to do in Apulia." All the harshness had gone out of his voice and his eyes. "You remember?"

The emir nodded. "Often, I have looked out at the sea, toward Sicily, and thought of those happy days at your court. No other man I have ever met understands falcons, or men, as you do."

AFTER FAKHR-ED-DIN HAD returned to his tent in the embassy's encampment, Frederick walked back to his chambers. It was late, well past the twelfth hour. The guards in the passages stood to attention as he passed, silent shadows in the light of the torches.

Frederick walked over to the window. The night sky was dark and velvety, with brilliant stars. Above the sea hung the thin sliver of a waxing moon. The growing crescent of Islam.

He turned from the window and stopped to look at the astrolabe on the table. Of all Al-Kamil's splendid gifts, this astronomical device was the one he valued most. He turned it idly with one finger. Uncertain of the result of his attack on Damascus, Al-Kamil was procrastinating. If Damascus fell quickly, he'd be able to face a war in Palestine. If, however, Damascus held out, if the attack turned into a long siege, he'd have to accommodate Frederick.

What was needed now was a show of force, to reinforce his threats to the sultan. It was time to march to Jaffa.

He picked up a cup and poured some of the sweet, ruby-red wine of Palestine into it. Like a libation to a pagan god, he raised the cup. "To the walls of Damascus!"

WHILE THE CRUSADERS were preparing to strike camp and march toward Jaffa, two Benedictine friars arrived in the port of Acre aboard a fast galley. In a city filled with pilgrims and friars of every description, they excited little notice. They stayed just long enough at the house of their order in Acre to obtain horses from the prior's stables. Before vespers, the two knelt before the patriarch of Jerusalem in his palace in Caesarea.

The patriarch stared at them: "But this will destroy the crusade."

The elder of the two friars nodded. "That is the Holy Father's wish. The emperor is the personification of evil. A crusade led by him without the pope's blessing is a mockery of heaven. God's wrath will come down on the crusaders. It will end in defeat and the death of thousands of innocents."

The patriarch nodded. "There have, of course, been rumors for a long time. The sudden death of the Empress Yolanda, his Saracen ways . . . it is even whispered that he never makes confession . . ." He rose from his thronelike chair with surprising agility for a man of his age and girth. "If we are to ensure that the pontiff's will be done, we must make haste. Come, brethren."

AT SUNRISE THE following day, the patriarch, accompanied by the officers of his household and the archbishop of Caesarea, arrived in Acre. The army, Gerold knew, was set to march south the next morning. The pope's letter was read by the patriarch in the great square outside the castle to the clergy and the assembled crusaders.

The excommunicated emperor was to be given no allegiance by either clergy or the religious orders. Under pain of losing the remission of sins granted to those who took part in a crusade, all crusaders were forbidden to obey the emperor.

WHEN FREDERICK RECEIVED the news, he called for his sword and cloak. Vaulting onto his horse, he galloped to Acre, followed by his guard and a breathless Berard riding beside Hermann. Night had fallen by the time his heralds summoned the crusaders to an urgent meeting.

Frederick's eyes scanned the faces that filled the torchlit hall. Some were clearly ill at ease, torn between their duty to him and their fear of God. The secret traitors shifted their eyes. Yet others showed open triumph. The grand master of the Templars, a tall, hook-nosed French nobleman, stared at him with unconcealed enmity. Frederick held his gaze until the other lowered his eyes. A few smiled encouragement. A small group of his own men, Thomas of Acerra, the Duke of Limburg, Richard Filangeri, and, surprisingly, Balian of Sidon, clustered around him as if they feared that he would be attacked. Hermann von Salza too stood at his side, with that magnificent bearing that commanded the respect of even his enemies.

"My lords, I have heard your case," Frederick said after a pause. "As you know, I have done everything in my power to make peace with the Holy Father. I have offered to accept any religious penance he wishes to impose, I have redeemed my vow to go on crusade, all to no avail. While the pope's attitude seems to me to be that of an old man whose mind has become addled so that he can no longer see where the real weal of Christendom lies, I understand the terrible predicament that you are all subject to. In order to save this crusade," Frederick continued, "so that we may still accomplish what we have set out to do, for the greater glory of God, I hereby relinquish its leadership."

With a slow, deliberate gesture, he unbuckled his sword and laid it carefully on the table in front of him.

Frederick leaned forward, his palms on the table. He looked at the men before him: "The orders to the army will be given by the Duke of Limburg, in the name of Jesus Christ. We march as arranged at dawn." With that, he turned and strode out of the hall.

* * *

AND MARCH THEY did, to Frederick's own surprise. At dawn, with blaring trumpets and flying banners, the endless line of men and beasts, knights and foot soldiers, carts and camp followers lumbered along the coast toward Jaffa. The Templars and the Hospitallers, unable to resist the lure of war but unwilling to associate themselves too closely with the anathematized emperor, followed in the distance.

Frederick was jubilant. Despite the pope's efforts, most of the crusaders were still behind him. Thanks to a simple ruse, they were willing to fight.

At their approach, the small Saracen garrison of Jaffa fled. Frederick marched into the city where he was joyously received by the Christian population. He immediately began to rebuild the walls that the Saracens had dismantled.

JAFFA WAS A pleasant town clustered around a lovely bay, surrounded by orchards of lemon and orange trees. The only problem was a shortage of food. Many of the crusaders and pilgrims refused to eat unaccustomed foods. Although the days were warm and sunny, interspersed with soft rain, the nights were bitterly cold. Looking up at the bleak hills of Judaea, they could see the snow that lay on the rocky land. Up on its plateau, Jerusalem, too, would be dusted with snow.

At Frederick's Christmas court, gaiety was forced. The city they had come to conquer seemed further out of reach than ever. Negotiations with the Sultan came to a halt. Incensed by what he termed Frederick's aggression, Al-Kamil broke off discussions. A melancholy Fakhr-ed-Din embraced Frederick and rode off once more into the hills of Samaria toward the Sultan's court at Nablus. This, Frederick told them, was just one more maneuver of an oriental mind. The crusaders, however, demanded action. Frederick temporized. The troops he could still rely on were too few to take Jerusalem.

To distract himself, Frederick invited the famed Talmudic scholars of Jaffa into the fortress. Seated among them, he questioned them about Jewish law and customs. Taking his leave, the chief rabbi said to Frederick, "Previous crusaders have at best ignored us and at worst massacred us; you have treated us with courtesy and inquired about the law of Moses!" The leaders of the small Jewish community in Palestine left that evening shaking their heads. Never before had they come across a Christian prince who wanted to know why Jews were not allowed to eat fish without scales!

Then came the dread news that the supply fleet bearing the desperately needed Sicilian corn had perished in a storm. All but two transport vessels had sunk. The price of bread soared. There were food riots. This exacerbated the dissensions in the camp. Frederick pointedly continued to go about without a sword, but by now even the ordinary footsoldiers, incited by the clergy, had begun to mutter that only evil could come from fighting in the army of an excommunicate.

In the middle of January he left Jaffa, well garrisoned and with her walls refortified, to return to Acre. As he rode out of the gates, he looked up in the direction of Jerusalem. For the first time since his arrival in Palestine, he asked himself whether he too, like the Lionheart, was fated to never set eyes on the Holy City.

As he approached Acre, the weather improved. The clouds lifted and a pallid sun tinged the gray sea with gold. Above the great tawny walls of Acre flew the Hohenstaufen eagle. Lush sugarcane as high as a man, its spear-shaped leaves glossy with rain, lined the side of the sandy road. Soon it would be cut and its juice turned to sugar. The abundance of sugar here had astonished the crusaders. Sugar was a costly luxury in Europe, unknown to anyone but the very rich.

Despite the wet cloak that dragged on his shoulders, Frederick's gloom began to lift, too. The coastal towns were in his hands. And the sultan was having difficulties of his own. All that was required now was patience, and time.

SEVERAL DAYS LATER, on a cold, clear morning, a Sicilian galley docked in the harbor. Within hours a second galley, having been sent by a different route for reasons of safety, arrived as well. Both bore identical messages from the regent of Sicily, Rainald of Spoleto.

Frederick, reading the duke's letter, turned white. He handed the parchment to Berard. "The pope has invaded Sicily."

"I can't believe it," Berard said. His hand holding the letter shook. "He must be mad."

"He's your pope, head of your Church!" Frederick yelled.

"The pope is but a man."

Frederick crashed his fist onto the table. "He's a vicious, self-seeking old fool. I'll sweep his soldiers like vermin off the soil of Sicily, and cast him into a black dungeon, to rot forever!"

The hatred in Frederick's eyes was so palpable that Berard took a step back. Where would this battle end? In death? With terrible certainty, he knew that this was to be the greatest crisis of Frederick's life. And of his own.

Frederick paced up and down. He was clad in a Syrian robe of saffron-colored wool. On his bare feet he wore slippers of red leather, with curling toes. A large topaz, a recent gift of Al-Kamil, gleamed on his left hand.

His first impulse was to leave at once for Sicily. However, the more he thought about it, the more he realized that he couldn't triumph over Gregory without having recovered Jerusalem. Rainald assured him in his letter that he could contain the papal armies, mostly Lombard mercenaries led by Yolanda's father, Jean de Brienne. In the north, they had attacked the March of Ancona, near Jesi. In the south, the great abbey-fortress of Montecassino had been surrendered by its spineless abbot. Clearly, Gregory's aim was to extend his own territories, pushing the boundaries of Sicily further south. How he hoped to maintain his gains puzzled him.

What sinister plan had Jean de Brienne and Gregory hatched together in the Lateran? Surely the pope, who despite his age was highly astute, couldn't delude himself that he would let him keep these lands upon his return. Was it possible that Yolanda's father imagined that if Frederick were deposed or assassinated, he could rule Sicily as a papal vassal, in the name of his grandson?

But could he leave the defense of Sicily in the hands of another, even a man as able and as loyal as the Duke of Spoleto? He must recover Jerusalem as fast as possible. Thoughtfully, he looked at the topaz on his hand, turning the golden stone so that its facets caught the sun.

"Mahmoud," he called, "send a messenger to Acre to fetch Thomas of Acerra. Meanwhile, go and call Balian of Sidon. They will leave for the sultan's court at dawn."

He had one last concession to make that he had so far kept back. This he would now offer to the sultan.

* * *

"WHAT MANNER OF man is this emperor of the Franks really?" the Sultan asked.

Fakhr-ed-Din smiled at his cousin, his teeth gleaming white in his dark face. "I've told you many times."

The sultan nodded. "Yes, yes, I know, but what I want to know is, how honorable is he? If he gave his word, would he keep it?"

The emir thought for a moment. "Yes, if he thought that you had used him honorably too."

The sultan, several years older than his cousin, sat cross-legged on a low dais covered in carpets. A large uncut emerald gleamed in his cream-colored turban adorned with a white ostrich feather.

His cousin reclined across from him against a brocaded bolster. Between them stood a silver platter with sweetmeats.

The walls were painted deep blue, with bright orange and yellow flowers on twisted golden stems. The domed ceiling, of the same intense blue, was sprinkled with golden stars. Through the central horseshoe arch the green valley of Nablus was visible, its almond trees white with blossoms.

Al-Kamil's hooded, melancholy eyes, at odds with the imperious sweep of his aquiline nose, looked north, toward Damascus. That great prize, which he had thought within reach, continued to elude him. His brother's widow had recently wed a Muslim convert from Christianity, who had once been a Hospitaller. This man was proving an exceptional general. Taking Al-Kamil's troops by surprise, he had inflicted a terrible defeat on them and was now threatening their supply lines.

With a grim smile, Al-Kamil thought that like Frederick, he, too, was stretching out his hand toward a city that refused to yield to his will. The only difference was that what the Frankish emperor so persistently demanded was a half-empty agglomeration of crumbling churches and mosques, fed by a single spring and devoid of all wealth. Damascus, however, was a city rich beyond the dreams of avarice, paved with marble and gold, with splendid mosques, palaces, and gardens, surrounded by bountiful fields and palm groves.

Frederick himself said so. Al-Kamil picked up the parchment beside him and reread the emperor's words.

"... turn your eyes and all the strength of your invincible armies toward Damascus, fount of beauty and riches, gateway to the East, and surrender to me what is rightfully mine. All I ask is a city built on rocks, without water or greenery, filled with rubble and old buildings. My need, oh friend, is greater than yours and so is my desperation. Do not force me to fight you, which I now must, but rather return Jerusalem to me, so that I may again hold up my head with pride. If you do this, I will even permit the holy places of Islam to stand and your people to worship there."

The sultan shook his head. "He humbles himself like no other ruler I know."

"Yes, but there is great courage in his humility." Fakhr-ed-Din cast an appraising glance at his cousin. He could see that sharp mind weighing the benefits and calculating the risks. The sultan leaned forward and took one of the little cakes.

"The emperor has offered to leave the shrines of Islam in Muslim hands," Fakhr-ed-Din said. "Give him Jerusalem, and instead of more warfare, which you can ill afford right now, you'll have a loyal ally."

The sultan knitted his thick brows. "You have always given me wise counsel, cousin. I think I'll take your advice and rid myself of this Frankish emperor, who disturbs my sleep." He smoothed his beard. "I almost regret never having met him. Although he's a Christian and I am a descendant of the Prophet, I think we would have had much to talk about. I, too, am bedeviled by power-hungry old men who in the name of Allah are trying to stifle thought."

With a twinkle in his eye, the sultan added, "You may bring the proposal for a treaty to your friend the emperor yourself."

JERUSALEM, MARCH 1229

The road ran steeply up into the hills of Judaea through barren, rocky terrain. Here and there, brown mud villages hedged with low stone walls sat among figs and olives. Scrawny black goats, beards quivering, scrambled over the rocks.

At the infrequent wells, tall Bedouin in voluminous sand-colored robes, lords of the desert who owed allegiance to no one, watered their surly-looking camels or filled their waterskins. The Bedouin cast disdainful glances at the great host of Christians, while sullen-faced fellahin gathered outside their villages, staring at the endless line of men and horses that climbed the road to Jerusalem in a great choking cloud of dust.

The banners hung limply in the still, warm air of the afternoon. Frederick rode at the head of the cavalcade, flanked by Hermann and Berard. Behind the mounted knights and men-at-arms followed more than a thousand pilgrims, mostly Germans, on foot. Men and women, clad in gray homespun, wearing wide hats with turned-up brims, satchels slung over their shoulders, and the traditional wooden pilgrim's staff in their hands, labored on through the hills. Footsore and weary, they were sustained by a single hope: to reach Jerusalem. As a precaution against brigands who often attacked stragglers, Frederick had ordered a detachment of mounted knights to follow behind the last pilgrims.

The scent of wild thyme that grew in drifts between the rocks mingled with the smell of dust, a fine, white dust particular to Judaea. It's like the dust of marble, Frederick thought, the dust of vanished ages ... They reached a high ridge called the Mount of Joy. From here, for centuries pilgrims from the west had had their first glimpse of the Holy City. Frederick reined in his horse. "Jerusalem!" he cried.

Berard's heart filled with joy. He turned to Frederick. They exchanged a smile, before turning back to stare at the city that meant so much to both of them, for such different reasons.

The great lion-colored walls of Jerusalem rose atop a barren plateau of rock. Stony ravines and bleak, deep wadis ran off to the sides. Here and there, sparse tufts of vegetation had found a foothold in the crevices between the rocks, rounded and smoothed by the winds that had swept over them since the time of Abraham.

Jerusalem. Frederick had long ago wearied of the name. Yet, now that he beheld her, he was spellbound. Before him lay the city of David, of Solomon and Herod, where Christ had perished on the cross. Jerusalem had been destroyed and rebuilt many times in her long history. Titus razed her to the ground less than forty years after the crucifixion, scattering her Jewish inhabitants to the four corners of the earth. Under Hadrian, Jerusalem became a Roman city. Three hundred years later, when Constantine adopted Christianity as the religion of the Empire, the holy sites were searched for and turned into places of pilgrimage.

With the advent of Islam, the Byzantines lost control of the city. Although Christian pilgrims were permitted by the Saracens to visit the holy shrines against payment of a tax, they were increasingly attacked, robbed, and murdered. Europe, too, was plagued at that time by unprecedented violence, often committed by roving bands of unemployed mercenaries or landless younger sons of the nobility. As a remedy to both problems, Pope Gregory the Great launched the first crusade. The result was the foundation of the kingdom of Jerusalem and the Christian principalities in the East. Their fate had been one of constant battles with the Saracens, of lands gained and lands lost . . .

At length, Frederick gave the signal to continue. His entry into Jerusalem would surely be the strangest in her long history. An excommunicated emperor being handed the keys to the most sacred city in Christendom by the sultan's representative!

By his treaty with Al-Kamil, after much haggling back and forth, he had obtained not only Jerusalem, but Bethlehem and Nazareth as well. He had thus recovered the three holiest shrines of Christianity: the places of the Annunciation, the Birth, and the Crucifixion. In addition the sultan had ceded other lands and several important crusader fortresses, including the great castle of Montfort. While it was true that Jerusalem was linked to the sea only by a narrow corridor of Christian land, the treaty was nevertheless a resounding success. The truce was valid for ten years, ten months, and ten days, the longest period for which Islamic law permitted a truce with the infidel.

Incredibly, neither the clergy nor the princes of Outremer had been pleased. The princes, resentful of his secretive negotiations with the sultan, were furious that he had signed the treaty without consulting them. The patriarch Gerold, still seething with anger at being outwitted, condemned it because Frederick had granted the Muslims possession of their holy shrines. Not only had the enraged patriarch refused to accompany him to Jerusalem, but he had also threatened to place the Holy City under an interdict if Frederick were to set foot in the city. The Templars and the Hospitallers refused to follow him to Jerusalem. Frederick had been unperturbed. He no longer had need of their fighting capacity. Jerusalem was his.

Without so much as drawing his sword, he had accomplished what the third, fourth, and fifth crusades had failed to achieve with a great deal of bloodshed.

THE SUN WAS beginning to set as they entered the city gates. The pilgrims, beside themselves with joy, swept forward, past the riders. They sank to their knees to kiss the ground that had been hallowed by the footsteps of Christ. Many began filling their satchels with stones.

"What are they doing?" Frederick asked Hermann.

"The stones of Jerusalem are venerable, my lord. Some they keep for themselves, but most they sell when they get home. They're considered almost as holy as relics."

The local population, dark-skinned, bearded men and veiled women, Jews, Christians, and Arabs, surrounded by ragged children, stared at them with appraising eyes. Frederick thought how similar they looked despite their different beliefs. During centuries of foreign domination, Jerusalem had changed masters and religions innumerable times. After satisfying themselves that no immediate danger was to be expected from this latest change, they melted back into the warren of vaulted streets sunk in age.

The sultan's representative, the elderly Qadi of Nablus, received Frederick on a dusty square laid with carpets. With a solemn gesture, he handed him the keys of the city. Beside him stood Fakr-ed-Din. As his eyes met Frederick's, the emir permitted himself a flicker of complicity.

A hook-nosed man with the proud bearing and leathery face of a desert dweller, the qadi bowed. "My lord, as there is no suitable palace to lodge you, I would be deeply honored if you would accept the hospitality of my worthless home."

Frederick replied in Arabic, "I am sure that in your splendid home I will enjoy all the blessings of Allah."

Frederick's attention had been caught by a building that rose behind the square.

"The Dome of the Rock," the qadi informed him, following his eyes, "whence the Prophet Mohammed, peace and benediction be on his name, ascended to heaven."

A masterpiece of architectural simplicity, it resembled a crown of stone, with an octagonal base sheathed in white marble, capped by an immense golden dome. One day, Frederick thought, I'll build a castle such as this. I'll set it like a circlet above the hills of Apulia.

Hermann cleared his throat. "The horses are here."

Frederick started. "Yes, of course."

"You might be interested to know that the building before you occupies the site of the Jewish temple where Christ preached to the Pharisees," Hermann said.

"The temple of Solomon?" Frederick's eyes widened.

"Well, yes. It had been rebuilt by Herod before then, I believe, but it was the same temple. Over there, beyond that arcade, lie the ruins of a huge wall of great stone blocks. That is all that is left of the temple. The few Jews who remain here call it the Wailing Wall and go to pray there, bewailing the fate of their dispersed nation. The rock that is now within the dome was below the altar in the Jewish temple. The Knights of the Temple had their first quarters there, in the early days of the kingdom, hence their name."

Frederick grimaced at the mention of the Templars. "Have you been inside?"

"Christians aren't allowed in Muslim shrines." He added, "Not that I've ever had any desire to."

Frederick turned to the qadi. He smiled. "That building is a marvel such as I have rarely beheld. I would very much like to visit it tomorrow."

The qadi bowed. "It shall be done as you command, my lord."

Hermann, aghast, touched Frederick's elbow. "Tomorrow, my lord, you will be crowned. I do not think . . ."

"Nonsense!" Frederick interrupted him. "There's no reason why I can't be crowned in the morning and pay my respects to the temple where Jesus preached in the afternoon, now is there?"

Hermann looked at him, clearly exasperated: "If you put it that way," he said.

* * *

FREDERICK COULD SCARCELY believe his eyes. The Church of the Holy Sepulcher, the holiest shrine in Christendom, resembled a gloomy, smoke-blackened labyrinth of low little chapels and dark passageways. Narrow, worn stairways led upward into yet more chapels or down into damp rock caverns. Crumbling mosaics and moth-eaten tapestries covered the walls. The Byzantines and Latins shared custody of the church, bickering over every inch of holy ground.

The church, built by the crusaders on the remains of the original basilica erected by Constantine, covered the hill of Golgotha. At the western end was a pillared rotunda above which soared a dome. Under this stood the tomb of Christ.

The last echoes of the choir faded away. The thanksgiving Mass for the delivery of Jerusalem, celebrated by Sicilian clergymen because no local prelates dared to do so, came to an end.

The huge crowd of pilgrims and soldiers shifted their feet. To one side stood the superiors of the religious orders, who ran hospices, convents, and monasteries in Jerusalem. Despite the pope's ban and the patriarch's interdict, they had come that morning to thank Frederick for delivering Jerusalem.

On the altar, on a cushion of blue damask, lay the crown of Jerusalem, glittering in the light of hundreds of oil lamps suspended from the ceiling.

Frederick, following a sudden inspiration, turned and walked toward the tomb of the Redeemer. Bending under the low doorway, he entered the sanctuary. He knelt in the tiny chamber. The Stone of Resurrection on the tomb was worn and dented, eroded by centuries of veneration. He pressed his forehead against the rock. The stone was cold, as cold as death. He, too, felt cold, chilled to the bone. He shivered. The terror that for months he had forced into the deepest recesses of his soul suddenly overwhelmed him. Frederick gripped the Stone of the Resurrection with both hands. "I beseech you, Oh Lord, protect Sicily . . . Protect my people from this madman and the terrible power he wields over the minds of men . . ." To his astonishment, a great peace flowed into him. All fear, hatred, and bitterness left him. Warmth returned to his body. He closed his eyes. To remain thus, at peace, forever . . .

This, then, he thought full of awe, is the meaning of God. Not perpetual happiness, but instants of light . . . Yet it could not last, the outside world waited for him, splendid in its terrible beauty. At length, with an effort, he rose and stepped back into the church.

He halted before the altar, and looked down at the crown of Jerusalem. There was a sudden, tense stillness. He reached for the crown. Then, with both hands, he placed it on his head.

Cheers in a babel of different languages went up. The German pilgrims broke into "*Heil dem Kaiser, Heil dem Kaiser!*" The Sicilians and English shouted, "*Ave Imperator, Ave Fredericus Rex et Imperator!*" The few princes of Outremer who were present hailed him in French.

Berard's eyes stung. He saw both the triumph and sadness in Frederick's eyes. By crowning himself, he had just defied a thousand years of Christian tradition.

Frederick raised his hand, commanding silence.

"My lords, venerable princes of the Church, good people," he began in Latin, "I vowed I would recover Jerusalem, and I have done so. I did not wish to place a burden on the conscience of the churchmen here today. That is why I have set this diadem upon my head myself. I have not done so out of insolence, but in deep reverence of God, who has chosen me to wear it." His voice echoed through the nave.

He went on to describe the events since he took the cross in Aachen, and how he had redeemed his crusading vow and recovered the holy places despite the obstacles placed in his way, aided by God. He ended on a conciliatory note, saying that the pope's attitude could be due only to ignorance of his real intentions and that the pontiff would surely grieve over the hostile letters he had sent to Outremer now that Jerusalem had been delivered. Out of his reverence for the Most High, Frederick said, he was prepared to make peace with His representative on earth, once the pope had seen the error of his ways.

His words were greeted with joy by the congregation, promising as they did a healing of the rift between Empire and papacy. Berard, glancing about, told himself that pessimism must be a sign of old age. He alone seemed untouched by the euphoria. Gregory, he knew, would never sue for peace, and Frederick wouldn't rest until Gregory was either dead or so humiliated that he would be deprived of power forever.

On his way out, Frederick paused in the pillared vestibule before the tomb of Godfrey of Bouillon. As he looked at the simple stone slab under which lay the first Christian king of Jerusalem, he felt a chill premonition.

AFTER INSTALLING A garrison in Jerusalem and ordering the reconstruction of her walls, Frederick left the city two days later with a small escort. His aim was to return to Sicily as quickly as possible. He intended, he had told his lords the night before, to sail from Acre in two weeks' time.

The emir accompanied the imperial cavalcade for several miles outside Jerusalem. On a bleak hill they embraced.

"Farewell, Frederick. May the blessing of Allah always be with you."

"Farewell, my friend." Frederick smiled. "One day you'll come again to my court and we'll play chess till late into the night!"

Fakhr-ed-Din looked at him. There was sadness in his dark, expressive eyes. "I do not think so, Frederick, but I will wait eagerly for your tidings." He swung himself into the saddle and raised his hand in a last salute. Turning his mount abruptly, he galloped back to Jerusalem, the red cloaks of his guard billowing on the horizon.

Taking a shortcut through the mountains, they rode through wild, un-cultivated country. The March sun stood at its zenith, burning down on the riders in their heavy armor. Frederick guided his mount along a narrow, stony path, more suited to goats than horses. The horse, an Arab stallion named Dragon, had been a gift from Fakhr-ed-Din.

They entered a narrow, rocky ravine. A brook, swelled by recent spring rains, ran along its rocky bed. In the distance, beyond the gorge, rose a bare brown mountain whose crest was still sprinkled with snow. A pair of goshawks hung in the cobalt blue sky, ready to swoop down on their prey. A few stones rolled down the steep side of the defile.

Frederick tensed. He looked up and saw that his Saracens, riding in single file ahead, were looking around uneasily, too. Suddenly a hail of arrows whistled down on them. One bounced off Frederick's helmet. Armed riders in brown tunics and chain mail skidded down the steep slope toward him in an avalanche of soil and stones. Turning his head, he saw that the same was happening behind him. His horse reared in fright. He pulled the animal away from the path, down into the river bed, yelling to the soldiers in front of him to do the same. If I can lure them across to the other side, he thought, provided they don't have reinforcements, they'll be out in the open and will provide a target for my men.

With his back against the other side of the gorge, he faced the attackers. A giant of a man galloped toward him with his couched lance, uttering bloodcurdling cries. Hemmed in by boulders, Frederick ducked. The lance flew through the air and splashed into the water beside him. The two horses were side by side. Frederick plunged his sword into the brown cloak. Blood bubbled from the man's mouth before he fell off his horse into the river. Hermann appeared, still on his charger but without his helmet. There was a nasty gash above the grand master's right arm. A lance had torn through the chain mail that hung in metal shreds. Despite his injury, he gripped his bloodied sword, ready to defend Frederick.

The gorge echoed with the clanking of swords and the terrified whinnying of horses. Frederick's Saracens had rallied around him in a protective circle. The attackers, fewer than he had at first thought, having lost the advantage of surprise, turned and scrambled back up the hill. Faceless brown shadows, unreal under the broad noseguards of their steel helmets, they melted away as swiftly as they had come. An eerie silence descended on the gorge. The hawks still glided in the blue sky.

Frederick leaped off his horse and waded to where his dead assailant lay facedown in the shallow, crystalline water. With his foot, he turned the man over. A young, aristocratic face with a thin nose, pale now in death. With a start, he recognized him. It was the French knight who had so rudely interrupted him at the meeting in Acre. A Templar.

Hermann bent over him. "Armand de Coucy. It is as I thought. They have plotted to assassinate you."

"At the instigation of the pope? Aided by Jean de Brienne? So that I would never return to defend my realm?" Frederick spat the words.

Hermann looked with disgust at the dead man. He nodded. "Aye, my lord."

The rest of his escort, some injured, others merely disheveled, waded toward him. Berard's tunic was torn and smeared with mud. He had been unhorsed. The archbishop, up to his ankles in water, stared at the dead man. He looked at Frederick, arching his brows.

"Templars," Frederick kicked the corpse contemptuously. "Take this vermin along as evidence."

I'll stamp this evil out forever, he thought as he swung himself back into the saddle. Not just in Acre, but at its very roots, in Rome.

APULIA, JUNE 1229

The sentry in the watchtower peered over the parapet into the darkness. The faces of the riders at the gate were blurred shadows dancing in the torchlight. Their banners hung limp and unrecognizable.

"Open in the name of the emperor!" a voice bellowed.

The sentry shook himself awake. The emperor? The emperor was on crusade in the Holy Land. He had died there, some said. In these dangerous times, betrayal and subterfuge were commonplace. None of the Pope's accursed mercenaries had yet penetrated this far into the Apulian mountains, but they might well employ such a ruse.

"The emperor is in the Holy Land. Show me the emperor, if he's here!" he called down.

A rider threaded his horse through the others. Taking a lantern from one of the soldiers, the horseman held it up to his face.

The sentry stared down. "It's the emperor!" he cried to the other guards. "Open for the emperor!"

THE DOOR WAS flung open. The old nurse sleeping at the foot of the bed was instantly awake.

"My lady!" she screamed, "my lady!"

Bianca stirred in the bed, its curtains left undrawn because of the heat. "What is it, Peppa?" she asked, sitting up slowly. Then she saw the figure in the doorway, outlined by the light in the passage behind. "Frederick!" Bianca threw off the sheet and flew toward him.

He caught her halfway across the room. "My beloved, my precious," he murmured as he held her to him, kissing the top of her head. He could feel the sobs that racked her while her arms encircled him. She raised her face, streaked with tears, and smiled up at him. "You're back!"

"So I am, my love, but alas, I have to leave at dawn." He kissed her wet cheek. "I'm on my way to Capua." Peppa, after lighting the candles on the table, tiptoed from the chamber, closing the door.

They sat down beside each other on the bed. In the dim light Bianca could see lines of fatigue etched on his face. He still wore his riding tunic and dusty boots. She rubbed his forehead where the steel of his helmet had left a red weal.

He caught her hand. Turning it over, he kissed the inside of her wrist, the white skin untouched by the sun. He looked up. "I've come here just to be with you for a few hours, when I should be riding through the night."

"Is it true that you have won Jerusalem?"

He nodded.

"The whole of Europe will pay homage to you!" Her eyes glowed.

"I wouldn't be so sure of that," he said with a twisted smile. "The pope has done all he can to blacken my name."

"Can you prevail against the pope?" she asked.

"Yes, but it will take time. He has freed Naples, Gaeta, and other southern cities from their allegiance to Sicily, and promised them autonomy under his suzerainty. The March of Ancona is occupied by papal troops. But for Manfred, they would have advanced even further."

"My brother had us all brought to this mountain fortress in secret. Conrad cries for his wet nurse. He hates goat's milk . . . But Manfred's wife thought she couldn't be trusted."

Frederick's eyes lit up. "How is my son? And Enzio? And Catherine? We'll have to wake them at first light. Wait till they see the toys I've brought them. Mechanical marvels from the East . . ."

She smiled. "Conrad is growing like a mushroom. The others are fine. But what about you? You look tired."

"I've never felt better." He grinned. "All I need is sleep."

"You know that the pope's agents were spreading the word that you were dead?"

He nodded. "An old trick. But he was hoping it was true; he had set the Templars to assassinate me. I had their grand master arrested in Acre and their treasury confiscated. Some extra gold will come in very useful."

"Men are torn between loyalty to you and fear of the pope. Many are afraid that they'll be damned if they resist soldiers who wear the keys of Saint Peter on their tunics. Is that not a weapon more powerful than the strongest army?"

"Once the people see that I am alive, and recognize the pope's lies for what they are, they'll rally to me, some out of loyalty and others out of self-interest. The threat of earthly retribution is for more immediate than the heavenly kind! After I landed in Brindisi, the people danced in the streets. The news of my recovery of Jerusalem is spreading like wildfire, further undermining Gregory. Fear not, I'll rout the papal mercenaries. And then I'll wring Gregory's shriveled neck with my own hands!"

He slipped the nightgown from her shoulders. Bending his head, he murmured, "Tomorrow, we'll worry about the pope. Tonight, let us be in paradise." With the hunger of a man long starved, he closed his lips around one delicate nipple. Bianca pressed his head against her in a gesture that was both voluptuous and protective.

He's mine, he'll always be mine, she thought, as her body dissolved under the onslaught of his.

As THE FIRST rays of the sun tinged the horizon, Bianca stood beside Frederick in the lichen-covered courtyard. After he had hugged his sleepy children, she had insisted on staying with him until the last moment. "I may never see you again. This time you won't deny me as you did when you left for the Holy Land."

He swung himself into the saddle. Bianca reached up to touch his horse, her eyes moist. "Frederick, may God watch over you." With the stubborn pride he so loved about her, she shook her head, determined not to weep.

He leaned down. "Don't cry, beloved, no harm will befall me, I promise you."

Her right hand lay small and pale on the black stallion's neck, as if to ward off any evil from him. He laid his hand on hers for an instant before reaching for his reins.

With a last look at her slight figure in the mulberry cloak, he wheeled his horse around and clattered across the drawbridge.

SORA, AUGUST 1229

Mahmoud removed Frederick's coat of mail and unbuckled his steel knee-guards. Clad only in his padded gambeson, he let himself fall into a camp chair. A page knelt and began to pull off his boots while Mahmoud left to prepare hot water.

A bath, Frederick thought, a bath to wash off the blood and the grime. So much blood . . .

"Ah, there you are." Manfred walked into the tent. He waved a rolled parchment. "I've got the list of papal prisoners. Some noble names. The ransoms will be substantial!"

"Pour us some wine. My throat's parched." Frederick wiped the sweat off his face. The heat had not abated with the setting sun. All day it burned down on men stifling in armor as they breached the walls and took the town street by street. It seemed as if the very soil, soaked in blood, had absorbed the rays of the sun.

Manfred mixed wine and water in two silver cups and handed one to Frederick. Pulling up a stool, he sat and waited for Frederick to speak. He's aged in the last year, Manfred thought. He felt a stab of sadness. Somehow, he had never thought that Frederick could ever change, grow old, die . . . There were two lines now running along his nose and his hair was touched with gray. The last months had been tiring, but also exhilarating. Frederick had reconquered town after town. Jean de Brienne was routed. Most soldiers of the Keys fled back to Rome. The pope had taken refuge in the Castel Sant'Angelo.

It was strange that Frederick never took pleasure in his martial success. He was often glum after a battle. Unlike most princes, whose passion for war was bred into them, Frederick disliked bloodshed. He saw the slaughter of men as a waste of resources. A competent general, he organized his campaigns with great attention to detail. Cool-headed and valorous in battle himself, he nevertheless lacked the strategic brilliance of his grandfather Barbarossa, whose soldiers had loved him with a legendary devotion. Frederick, instead, paid his soldiers well, and on time.

Through the open tent flaps, Frederick stared at the city burning against the darkening sky. It was a spectacle of dread beauty. He had ordered Sora razed to the ground and all male citizens of fighting age put to the sword. Sora, close to Montecassino, was one of the Sicilian towns that had yielded to the Pope's blandishments of autonomy.

From the camp came the usual din of a victorious army. The noise of men, thousands of men. Raucous song, and laughter too, the laughter of men drunk on wine, blood, and pillage . . . Why did perfectly normal men turn into raging animals during war? They killed and maimed and raped in a frenzy of destruction. What had happened today had been a necessary lesson. Yet, as he watched the women and children and old men depart the city in long lines, carrying their miserable bundles, he had felt sad. Afterward, the soldiery had been allowed to pillage the town before setting fire to it.

The one thing he wouldn't allow was rape, on pain of death, no matter how much his lords argued that it was the common soldiers' right, an inevitable evil of war. He'd never forgotten, as a young man, during a raid on a rebel stronghold, the sight of a peasant girl, beaten and torn, being mounted by a line of men in the village square. As they rolled off her with their bloodied members, he had felt such disgust that Alaman had to restrain him from rushing at them with his sword.

Recently, he had a nightmare about Bianca, a dream so horrible that he woke in a cold sweat. He rubbed his forehead with both hands. He had moved her and the children, with Manfred's family, to the safety of Palermo. He yearned for her as he had never yearned for anyone. Manfred had been to Palermo, but had not said a word. He turned to him now. "How is Bianca?"

Manfred stared at him. He knew that every courier to Palermo carried letters from Frederick to his sister. Despite this, he still hoped that Frederick would tire of her after his long absence in Palestine. Bianca's reputation had already been destroyed. Sooner or later, her heart would be broken, too. Frederick's own troubles were exacerbated by his infatuation with her. His adultery had figured prominently in the pope's catalogue of outrages at the time of the excommunication. Manfred, too, was affected.

The more privileges Frederick heaped on him, the more jealous tongues wagged. Yet he loved them both. He shrugged. "She was well."

"You don't know how often I think of her."

Frederick's candor riled him. He didn't want to hear more. He was about to make a curt reply when Hermann strode into the tent. Manfred, relieved, rose to bring another camp chair.

"Some wine, my lord von Salza?"

The grand master smiled. "Please, Manfred, but do not forget to mix it with water!" Hermann never drank unwatered wine.

"We'll strike camp tomorrow," Frederick said. "We should reach the papal lands by noon." For weeks, Hermann had resisted marching on Rome, pleading with him to find an alternative solution.

The grand master regarded him from under his bushy eyebrows. "Frederick," he said, "will you grant me a request?"

Frederick looked at him. "If you want me to abandon my intention to teach Gregory a lesson, I can't."

Hermann leaned forward, his big hands on his knees. "Frederick, I beg you, let me make one last attempt. I'll go to Rome while you remain here. You have nothing to lose. If he still won't make peace, then you will have no reason not to invade his territory."

"You'd be wasting your time. The German princes, the Sicilian bishops, even his own cardinals have all pleaded with him. Louis of France has written to him in vain. Gregory will only change his mind when he feels the tip of my sword at his throat!"

"And if he doesn't?"

"Then he'll be dead and I can have a sensible man elected in his place!"

"You'd kill the pope?"

Frederick smiled. "Well, perhaps I'll just have him incarcerated and declared insane, which obviously he is."

"Please let me try once more. I've been Gregory's friend for many years; this time he may listen to me. He knows he has lost; if one offered him an honorable way out, he might accept. In his obsessive hatred of you, he has lost his senses. I think I can make him regain them."

Frederick studied his hands.

"For your sake and his, let me try," Hermann said. "It's a terrible thing to make war on the vicar of Christ. Christendom will condemn you."

Frederick sighed. "Very well, Hermann. I give you one week. If in seven days you have not returned with a written peace proposal, I march on Rome."

ANAGNI, AUGUST 1230

Through the mullioned windows of the papal summer palace the sun could be seen setting over the green vineyards in the valley below. A pleasant breeze fanned the three men dining at a long oak table. The servants had been dismissed. They were alone.

"A little more bread, my son?" the pope asked, pushing a silver platter heaped with little loaves made of costly white flour toward Frederick.

"Thank you, Holy Father." Frederick helped himself to another.

Hermann wiped his pewter plate clean with a piece of bread. Gregory normally subsisted on a Spartan diet, to which he ascribed his longevity, but today he had instructed his cook to prepare a sumptuous meal. Snails in onions and red wine, a stew of lampreys flavored with cinnamon, ginger, and sage, and roasted swan. The grand master sat back to ease his stomach, and eyed his two companions.

The bearded, ancient pope, eighty-seven years old, and the clean-shaven emperor of thirty-six were an extraordinary pair. Gregory, tall, thin, and stooped, with shaggy brows and sharp hazel eyes, chewed the food with his remaining teeth. He nodded as he listened to Frederick tell an anecdote about Jerusalem.

Frederick leaned across the table to make a point, smiling. The pontiff, not normally given to frivolity, laughed heartily. Hermann was astounded at the pope's transformation. This morning Gregory had still been the aloof vicar of Christ. Then, incredibly, the old man had begun to soften, swayed by Frederick's manner. Was it that alone, Hermann asked himself, or had Gregory, this son of a small landowner, been overcome by the affability with which this successor of the Caesars treated him? Gregory's invitation to the emperor to dine with him had been unexpected. He had seemed genuinely pleased when Frederick accepted.

Now, as Frederick, over a dish of figs stewed in honey, outlined his belief that pope and emperor should jointly rule the world for the welfare of mankind, Gregory nodded several times in quick succession.

"Well, my son," he said, "mayhap it is possible to bring about this ideal state you describe."

"It must be, Holy Father," Frederick said. "Chaos and lawlessness would result if ever Church and Empire were permanently divided. I wield the temporal sword that protects the world from anarchy, while you enforce the spiritual laws that keep men from sinking to the level of beasts."

Hermann could scarcely believe what he was hearing. Even if each privately still harbored grave doubts about the other, what he was witnessing seemed close to a miracle. Praise be to God, Hermann thought. These implacable enemies, who had not long ago vowed to fight each other to the bitter end, appeared to be in perfect amity tonight.

It had taken Hermann, Piero della Vigna, Frederick's new chancellor, and a delegation of Sicilian bishops headed by Berard a year to negotiate this treaty. Frederick's excommunication was lifted, the pope recognized him as king of Jerusalem, and the interdicts on the holy places in Palestine were rescinded. The patriarch of Jerusalem was to ratify the treaty Frederick had signed with Al-Kamil. The grand masters of both the Templars and the Hospitallers were ordered not to endanger the truce in the Holy Land by acts of hostility.

Frederick had to concede to Gregory that the property of the Templars in Palestine and Sicily, which Frederick had confiscated, be returned, as were the Church's possessions in Sicily. A general amnesty for all papal supporters in the kingdom was to be declared, and Frederick had been forced to make concessions on the thorny issue of his right of veto in the election of Sicilian bishops.

The treaty had been signed that morning near the town of Ceprano, not far from Anagni. The pope rode into the valley from his summer palace on his white mule, while Frederick issued forth from his encampment under a purple canopy. They signed the treaty in an open field, on a table covered with cloth-of-gold beneath a cloudless summer sky, cheered by their respective retinues.

After giving each other the kiss of peace, pope and emperor proceeded to a small chapel where Gregory, assisted by two cardinals and an archbishop, lifted the ban of excommunication that had lain on Frederick for three years. Couriers were immediately sent to inform the world that the rift between pope and emperor had finally been healed.

THAT EVENING, AS the small party rode back toward the camp at Ceprano, Frederick let his eyes wander over the moonlit fields and terraced vineyards. Hermann dozed on his horse, lightly holding his reins. Without him this treaty would never have come into being. Hermann, whose advancing years were beginning to weigh on him despite his iron constitution, had spent most of this last year in the saddle, pleading, cajoling, and occasionally crashing his large fist down on both imperial and papal tables.

There was a stillness, a soothing quiet in the warm night air, interrupted only by the beating of hooves on the dry soil. Raising his eyes toward the inky sky, he felt a heady sensation of relief. He was free! Free to devote himself to Sicily and the Empire.

Was it really possible to weld the German principalities into one nation? He had pondered this question now for fifteen years and still not found an answer. Their loyalty to a strong emperor, a first among equals, bound them together. But could these unruly princes remain united for longer than one man's lifetime? Perhaps, if their allegiance could by transferred to a dynasty.

Yolanda's little son Conrad had grown into a robust little boy of three. Frederick had been relieved to see that the child hadn't inherited Yolanda's frail constitution. He was his only legitimate heir after Henry. Henry had recently been betrothed to the Duke of Austria's daughter Margaret. Frederick had long been searching for a means of incorporating the duchy, which controlled Germany's access to Italy, into the Empire.

Whenever he thought of Henry he felt vaguely guilty. He hadn't seen his son for ten years, since the day he and Constance left Germany. His last image of him was of a nine-year-old hiding his tearful face in the archbishop of Cologne's cope. It wasn't his fault that every time he planned a reunion, fate thwarted his efforts. The Saracen rebellion, the Lombard closure of the passes, the crusade . . . He wrote to Henry frequently, admittedly mostly about matters of government. Yet a voice at the back of his mind told him that this was not all, that since Henry's infancy he had felt a distaste for his son's whining ways. Then there were his natural children, among them Richard, as dark as his mother Leila, a broad-chested young man of twenty, with an unbending sword arm.

There was little Frederick of Antioch, the child of Yolanda's vivacious cousin, born after his mother's precipitous return to Palestine. The ruse hadn't worked. Her ship had been delayed and she had been visibly pregnant upon her arrival in Outremer. Her husband had been prevented from burning his wife for adultery only by the threat of having his lands confiscated by Frederick's regent, to whom she had appealed. No sooner had Frederick landed in Acre than the count sent the boy to him in a basket, with a note to say that he could care for his own hell's spawn. He picked up the frightened child and hugged him. "I'll give him the title of prince of Antioch, like my uncle Bohemund," he had said to Mahmoud, "that will make the old ass of a count even angrier."

There was Catherine, Adelaide's daughter, a pretty little thing of thirteen. Soon, he'd need to find her a husband.

However, despite the affection he had for all his children, it was Enzio who was his favorite. He had inherited his mother's beauty, except that unlike Adelaide, he was dark-haired, with large, dreamy eyes. He was a devil in the lists. He had a quick brain and a talent for poetry. Frederick sometimes allowed the boy to join him when he entertained his circle of poet friends, such as Giacomo da Lentini, laureate of Sicily, or Percival Doria, the Genoese prince. As they sat around the fire, listening to a lute player, the group would compose poems in the vernacular. Enzio's compositions were invariably outstanding, almost as good as Giacomo's and far better than his own. Enzio would be fifteen this year. It was time to entrust him with greater responsibilities.

Responsibilities . . . Frederick sighed. There were so many. So much of what he had planned had been left undone during the years of his strife with Gregory. But now he could devote his energies into refashioning Sicily into the marvel it had once been.

He felt a sharp longing as he thought of Palermo. He could see the city, her flat rooftops and minarets, her shores washed by a blue sea, her gardens lit by the same moon that was here turning the bunches of unripe grapes into clusters of silver. A face imposed itself on the image of the city, a beloved face, with dark brows and large, searching ink-blue eyes.

Frederick gave spurs to his mount. He was suddenly in a hurry.

MELFI, APULIA, JULY 1231

"Frederick II, Holy Roman Emperor, King of Sicily, Jerusalem and Burgundy, to his people . . ."

Piero della Vigna's magnificent orator's voice echoed through the pillared hall of Melfi Castle as he read out the introduction to the new code of laws. When the chancellor had finished, Frederick dipped his pen into the vermilion ink and affixed his signature to the parchment. A great cheer went up. The Constitutions of Melfi had assumed force of law.

Roffredo of Benevento, on Frederick's left, beamed. It had taken him, Piero, and a team of jurists years of labor, of long discussions with Frederick, of arduous travels investigating arcane customs and local laws, and of consultation with princely bishops and unlettered village elders, to compile the work. It was the first legal code promulgated in Christendom since that of the Byzantine Emperor Justinian more than seven hundred years earlier.

Berard, watching Frederick's face, thought how little he had changed despite the passing years. He was smiling that peculiar half-smile he had had since boyhood whenever he achieved an objective.

Since the peace of Ceprano, Frederick had devoted himself to Sicily's prosperity. The Messina mint had made a gold coin called an *augustalis*. It was the only gold coin in Europe and caused a great stir, accustomed as people were to adulterated and clipped silver coins. Frederick accumulated the gold by forcing foreign merchants to pay for Sicilian goods in gold, but allowing payment for local trade to be made only in silver. On the obverse, the *augustalis* bore a likeness of himself, crowned by a laurel wreath, and on the reverse the imperial eagle. Gregory was sure to look on this with misgivings: little imagination was needed to realize that it proclaimed Sicily and the Empire as one, united in Frederick.

As much as he had been against the images on the coins, Berard shared Frederick's pride in the new legal code. An amalgam of centuries-old customs and new laws, the code was Roman in spirit. But it also contained radical concepts that were Frederick's own. The status of women, villeins, and orphans was improved. Trial by combat was abolished, as was payment of blood money for murder. Most importantly, all would be treated equally under the new laws, be they Saracen or Lombard, lord or villein. This, unheard-of in feudal law, sprang from Frederick's conviction that the foundation of justice was impartiality.

It remained to be seen what Gregory would make of it. With an eye to appeasing the pope, Frederick had introduced more severe measures against the growing number of heretics. The Albigensians, or Cathars, as they sometimes were called, had begun to spill over into Italy and Sicily to escape the Inquisition. In Languedoc, where they originated, they were being hounded by the Inquisition.

The Office of the Inquisition, recently established by Pope Gregory and encouraged by King Louis and his pious mother, was becoming very powerful in France. Frederick worried that the Inquisition's tentacles would soon reach into Italy, Spain, even Germany. Independent of the local clergy, the Inquisition was ostensibly an instrument for extinguishing heresies. So far, there had been no torture to extract confessions. But as Frederick said, the Inquisition was an ideal tool for the papacy to terrorize opponents and stifle thought. Torture was bound to follow.

A movement caught Berard's eye. A page approached Frederick and was whispering to him. Frederick broke into a smile. He beckoned to Piero. "She's been delivered of a daughter. See to the lords and the English ambassador. I'll join you at the tournament." He instructed the officers of state who were to sign the document to witness it in his absence.

Although Frederick had spoken in a low voice, others, too, had heard his words and were casting looks at each other. Surely the birth of a bastard was not a reason to disrupt an occasion such as this. Frederick flashed Berard a broad smile as he passed him. There was no doubt of the happiness Bianca brought him. Last year, she had given him a daughter he had named Constance. Now she had born him another child. Frederick knew he could never wed her. If Bianca's insignificant rank would have barred him from marrying her before, now that she had born his bastards, it was unthinkable. Despite this, Bianca Lancia was the uncrowned queen of Sicily. Troubadours sang of her beauty, and foreign envoys carried tales of her back to their courts.

Berard noticed Piero's narrowing eyes as he, too, watched the haste with which Frederick disappeared. The chancellor disliked Bianca. He was used to women succumbing to his suave charm. Malicious tongues accused him of bedding not only a large number of the ladies at court, but some of their husbands, too. Berard, observing him in unguarded moments, often asked himself what the real cause of his resentment of Bianca was.

Piero was turning to the English ambassador with great affability. Drawing him aside, he engaged him in conversation. Piero's mind was as devious as it was sharp. Yet there could be no doubt of his loyalty to Frederick, who had raised him, on merit alone, to the office of chancellor after Walter of Palear's disgrace. What Berard disliked about him was his hubris. His strutting gait and flamboyant cloaks put him in mind of a peacock. But Piero wrote excellent sonnets, a new form of poetry invented by Giacomo da Lentini. Piero declaimed them with a flair rivaled only by Frederick's son Enzio. From dark-haired Enzio, Berard's mind wandered to Frederick's eldest son Henry.

Berard maintained a correspondence with the bishop of Ratisbon, chancellor of Germany since poor Conrad's assassination, whose task it was to ensure that Henry followed his father's advice—advice that, of late, Henry seemed to be ignoring more and more.

Now twenty, Henry had inherited his father's willfulness but none of his astute political sense. Frederick, despite his independence of mind, had always surrounded himself with able men and known when to follow their counsel. Henry appeared to be sadly lacking in this regard. Resentful of the curbs imposed on his authority by the German princes, he had been making overtures toward the burghers of the free cities, setting himself up as their protector. From the reports he heard over the years, Berard had pieced together a fair picture of the young man. It was not one that bode well for the future.

He made his way in a somber mood through the throng of guests to the adjoining hall. His eyes lit up at the tables laden with choice wines, Saracen sweetmeats, delicate pasties, and above all, sherbets. Made with snow brought down from mountaintops and stored in deep underground caverns, they were his special delight. He suddenly realized how hungry he was.

A cup of spiced wine in one hand and a flaky boar pasty in the other, Berard chewed appreciatively, while his eyes scanned the company. Most were Sicilians, with a few tall German noblemen and one or two portly Rhenish prelates. This reminded him again of his friend Siegfried. It had been a long time since he had seen the bishop. They had spent many pleasant hours together during his years in Germany. Well, he'd see him soon enough. As chancellor of Germany, Siegfried would be a prominent member of Henry's retinue at the Diet in Ravenna that autumn.

THE RED-WALLED CITY of Ravenna was preparing for the first imperial Diet to be held in nearly eleven years. Every German prince, as well as King Henry, would be present.

Frederick took up residence in the bishop's palace on the marketplace. While awaiting the delegates' arrival, Frederick, accompanied by Norbert, explored the monuments of Ravenna's past. He hoped that Ravenna, once capital of the Western empire after the barbarian conquest of Rome, would yield antique columns, plinths, and perhaps statuary for the palace he was building in Foggia.

The pleasant autumn weather turned and rain fell for days, shrouding the city and the surrounding marshes in gray mist. All Saints' Day came and went, and still not a single delegate had arrived. Three days later, a fast-riding courier sent by Henry of Brabant brought calamitous news: the Lombard communes had once again blockaded the Brenner Pass. The duke and the other princes were making their way by the much slower and by now snowbound Styria-Friuli route. They wouldn't be in Ravenna before the middle of December. The Diet was postponed until Christmas. Frederick began to plan the only solution to the Lombard problem: war.

On the second day of Christmas, Frederick's birthday, an exhausted, much aged Henry of Brabant arrived with an escort suffering from the ill effects of cold. Conditions were so bad, he reported, that most of the other princes had turned back. After embracing the duke in the vestibule of San Vitale, where he was attending mass, Frederick asked, "And Henry?"

He blanched when he heard that his son had never left Germany. Instead, Henry had sided with the burghers of Liège in a dispute against their bishop. Staring at the floor mosaic, he muttered, "A fitting birthday gift . . ."

The Diet was postponed once more until the spring, in Aquileia. Frederick issued an imperial summons, worded in the harshest terms, for

Henry to present himself at Easter in Aquileia. Milan, head of the Lombard League, and her allies were placed under the ban of the Empire.

"WHAT AM I to do with him?" Frederick put the fragment of a marble hand back on the pile of Roman remains.

Bianca was sitting on the stump of a column. Thoughtfully, she scraped the earth at her feet with the tip of her shoe.

"He's behaving like a willful child," she said, "so a good spanking is the first thing that comes to mind. What, I wonder, is the equivalent of a good spanking for a king?"

Frederick sighed. "Berard thinks that I should talk to him, not as emperor, but as father. I've left him alone too long. Now that he's a man, he thinks he needs no one's advice any more. In a way, I can understand his irritation with the churchmen around him." He smiled. "When I was young, they nearly drove me mad. If it hadn't been for Berard, I might also have rebelled against all common sense simply because its source was a fusty prelate."

"No, you wouldn't. You're too clever for that."

"Bianca, I want to make peace with him. He's my son, my heir, the next emperor of my blood. But I can't tolerate open defiance!"

"You've another son, little Conrad. You can depose Henry and have Conrad elected in his stead. The German princes won't stand in your way; they dislike Henry as much as he dislikes them."

"I can't do that. First of all, it would disgrace the Hohenstaufen name, and second, Conrad is heir to Sicily. While I live, the Empire and Sicily are one, united in my person, even if not in law. But after my death, they must be separate."

"Must they really?" Bianca held his eyes.

It was uncanny. At times she read his innermost thoughts, thoughts that he himself only half acknowledged.

Slowly, she added, "I don't think Henry will be emperor, Frederick. I don't know why. I had a disturbing dream about him a few nights ago. He was wearing shackles."

Frederick shivered. Did she have the gift of prophecy, too?

Although it was a mild winter's day, the ground was damp and cold. He bent down and pulled the furred hood of her cloak over her head. "There,

314 M A R I A R. B O R D I H N

my sweet. You mustn't catch cold." Although their third child was not due for another five or six months, he worried that she didn't rest enough and still rode, even hunted. Bianca had given him two daughters in as many years and now she was once more with child. It was too soon. Although she was young and strong and her confinements had been easy, he was tormented by a secret dread that she would die in childbirth. He told himself that she was happy, happier than most queens wedded to unloved husbands, yet the fear of retribution never quite left him, no matter how much he scoffed at it. Her beauty had increased with maturity, acquired definition, dignity. Even on a broken column, she looked the queen she could never be.

Norbert and Bartolomeo da Foggia, his talented new assistant, were coming toward them.

"My lord, come quickly." The Rhinelander's lively brown eyes shone.

At the excavation site they looked down in wonder. Lying in a grave of mud was a life-sized marble statue of a woman. The workmen had cleaned her with rags, leaving smudges of dirt. A lady of delicate features, her hair piled in a Grecian knot, her limbs and features perfectly proportioned, she looked up at them with a smile that seemed to mock the passing of the ages.

Frederick, whose delight in ancient artifacts bewildered his courtiers, who had little use for the remains of antiquity other than to use them as building materials, couldn't contain his excitement. Was she Greek or Roman? Perhaps it was Placidia herself. . . . "Raise her quickly," he cried. "If it rains again, the shaft might cave in."

He had begun excavating a half-buried brick building beside the Church of San Vitale, said to be the tomb of Galla Placidia, a Roman empress of the fifth century. He was astounded by the fragmented statues, utensils, and even glass the workmen had turned up alongside the mausoleum.

The statue was transported to the palace on a straw-covered litter. Frederick named her the Lady of Ravenna, and had her set on a plinth of pink marble carved for her by Norbert. She would always remind him of the Diet of Ravenna that never took place.

FROM RAVENNA, FREDERICK decided to go on a progress along the Adriatic coast toward Ancona. From there he would take ship for Aquileia. On the way, he planned to halt in Venice. The Republic of Venice controlled access to the Friuli-Styria route over the Alps, the only alternative to the Brenner Pass. If he were to engage in a Lombard war, it was essential to strengthen the Empire's tenuous bonds of friendship with the wily Venetians.

They left Ravenna on a windy March morning. A few miles south of the city they reached a narrow stone bridge. Berard reined in his horse. He pointed. "That, Frederick, is the Rubicon."

Frederick stared at the brown, sluggish waters that flowed under the bridge. Once this insignificant-looking river had been the boundary between Cisalpine Gaul and Rome. For a general to cross it with his legions without the Senate's permission was treason. Caesar, aware that his enemies in Rome were plotting his downfall, had to either ford the Rubicon or perish. Caesar took the greatest gamble of his life. He ordered his legions to advance on Rome. Within a few months, Caesar was lord of the Roman world.

Frederick twisted his lips in a bitter smile. His enemies too, like Caesar's, were biding their time in Rome. The struggle with the papacy wasn't over, not yet. Only when the pope's Lombard allies were cowed forever, their lands integrated into the Empire, and the papacy totally isolated, could there be real peace. That is, he thought, if my enemies don't destroy me first, as they destroyed Caesar in the end.

As if to rid himself of so grim a vision, Frederick spurred his horse over the bridge, across the Roman cobbles that still paved it. Beneath him, the Rubicon continued to flow toward the sea, unconcerned with the fate of men or empires.

LIKE A FLOATING mirage of palaces, churches and squares, arching bridges, and latticework windows of terracotta-colored marble, Venice rose out of the waters that nurtured and protected her.

The March breeze was crisp and bracing, whipping the surface of the water as the convoy of galleys made its way down the Grand Canal.

Frederick, standing beside the doge under a fringed canopy of purple silk on the deck of the *Bucintoro*, the gilded state galley of Venice, breathed in the sea and marveled at a city built on water. A fitting setting for a

republic that made her dominion of the sea the basis of her greatness . . .
The Venetians' achievement was a remarkable one. The usual result of
democracy was internecine strife and chaos. In Venice, ruled by an oligar-
chy of patrician families, this had not occurred. How odd, he thought, that
such a unique city should have been created by an accident of history. The
marshy islands in the lagoon had first been settled by the inhabitants of the
mainland fleeing from the invading hordes of Attila.

"There, Your Grace, the Fondaco dei Tedeschi, the trading center and
warehouse of the German merchants." The doge pointed toward a huge
square wooden building with double-tiered arcades on the left of the
Grand Canal, its arches hung with imperial banners and crammed with
cap-waving merchants from Germany.

The doge, Francesco Dandolo, an elderly man with small black eyes and
yellowish skin, his deep voice at odds with his slight build, wore the char-
acteristic horn-shaped brocade headdress that was the sign of his office.

On the piazzetta at the waterfront, dwarfed by the winged lion of Saint
Mark and the statue of Saint Theodore on their antique columns, the
doge's council, the Signoria, and the noblest citizens awaited Frederick.
Their doyen, Leonardo Tiepolo, bowed and spread his beringed hands.
"Welcome, Your Grace, to our unworthy city. We are honored by your visit."
His mellifluous voice betrayed no uneasiness.

Frederick's presence, with a considerable armed escort, was a cause of
concern for the Venetians. His spies had reported that members of the
Signoria referred to him in private as "the Hohenstaufen tyrant." Yet they
could hardly have refused his request to pray at the shrine of Saint Mark
on his way to Aquileia without giving offense. They knew the motive for
his visit was to safeguard access to the Empire; as long as that was his only
reason, he'd be welcome.

Frederick smiled. "It is I who am pleased to feast my eyes on the beauty
of your city, a marvel of the stonemason's art. I am filled with impatience,
too, to pray at the shrine of the holy apostle Mark."

He recalled with amusement how Venice had come by this treasure: the
Venetians had purloined the remains of the apostle from his tomb in Alex-
andria, smuggling the relic out from under the nose of the sultan's port
officials by hiding it under a consignment of salt pork. Not, of course, that
stealing saints was a Venetian prerogative. Hallowed relics had been plun-

dered down the ages: entire bodies or parts thereof, fragments of the True Cross, bottled milk of the Virgin, holy teeth or hairs of venerable beards, had all fallen prey to pious theft.

With a twinkle, he added, "I've also noticed that the women on the balconies of your city are as beautiful as the palaces they grace."

This brought forth laughter and a round of applause from the patricians who filled the piazzetta.

LATE AT NIGHT, as Bianca nestled against him, sleepy from their love-making, her mind drifted back to this astounding city.

She and Manfred's wife had that morning paid their respects to the doge's wife. The dogaressa, a fat, overly rouged woman with a front tooth missing and kind eyes, had received them in the women's wing of the palace, amid frolicking grandchildren, lapdogs, and a pet monkey. They all sat on huge round silk-covered cushions on the floor. When the time came to eat, a black eunuch cut up the dogaressa's food into little pieces. Making use of a small golden implement shaped like a snake's tongue with a handle, the doge's wife impaled each morsel on it. She had explained that it came from Constantinople, where it was very fashionable, and that it was called a fork. The Venetians might be a nation of wily merchants, as Frederick called them, but they were fabulously rich.

His voice interrupted her thoughts. "Bianca?"

"Yes, my love?"

"I've been thinking. Why don't you return to Foggia with the bishop of Caserta? He leaves next week. The Diet at Aquileia could last for weeks, if not months. By that time you'll be too far gone. The return journey might be hard on you and the babe . . ."

Suddenly she was wide awake. "You mean you don't want to be embarrassed by my presence."

"Bianca, you know that's not it. The whole of Christendom knows about you, and is envious of you."

It was true, Bianca thought. He had heaped jewels and lands on her. In the guise of the Marquis Lancia's sister, he allowed her to meet lords and princes, ambassadors and scholars. She had a court of her own, with waiting-women, dwarves and falcons, a chaplain, and a chamberlain.

Yet his devotion to her hadn't precluded him from keeping the troupe of Egyptian dancers he had brought back from the East. Like the exotic animals and the celebrated elephant, they were a gift of Al-Kamil. They lived in secluded quarters, guarded by towering black eunuchs and, together with the elephant, followed every imperial progress. At night they danced for Frederick and his friends. He maintained that they were only entertainers.

She often joined him in a progress. Why had he now decided it would be too dangerous? It was true that travel over bad roads in an advanced stage of pregnancy could be dangerous. Frederick himself had been born in a tent because his mother had been overtaken by the onset of childbirth while traveling. And yet . . .

The stillness was interrupted now and then by the crackling of a log in the fireplace. At length she said, "It's Henry, isn't it? He's the reason you don't want me there."

Frederick sighed. "Yes, my sweet. I don't know how to say this, but . . ."

She laid a hand on his bare chest. "I understand," she said. "I'll wait for you in Foggia, if you'll promise to send me news of the Diet, and above all, of Henry. I would have liked to meet him, but no matter, you'll tell me everything about him later." She closed her eyes to hide her tears.

FREDERICK SPENT TWO weeks in Venice, holding meetings with the doge and the Signoria. As expected, the Venetians demanded further trading concessions in Sicily and Palestine in return for their neutrality in the Lombard war. After a show of reluctance, Frederick agreed and the pact was sealed. On the day of his departure, he prayed at the shrine of Saint Mark, offering gifts of gold and silver to the basilica. The city presented him with an enamel reliquary pendant containing a splinter of the True Cross. Frederick allowed the doge to slip it over his head, thanking him gravely.

THE IMPERIAL CAVALCADE arrived in Aquileia at dusk to find the town and its immediate surroundings overflowing with the retinues of the German delegates. The patriarch of Aquileia, accompanied by the officers of his household, greeted Frederick outside the gates and escorted him to the patriarchal palace.

Many of the delegates had arrived a week or two earlier. They lodged in palaces, monasteries, and merchant's houses, while some of their more extravagant suites were obliged to stay in tents outside the walls. The duke of Carinthia, the patriarch told Frederick, arrived with a suite of more than three hundred, while the archbishop of Cologne's retinue numbered more than two hundred servants, chaplains, and secretaries. The only modest one among them was the archbishop of Salzburg, with a retinue of just twenty. This was without counting the mounted men-at-arms that accompanied each lord. Unfortunately, the patriarch said, there was no word yet of King Henry.

Frederick forced a smile. The Diet wasn't scheduled to begin for another week. This time Henry would come, must come. "He'll be here in good time," he said brightly, waving to the cheering crowds.

That evening, Frederick took Hermann von Salza aside and handed him the Venetian reliquary. "This'll sit much better on your chest than on mine."

The grand master stared at him. "But Frederick, it is of great spiritual and material value."

Frederick shook his head. "It'll look splendid on your white robe. Keep it."

THE MESSENGER FROM King Henry had barely left Frederick's presence before a page was sent to call an immediate meeting in his privy chambers.

When Piero, Berard, Manfred, Henry of Brabant, and the patriarch arrived, they found Frederick in a towering rage. Henry, he informed them, assumed that he would lodge in the same palace as his father. He had sent his chamberlain ahead with his household to prepare his quarters in the patriarchal palace.

Frederick's voice cut through the silence. "Henry and his retinue will have their quarters in Cividale across the marsh. He is not to set foot in Aquileia."

"But Frederick, he's your son, you can't—" Manfred objected.

"I can, and I will. He's a rebellious subject and I won't allow him into my presence until he takes a public oath that he will refrain from further insubordination. You," he pointed to the patriarch, "the archbishops of Salzburg and Magdeburg, and the dukes of Meran, Saxony, and Carinthia, will be the guarantors of his good behavior, on the understanding that should he break his oath, you are to take up arms against him. Furthermore, he is to write to the pope stating that if he relapses into rebellion, he'll accept his own excommunication. Those are my conditions, and unless he agrees to them, I shall have him imprisoned for treason. You, Piero, see to it that he's separated from his troops and kept under guard."

They stared at him. This was harsh medicine indeed. The patriarch, who obviously didn't relish this unpleasant duty, pressed his lips together.

Only Henry of Brabant nodded. "You're right, except you're being too lenient," the duke said with his old outspokeness. "That boy has inherited the Hohenstaufen frivolity without any of their greatness. He's a foolish, headstrong fop. You should replace him before he does more damage."

Frederick lowered his eyes. The duke, alas, was right.

Berard took a deep breath. "Frederick," he said, "I think you're being too harsh. You will only incite him to further mischief if you trample his pride thus."

"If such is his mettle, let him show it, the sooner the better." Frederick said. "He'll be watched closely from now on. I can't allow my feelings as a father to intrude upon my duties as emperor. Henry will be punished, and if he isn't man enough to accept it and see the error of his ways, then so be it."

"Who," Manfred asked, "is to bring Henry your conditions?"

Frederick jerked his chin towards Henry of Brabant. "You," he said.

The duke raised his brows. "But he dislikes me intensely. Why me?"

"For precisely that reason. You, Henry, are not likely to pity him, as some of my other friends here might." He shot a pointed glance at Berard and rose.

"Leave me, all of you. I wish to be alone."

He turned to the mullioned window and looked out across the battlements, over the rooftops to the sea. Aquileia was the largest ecclesiastical principate in the Empire, and its patriarch, the second most powerful bishop after the bishop of Rome, a loyal vassal of his. Wedged in a narrow strip between the Eastern Alps and the Adriatic, the patriarchate was the back door to the Empire, crucial in the coming war with the Lombards and his confrontation with Henry.

Frederick passed his hand across his eyes. All anger had gone out of him, leaving only sadness, and a tiny glimmer of hope. Perhaps he'd still change his ways. Perhaps Berard was right. Berard, who always saw the other side of every argument . . . Oh, Henry, my son, what is to become of you? What manner of man are you, whom everybody criticizes so harshly?

He turned away from the window. It was useless to allow his feelings to weaken his resolve. He would soon be able to judge Henry with his own eyes. Then he would take appropriate action.

A HUSH FELL over the hall. The minstrels stopped playing. The crowd parted. Princes, prelates, and officials tried not to stare as King Henry, announced by three fanfare blasts, entered the hall.

Tall and well formed, with Constance of Aragon's golden hair, Henry of Hohenstaufen was an extraordinarily good-looking man. His head held high, he walked slowly past the throng of courtiers, eyes fixed on the figure of his father enthroned on the dais. From Henry's shoulders trailed a superb mantle in deep blue velvet lined with miniver. Jewel-studded armlets encircled his wrists. His young wife, Margaret of Austria, was a slight, brown-haired girl with good skin, a plucked forehead under a cloth-of-gold wimple. She had nervous brown eyes and despite being sumptuously dressed, she appeared dowdy in comparison with her dazzling husband to whose arm she clung.

As Henry halted before the dais, the tension was palpable. Would Frederick rise to embrace his son, or just acknowledge him from his throne?

For a long moment they stared at each other in silence. Henry's knees gave way under his father's implacable stare. Slowly, he knelt down and bowed his head. Only then did Frederick rise.

Ignoring his son, he took two steps toward Henry's wife and raised her from her curtsy. "Welcome, Margaret, to my court," he said with a smile. "Sadly, the onerous duties of state have kept me from embracing you till now." He embraced and kissed the girl, who seemed on the verge of tears. Then he turned to the still kneeling Henry.

"Rise, my son," he said, trying to subdue the surge of deep irrational pride he felt at the sight of the splendid man his son had become.

Henry stared at his father. "Am I forgiven?" he asked in a soft voice strangely at odds with his magnificent physique.

Frederick, by way of reply, hugged him tightly. Pray for him, Constance, he thought, pray for both of us.

SIEGFRIED OF RATISBON and Berard walked side by side in the little garden atop the ramparts of Aquileia's patriarchal palace, with its rectangular herb beds and a pear maze at the far end.

"It's a pity," the chancellor said, "that he's got only one other son."

Berard nodded. "True, but at least little Conrad is robust and has outlived the worst dangers of infancy."

The chancellor halted and turned to look at Berard. "Why hasn't he taken another wife? It's five years since Yolanda's death."

Berard smiled. "You have doubtless heard of Bianca Lancia?"

Siegfried resumed walking. "Aye, so I have. Tell me," he asked with a gleam in his eyes, turning his head toward Berard, "is it really true that he has a harem of Saracen girls that accompany him everywhere?"

Berard smiled. His old friend was an upright churchman and an excellent diplomatist. His only failing was a fondness for gossip. "I'm afraid it is. And to tell the truth, a harem full of comely girls must seem tempting to any full-blooded man, don't you think?"

Siegfried nodded. "I'm not saying that other princes don't indulge their lusts—alas, it's men's nature to do so—but Saracens, Berard, followers of Mohammed, in the bed of the Holy Roman Emperor?"

Berard smoothed his beard. "He grew up with Muslims and doesn't find their company distasteful. Frederick stands above the petty bigotry of other men."

The chancellor swallowed the rebuke with good grace.

"Well now," he said, changing the subject, "to whom shall we wed him?"

"I don't think your project will find much favor with Frederick, but Piero has been talking of an English alliance for some time."

They reached the end of the walk. "Shall we sit awhile?" Siegfried indicated a stone bench beside the maze.

The two men sat in silence, each contemplating the little garden in the afternoon sun. Both had reached the autumn of their lives, and were glad of the warmth. The chancellor in particular, who suffered grievously from gout, found that irritation and cold aggravated his pain. Here, in the sunshine of Italy, far from the strains of trying to rule Germany and Henry at the same time, life seemed almost the way it had been in his youth. He watched a sparrow fly across the lavender and settle on the lichen-covered parapet beside them.

"It's a long time, Berard, since you and I first met. It must be more than twenty years since I received young Frederick at the gates of Basle. We all prayed then that he'd turn out to be a true Hohenstaufen. He's a great man, our Emperor, but a strange one, too."

"Alas, God hasn't seen fit to give him an heir of his own mettle." Berard said. "Henry will never rise above his own mediocrity."

Siegfried sighed. "We haven't seen the last of that business yet. I've known Henry since boyhood, and I don't think he'll remain as submissive as he now appears for long. It's my opinion—"

Frederick waved at them from the end of the walk. He strode toward them in a moss-green hunting cloak.

He's nearly forty years old, Berard thought, and still he cannot walk but must run.

"I was told that the two of you were taking exercise. Instead I find you sitting in the sun like plotting lizards. What have you been up to?"

"We've been marrying you, my lord." The chancellor's eyes sparkled. "It is high time you took a wife. We can't have the people getting into this habit of not getting married any more, it's a bad example."

"And who, may I ask, have you picked as my bride?"

"We've considered several candidates, but I think we settled on the King of England's sister, didn't we?" Berard cast a look at Siegfried.

"I'll tell both of you, as I've told Piero before: I don't need a wife and I'm not going to take a wife!" An angry nerve twitched above his left eye.

The outburst was so unlike Frederick, who enjoyed banter, that they could only stare. The strain of the last few weeks must have overtaxed him, Berard thought. After Henry's public submission, father and son had attended banquets, jousts, and hunts together, tight smiles on their lips.

Then, suddenly, with that mercurial changeability he'd always had, but which was becoming more pronounced, Frederick smiled. He extended his hand to help Siegfried up from his seat. "Come, my lords, let us walk a little. I wish to deliberate some matters with both of you that are best discussed in the fresh air. The walls, here as everywhere, have ears."

THE NEXT MORNING, a meeting was held in the great hall at which all the delegates to the Diet were present. By the time Frederick rose at the end of the session, the German princes had unanimously pledged themselves to raise an army against the Lombard Communes in the spring of the following year.

GHIOA DEL COLLE, APULIA, SUMMER 1232

The wheat stood high and golden that year, bent under the weight of a rich harvest. In the hot stillness of the afternoon, an eagle glided toward the horizon above a few solitary olive trees on the crest of a hill.

Frederick, leaning against the trunk of an ancient cork oak, sighed with contentment. "What," he asked, removing the stalk of wheat he had been chewing, "is God's price for such bliss?"

Bianca opened her eyes. Her head lay cradled in his lap. How typical! Frederick, who professed to scorn them, would have made a first-rate merchant. He was forever totting up ledgers, real and imaginary. His friend the mathematician Leonardo Fibonacci had introduced him to a new counting method with Arabic numerals. There were nine numerical signs. But the real innovation lay in the tenth, called a zero. This, according to Frederick, revolutionized mathematics, making it possible to reckon unimaginably large figures without the aid of an abacus. Frederick had introduced it into all the royal counting houses.

"What are you thinking, my love?" she asked.

He laid a hand on her bulging belly. "I was thinking how beautiful Sicily is. How much more beautiful and promising than the so-called Promised Land."

Bianca smiled. "You mean the Holy Land doesn't flow with milk and honey?"

"In most places, particularly Judaea, it doesn't even flow with water. It's arid and stony, with a harsh, blinding light that hurts the eye and burns the soul. Maybe it even deranges the mind. Perhaps that's why it has brought forth so many prophets . . ."

Dangerous ground, this. When Frederick expounded on religion he tended to say fearful things, things that could harm his soul and his reputation. Quickly, she said, "Tell me about Henry. What news of him?"

"He's behaving himself, for the time being."

After a moment, he added, "Henry's problem is that he looks like a Hohenstaufen but doesn't think like one. You see, it's a little like breeding horses." Noticing her frown, he said, "The more often you cross a superb horse with an equally exceptional one, the better the offspring."

He pulled off another blade of wheat, and began to chew. "Recently," he said, "Matteo of Santa Eufemia proved to me that it even works with plants. Wheat, for example. The abbot grows wheat that yields far more than its ancestors. The Cistercians are making great advances in this. But you see, there's a rub. When you've succeeded with so many generations of wheat or men or horses, the strain exhausts itself. That's happened with Henry. It happens to civilizations, too . . ."

Bianca laid her hand on his. How lightly he had condemned his son, and yet how much bitterness that knowledge must cause him.

With his eyes on the distant eagle still circling above the olive trees, he said, "Perhaps the son you carry will one day redeem my race."

Bianca caught her breath. She'd given him two daughters, and still he dreamed of a son. But what did he mean . . . "Oh no," she muttered, closing her eyes as another stab of pain shot through her.

One glance at her told him what the matter was. He put two fingers in his mouth and whistled once, a sharp piercing whistle. A pack of hounds shot out from behind a nearby hillock. An instant later, armed men came running.

"The lady Bianca is unwell. Make a litter. We must get her to her waiting-women fast."

The horse-litter in which she followed him this morning would jolt her too much. Frederick chewed his lip. He watched his men make a makeshift litter of a cloak tied between two lances. How could he have taken a pregnant woman, only a moon away from her time, on a hunt over rough terrain, even if she insisted on coming?

A HUSH FELL on the lying-in chamber as Frederick entered. Although it was only early afternoon, the chamber was lit by dozens of candles, the shutters closed to protect the newborn from the evil eye. On a portable altar against the wall, grains of incense burned in a silver censer before an effigy of the Virgin.

The women surrounding the bed backed away. Only Peppa continued to brush Bianca's hair.

In the bed, hung with coral silk, Bianca was propped up against the cushions. In her arms she held her son, tightly swaddled in white linen.

She looked pale, more so than after her other two confinements. Frederick felt a stab of fear. He raised her free hand to his lips. "How is my swallow?" he asked, trying to banish the image of the dead Yolanda from his mind. "May I hold my son?"

Bianca attempted a weak smile. There were purple shadows under her eyes.

He picked up the child. Big eyes of an inky color between black and blue looked up at him. "He's beautiful. I can already see great talent and good looks."

"Is he at the beginning or the end of the wheat cycle?"

"The beginning, without any doubt," Frederick laughed. "New blood, you see." He studied the infant. "His eyes will be like yours and Manfred's. Let's call him Manfred. Maybe his uncle will then finally forgive me."

Bianca lowered her eyes. She was tired. She should feel elated that after two daughters she had finally borne a son. Instead, she just felt a terrible weariness. To Frederick, despite what he had said to her in a moment of wistfulness, the child's sex didn't matter . . . She tried to fight the tears that stung her eyes.

Frederick looked at her. He sensed her unhappy mood and was at a loss what to do.

She began to cry. "Please go away," she sobbed. "Leave me alone."

He glanced at Peppa, on the other side of the bed, for guidance. The old nurse had helped bring each of Bianca's children into the world, to the annoyance of the midwives, who had been relegated to the role of spectators. She must know what this was all about.

Peppa shrugged. "It's best that you leave my lady to rest now." She turned and busied herself with a pile of linen. After all these years, Peppa still didn't approve of him. She was a formidable old dragon. Yet, for a reason he couldn't fathom, he would have liked her acceptance. He kissed Bianca's forehead. "Sleep now, my sweet. I'll come back tonight."

Bianca stared at the door, tears trickling down her cheeks, while the women in the chamber pretended not to notice. She looked down at the tiny face of the baby in her arms. His eyes were closed now. In the corner of one eye was a dark red mark. Peppa assured her it would disappear in a few weeks. Even if he turned out to be as talented and handsome as Frederick had said, it would avail him nothing. He would always be a bastard, while his two half-brothers wore their crowns in proud splendor. A new sob racked her. *I, through my sin, am the cause of the curse this child will bear all his life.* She felt a chill run through her.

Her head spun. Before her eyes rose the scene of a battle's aftermath. The stony ground was littered with dead and dying men and horses. Sprawled on the ground beside a trampled gorse bush was a man, auburn-haired and clean-shaven, in an emerald cloak. Beside him lay a golden crown in the muddy grass. The face was white in death, the hand still clutched a bloodied sword.

With a scream, Bianca fell to one side in a dead faint.

THAT YEAR, A fierce summer gave way to an unusually cold winter. Bianca recovered from her malaise. Little Manfred flourished and his mother, watching him grow, forgot the foreboding she had felt on the day of his birth.

Frederick was engaged in preparations for the Lombard campaign in the spring. The court had taken up winter quarters in Foggia. This flourishing city in northern Apulia was now the capital of Frederick's empire. In its vaulted chancery, all the threads of government came together.

* * *

DUSK HAD FALLEN by the time a blast of fanfares from the sentries announced the emperor's return with his huntsmen. The huge iron-banded
gates of Foggia's palace creaked open. Frederick and his lords, amid much
laughter and banter, rode into the torchlit courtyard.

After he had dismounted, Frederick clapped Piero on his back. "Well
done! You excelled today, my friend."

"Only because you held your falcons back." Piero felt a surge of pride.
To hunt as well as a nobleman had long been a dream of his, one that he
had turned into reality by hard training. Not that he was particularly interested in either falconry or the dangerous business of killing a boar, which
so entranced those of noble birth. But Frederick's approval was another
matter.

"He's bagged more than anyone else, including myself," Thomas of
Aquinas said.

Frederick rubbed his hands together. "I'm famished." The stars glittered in the clear sky. The air was cold and bracing.

They walked through the great marble arch, their boots clattering on
the inlaid breccia floors. From here they passed into an open courtyard
with an octagonal fountain flanked by six griffins. The palace, which had
taken nearly eight years to complete, was a blend of Saracenic and classical architecture. Greek and Roman statues stood in niches. The privies and
bathing chambers had water channeled to them in lead pipes.

"Your Grace!" A steward ran toward them, followed by a messenger in
a foreign livery. "A message from the bishop of Ratisbon." The messenger
drew a letter from his cloak. Kneeling, he handed it to Frederick.

Frederick glanced at it. It was sealed with the German chancellor's privy
seal, employed only for personal correspondence. He broke the seal and
began to read. He turned to Piero. His face was grim. "Come."

The chancellor followed Frederick's brisk stride to his private apartments. From a large fireplace came the scent of burning olive wood. Eastern rugs covered the floors. Cushioned divans lined one wall. There were
book chests and a carved lectern. In a corner, upon her plinth, stood the
marble Lady of Ravenna.

Mahmoud, a linen towel over his arm, appeared in the doorway to a smaller chamber. He salaamed. "Your bath is ready, oh sultan."

"The bath can wait. Leave us." Frederick threw off his cloak. When the door had closed, he turned to Piero.

"It's Henry. He's freed the inhabitants of three Rhineland cities from allegiance to their overlords. With his wife's father, the Duke of Austria, he has attacked the Duke of Bavaria."

Piero's dark eyes clouded. "He's trying to wrest control of Germany from the princes, and then . . ." he halted, afraid to finish his sentence.

". . . from me." Frederick completed it for him.

"It is treason."

"Aye," Frederick said, his voice husky with pain, "treason."

"You must act immediately, send an army to halt him."

Frederick shook his head. "No, Piero. I must go to Germany myself. Conrad will come with me. He must be elected king in Henry's stead."

Frederick sat down on a settle. He stared into the fire. At length, he said, "First, I must meet with Gregory. I must secure his consent to Conrad's election. Fortunately, he still has need of the troops I sent him. He'll have to agree, whether he likes it or not."

Piero nodded. At least the moment was propitious. The Roman populace had once again rebelled against papal rule. Burning and plundering, the mob made its way to the Lateran, threatening the pontiff himself. Gregory, dressed as a groom, managed to escape to Rieti. From there, he had called on Frederick for help.

"My lord, forgive me. While it is true that today he has great need of you, that may not be so tomorrow. Gregory is the wiliest of men. He—"

"I know," Frederick snapped, "better than anyone else."

"What I mean is," Piero said, "you must reassure him that you'll take immediate steps to secure the succession of Sicily, that the current situation is only a temporary one, until such time as you have a new heir."

Frederick sighed, "Pour me a cup of wine. My throat is parched. I can't contemplate what you're about to tell me with a dry gullet."

Piero poured wine into a cup and handed it to him.

Frederick drank deeply, then put the cup down on the floor. "Sit," he said. "It's the English alliance again, is it not?"

Piero leaned forward. "My lord, you must reassure Gregory. The only way to do that is to have another heir. You must marry again. An English alliance will also strengthen your power, and the rich dowry of King Henry's sister will go a long way to defray the expenses of the Lombard war."

Frederick stared into the fire again. After a while, he asked, "How much would such a dowry bring?"

"Twenty, perhaps thirty thousand gold marks."

"Thirty thousand gold marks and a few sons, if I'm lucky, to appease the pope."

"Precisely, my lord." A smile flickered over Piero's lips. "I am told by the English ambassador that the princess is very comely."

"They all are, till you see them," Frederick said, studying his boots.

TRANI, SUMMER 1233

"Greetings to the emperor of the Franks!" White teeth flashed in the dark bearded countenance.

"Greetings to the cousin and envoy of the great sultan, may the peace of Allah be upon you!" With outstretched arms, Frederick stepped onto the gangplank and embraced Fakhr-ed-Din in the harbor of Trani. He held him at arm's length. The emir had hardly changed since the day, almost five years before, when they said farewell to each other on a height overlooking Jerusalem.

The sultan's continued friendship was an important element in the network of alliances he was forging. Al-Kamil had emerged victorious in his battle for supremacy with his kin. He now ruled the Arab world from the Nile to the Tigris. In Europe, Frederick had recently signed a new treaty of friendship with the French king. And in England, Piero was conducting the negotiations for his marriage to Henry III's nineteen-year-old sister Isabella.

He steered the emir away from the jetty toward the waiting horses that were to convey them to the half-finished castle that stood beside the Norman cathedral. "I have brought a friend to welcome you," Frederick said, gesturing toward his own mount, a black Arab stallion with vermilion saddlery. "Dragon, you remember your old master, don't you?"

The emir stroked the horse's head. He smiled, "I see you have taken good care of him."

"IT'S A MARVEL!" Frederick examined the sultan's gift, a planetarium in the form of a golden tent, in which astral bodies wrought in gold and jewels moved within their circuits by means of hidden mechanisms.

Michael Scot, whom he had hurriedly summoned, couldn't contain his astonishment either. Walking around it in the audience hall, Frederick's physician and astrologer exclaimed, "And it's a clock, too, my lord! See here," he turned a knob and a chime sounded the fifth hour of the afternoon, "it keeps time!"

"There are only two in the world," Fakhr-ed-Din said. "The other stands in my cousin's palace in Damascus. His sages tell me that this clock is a hundred times more accurate than the best waterclocks."

Frederick turned to those gathered in the hall. "My lords, next week is the feast of the Hegira. I will hold a great banquet in Foggia in honor of the Prophet Mohammed and the sultan's illustrious ambassador." For the benefit of the German lords, he added, "The Muslims celebrate each year the anniversary of the Hegira, the prophet Mohammed's journey from Mecca to Medina."

They stared at him in consternation.

IT WAS LATE at night. Through the open arches came the bittersweet scent of cypresses. Somewhere, a fountain splashed. The palace was silent except for the sentries, somber helmeted figures pacing the walkways.

Frederick and Fakhr-ed-Din were seated cross-legged on the carpet in Frederick's apartments. They had just finished a last game of chess.

The emir reclined. "Nowhere in the Christian world except in your realm could a feast like the one today have been held." After a great hunt, more than four hundred noblemen and prelates from Sicily and the Empire had sat down in three crimson tents with the sultan's envoys to celebrate the feast of the Hegira. Frederick himself, to honor his guests, had worn a green tunic embroidered with Koranic verses.

Frederick smiled. "My lords were a little reticent at first, but eventually, with the aid of a fair amount of wine, they enjoyed themselves. The differences between people are far smaller than they themselves imagine, imprisoned as they are in their own worlds. I like to fool myself that by showing respect for the Prophet, I've broadened their minds just a tiny bit. I shall miss you. My true friends are few and I treasure them."

Fakhr-ed-Din inclined his head. "Your friendship is a precious gift. Know, Frederick, that should you ever have need of me, I and all I possess are yours."

"I thank you, my friend." He stared at the carpet. "I have a great sorrow, Fakhr-ed-Din," he said, "that I carry within my heart."

The emir raised his brows.

"My son Henry has disgraced me. He has rebelled against my orders. Even worse, a few weeks ago, I received news that he has plotted against me with my enemies, the Lombard cities."

The emir had some knowledge of this incomprehensible thing called the Lombard League. "But why would your son wish to do so? Are they not his enemies as much as yours?" he asked.

"The Lombards are serpents in human form. The emperor is by rights king of Lombardy. But the Lombards' power increased greatly after my grandfather Barbarossa's death. For years, they've refused me their crown. To entice Henry to side with them against me, they have offered to crown him king of Lombardy. I'm sure they have no intention of keeping their promise, but my son isn't only a traitor, he's a fool, too."

"So you will have to take up arms against your son?"

Frederick nodded. "In the spring. Most German princes are with me. The campaign will be short. The rebels backing Henry, with the exception of one or two princes blinded by greed, are common burghers unaccustomed to fighting. They'll soon lose their courage. But the worst is to have to sentence my own son as a traitor . . ." He stood up and paced. "The pope has agreed to my son Conrad becoming German king. But the pope, too, is a serpent. He, who has repeatedly offered to mediate between myself and the Lombards, has been making secret overtures to them. At times I wonder whether Gregory is involved in Henry's plot, too."

The emir stared at him, wide-eyed. "Is it possible?" he asked.

Frederick said, "With the Vicar of Christ anything is possible."

GRAVINA, APULIA, APRIL 1235

Bianca stood on the parapet of the south tower and watched as Frederick left on the first stage of his journey to Germany. It was a glorious April morning. The day was clear and crisp, cool still, but with the promise of the sun already in the air. Mounted Saracen crossbowmen clattered over the drawbridge, four abreast. A solitary figure on a black steed appeared from under the gate arch. He was dressed in moss-green huntsman's clothes, his head bare, in yellow boots.

Behind him, in a wooden wagon with scarlet leather curtains, traveled little Conrad and his nurse. Beside the prince's conveyance rode his valets and two of his tutors. Conrad was now Frederick's only heir.

Apart from his son and his menagerie, he's also taking his Egyptian dancers, she thought, remembering Peppa's words. What would his new wife make of his odalisques? Strangely, the thought of the English princess who was to become Frederick's wife no longer hurt. When he had first confessed to her that he was to marry again, she had walked about for weeks with a burning ache in her stomach, unable to eat, think, or sleep. Master Scot had prescribed thin gruel and ship's biscuit, which for the sake of her children she had forced herself to eat.

When all his efforts at comforting her failed, Frederick did what came naturally to men when faced with guilt: he attempted to buy her acquiescence with gifts of jewels and more lands. When that tactic, too, failed, he stayed away.

The week before he came to bid farewell to her and the children. He would be gone for at least two years, he said. When she stared at him in silence, he took her hands.

"Bianca," he pleaded, "don't send me away like this. I may not see you for several years. My heart is heavy with what I must do to Henry. My marriage to Isabella of England is naught but an affair of state. She's probably as plain and boring as Yolanda was, but even if she were comely, it would change nothing. I give you my word as emperor that no other woman will ever take your place in my heart."

Against her will, she had smiled. Only Frederick would offer his word as emperor as a pledge of love. He took her in his arms then. And her body, like her heart, once again betrayed her. For seven days and nights they hunted, talked, and loved together.

At dawn this morning he awakened the children in the chamber where they slept with their nurses, and kissed them. Constance, the eldest, a serious child of five, curtsied before her father like a great lady. Violante, who was nearly four and used to her father's erratic comings and goings, sleepily kissed him back. But two-year-old Manfred clung to him with heart-rending cries of "Take me! Take me!"

When the moment came for Frederick to bid farewell to Bianca, she had turned away.

"Farewell, my emperor," she now whispered into the breeze. She felt a presence and turned around. Beside her stood her brother. In the din of the baggage train she hadn't heard his footsteps.

"Manfred!" She was ashamed of the tears that were running down her cheeks.

"I hope I haven't startled you," he said, averting his eyes from her face. "I, too, wanted to watch him leave."

After a moment's silence he added, "Only God knows when we'll see him again."

"Or what may befall him in Germany." Bianca bit her lip. "He says that defeating Henry will be child's play. His trust in his German vassals is such that he isn't taking enough troops. And next year he'll lead a German army against the Lombards. That, too, is fraught with danger."

"He must leave Sicily well garrisoned, Bianca. He doesn't trust the Pope, and rightly so."

She turned to her brother. "I fear for him, Manfred. Even for Conrad. If he were to fall into his brother's hands . . ."

Manfred put an arm around her. "Frederick takes only calculated risks. Riding in a show of oriental splendor across Germany, with little Conrad by his side, is such a calculation. The burghers and nobles of Germany will, I promise you, succumb to him as they did once before. No one understands the German soul as Frederick does. Mark my words. The princes will elect Conrad king of Germany."

Manfred's eyes followed the distant figure in the green cloak. He had served him now for more than twenty years. From a young nobleman with few prospects he had risen to become one of the most powerful lords in Sicily. He would never betray Frederick's trust. And yet he sometimes asked himself if he hadn't sold his soul. Was not the pain he had just read in Bianca's eyes the wage of his weakness?

Together they stood watching the long lumbering line of the baggage train slowly disappear over the crest of a hill. Neither mentioned the English marriage.

SPEYER, GERMANY, JULY 1235

In the beauty of a German summer's day, with the beeches and chestnuts and oaks all clad in dappled greens and the Rhine flowing past the red-walled city like a stream of molten silver, Frederick made his entry into Speyer.

Cymbals clashed and trumpets blared as the Saracen cavalry rode across the bridge onto the left bank of the Rhine. Mounted on black Barbary steeds, the fierce-looking horsemen were a splendid sight in their red and green striped tunics and crimson turbans.

After an interval that allowed the dust to settle, the emperor appeared. Frederick, mounted on Dragon, in a purple mantle embroidered with the eyes of peacock feathers, acknowledged the cheering crowd with a gloved hand. He bent down to whisper something to seven-year-old Conrad, riding beside him on a gray palfrey. The curly-haired prince, who handled his mount with assurance, smiled shyly and raised his right hand in a salute. The effect was immediate. "Long live Prince Conrad, Long live Prince Conrad!" the crowd roared. Behind Frederick and his son rode the German princes and prelates in a sea of flying banners.

Then came the falconers in moss-green tunics and peaked hats. On their wrists sat the falcons, their heads sheathed in embossed leather hoods with red feathers. The imperial hounds, sleek and well groomed, were led in pairs on scarlet collars and leashes. In their midst padded a line of camels. Upon their backs, in curtained palanquins, traveled the Egyptian dancers. Here and there, the people caught a glimpse of a dark-eyed veiled beauty peering down at them. The eunuchs of the imperial household, towering black men of huge girth, rode on richly caparisoned mules beside the camels. They were followed by the hunting cheetahs. Mounted on special seats affixed to the cruppers of their Saracen keepers, their eyes were hooded like those of the falcons. The people clapped and cheered at their sight.

As the elephant lumbered into view the crowd fell silent. On its back it carried a red wooden tower filled with Saracen crossbowmen. Behind ambled a giraffe, led on a leash like a giant dog by a groom on horseback. More animals of the imperial menagerie appeared in cages that rattled past on wooden wheels: spotted lynxes, a lion, and a polar bear.

"Father," Conrad said, raising his voice to be heard above the din of hooves and wheels and bridle bells, "I've never seen so many people."

Frederick laughed. He laid a hand on Conrad's shoulder. "This is nothing. Wait till we get to Cologne. The Germans have never seen anything like this. And they love their emperor. They'll love you, too."

The boy looked down on his embroidered gloves. His father had explained to him that he was to be king of Germany because his brother Henry was to be deposed. He did not quite understand the fearful thing that had befallen Henry, whom he had never met. People talked in whispers about Henry and fell suddenly silent when Conrad appeared. Just as they did when they talked about his Aunt Bianca. Well, she wasn't really his aunt, but she had brought him up until he had received his own separate household a few months ago. Although traveling with his father was great fun, Conrad missed her. She had given him a brightly colored psalter as a farewell gift, and hugged him. Father had wanted to hug her, too, but she had turned away. When he lay in his bed in some strange German castle at night before falling asleep, he sometimes imagined that she was there. In the glow of the embers, he'd watch the door slowly open. She would sit down on his bed with a smile, to say his prayers with him, as she often used to do.

Did Henry pray? Probably not. Maybe that was why he had been imprisoned. How could his brother have done anything hurtful to his father? Everyone loved his father. He had even allowed Conrad to bring his new tiercel, a small, tame falcon he was teaching him to hunt with. It was exciting riding beside his father across Germany. Everywhere, huge crowds acclaimed them. Every day, different princes came to pay their respects.

Conrad felt very important and adult. The only part he didn't like was the one about living in Germany. His father had explained to him that one day, when he was king, he would have to live there, because a German king had to live in Germany.

OUTSIDE THE GREAT cathedral of red Rhenish sandstone, the clergy and dignitaries awaited them. As he dismounted, Frederick noticed a familiar face. He bent toward Siegfried of Ratisbon. "The fat bishop with the violet cope, isn't that Landulf of Worms?"

"I'm afraid so," Siegfried whispered.

Frederick clenched his fists. "How dare he appear here after having been Henry's counselor! Remove him and have him stripped of his episcopal insignia!" Two sergeants went up to Landulf and grabbed him by either arm, dragging the protesting bishop down the steps while the townspeople cheered.

Frederick took Conrad's hand. Together they ascended the steps. In the dimness of the double-choired basilica, Frederick closed his eyes as he listened to the Te Deum. Soon he would have to sit in judgment on another, far worse traitor than Landulf, one whose betrayal could not be forgiven.

A THICK MIST hung upon the mountainside. The fog was engulfing the trees, creeping down toward the Neckar River. Below the castle's ramparts, the roofs of Heidelberg had nearly vanished in the swirling grayness.

Frederick slammed the shutter closed. And this in June! The castle's cavernous chambers were as dank within as the weather without, a penetrating cold that froze one's bones and sapped one's spirit. In the hearth smoldered a fire of damp logs that gave off only smoke.

This impregnable fortress, with walls twelve feet thick, was his son's prison. Putting down the rebellion had been easy. Henry's supporters had deserted him one by one. The rebel Rhineland cities were brought back under the control of their bishop-princes. In most cases, armed intervention hadn't been necessary. At Frederick's approach, the citizens flung open the gates and begged for mercy.

Henry sought refuge in the castle of Trifels. It took Hermann's repeated intercession to convince him that resistance was useless and would only lead to starvation. Finally, Henry surrendered. He was clapped into fetters. In a barred wagon, jeered at and pelted with refuse by the same populace who had recently acclaimed him as their protector, Henry was brought to Heidelberg.

Thus was, must be, a traitor's fate. Yet he couldn't blot the image from his mind. He kept on hearing Hermann's voice describing the journey. He saw the contorted faces of the crowd, ordinary men and women turned into a savage mob, gloating over the fall of an anointed king.

He adjusted his sword and opened the door to the antechamber. Hermann von Salza, Henry of Brabant, and the archbishops of Cologne and Salzburg stood waiting. They all wore ceremonial dress. Their faces were grave.

He squared his shoulders. "Let us proceed, my lords."

FREDERICK, ENTHRONED BENEATH the dais, looked toward the doors through which Henry would be brought any moment now. The throbbing in the left side of his head, which had started that morning, was worse. For the first time in his life he felt the weight of the imperial crown a burden on his head.

The hall was crowded. Every German lord of note was present. Glancing about the hall, Frederick recognized many of his friends. Henry of Brabant, the Duke of Meran, and Siegfried stood to his right. His eyes met Hermann's. He understands, Frederick thought, better than anyone.

The doors swung open. Henry, a purple cloak on his broad shoulders, had lost none of his bearing, except for his gait. The chains around his ankles clanked with each shuffling step. Beside him walked his jailer and arch-foe, Wilbert of Bavaria, the Duke of Bavaria's brother.

Henry flung himself to the ground before the throne. "I am your son, father, I beseech you, have mercy on me!" His back shook. The lords glanced from Henry, sobbing into the floor rushes, to Frederick. Silence hung heavily in the room.

Hermann turned to Frederick. "Allow him to rise, Frederick."

"We beg you, Your Grace," the Duke of Meran put in, "let the king defend himself standing."

At length, Frederick spoke. "Rise, traitor," he said in a voice he didn't recognize as his own.

With Wilbert's help Henry managed to stand. Rushes stuck to his cloak.

Frederick signaled to the chancellor, who stepped forward. Siegfried's voice carried across the hall: "You, Henry of Hohenstaufen, king of the Germans, are accused of rebelling against your father the emperor. You are accused of treacherously taking up arms against your own vassal, the Duke of Bavaria, as well as the Rhineland bishops. You are further accused of having conspired with the Lombard communes against the emperor, and of coveting his crown of Lombardy. What have you to say?"

For a moment, it looked as if Henry would begin to sob anew. Then he straightened his shoulders. For the first time, he raised his eyes.

An image of Constance flashed through Frederick's mind, her fair hair, Henry's hair . . .

"Father, I . . ." He bit his lip. "I never wanted to betray you," he said in a barely audible voice, "I just wanted to be king not only in name, but in reality. You and your officials have controlled every move of mine, every moment of my life. I am king, but I have never been allowed to rule."

Frederick's lips were pressed together. His finger stroked the armrest of his throne. There was some truth in this. Yet, if only he had controlled him more . . .

Henry, emboldened by his silence, continued, "I truly wanted to help the burghers. The bishops," he glared at the bishop of Worms on his left, "the bishops exploit the people. It is they who really rule Germany, father, not you."

There was truth in this, too. And it stung. But it didn't justify betrayal. Nothing justified that. "And the crown of Lombardy? You thought to be all-powerful king of Germany and of Lombardy, too?"

"Father, the Lombards, they promised, it seemed so easy, you're not their king anyway, they've always refused you their crown, so I thought—"

Frederick leapt up, his face contorted. "It's treason, treason of the most abominable kind! Treason of a son against his father is a violation of both God's and man's law!" Over Henry's head he addressed those gathered in the hall: "My son has conspired against my imperial authority and against yourselves. From this moment onward, he is no longer my son or king of

Germany. I myself will again assume the German crown." He gathered his mantle, about to depart.

"Your Grace, you must pronounce sentence," the chancellor whispered.

"For the sake of his mother's memory, I will spare his life, but he is to be imprisoned for the rest of his days."

Henry turned white. "And my wife, my children?"

"They'll be treated with the honor due their station."

Frederick stepped down and walked past Henry. Before the doors he halted. He looked back at his son for the last time. Then he strode out of the hall.

FREDERICK LEFT HEIDELBERG CASTLE immediately, and rode back in a pouring rain to Worms. There he went straight to his apartments, giving orders that he was not to be disturbed. His head throbbed so badly that his vision was blurred.

After Mahmoud had divested him of his wet cloak, boots, and gloves, he asked him to leave.

"Would my lord wish for some food or drink ?" Mahmoud asked.

Frederick, holding his hands before the fire, shook his head.

"No, Mahmoud, I have no desire to eat."

Mahmoud salaamed. "May the peace of Allah be with you."

"Thank you, Mahmoud, and with you, too." The compassion in his childhood friend's voice brought a lump to Frederick's throat. He too, like Berard, knows of my pain, he thought.

After Mahmoud left, Frederick lay down on the bed, fully clothed. The shutters were closed. He watched the fire, its leaping flames. He should have called for Michael, asked for a draft of henbane. Yet he didn't want the physician around him. He didn't want anyone. He wanted peace. The chamber was still and dim. His head felt a little better. Silence always helped. Silence and darkness.

Maybe it was age. Forty was the threshold of old age, yet despite the headaches he had been getting, he didn't feel any older. It wasn't so much the physical ravages of age that frightened him. They were part of nature's cycle. Long before death, things began to wilt, shrivel, draw closer to the earth whence they came. It was the weight of experience that oppressed him. The understanding of others, and of himself.

His stomach was still knotted. In rage. Humiliation. Guilt. And regret. He turned over, away from the fire, and closed his eyes.

Dwelling on the past was the most futile of weaknesses. The heir Constance had born him after long hours of labor on a hot summer's day in Palermo, the curly-haired indulged boy frightened of horses, the handsome young man who wore his crown with such dignity and so little sense, had ceased to exist. He must efface him from his mind.

He would look to the future instead. To Isabella. To a new son.

THE FOLLOWING MORNING, Frederick, despite a night of fitful sleep, felt somewhat better. He was being shaved by his barber, a fat jolly Saracen named Rashid who had been trained by Mahmoud, when Henry of Brabant appeared in the doorway.

"I beg your pardon. I'll wait outside." The duke stepped back.

"I'll be ready shortly. Sit." Frederick said, with his head reclining on the back of his chair.

Henry, booted and spurred, gloves in hand, remained standing. The Saracen deftly wielded the sharp shining razor, scraping it with consummate skill over the imperial cheek.

When Frederick finally sat up, Henry said, "We're about to leave. The others are waiting. We must make haste if we are to reach Antwerp before the princess's ship."

"Ah, Isabella." Frederick sighed. "You have my gifts?"

Henry nodded.

Frederick rose. He was still wearing his mustard chamber robe and curly-toed Egyptian slippers. There were dark shadows under his eyes.

"Have you a message for the princess?" Henry asked.

"Tell her that I await her arrival in Cologne with great impatience."

Brabant gave him a long look. Frederick twisted his lips. "I'll get used to her. God knows I need another heir. Thirty thousand marks sterling and an English alliance aren't to be sneered at either." He clapped Henry on the back. "Godspeed, my friend. I'll wait for you in Cologne."

After Henry had gone, Frederick sat down. He rubbed his forehead with both hands. He didn't want to think of his son, or of Bianca. Both kept coming back into his mind, however hard he tried to banish them. Henry's eyes would haunt him forever, just as Bianca's bitterness on the morning of their parting was etched into his memory. He had written her several letters, to which he had received replies inquiring after his and Conrad's health and the weather in Germany. Neither had ever understood what he was trying to achieve. Neither understood that personal considerations were of no consequence where the Empire was concerned.

The barber was cleaning his instruments in a corner, packing them into their casket till tomorrow.

"Rashid," Frederick asked, "tell me, you have a wife?"

The barber turned around. "Two, my lord, in Lucera."

"And children?"

"Six, my lord."

"And you can marry another wife any day you like?"

"Yes, my lord. According to the Prophet's law, a man may have four wives, as long as he can afford to treat them all equally."

"And the first two won't make your life a misery because you've taken a third wife?"

The barber shook his head. "They they wouldn't dare to speak against God's law."

Frederick smiled. "You Muslims are blessed."

THE WEDDING FEAST was held in Cologne. Long rows of trestle tables laid with immaculate white napery were arranged under the great stone arches of the covered market. There were more than a thousand guests. The young princes of the Empire served at the high table. Henry of Brabant's eldest son acted as Frederick's cupbearer. French troubadours, Sicilian *trovatori*, and German minnesingers sang and strummed their lutes. Isabella, whose love of music was known, rewarded them with smiles and a gracious inclination of her head.

Frederick observed his new wife. When he had seen her for the first time that morning, he had been taken aback by her fairness. She had a skin like translucent alabaster, hair so blond it was almost white, a pert little nose, and large blue eyes fringed by dark lashes. Her only defect appeared to be crooked front teeth, which she managed to hide most of the time by sketching just the shadow of a smile in a way that was fetchingly mysterious.

If her ancestry was anything to go by, she might prove as spirited as she was lovely. For Isabella Plantagenet carried in her veins the blood of two of the most tempestuous women of the age. She was the granddaughter of Eleanor of Aquitaine, who had wed Louis VII of France and then divorced him to marry Henry II of England.

Her mother, Isabella of Angoulême, eclipsed even her grandmother with the scandals she caused. At the age of eighteen, affianced to one of King John of England's French vassals, she eloped with the English king when the latter paid a visit to his liegeman. After John's death the unpopular queen was made to retire to her French domains, where she married Hugh de Lusignan, the man she herself had betrothed to her daughter.

Isabella turned her head and caught his look. Frederick smiled at her, a lingering smile. A shell-pink flush rose from her slender neck to her cheeks. She smiled back briefly and then, with a self-assurance he thought admirable in a virgin, resumed her conversation with the Duke of Bavaria. Not, he thought with a flicker of anticipation, that there was anything virginal about her well-rounded bodice of garnet-colored velvet embroidered with pearls or the sensuous curves of her full lips.

Her trousseau was as sumptuous as the golden crown on her head. King Henry had outdone himself to ensure that his favorite sister would impress her husband. Apart from the thirty thousand marks sterling, Henry had given Isabella chests filled with furs, robes of wool and silk lined with miniver and marten, cloaks of "triple" camel hair from Tripoli, Eastern carpets and silver plates, silken bed hangings and caskets filled with jewelry. He had even included a set of cooking pots of unalloyed silver.

Frederick relaxed against the throne. He raised his cup and drank a silent toast to his new wife. May she be fruitful, he thought. Her potential spirit didn't disturb him—on the contrary. And if her thoughts should turn to infidelity, like her grandmother's, or to ambition, like her mother's, he would soon put them to rest.

* * *

THE CHAMBER WAS in semidarkness, illuminated only by a slow-burning log fire in the fireplace against the far wall. The scents of wilted roses and frankincense filled the air.

Isabella of England lay stretched out on the great bed hung with cloth-of-gold and strewn with rose petals. She was clad in a shift of cream linen embroidered with gold threads.

She shivered. Despite the fire and the July sun that had made Cologne stifling today, the chamber was cold. The archbishop of Cologne and his acolytes had left after blessing the nuptial bed with holy water and praying for her fertility. Her ladies, after dressing her for the night and brushing her hair till her head hurt, had all withdrawn. Margaret, her favorite, had been the last to leave. Now she was alone with the dancing shadows on the walls and the deep silence interrupted by the occasional crackling of the fire.

How much longer would she have to wait? The emperor both frightened and fascinated her. Despite his age, for he was twenty years older than she, there was an undercurrent of feral vitality in him that made her shudder. Some said that he was in league with the devil. She thought uneasily of the ill-fated young queen of Jerusalem, his second wife. Rumor had it that he had her poisoned so that he could carry on with Bianca Lancia, his famous mistress.

Her brother had assured her that those were envious tales put about by his enemies. He was, after all, the greatest monarch in Christendom, a man renowned not only for his crowns, but also for his learning. It was said that he spoke and wrote in six languages, that he could read the stars and chart the heavens, and that he knew every book in existence. He conversed with her in oddly accented, but otherwise excellent, Norman French.

At the wedding banquet she had caught him repeatedly watching her. His eyes, an unusual aquamarine color, had the same intensity as those of the two hunting cheetahs he had sent her brother as a gift. Henry had been so taken by the beasts that he built a special enclosure for them at the Tower. The cheetahs supposedly came from Abyssinia, the land of Prester . . .

The door creaked open. Her heart began to race. From under half-closed eyes she watched him enter. Unable to take her eyes off him, she followed his movements as he undid first his crimson mantle and then his tunic.

He cast off his clothes with his back toward the bed. For a moment she had a glimpse of his naked body as he turned to pick up a robe. In the glow of the fire his arms and legs seemed cast in bronze. Isabella swallowed. She had never seen a naked man before.

He came toward her with that loose-limbed gait she had noticed before. His wide-sleeved chamber robe was open down the front. Clutching the coverlet, she became stiff as a board.

He sat down beside her and stroked her hair. He smiled. "There's no need to be frightened." Then he sought her lips. She turned her head away brusquely.

"I'm afraid this won't do, my beauty." With both hands, in a single movement, he pulled her shift up to her neck. He stared at her. "God's word, Isabella. Do you know how lovely you are?"

He began to caress her stomach with slow, circular movements. "This smooth belly will swell with our sons . . ." His voice was suddenly hoarse.

She hardly heard his words. She closed her eyes. Flooded with an inexplicable languor, she felt every taut muscle relax. His hand, still stroking, slid lower. Dreamily, she willed him to continue, to continue forever . . .

Suddenly he stopped. Isabella, startled, opened her eyes. What was wrong? Then she gasped. Despite her shock, she couldn't avert her eyes. His member had risen as if it possessed a life of its own. Its shadow loomed on the wall.

"Turn over." He whispered. "Get on your knees."

Knees? What in God's name was he asking? Serving maids went down on their knees to scrub floors. Surely he could not, like that . . . only beasts . . .

"Come, my sweet, do as I tell you," he said. "That way I'll hurt you less. Don't resist, yield to me, let yourself go, and it will not hurt at all."

Lulled by his voice, she obeyed. She was yearning to feel his hands on her again, to feel their pressure. There was a quick, searing instant of pain. Then a fierce wondrous warmth filled her belly. Why ever, she wondered, had Margaret told her to clench her teeth?

AFTER THE WEEKLONG wedding festivities, Frederick and Isabella went to Mainz, where he had called a Diet. Among other decrees, the Diet promulgated a law stating that any son who took up arms against his father forfeited his inheritance. The Diet's last event was the reconciliation between the houses of Guelf and Hohenstaufen. In a ceremony that had many older princes unashamedly wiping their eyes, Frederick passed the territory of Brunswick over to the Guelf heir, making him Duke of Brunswick-Lueneburg.

At the end of November Frederick and Isabella moved to Haguenau, to hold their Christmas court and spend the winter. Frederick found his favorite German palace unchanged. Barbarossa's marble-floored library lined with book cupboards was just as he had left it fifteen years earlier. The storks, a new young chamberlain assured him, continued to come, nesting year after year in the same west tower.

Every few days, couriers, part of a new postal system, brought news of Sicily. Berard told him in long personal letters much of what the official reports didn't say. Bianca's children wrote regularly, in stilted Latin formulated by their tutor. Their mother remained silent.

The halls of Haguenau resounded with the voices and spurs of vassals coming and going in preparation for the war against the Lombard League. In threatening to free the German cities and permit them self-rule on the Lombard model, Henry had unwittingly performed a great service for Frederick: the German princes' old hatred of the Lombard communes had taken on a personal element it had lacked before.

On the day before Christmas, he granted an audience to Margaret of Austria and her children. He received Henry's wife in private, seated alone in the library. The pale girl with the plucked forehead he remembered from Aquileia had turned into a plump woman with sad eyes and a double chin.

Margaret sank into a deep curtsy. She raised her eyes. "My lord, I have come to beg your mercy. My father and my husband have gravely wronged you, but neither I nor my children have ever been disloyal to you. It is true that by Your Grace's magnanimity, our lands and titles have been left us, but we are outcasts." Her voice trembled. "No lord will take my sons into his household. My daughter has no hope of finding a husband when she's grown. She'll be condemned to a nunnery . . ." Margaret began to cry.

Frederick rose. He took her hands. "No Hohenstaufen shall become a nun unless she feels called by God. You and your children shall come to court. I myself will take your sons into my service."

She wiped her eyes. "Thank you, my lord. I thank you with all my heart."

Poor girl, he thought. To have a father and a husband who were traitors was a harsh fate indeed. Her father, Frederick of Austria, had sought refuge in a fortress in Graz, from where he dispatched emissaries suing for peace. At first, he suspected that the duke sent his daughter in an attempt to soften him. He didn't think so now. Margaret's concern was for her children. In any case, it would avail her nothing to plead for her father.

He pointed with his chin. "Those are your children?"

"Yes, Your Grace."

"Tell them to approach."

She turned and beckoned to two boys and a girl clustered beside their attendants.

Three pairs of huge eyes stared at him. He ruffled the boys' hair. They were twins. One was slightly taller than the other. Both had golden hair. "How old are you?"

"Six, Your Grace."

He picked up the smallest child, a little girl of three or four with unruly auburn curls and a freckled nose. He smiled at her. "Would you like to see where baby Jesus was born?" She nodded, sucking her finger.

"Come, Lady Margaret, bring your sons." He led the way down a spiral staircase into the hall, carrying the child.

At one end of the hall, between two twisted columns of gray marble, stood a stable the size of a small shepherd's hut. Inside, life-sized figures of Mary and Joseph flanked a straw-filled cradle with a swaddled baby. Three wise men held out jeweled caskets. An ox and an ass stood on either side of the entrance.

The boys ran up and touched the roof, thatched with real straw. They went around the side and peered through the window at the back. The little girl stroked the ass's scarlet saddle.

"Saint Francis fashioned the first such Christmas nativity, so that people could imagine Christ's birth," Frederick said. "The humble chapel he and his brothers built in the field beside their huts had no frescoes or colored windows to tell stories, so Francis set a carved stable below the altar. Today, during the twelve days of Christmas, such scenes are found in many churches in the south."

Margaret smiled. "It's so much more real than a mural. One feels transported to Bethlehem. You, I believe, knew the saint?"

"Yes. I met him twice. It was shortly before he went blind. He contracted an eye disease in Egypt. . . . I have a nativity set up every year in his memory. It brings people closer to God than thundering sermons delivered by men in brocaded vestments."

Margaret's eyes widened.

She, too, has been fed tales about me, he thought sadly, from Henry, no doubt. He turned to the little girl, who was holding the donkey's bridle. "Would you like to ride on him?"

She clapped her hands, "Please, please!"

He hoisted her up and adjusted the saddle strap. "What's your name?"

She fixed him with wide blue eyes. "Constance."

He pressed the child against him for a moment.

THE HORSES' HOOVES beat on the frozen path. They left the forest with its dark snow-burdened firs and emerged into an open landscape of glittering whiteness.

Frederick swept the horizon with his arm. "It's beautiful, isn't it?"

Isabella looked at him and smiled. "It is indeed, my lord."

"But wait till you see Sicily. God would never have called Palestine the Promised Land if he had seen Sicily first!"

Did he make such remarks only to shock people or because he half-believed them? She wouldn't give him the satisfaction of asking, unlike those stuffy prelates he enjoyed baiting. When he wasn't being too serious, Frederick was great fun. To her surprise, she had discovered that she could quite easily divert him. She wanted him to be in a cheerful mood. She threw her head back. "Come, I'll race you."

Galloping across the snow, horse and woman seemed one, so perfectly did they blend together. Frederick spurred his horse on. Catching up with her, he grabbed her reins and brought the gray mare to a shuddering halt. Isabella, flushed and out of breath, laughed. Her hair had become undone and cascaded down her sky-blue riding cloak.

He leaned over to kiss her icy cheek. "I really am beginning to think that you've inherited your grandmother Eleanor's wildness," he said. "Next thing, you'll want to go on crusade too!" He slid off his horse and draped his reins over the animal's neck. "Let's wait here for the others." He stamped his feet, rubbing his gloved hands.

Isabella took a deep breath. "Frederick," she said, "I . . . I have something to tell you."

He raised his face, suddenly alert.

She held his eyes. "I am with child."

He swung her out of the saddle and hugged her. "Oh, Issy, that's the most wonderful news! You'll give me a son, won't you?"

"I'll try, Frederick," she replied, taken aback. What if she disappointed him?

"No more riding, my sweet. You now carry a burden more precious than all my crowns. You promise not to do anything foolish, such as racing your husband over fields full of hidden boulders?"

The expression in his eyes overwhelmed her. She felt herself loved and cherished. She closed her eyes as he kissed her. Please, dear God, she thought, never let it end.

VERONA, JUNE 1236

In the summer of 1236 the imperial armies swept across the Brenner Pass down into Verona. Ezzelino da Romano, lord of the Trevisan March and ruler of Verona, welcomed Frederick outside the city.

Frederick's intimates, particularly Hermann, disapproved of his alliance with a man of such sinister reputation. He shrugged off their objections: "My gold has made him lord of Verona, which gives me access to the Brenner Pass. I don't care if he's Lucifer himself. He's so hated by the Lombards that I needn't fear his betrayal!"

Upon meeting him for the first time, Frederick had actually found him much to his liking. The towering Ezzelino would have been darkly handsome had it not been for a livid scar that ran from his left cheek to his chin. Frederick confided to Hermann, "Maybe he's a monster, but he's amusing, and far more cultivated than most devout princes."

While the army camped outside the city, Ezzelino offered Frederick lodging in the fortress built by the barbarian king Theodoric centuries before. In view of the hostile mood of the populace, Ezzelino had decided that they would be safer behind its ramparts than in the city itself. Together they rode past the amphitheater turned-quarry, through the narrow streets of this city of ancient red brick. The people of Verona looked on in sullen silence as Frederick rode beside their new lord. Their faces were stony as they listened to the Saracen drums sounding the death knell to their dreams of independence.

Frederick pressed his lips together. Twice, the Veronese had defied him by blockading the Brenner. Now they were paying for their daring. The cavalcade crossed the Adige over a graceful Roman bridge and made its way up the hill toward the castle.

FROM ITS HILLTOP, Verona's castle had a sweeping view over the city and the plains of Lombardy. Frederick stood on the loggia and watched the sun set over the haze-shrouded fields. The sun was dipping west, toward Brescia and Milan.

Brescia, a bastion of the Lombard League, was the last major city before Milan. With the league's dissolution, the Empire would stretch in an uninterrupted swathe from the Baltic to Palermo. The Lombards were the pope's last allies. Their subjugation would put a final stop to the papacy's territorial ambitions. The pope, confined to Rome, would become what God and the Church fathers had meant him to be: a shepherd of souls, not a ruler of men.

In Rome, the nonagenarian Gregory was still ostensibly mediating with the Lombards on Frederick's behalf, in an effort, so he said, to avoid the bloodshed of war. In reality, the pope was secretly supporting the Lombards.

Frederick turned back to the room. "How long," he asked Ezzelino, "will it take to capture Brescia?"

Ezzelino put the yellow plum he had been about to eat back on the platter. "That, my lord, depends on whether we can lure them out of their city. The walls of Brescia are almost as stout as those of Milan."

"Sieges are a slow business, costly in men and provisions. Can we taunt them to come out and fight?"

Ezzelino pursed his fleshy lips. "The Lombards are a dour race, Your Grace. They're not easily inflamed. However, I think if we—" he broke off, interrupted by a knock at the door.

A mud-splattered messenger stood in the doorway, hat in hand. Frederick recognized him as one of Isabella's heralds. The man knelt. "I bring tidings from Haguenau, Your Grace."

Frederick broke into a wide grin. Isabella's time had been drawing near. "I have a son?" he asked.

The messenger lowered his eyes. "A fortnight ago, on the Feast of the Transfiguration, the empress was delivered of a daughter. Both are in good health."

Frederick's face fell.

Ezzelino, about to voice his congratulations, closed his mouth.

Frederick dismissed the herald. He remained on the spot, staring at the floor. At length, he sighed. "'Tis a chancy business, this breeding of heirs."

"Next year the empress will give you a son. Daughters also have their uses. The Count of Provence married one daughter to the king of England and another to the king of France. No mean feat for a count, wouldn't you say?"

"He has a brilliant chancellor. He's promised to make each of his lord's daughters a queen!"

"Well, there you are. Your daughters, too, will provide great alliances for you, while your sons wear your crowns. Patience, my lord."

"You're right, Ezzelino. I must write to the empress. It's not her fault."

Ezzelino raised both brows.

"I know it's supposed to be the woman's fault. But I'm not so sure. Eleanor of Aquitaine bore King Louis naught but daughters in many years of marriage and then gave Henry of England five sons!" He shook his head. "No, I shan't scold poor Isabella. She's a lovely girl. She had an unhappy childhood, you know. She was only two when King John died and her mother went back to Angoulême, leaving her children in the care of William the Marshall." With a faraway look in his eyes, he added, "When Louis of France nearly ousted the Plantagenets from the English throne, the children often had to flee from one castle to another in the dead of night."

He raked his hand through his hair. "Let's celebrate the birth of my daughter. We'll hold a banquet tonight. Have wine and bread distributed in the city!"

The lord of Verona was astounded: "You would use the army's provisions to feed that traitorous scum?"

"Let them see how sweet my yoke can be. They might like the taste of it. As for provisions, the fields and orchards of Lombardy are heavy with the harvest of summer."

A WEEK LATER, Manfred arrived in Verona at the head of six thousand Saracen troops from Lucera. Frederick strode into the great cobbled courtyard. He embraced him, while his eyes scanned the crowded bailey. Servants and men-at-arms staggered past with chests. Horses were led away by grooms.

"Where's Bianca?" he asked finally.

Manfred held his gaze. "In Foggia."

"Gesùmmaria, she can't still be angry!" He had been certain that she'd come, that within moments he'd see her, hold her in his arms. Bianca wouldn't, couldn't defy an order of his.

"She's not just angry, Frederick, you've broken her heart. She's a woman. She was so furious when she received your letter that she actually told me she'd come to Verona only in chains."

Frederick swallowed. "If that's her attitude, she can go and sup with the devil."

HAGUENAU, NOVEMBER 1236

Isabella stared into the fire. She smoothed the blank parchment. The little dog at her feet whimpered in his sleep. Pursing her lips, she dipped the quill into the ink and began to write in an elegant flowing script:

> To her excellent and most dear brother Henry, King of England: Isabella, Holy Roman Empress, his devoted sister, greetings.
>
> Both we ourselves, our dear husband the emperor and our infant daughter are, thanks be to the Lord, in good health. We trust that by the grace of God and all the saints this letter will find you, too, dearest brother, in good health.

Knowing how greatly you will rejoice at our good fortune, may you learn of the resounding victories which our dear husband and lord hath recently achieved over his Lombard enemies. Soon this rabble which threatens the peace of the world will be wiped out.

Beloved brother, we give you thanks for your warm words of affection. We also thank you for your splendid gifts. We play daily upon the sackbut you sent us. It is an instrument of wondrous workmanship, whose sound delights our ear and our heart, knowing as we do that you, dearest brother, have chosen it for us. Our pets and our musical instruments provide much solace for us during these long days of autumn.

We pray that our English retinue, and in particular our dear waiting-women, whose presence here our dear husband the emperor deemed unnecessary, have reached your court safely.

Your little niece, Margaret, is a bonny child, joyous and healthy, suckling vigorously from her wet nurse. She will be five months old next week, and already she is smiling. Although he must have been greatly disappointed, our dear husband the Emperor wrote kindly to us upon her birth. I . . .

Isabella replaced her quill in the inkhorn. Her hands were stiff with cold. She slipped them into the fur-lined sleeves of her gown and read the words she had just written. Had she said anything to which Frederick's officials might object? She had long suspected that her letters to Henry were read in the chancery before being dispatched. Just as he had removed her English retinue, Frederick would make sure that no untoward information reached her royal brother in England.

She hadn't seen Frederick for months. She was to meet him in Vienna before Christmas. His letters were penned by a secretary. She imagined him, walking up and down, his hands slicing the air. She had often seen him dictate to several scribes at once. The only letter he had ever written personally had been after Margaret's birth, a missive of charming platitudes that hadn't masked his disappointment.

She missed him. During the long winter nights she ached with yearning for him, for his hands, those hands that sent currents of delight through her. The memory of their togetherness made her as giddy as the sweet wine of Alsace.

Isabella took another sip of wine from the silver goblet by her side. Its stem was as icy as her hands. She glanced at the hour candle. It was already past noon. Outside the closed shutters, she could hear the wind howling. Soon, there'd be snow.

If only she were already in Vienna. If only she could escape the monotony of life in Haguenau. There were no hunts or dances, no amusing gossip. And as for those dreadful black men with high-pitched voices Frederick had appointed to serve her, they, too, were depressing. Margaret, her only real companion, had whispered to her that they were eunuchs. Oriental potentates, she said, used them to guard their harems. The thought of Frederick worrying about her chastity was so absurd it amused her.

Isabella smiled to herself. She felt better. The wine was beginning to take effect. Did he really think that she, a Plantagenet princess, could . . . She dipped her quill into the ink again. She had better finish her letter.

THAT YEAR, FREDERICK held his Christmas court in Graz, in the company of Isabella and his son Conrad. At the beginning of the new year the court moved to Vienna. There, at a Diet of imperial princes, the nine-year-old Conrad was elected king of Germany. Two weeks of feasts and tournaments followed, during which Frederick declared Vienna an imperial city. He also appropriated the dukedoms of Austria and Styria, erstwhile fiefs of his son's father-by-marriage, Frederick of Austria.

With the problem of the succession solved, and the German princes firmly behind him, he left Isabella behind at the beginning of September and crossed the Brenner again to continue the Lombard war.

On a hill outside Innsbruck their cavalcade was overtaken by a courier who handed him a letter. Frederick broke the seal. Isabella was with child again. He smiled to himself. This time she would give him a son.

LOMBARDY, OCTOBER 1237

Frederick stepped out from his tent and let out an obscenity. A soft drizzle fell. Swathes of mist rose from the marshes, drifting over the bare autumn fields. This abominable weather was all he needed. For the past four weeks his army and the Milanese forces had been circling each other like two weary antagonists at a dogfight. They had been facing the enemy for two days here at Pontevico, separated only by a small tributary of the Oglio. The Milanese, on the other side, refused to be drawn from the swamps that protected them.

"Enzio!"

"Yes, father?" His son came out of the tent, pulling up his hood.

"Fetch Ezzelino, the landgrave, and Manfred." Enzio had just passed his twenty-second birthday. He had distinguished himself at the recent siege of Vicenza.

Enzio returned with the three men. The landgrave Conrad of Thuringia, Frederick's kinsman, was the son of that other landgrave who had perished in Brindisi many years earlier during the crusade. Frederick scowled. "I've had my fill of playing hide-and-seek with the Milanese. We'll raise camp and march to Cremona."

The landgrave stared at him. "Retreat, Your Grace?"

Ezzelino, whose courage in battle was eclipsed only by his cunning, nodded in comprehension.

"Will they swallow it?" Manfred asked.

"If we bait the hook properly, they may," Frederick said. "Spread the word among the camp followers that I'm disgusted with the Milanese and the weather and wish to sleep in a real bed till spring. We'll march off. Before Cremona, we'll divide our forces. Part of the army will go on to Cremona, an obvious choice for winter quarters. We, with a striking force of knights and the Saracen archers, will creep after the Milanese. Once they break camp, we attack."

THE MILANESE WAITED for the middle of the night before emerging from the swamps. In the small hours, Frederick was awoken by Manfred with the news that they were marching north, toward Milan.

Frederick, who had been sleeping soundly, swung his legs over the edge of the camp bed. "Give the order to mount."

Mahmoud slipped the chain mail hauberk over Frederick's head and secured it with leather thongs. He and a page laced up his mail gauntlets. A padded arming cap designed to ward off blows and absorb the weight of the steel helmet was tied under his chin. Over this he wore a coif of chain mail. His helmet, of a new design that covered the entire face, with slits for the eyes, would be carried by his squire until it was needed in battle. His legs were encased in chain mail chausses, with circular plates of solid steel to protect his knees. Finally, they girded him with his sword.

He stepped out of the pavilion. The rain had stopped. A smell of moist earth and crushed grass hung in the air. A breeze fanned the torches. His lords stood in a semicircle, waiting. The chaplains had finished. The heralds and banner bearers were already mounted, their steeds protected by padding. The Saracen archers swung themselves into their saddles, their banner, the green flag of the Prophet, flying beside the imperial eagle. They were on their way. All lanterns were extinguished as they followed the road north in the first light of dawn.

In the early afternoon their scouts sighted the Milanese less than a league from Cortenuova. No time was to be lost if they were to be prevented from sheltering in the town. They came upon the Milanese suddenly, beyond an incline in the road. Frederick's mouth went dry as he stared down at the multitude before him. His heart pounded with savage elation. Finally, after months of waiting, he had them in the open, on a flat expanse of land that offered no cover and no escape.

The Milanese were fanned out in a wide swath. They hadn't even bothered to post scouts. Archers and knights were mounted but thousands of soldiers marched along on foot, singing gaily, their round shields slung over their backs. In their midst rumbled their most precious possession, the Carroccio, or battle chariot, of Milan. In the distance rose the fishtailed battlements of Cortenuova.

An imperial herald in scarlet and gold spurred his horse forward. Galloping past the startled Milanese, he drew rein halfway along their lines, shouting at them to be ready.

At a signal from Frederick, the Saracen archers loosed volleys of arrows with deadly precision before surging forward amid an answering hail of arrows from the Milanese, who had managed to regroup.

On the hill, Frederick sat on his mount and watched. The Saracens abandoned their bows and struck out with their scimitars. Inferior in number to their adversaries, ell by bloody ell they pushed the Milanese lines back. Frederick dropped his raised hand. "Now!" he roared. Brandishing his sword, he gave spurs to his horse. "God and the Empire!" the knights yelled, following him down the slope. They thundered past in an avalanche of steel and hooves, scattering turf and stones as they raced forward with flying banners, their lances level.

The battle raged for several hours. Slowly, the sun dipped in the west. Swords clashed on swords, axes on helmets. The groans of dying men and the terrified screams of horses filled the air. The Milanese fought with grim determination in their entrenched positions, while the imperial knights who had their horses killed under them battled on foot. Frederick, with Enzio holding his banner riding beside him, galloped across the field, lashing out with his sword, shouting to some to regroup, ordering others to attack on another flank, warning yet others to protect their rear.

Ezzelino rode on his black charger, swinging his ax with murderous precision, slicing off heads and arms while yelling with glee as he wreaked havoc amongst the Milanese.

The sun set. It seemed to Frederick, as he finally took off his helmet and wiped the sweat from his eyes, as if the crimson sky were a reflection of the blood-soaked battlefield littered with corpses. In the dusk, vultures circled, black shadows against the fiery sky. They always picked out the eyes first. . . . Among the overturned wagons around the final Milanese entrenchment stood the hallowed Carroccio, the standard-bearing battle chariot, abandoned by the routed Milanese.

The next day, more than two thousand Milanese were counted dead. Frederick ordered his heralds to identify the noblemen by their armorial bearings. They were to be buried in consecrated ground in Cortenuova. The town's garrison had fled with the remnants of the Lombard army. Among the many illustrious prisoners taken for ransom was the governor of Milan, Pietro Tiepolo, son of the doge of Venice. Venice, fearful of Frederick's rising power in northern Italy, had joined the Lombard League.

FOGGIA, JANUARY 1238

The rain slanted down in gray sheets. It had rained the previous day and night. Still the rain kept falling. It swirled in the castle's courtyard, and shrouded the walkways and watchtowers in a veil of mist.

The weather matched Bianca's mood, gray and listless and bleak. Her anger had long ago been spent. All that remained was emptiness. She hadn't seen Frederick for nearly three years. The terrible longing she had felt for so long had left her. It hadn't been difficult to refuse his summons, when it finally came, to go to Verona. Yet try as she might, she couldn't escape the gossip about him and Isabella. In less than three years, and despite the fact that she spent much time away from him, Isabella had already given him two children, the second child the long-awaited son. Between that and his victory over the Lombards, Frederick must be a happy man indeed.

She picked up her embroidery again. As she pulled the stitches through the fine linen, one after another, each identical to the one before, she saw her future stretched out before her like an endless row of stitches, each a day of life, mechanical and empty.

She might be allowed to remain as his mistress, kept out of view and visited when the fancy took him. But even that was unlikely. Isabella of England wasn't poor Yolanda. Frederick seemed to think that all would remain the same. But Frederick was a man. Men didn't understand that women had pride, and dignity, too.

Bianca bit off a thread. He would soon be returning to Sicily. He'd sent Manfred a German toy horse and a letter in which he promised to be back before spring. He wrote regular letters to the children, in his own hand. Since Verona, he had ceased writing to her, which was a relief. After each letter, she had been in turmoil for days, her hard-won serenity gone. It was one thing to defy him when he was far away, but what would she say when he stood before her?

Bianca laid the embroidery beside her on the window seat. "Have my litter readied. I'm going to see the archbishop." Her ladies glanced up from their loom. The younger, Elvira, rose to ring the handbell.

For a long time Bianca had been considering this, restrained from action only by the thought of her children. But her children had their own households already, their tutors and companions. They had a loving father, and siblings of all ages. For once, Frederick would not have his will. He had a beautiful new wife, he had a harem, he could have all the noblewomen who fluttered around him like butterflies, but he would never have her again.

* * *

BERARD, WHO WAS recovering from a severe cold, sat in his study, wrapped in furs, with hot bricks under his feet. He coughed and asked her forgiveness for receiving her thus. With a smile that betrayed no surprise, he gestured to a settle beside the fire.

Bianca sat down on the edge of the bench. She lowered the hood of her sable-lined cloak.

"My lord Berard, I have taken a decision of grave import, a decision over which I have long agonized. I wish to take the veil. I want to enter the house of the Benedictine nuns at Caserta. But I need your help. I must find a way to dispense with the novitiate. There's no time. Frederick will be back soon. But even he cannot undo final vows. Will you help me?"

Berard knitted his brows. "Frederick will be beside himself."

"My concern is not with Frederick, but with God. Surely he takes precedence over the emperor?"

Berard smiled. "Very true, but I'm not sure Frederick always remembers that. You do know that this is a grave step, one not to be undertaken lightly?"

Bianca nodded. "I know. You are thinking that I am guided by revenge alone, but you are wrong. I own that revenge is part of it, but mostly, I need to survive, survive in dignity. There never was a place for me by his side. Frederick has given me the happiest moments of my life. It was foolish of me, but for years I hoped against hope that he would wed me after all. Yet a world I don't share with him isn't worth living in. I would rather dedicate myself to God."

"And your children?" Bianca was a loving mother. How could she part with them?

"My brother's wife will take care of them, and their father. The emperor," she said with a smile that lit her face, "dotes on his children."

Berard looked at her. He folded his hands over his stomach. While her vocation might be doubtful in God's eyes, it was more genuine than that of many who entered nunneries. Convents were the only places where women unwed or unwanted, seeking freedom from marital or parental tyranny, could find a safe haven. "Very well," he said at last, unfolding his hands, "I myself will take your vows."

Bianca reached out and kissed his ring. "Thank you."

Berard said, "I am to see him in Verona. I'll tell him."

"Then he's not coming back?"

Berard shook his head. "He still has unfinished business in Lombardy."
Bianca's eyes widened. "But I thought the Lombards surrendered."

"He refused to accept because their surrender wasn't unconditional. They wouldn't dismantle their walls. At this moment, he is negotiating with the Milanese." Berard smiled. "Such matters take time, my lady. As soon as the rains cease I'll be leaving for Verona. I'll tell him about your decision."

Bianca stared into the fire. Softly, as if to herself, she said, "You see, it's not that I no longer love him. It's that I love him too much."

"I know." Berard said. "I salute your courage. There aren't many who dare defy Frederick."

BERARD ARRIVED IN Verona six weeks later, after an arduous journey over mud-clogged roads. Frederick was out hunting with Enzio and Conrad, the ten-year-old King of Germany. The victorious army's tents surrounded the city. Verona's castle had become an imperial headquarters, crowded with German and Sicilian officials.

Berard was glad to have time for his servants to unpack a set of clean clothes, and spread his carpets and hangings. When Frederick finally arrived, Berard was seated beside a brazier, his stockinged feet on a stool. After they greeted each other, Berard said:

"Frederick, I bear news you won't like."

Frederick laughed. "Nothing can upset me after Cortenuova."

"I think this will." Berard held his gaze. "Bianca has taken the veil."

Frederick's face remained expressionless. "She's done *what?*"

Berard nodded.

"I don't believe you."

"It's true. She has entered the convent of Benedictine nuns at Caserta, whose patron she is."

"She's gone mad! She's mine! She's the mother of my children!"

"Frederick, no one belongs to another. We all belong to God, and so does Bianca."

Frederick paced, a scowl on his face. "I'll send Manfred. If she doesn't agree to leave of her own accord, he'll bring her by force."

"You cannot violate the sanctuary of a convent."

"You mean I must let a mere woman get away with defying me?"

"Frederick, I have watched this mere woman struggle for a long time with the burden of living in sin. But what she saw as your betrayal was too much for her. She has sought refuge in God's love, which, unlike your affections, will never forsake her. Let her be."

Frederick glared at him. "Rubbish. She's just jealous, trying to revenge herself on me. Trying to make me the laughingstock of Europe. If I had married the Duke of Brunswick's fat plain daughter, she'd have pouted for a while and then accepted it. Let her stay in her convent. She'll come to her senses soon enough, after a few months of boredom and rising for matins in the middle of the night. I know Bianca. She may have faith, but she's not made to be a nun." He laughed harshly. "Gesùmmaria! Bianca a nun!"

Berard watched him, searching for a feeling other than injured pride. If it was there, it was well concealed. He reached for a parcel on the table. "She bade me give you this."

Frederick untied the ribbon. He stared at the contents. On the blue cloth lay a thick coil of gleaming chestnut hair. He flung it onto the floor. "Let her rot in her nunnery! I've got more serious cares than the antics of a jealous woman!" He stalked to the window.

Berard adjusted the cushion behind his aching back. He glanced from Bianca's lovely hair, scattered on the stone flags, to Frederick's broad shoulders. He stood like a statue, unmoved, unflinching. His power had never been greater. The Milanese had sued for peace, prostrating themselves before him. They even offered him the iron crown of Lombardy. To the watching world's consternation, Frederick refused. He demanded unconditional surrender and the destruction of their walls.

Meanwhile, in a warning to Gregory, Frederick dispatched the Milanese Carroccio as a gift to the people of Rome, who set it up in the Capitol. The significance was clear. Frederick's next goal was Rome. With the birth of Isabella's son, a few weeks after Cortenuova, his triumph had been complete.

Frederick turned around. He sat on a stool. His face was drained of all vitality. "She'll leave a terrible void in my life."

Berard was surprised. He hadn't thought him capable of such an admission. "Perhaps if you went to her yourself . . ."

Frederick shook his head. "No." His eyes clouded, "We won't speak of her anymore."

Berard felt tired. He didn't travel well these days. His joints troubled him more and more. Out of pride, he refused to travel by horse litter, subjecting himself to the discomforts of riding.

Frederick leaned forward. "I'll launch this year's campaign as soon as the weather improves. My first objective is Brescia. And after that, we'll besiege Milan herself. The Brescians are feverishly provisioning and fortifying their city."

"After what you did to the Milanese at Cortenuova, you'll have a hard time luring them into the open."

"I have a formidable new weapon, Calamandrinus, a Spaniard. The most talented builder of siege engines I've ever known. He has already built two superb wheeled towers, and is busy on a new kind of mangonel. It can fling Greek fire at five times the speed and distance an ordinary mangonel casts stones."

"Greek fire?" Berard's eyes widened. This mysterious flammable substance, said to contain sulfur and pitch, was a closely-guarded secret of the Byzantine army. No one in the West had ever succeeded in copying it. "How," he asked, "have you come by it?"

Frederick grinned. "I am negotiating to wed little Constance to the heir of Byzantium. Amongst other gifts, the emperor sent me canisters of the stuff. It's a hundred times more effective than burning arrows."

Berard would have liked to ask whether Bianca knew that her daughter might become empress of Byzantium. "What," he asked instead, "is Gregory going to make of a marriage between your family and the Greek emperor?" The schismatic Greeks, who had split from the Roman Church in a dogmatic dispute, were considered by the pope little better than heretics.

Frederick twisted his lips, "He'll rant that I'm behaving true to my godless nature!"

PADUA, FEBRUARY 1239

Piero della Vigna affixed his signature with a flourish to the creamy vellum. He knew that his letters and dispatches were held up in the chanceries of Europe as models of style. Not even the papal curia, those masters of mellifluous Latin propaganda, could compete with him.

His two secretaries withdrew with an obeisance. Piero picked up another parchment from his worktable. He studied it, frowning. It was a letter to the College of Cardinals, in which Frederick stated that he would hold them responsible for any ill-considered action the pope, in his dotage, might take against him. It was ostensibly addressed to the pro-imperial party within the college, but in reality it threatened those who still stood by the ancient pontiff. Frederick would sign it himself, sealing it with his golden seal. Only the Holy Roman Emperor, the doge of Venice, and the emperor of Byzantium sealed in gold. The pope, as a sign of humility, sealed in lead, and all other sovereigns in silver. Piero, rereading the letter in its final version, sighed. Frederick's relations with the pope had reached their breaking point.

Despite his furred gown and beaver cap with earflaps, he felt cold. Silence filled the long rush-strewn chamber occupied by the chancery in the abbey. The tall writing desks at which the secretaries stood were deserted, inkhorns stoppered and bundles of quills sharpened, ready for the morning. In the hearth a neglected fire smoldered, giving off a glow but little warmth. Through the small windows, glazed with costly roundels of glass, fell an opaque gray light. The day was nearing its end. The leaden skies and fierce cold portended snow again, unusual in Padua. But then this was one of the worst winters Italy had experienced in living memory, further aggravating Frederick's woes.

After the victory of Cortenuova Frederick's fortunes had been at their zenith. Now, a little more than a year later, his failure to capture Brescia had given new hope to the Lombard rebels. For three months the imperial army had ringed Brescia in a siege dogged by misfortune. First, the Spanish engineer Calamandrinus was captured by the Brescians and forced to work for them. Then a mysterious equine sickness broke out, caused by infected mares smuggled in by the enemy. Finally, even the weather turned against Frederick. With his men bogged down in unseasonable torrents of sleet and mud, he raised the siege at the end of October.

In Piero's view the siege should have been continued at any cost. But Frederick, infuriated by his vassals' insistence that their period of annual service was over, retired for the winter to the abbey of Santa Giustina near Padua. Although the abbey was wealthy, the monks were sorely tried by this prolonged imperial sojourn. Not only did they have to put up with

Frederick's retinue, but they also were forced to deal with an elephant, stables full of camels, hunting cheetahs, and falcons. Frederick hunted in the surrounding forests with Isabella and his sons. Despite the cheerfulness he professed, he was often irritable and short-tempered in private. He still hoped that a negotiated settlement with the Lombards might be possible.

Hermann had been riding to and from Rome, trying to arbitrate between Frederick and Gregory. However, during the second half of the year it became obvious that Gregory was wholly on the side of the Lombards. Strange rumors began to circulate about Frederick. To the scandalous tales of his private life, which included every imaginable depravity, were added new, and more serious accusations. It was said that his mistress had to seek refuge in a nunnery from his impiety. He was accused of having said that Christ was an impostor, and of denying the miracle of transubstantiation.

Unlike most other rumors, this one was true. Piero remembered the occasion well. It had been the first time he had realized just how far Frederick's conceit went. Frederick's friend, the aged bishop of Winchester, brought up this new doctrine. It stated that at the moment of elevation, the host and wine actually became the body and blood of Christ, rather than being the mere symbols they had hitherto been. Peter of Winchester only wished to discuss its finer theological points. Frederick, however, laughed harshly, "Ha," he said, "what a clever ploy to increase the clergy's power. Formerly priests were just intermediaries between God and man. Now they've been endowed with divine attributes themselves, conjuring up miracles before the eyes of the faithful!" Stunned silence had greeted this outburst.

Piero leaned against the back of his chair and rubbed his forehead. He was forty-five, Frederick's senior by a year. The burden of running the imperial administration was beginning to show in deep horizontal lines on his high curved forehead and thinning hair. He eschewed no expense in dress, horses, or servants. He owned two great estates in Apulia and a town with a lucrative manufactory producing pottery. Risen from small beginnings—his father was steward to a bishop—he owed everything to Frederick, who treated him with the same magnanimity he accorded all those he valued.

There had been a time, after Palermo, when he tried to overcome his growing resentment of Frederick, of his manner of never doubting his right to override every sacred tenet. With the years Frederick's vicious streak, long hidden under a veneer of cultivated affability, emerged further. At the recent hanging, in revenge for Venice's betrayal, of the doge's son who had been captured at Cortenuova, Frederick had thrown back his head and laughed, a demonic laughter. At that moment, Piero had felt something black, like a bat's wing, brush his heart.

It was Piero's greatest secret, a secret so deeply concealed that at times even he forgot about it. Yet for years, since first meeting the emperor as a poor young notary, he had been under his spell. At a banquet given by the university of Bologna, Piero had been selected to read some of his poetry. Frederick, at the end of the reading, beckoned him onto the dais. He offered him praise, wine in a silver cup, and a little later, a post at the university he had just founded in Naples.

During the years of compiling the Constitutions of Melfi, they had often worked together in Frederick's apartments till late. One sweltering night in Palermo, after the others left, Frederick had unlaced his shirt. He flung it over the back of his chair. Piero could see himself staring at the bronzed muscular torso glistening with sweat. He remembered the dryness of his mouth and the surge in his loins. The auburn head had been bent over the draft of a law, the quill scraping the parchment.

Frederick raised his head. He hesitated for a moment, as if taken aback, then smiled. Frederick's hand, with the seal of Sicily, reached out to him across the table. Time and Piero's heart stood still. He imagined the taste of skin, the feel of thick, curly hair, of hard muscles. An owl hooted outside. The spell was broken. The hand touched his arm, lightly.

After all those years he could still hear Frederick's voice: "You don't look well, Piero. Go and sleep." There had been a strange look in Frederick's eyes, somewhere between contempt and compassion.

Yet Frederick had never changed his attitude to him. He, who possessed such insight into men, continued to single him out as one of his closest friends.

Piero slipped his hands into his sleeves. Frederick would need all the friends he could muster. Two weeks ago, four bishops, two Italian and two German, arrived in Padua from Rome. Ostensibly sent to discuss a list of papal grievances, including that hardy perennial, Frederick's treatment of the Sicilian Church, their real aim had been to question him about his faith. Frederick, aware that a breach with the pope at this stage would cripple his efforts in northern Italy, resisted the impulse to cast the bishops into a dungeon for their temerity. Instead he submitted with amazing good grace to what amounted to an interrogation.

The bishops had departed, reassured of his orthodoxy. But to Piero it had been obvious that this was not the end, but rather the beginning of a storm soon to break.

UNBEKNOWN TO HIM, the storm Piero had foreseen was unleashed several weeks later a few hundred miles south of Padua, in Rome.

The mosaics in the apse of the Lateran basilica glimmered in the candlelight. The cardinals stood around the high altar, lighted tapers in their hands. They looked on with solemn faces as the ancient pontiff was helped up the altar steps by Matteo Orsini, senator of Rome and Gregory's staunchest supporter.

Gregory raised his bony arms, invoking the Holy Ghost. "My brothers in Christ," he intoned in a voice shrill with age and fury, "we are gathered here today to call down the wrath of God on Frederick of Hohenstaufen. He is the enemy of the Church, and an incarnation of the Antichrist. Not only has he consorted with infidels and stirred up disaffection in our city of Rome, he has terrorized the Sicilian clergy, refused belief in the doctrines of the Church and denied Christ himself!"

Gregory pronounced the sentence of excommunication on Frederick. Sicily was to be laid under the ban as well. The sentence was to be read afresh, amid tolling of bells, at every celebration of high mass throughout the Christian world. Frederick's subjects were absolved from their allegiance and encouraged to rise up against his heretic tyranny.

Gregory, too, was handed a lighted taper. Silver trumpets blew three times. The pope and the cardinals dashed their tapers to the ground and stamped them out. Frederick's soul had been cast into darkness.

AS SOON AS it was possible to do so without arousing comment, Cardinal Giovanni Colonna slipped out of the basilica. Gathering up his robes of scarlet silk, the cardinal, tall, gaunt and hook-nosed, climbed into his waiting litter and told his bearers to make for his palace with all haste.

Once there, he called for parchment and ink. Within minutes, he handed a sealed letter for the archbishop of Palermo to a messenger, with the order to ride to Padua at all speed, but without wearing the distinctive livery of the princely house of Colonna.

THE MESSENGER, SPARING neither himself nor the mounts he changed at staging posts, arrived in Padua in a record time of five days.

Berard's hand holding the cardinal's letter shook. He felt a terrible tightness in his chest, a lack of breath. He put the parchment down and breathed deeply in and out a number of times. Then he lowered himself to his knees.

He prayed with a fervor he hadn't felt for many years. "Oh Lord in heaven, protect Frederick from the forces of destruction this madman has unleashed against him. Protect him from his own rashness. Give him wisdom and strength that he may emerge victorious, oh Lord, and accord him your divine compassion and support, I beseech you."

He rose to his feet. The blossom-clad apple trees in the spring sunshine outside were like a mockery of the leaden weight he felt within him. Frederick was presiding at a joust in the piazza. Berard had watched him earlier mount in the courtyard, followed him with his eyes as he and his friends rode through the gates. He could still hear their laughter, see the bright banners streaming behind them in the sun.

He squared his shoulders, then called for his escort. Once again, it fell to him to be the bearer of calamitous news.

FREDERICK SPENT THE next two years warring against the Lombards and their new allies, Venice and Genoa. Fearful of the encroaching imperial power, and lured by Gregory with promises of future trading bases in Sicily, these old rivals had found common cause and joined the Lombards. The navies of Genoa and Venice now threatened the island of Sicily.

The Sicilian Church was forced to finance the war. Frederick ordered the Sicilian clergy to provide religious services despite the papal ban. Those who refused had their lands confiscated. Several who incited the population against him were hanged for treason.

Although Frederick was turning bitter, he could still amaze the world. When, after a long and bloody siege, the Lombard city of Faenza capitulated, expecting to be put to the sword, Frederick pardoned the stunned citizens. From Faenza, Frederick marched south, to lay siege to Rome. The Romans, with whose leaders he had been negotiating, were on the verge of opening the gates to him, when, at the last moment, the pope was saved by his own courage. Knowing that the populace favored Frederick, Gregory issued from the Lateran at the head of a procession bearing the heads of the apostles Peter and Paul. When the people began jeering, the old pope removed his tiara and set it upon the sacred relic.

"If you, the people of Rome, will not defend her against the Antichrist at her gates," he thundered, "the holy apostles of Christ shall do so!" In an instant, the mood of the townspeople changed. With tears of contrition, they pressed around the pope, crying their willingness to defend the Church and Rome. Frederick, unwilling to drench the holy city in blood, raised the siege.

Gregory called a general council of the Church, for Easter the following year, to arbitrate between himself and the emperor. Frederick, who would not have been averse to a council composed of the College of Cardinals, many of whom had imperial sympathies, knew that Gregory had invited mostly those foreign prelates who would do his bidding. Since Frederick controlled all the land routes to Rome, he warned his fellow sovereigns that he would grant no safe-conducts for their churchmen to cross his territories.

The churchmen, unable to ignore a papal summons, gathered apprehensively in Genoa, to be ferried by sea to Rome. Frederick ordered his fleet to intercept the Genoese galleys off the Tuscan coast. A large number of prisoners, including nearly a hundred prelates and two cardinals, were taken to Apulia, where they were imprisoned as pawns in the deadly game of chess being played between himself and the pope.

In August 1240, at the age of almost a hundred, Gregory finally died. The danger from Venice and Genoa disappeared with the death of the formidable old man who, by his will alone, had held together the rival factions. Frederick closeted himself with Berard and Piero to plan the election of a pope of his choosing. Satisfied that he had done all he could, Frederick went to spend the winter in Sicily, the first time he had set foot in the realm in five years.

CAPUA, JUNE 1241

The trestle tables were cleared away to make room for the entertainers. Frederick watched Richard of Cornwall's well-formed lips curl in a smile as his eyes followed the dancers in their diaphanous pastel silks. It wasn't the first time they had performed for the earl, but today they were outdoing themselves. Golden anklets and bracelets clinked as the girls swayed to the soothing Saracen music.

The chamber, a small mosaic-floored hall whose groin-vaulted roof was upheld by fluted columns of pink breccia marble, lay within the private apartments of Capua's nearly completed palace. Cushioned marble seats ran along two sides of the room. Piero, Berard, Manfred, the counts of Aquinas and Caserta, Enzio, and several English barons of Richard's suite were seated on either side of Frederick. Servants refilled their cups with smooth, ruby-red wine from Samos. Through the arches of the loggia the June night sparkled with stars.

Did Richard, who had recently spent time in Palestine, find it odd to be watching Saracen dancing girls here? Frederick, glancing at his brother-by-marriage, thought not. Like most men, Richard, too, had fallen under their spell. They were a handsome race, these Plantagenets. Handsome, and fertile.

Isabella was with child again, the fruit of an almost accidental joining. As often before, Isabella had been slightly in her cups one afternoon when he had paid her one of his infrequent visits. To his surprise, the regal Isabella embraced him with all the abandon of an alley cat. His mind had been elsewhere, and his body sated from a night spent in other company, yet he had felt honor-bound to give her what she so clearly asked for. It was odd that that delightful wantonness of hers didn't draw him to her bed more often.

Was it Bianca who came between them? Several times in the last two years he had been on the verge of casting aside his pride just to hear her voice, to touch her hand. Here in Capua, which was close to Caserta, the temptation to do so was even more frequent. Manfred, who saw her often, reported that she was well. She regularly wrote to their children, tender letters that he read avidly in the hope of gleaning some insight into her heart. Yet not once had there been a word for him, not even after his excommunication and war with Gregory.

Isabella remained mostly in the palace in Foggia, spending the summer in the shady gardens of cooler Melfi, playing her sackbut or trying on new garments or cosmetics from the East. Even in Melfi, she felt the heat in summer. She played with little Margaret, who was three, and Henry, who was two, but in a distracted fashion. Piero had told him that her long letters to her brothers, while never disloyal, were filled with yearning for England. Although she didn't complain and always received him with a smile, it was clear to him that Isabella wasn't happy. Whenever he appeared unannounced in her apartments there'd be a goblet of wine by her side and when he left, she'd cling to him. She had seemed far more content in Germany. His infatuation with her had worn off; Isabella's conversation bored him. Even her limpid blue eyes, so praised by others, appeared vacuous to him. Was it, he wondered, because he compared them to those other eyes, dark pools full of mystery?

After the dancers had left, Isabella's brother turned to him. "My lord, your dancing girls truly dance like angels. This news," he added, smoothing back his thick chestnut hair, "will greatly reassure Henry."

Richard wasn't being facetious. Frederick smiled, "I trust you'll tell my brother of England that the rumors that I am a monster are unfounded. He needn't worry about Isabella!"

Richard grinned back at him. "I shall do so with pleasure." He had been ill on his arrival from Palestine, but was now fully recovered. To Isabella's regret, he would soon return to England. The conversation, interrupted by the dancers, resumed. It concerned a subject more serious even than the deadlock of the papal election in Rome: the Mongols.

Frederick listened in brooding silence as his guests discussed the latest news from the Empire's eastern borders. They all agreed that the only answer was a crusade. Shortly before Gregory's death, an embassy of German princes had begged him to abandon his feud with him and instead call a crusade to fight the Mongols. Gregory, however, had been more interested in destroying Frederick than in saving Europe. The embassy had returned empty-handed. And now there was no pope to call a crusade. The chair of Saint Peter had been vacant for nearly a year.

The great Tatar empire of Genghis Khan had been further enlarged under his son Ogotay. After the Khan's death, Ogotay conquered Russia.

From there, his hordes turned to Hungary, overrunning it in the spring. Poland, Bohemia, Silesia, and above all, Austria were in deadly peril. Two months ago, the Mongols had been at the gates of Vienna.

At a Diet in May he had called the German princes to war, issuing a decree that every man with an income of three marks or more must take up arms to defend the Empire. At this moment the fate of Austria might already have been decided, while his army loitered in Italy, engaged in sporadic fighting with the Lombards and awaiting the outcome of the papal election.

Frederick tightened his hand around the cup. And he was here, a prisoner of Southern Italy just like those hapless cardinals in their conclave in Rome . . .

Manfred turned to him, as if he had read his thoughts. "How much longer can this situation in Rome last?"

Frederick looked at Manfred. Damn those eyes! "Soon, Manfred, sooner than we think," he replied with a calm he didn't feel.

"Have you had word from Rome?" Richard asked eagerly, leaning forward.

Frederick shook his head. "No, not yet. But I have a feeling that we'll soon have a pontiff. Whether he will be to my liking remains to be seen."

Berard cast him a long look. He, too, had read the letter, hidden in a cake of wax, that had arrived that morning from Rome. It hadn't boded well for the election of a Ghibelline pope.

STARING OUT INTO the inky night before retiring that evening, Frederick thought how savage an irony it was that while the Empire was being threatened, he was forced to remain here. He couldn't leave, risking the election of a Guelf pope and the invasion of Sicily while he fought the Mongols in Austria.

The Frangipani and the Colonna, two powerful clans who headed the imperial faction in Rome, had assured him that despite Matteo Orsini, the powerful senator of Rome and Frederick's foe, they would be able to bring about the election of a Ghibelline pope. This morning, however, a hastily scribbled letter from Cardinal Colonna's brother had reached him. Orsini had imprisoned the entire College of Cardinals, including Giovanni Colonna, Frederick's candidate, in the Septizonium, a crumbling Roman ruin on the Palatine.

There, the ten elderly cardinals were shut in a single room with only bread and water, while their guards urinated on them through the leaking floor above. Orsini's strategy was simple: as soon as they elected his Guelf candidate, he told them, they'd be free. How long could ten frail old men last in the heat of a Roman summer in conditions such as these? It was obvious that the cardinals would soon give in to Orsini.

He could march again on Rome, regardless of the bloodshed, and set Cardinal Colonna on the papal throne. It would be easy. The whole Campagna except Rome was in his hands. It would give him the city, and a pope of his own choosing. The Christian world would condemn him, of course, but for how long? The spiritual authority of a pope thus elected might be challenged by an anti-pope, as had happened before.

Frederick sighed. The East, too, gave him cause for concern. Matters in the Holy Land were in turmoil again. The local barons were fighting one another or fighting the imperial bailiffs. The Saracens took advantage of this. The truce he signed with Al-Kamil had expired. Everything he had gained would be lost if a Western army didn't soon come to the rescue of the Christians.

He looked up at the stars. It was a beautiful night, warm and velvety like a woman's skin. Perhaps she, too, was looking at the night sky at this very moment, peering up from the barred window of her spartan cell. It might not be all that spartan. The Benedictine nuns of Caserta, mostly widows or unmarried daughters of noble families, were canonesses. They took the vows of chastity and obedience but not of poverty. They were allowed personal possessions. Books, hangings, pets, even servants. They could have visitors. In the hope of receiving a sign from her, even if only a few words of thanks, he sent her a pectoral cross in gold and ivory, set with topazes. She hadn't acknowledged it. She'd probably given it to the convent's treasury.

The breeze caressed him like a hand. If only you were here, he thought, looking up at the starry outline of the Great Bear. He had once stood on this same tower, his arm about her shoulders, teaching her the language of the stars. He felt a pain in his chest, the gnawing pain of emptiness. He put the goblet down on the stone parapet. What was pride, after all, but a profitless emotion?

CASERTA, A LOFTY hill town surrounded by steep vineyards, rose above a broad plain shimmering in the heat. A dusty road wound up to it from the ancient Via Appia that crossed the plain.

The Benedictine convent was a rambling complex of buildings clustered behind high whitewashed walls. Centenary cypresses stood in its well-tended gardens, like admonitory fingers of God against the blue sky. The convent had a marble-pillared Norman cloister. The church was Norman, too.

Inside the church, Frederick stared at the mosaic floor. His left foot rested on the head of Saint Catherine, being martyred on her wheel. He moved the foot slightly, to the fronds of a nearby palm tree. Raising his eyes, he thought how serene Bianca's beauty was beneath the white headdress that covered her hair. Her brows were no longer fashionably plucked, her cheeks untouched by rouge, and yet she seemed lovelier than ever. On her breast she wore the jeweled cross he had sent her.

He longed to touch her, but the austerity of her habit kept his hand at bay. "I didn't betray you," he said, his voice flat. "I did my duty. I needed an alliance with England; I needed an heir, and I needed Isabella's dowry."

"After what I've heard about your wife, that duty can't have been too onerous," Bianca said.

"Yes, she's winsome and a pleasant bedmate," he said brutally, his voice rising, "but I don't love her, can't you understand that?" He took her by the shoulders and shook her. "I love you, and I'll love you till the day I die, otherwise I wouldn't be here now, begging, would I, I who have never begged anything from anyone?"

Bianca stared at him, her eyes dark and angry. "I will never," she said slowly, "be yours again. Enjoy your English princess and may she give you many more sons."

Just as she was about to turn, he lunged and took hold of her habit. With a sweep of his arm he gathered her to him and kissed her. For an instant, she struggled. Then all resistance left her. Her arms reached up and wrapped themselves around his neck, her body pressed itself against his with a yearning that took his breath away.

For a long moment they stood thus entwined in the dim side chapel before the altar of Our Lady. Then she disentangled herself gently from his grip. "I love you, Frederick," she said softly, "but our lives can never be joined again. I was wrong, you were never mine. You always belonged to the Empire, never to me. I shall pray for you." She raised her right hand in a gesture that was half farewell and half benediction. "May God be with you," she said, and was gone in a rustle of her black habit.

Frederick stared after her, his mouth dry, his heart still racing. Tears stung his eyes as he followed her starched white wimple along the pews and watched it disappear into a side door beside the choir.

AFTER SHE REACHED the vestry and turned the key in the rusty lock, Bianca sank to her knees beside a row of vestments hanging on pegs. She buried her face in her hands and cried, tears of pain and regret, of rage and love and longing, until she felt that she could cry no more. For a long time she remained kneeling. The vestry was cool and silent. She leaned her head against a chasuble. A faint musty odor of age and incense emanated from the faded silk. It was a smell both familiar and comforting, a smell of service to God, of holy rites, of peace. She dried her face and adjusted her wimple. Taking a deep breath, she left the vestry through the door that connected the church to the convent.

From the chapel on the other side of the pillared cloister she could hear the nuns singing vespers. This is my home, this is where I belong, she thought as she walked toward the soaring voices praising God.

FREDERICK SWUNG HIMSELF into the saddle. The sun glared off the convent's whitewashed walls. The gatekeeper, a wizened old monk with a frayed straw hat, opened the creaking iron-banded gates. He stared after the emperor and his small Saracen escort as they disappeared in a cloud of dust.

As he rode the seven miles of abysmal road that separated Caserta from Capua, Frederick's heart felt as heavy as the great boulders of granite that lay along the roadside. He hadn't really been surprised. Deep within himself he had known how she would react. He admired her strength, a strength he didn't have. Yet, seeing her, holding her, somehow had healed a wound. Berard was right. Unlike him, Bianca had found her peace.

What, he asked himself, guiding his horse around the potholes that pitted the road, is my life but an endless row of worries and battles, frustrations, intrigues, and rebellions? Did those whom he ruled feel any gratitude? Did the common people, mired in a perpetual cycle of apathy, poverty, and superstition, ultimately care whether their laws were just or not, their landlords and bailiffs corrupt or fair, their priests grasping and illiterate or virtuous and educated, their roads safe or infested with bandits? Did they understand the importance of storing grain, of repairing bridges, of paying taxes so that their homes and their livestock could be protected from brigands and invaders?

Did the nobles realize that every lordling couldn't rule for himself, that the resultant anarchy would be more detrimental to them than the freedom they craved, destroying the foundation of society? And these pig-headed Lombards, would not even they be happier if between them and their foes stood the might of the Empire, rather than just a few ells of breachable walls? And yet each man, from the highest to the humblest, thought that he could do it better if given half a chance.

He twisted his lips. Perhaps, he, too, should forsake the world. Then he and Bianca could sit together in a shady cloister, like Abelard and Heloise, those thwarted lovers, and compare the lives of Saint Jerome and Saint Catherine.

As tempting as it at times almost seemed, a leisurely life of chastity and contemplation was not for him. His friend Elias of Cortona, vicar of the Franciscan order, had painted its delights only last night at supper. But Elias was old and fat, steeped in erudition and the memory of Saint Francis, to whose work he had dedicated his life, carrying on the saint's work after his death.

We are all, Frederick thought wearily, born to a destiny. Francis was destined for sainthood, and Bianca obviously for a life of prayer. My fate is to shoulder the burdens of kingship.

The crenellated walls of Capua came into view above the loop of the river. It must have been a handsome town in Roman times. Capua had

once been as pleasure-loving as Sybaris. An entire street was devoted to
perfume vendors. Her women, then as now, were famed for their beauty.
Only once did the shrewd Capuans miscalculate: when, thinking that
Hannibal would conquer Rome, they allowed the Carthaginian army to
winter in their seductive city. After Hannibal's defeat, Rome's vengeance
had been swift and terrible.

Frederick was transforming the city, which had become a vast builder's
yard. Her walls had been entirely rebuilt, mansions and palaces were rising, there were new fountains, hospitals, almshouses, and a covered market. Norbert and Bartolomeo da Foggia, aided by Cistercian master masons,
had provided the castle with flushing privies, fireplaces with chimneys,
glazed windows, and mosaic floors. They were now working on the town
gate, a triumphal arch of white marble, the first Roman gateway to be
erected in Italy since the fall of the Caesars.

He had designed the gate himself. When he couldn't sleep, which happened with increasing frequency, he would work at night in his bedchamber, drawing statues, lintels, corbels, or entire floor plans. At the
moment he was designing a classical portal for an octagonal hunting lodge
he had begun in the forests above Andria. Its shape was inspired by the
Dome of the Rock in Jerusalem.

Well, he thought wryly, as he rode through the gate, monumental even
in its half-finished, scaffolded state, if posterity remembers me for nothing else, they'll remember me for the Capuan gate.

FOGGIA, DECEMBER 1241

The conclave Matteo Orsini had forced on the cardinals produced the inevitable result: after holding out for nearly two weeks in the heat and stench of
their prison, during which time one English cardinal died and several others
fell ill, the cardinals elected Orsini's candidate, Godfrey of Sabina, who took
the name of Celestine IV. Orsini's brutality, however, defeated his ends:
within seventeen days, Pope Celestine died from dysentery contracted in
the Septizonium. This time the cardinals took no chances. Within hours of
his death, the entire college had fled to Anagni. From there they begged

Frederick to release the two cardinals he still held, so that they could proceed with a new conclave. A round of negotiations now began between Frederick and the cardinals, which promised to drag on for months.

Meanwhile, the German princes had inflicted a crushing defeat on the Mongols, driving them back beyond the confines of the duchy of Austria, although the price had been a fearful loss of Christian lives.

Frederick established his court for the winter at Foggia. Isabella's time was approaching. He began to find solace again in her company. Most men fled their pregnant wives, but Frederick found the serenity of a woman far gone with child restful. To keep her amused as she became heavier, he ordered exotic trinkets and mechanical toys for her.

HE WOUND UP the bird. "Watch, Issy." The bird, studded with pearls, began to open and close its beak and flap its silver wings.

Isabella smiled up at him from the daybed on which she spent much of her time. "It's a marvel. Thank you. But you don't have to come and amuse me. Of course I like you to, but I know it is a duty for you." She looked down, adjusting her shawl.

He sat on the divan and took her hand. "In my own way, I do love you, Issy. No other princess could have pleased me as much."

She raised her luminous eyes. "That may be so, my lord, but it wasn't a princess your heart wanted."

ON A GRAY morning in December, as dark clouds hung over the city, Isabella's pains began. By the sixth hour of the afternoon, she lay dying. The bells of Foggia began to toll just as they had tolled years earlier for Yolanda, a somber, hopeless tolling that announced the approach of death.

Frederick, sitting beside her bed, his eyes dull with pain and disbelief, caressed Isabella's clammy forehead. Her face is already the color of death, he thought as he looked down at her. In her hands she clasped a rosary of pearls and amber beads. They had brushed her golden hair and spread it out upon the pillow. Her eyes were closed as if she were sleeping, the network of blue veins under her lashes showing through the translucent skin. Her eyes opened. Her bloodless lips formed a word he couldn't hear. He bent down.

"Frederick," she whispered, "don't fret. It is God's will."

"I shall always remember you with fondness in my heart, Isabella." It was true. Without realizing it, he had grown genuinely fond of his beautiful English wife. Now he bitterly regretted that he had left her alone too often with her music, her pets, and her wine.

"Henry . . . tell him that I have loved him well. Tell him that I yearn for England, for her cool green hills. . . . The children, love them, I know you will . . ." her voice trailed off and broke. A shudder went through her body, then it lay still.

John of Procida withdrew a little polished silver mirror from a pocket of his furred robe and held it to her lips. The mirror remained unclouded. The physician nodded gravely. Frederick closed Isabella's eyes.

A shrill keening went up in the chamber. Isabella's ladies and serving women began to tear their hair, swaying to and fro in their grief. In a corner beside the bed, the bishop of Trani, who had earlier shriven her, began to intone the prayer for the dead.

It was the terrible loss of blood that had killed her. The midwives had vainly attempted to stanch the flow of blood. Only when Frederick, bursting into the chamber, had bellowed in a rage to call his own physician, had the women consented to a male examining the empress. By then even John of Procida, whose renown extended throughout Europe, had been unable to halt the hemorrhage.

The lying-in chamber was oppressive. The smell of blood, sweat, and incense all mingled in a nauseating odor of death. Frederick felt his stomach heave. He made his way quickly to the door. In the open gallery outside he took a deep breath of clean cold air. His head, which had been spinning moments earlier, cleared. Following an impulse, he pushed open the door to Isabella's chapel.

In the dim chapel, a tall golden crucifix glowed in a halo of light upon a small altar covered in a cloth Isabella had spent years embroidering in Opus Anglicanum, that marvelous English embroidery of gilt silver threads and colorful silks.

Frederick sank to his knees. He closed his eyes, grateful for the silence. Only when he opened his eyes again did he behold a little black-draped bier at the foot of the altar. On it lay the tiny swaddled body of his stillborn son.

FREDERICK RECLINED IN the sunken basin of dark green marble. He closed his eyes. A scent of rosemary rose from the steamy water. Death. Death everywhere. What would his own death be like? Would it be swift, or long and drawn-out, by sickness, in battle, or by an assassin's hand? Strange, he thought, that men preferred a slow demise to a quick merciful one, just so that they could be shriven. Surely God couldn't deny a soul entry into paradise only because there hadn't been opportunity for absolution?

So many were dead. Constance, Yolanda, Al-Kamil, Mahmoud, Michael Scot, Hermann, Isabella . . . Time was inexorably drawing in her net, pulling it tighter with each passing year. Even Berard was approaching the venerable age of seventy. His flesh hung loosely now on his great frame, his jowls sagged, and there were pouches under his eyes. Only his smile remained the same. The archbishop's superb teeth had so far escaped the ravages of time that left most men toothless long before his age. Mahmoud, too, had died a few months earlier, felled as he was laying out his cloak for him in this very chamber. With his last breath, his old childhood friend, clutching his hand, had commended him to Allah's protection. And dear Hermann. On his way back from the Holy Land, the grand master had breathed his last in Salerno on the same Palm Sunday on which Gregory had pronounced his sentence of excommunication against Frederick. Mercifully, he had died unaware that all his striving for peace had come to naught.

Six months had passed since Isabella's death. Although the official period of mourning had ended and the black hangings been removed, the halls of Melfi seemed empty without her.

The throne of Saint Peter remained vacant. Although he had released the two cardinals and other prelates he had detained, the wrangling between the cardinals and him over a suitable candidate still dragged on in Anagni. Pressure was mounting on the cardinals to elect a pope who would be acceptable to him. In England, prayers were said for the resolution of the crisis. King Louis of France himself had written to the Sacred College, exhorting them to lay aside their political differences with the emperor and elect a new pontiff.

In Lombardy, the Milanese and their allies were lying low, watched over by Frederick's son Enzio, who commanded the army in northern Italy. As soon as the problem of the papal interregnum was solved, Frederick planned to go north again for another campaign against the Lombards.

Perhaps it was the narrowing circle of death, but his thoughts frequently turned to his firstborn son Henry. A prisoner for more than seven years now, Henry had first been held in Heidelberg. Then he had been brought to Sicily and imprisoned in Calabria. Although Henry was allowed every comfort, his existence must be dreary beyond belief. Had he ever repented of his treachery? If so, he had never addressed a word to him. Would he relent if Henry were now to beg his pardon?

He felt a yearning to see Constance's son. He couldn't set him free yet—perhaps he never could. But he could bring him to Apulia, see him, talk to him. Perhaps it was only Henry's pride, that obstinate Hohenstaufen pride, that kept him from begging for forgiveness. He is flesh of my flesh, blood of my blood. Maybe, if I take the first step . . .

He stood up abruptly in the octagonal basin, splashing water on the floor tiles. Two servant girls rushed forward with open towels, enveloping him in linen as he stepped out of the bath.

"Hurry up, you lazy daughters of Islam," he exhorted the girls in Arabic while they massaged his prone body with scented oils. He was impatient to be dressed. For the first time in months he felt cheerful. He'd send a messenger immediately to Nicastro, with orders that Henry was to be brought to Melfi.

HENRY STARED AT the count. "I have been summoned by my father?"

The count of Nicastro nodded. "Yes, my lord. The emperor's orders are for you to repair to Melfi immediately."

Henry frowned, suspicious. "Why?"

"I don't know, my lord. The emperor's message didn't say. It stated only that I was to convey you there myself."

Hope flashed in Henry's blue eyes. He smiled, a wistful smile, and turned away toward the hearth. For an instant, his smile reminded the count of the emperor. It was the first time he'd ever seen a resemblance to him in the man who had been his prisoner for five years. Henry hadn't given his jailer any trouble. He passed his time practicing archery in the castle's tiltyard, or playing drafts with the officers of the watch. Recently, he'd developed a liking for woodcarving. Fond of animals, his captivity was shared by a mastiff and two salukis. The shaggy beasts were stretched out contentedly before the fire. Outside, dusk was beginning to fall. The low-ceilinged, wooden-beamed chamber was darkening.

Henry stood before the fireplace, staring into the flames. He stroked the fur on his cuff. Just past his thirtieth birthday, he was still a handsome man, even if his confinement had led him to put on weight. Fond of food and drink, his well-cut features had thickened, and his once broad shoulders slouched forward, bent by years of hopelessness. Despite this, he still retained a vestige of the regal presence that had once rallied dissident princes to his cause.

Could freedom beckon at last, Henry asked himself, the freedom he had long ago given up hope of ever regaining? His hands began to shake.

He started as the count said, "We will leave in the morning, at first light." Hugh of Nicastro, a wide-shouldered Sicilian whose family had come out from Normandy with Robert Guiscard, sketched a perfunctory bow. With a glance at Henry's hands, he shouldered his way out of the narrow doorway.

After the door had closed, Henry sat down heavily on a chest. His heart was pounding.

As THE SUN ROSE, Henry, Count Hugh, and a company of mounted men-at-arms rode out under the raised portcullis.

They followed the road north to Salerno through hilly country. Below, to their left, lay the Tyrrhenian Sea under a sky of gentian blue. In the distance, Stromboli's smoke was visible. Vineyards covered in pale new foliage alternated with silvery olive groves, hedged in by low stone walls. Shepherds grazed their sheep, the new lambs bleating at the drum of the riders' hooves. They passed hamlets of ramshackle houses with ancient slate roofs. At the wells, women drawing water in leather buckets curtsied as they recognized the count's banner. Outside one village, a corpse had been left to rot on a gallows as a warning to would-be miscreants. Its flesh had been picked off by birds of carrion. Its blackened eye sockets crawled with maggots. Henry shuddered as they passed. The count laughed. "One brigand less."

The road climbed. Steep gaunt cliffs fell down toward the sea. Yellow gorse blazed between the rocks, filling the warm spring air with its scent. Was it possible, Henry asked himself, as he had asked himself through a night spent tossing, that his father would restore him to freedom, for no other reason than the goodness of his heart? Goodness was not a motivation that had ever animated his father. Surely a man who had recently poisoned his third wife, as Henry's chaplain had whispered to him during confession, a man who imprisoned and even hanged clerics like common criminals, wouldn't suddenly pardon his son in an access of goodness?

As he felt the wind in his face and took in the beauty of wide open spaces, of sea and mountains and sky, the soaring sensation of freedom, tears shot into his eyes. To forsake all this again for the gloom of barred chambers and the gray walls of another prison was unbearable. And such, to be sure, must be his fate. He suddenly felt certain that his father was moving him elsewhere only for reasons of greater security. Perhaps he was even planning to have him murdered. Why not kill him, too, just as he had done away with that poor English princess, to eliminate the threat of rebellious barons rallying around him again one day?

Never, Henry told himself, would he consent to be immured in another fortress. The count, riding beside him, was watching the road. Henry swallowed hard. He squared his shoulders. With a sudden savage thrust he dug his spurs into his dappled gray stallion. The startled animal flew forward, off the road into the heather. Henry raced through the air like a demon, a blur of flying golden hair and purple cloak, the horse's hooves barely touching the ground.

"After him!" the count shouted, spurring his horse forward. An instant later, horrified, he and his men reined in their rearing mounts. Too stunned to speak, they watched as the great gray horse and its rider raced ahead, making straight for the cliffs. Thirty, twenty, ten paces separated Henry from the abyss below. With a terrible scream—whether of defiance or terror no one knew—Henry and his horse plunged over the edge of the precipice.

THEY BURIED HENRY in the cathedral of Cosenza, in a shroud of cloth-of-gold interwoven with eagles' feathers.

Frederick arrived a month later to pray at the tomb of his son. He and Constance had been present at the consecration of that same cathedral twenty years earlier. They had given the cathedral chapter a jeweled reliquary in the form of a cross. It was one of the last times that he and Constance appeared together in public. A few weeks later, Constance had died in Catania.

Dry-eyed, Frederick rose from the marble slab. Berard, who had been waiting for him, fell in beside him. They were alone in the basilica, their escort waiting outside. In the pillared vestibule, Frederick halted. He turned. "I am weary, Berard," he said, "weary of grief. My heart is worn out. Every man needs one to share his joys and sorrows." He laid a hand on Berard's arm: "You have been my lifelong friend. For that I thank you with all my heart. But I need more."

Berard's brown eyes rested on him. There was compassion in them. "Go to her," he said. "Perhaps, in this hour of your need, she won't forsake you."

"You'll give me a dispensation?"

Berard looked at him. "Yes," he said after a moment's silence, "for your sake and that of those you rule. Whether God will agree with me is another matter. It will have to wait till I come face to face with him."

THE WHITEWASHED VISITORS' parlor behind the convent's thick walls was cool despite the blazing sun outside. A wooden crucifix hung on the wall, suspended above a long oak bench. Through the iron grille of the small window set high in the wall, Frederick could see the bell tower of the church.

A key grated in the lock. The door behind him creaked. His heart leaped. He was suddenly, absurdly, afraid to turn around. He hadn't seen her for three years.

"Frederick." The voice hadn't changed. It was as melodious, as entrancing as only the voice of a beloved woman could be. He turned slowly, fearful of how she would receive him.

She was smiling. "You haven't changed," she said.

My God, he thought as he looked upon her serene features, she is even lovelier than I remembered. "Isabella is dead, and so is Henry."

She nodded. "I have heard. I am so sorry. May God have mercy on their souls. I . . ." she paused, hesitant to add another platitude. She had felt nothing when Manfred brought her the news of Isabella's death. No elation, no triumph, not even compassion. She had forced herself to pray for the empress's soul. Wasn't it odd, she thought, they stood just a few paces apart, and yet they were strangers. Why, she wondered, had he come all this way to tell her about his wife's and his son's death?

"Bianca," he said, his face tense, "I need you more than God does. You can serve him far better by being my wife." He pulled out a parchment from inside his cloak. "I've secured a dispensation releasing you from your vows."

Her composure suddenly deserted her. "What?" She clutched the bench to steady herself.

"I am asking you to marry me. I cannot make you empress and our children will have no right of succession, but we will be married according to the rites of the Church." His face relaxed. With a smile, he added, "And this time, I won't accept a refusal. If you don't agree, I'll carry you off, roped and slung over my horse. I've got the convent surrounded."

For an instant, she stared at him, unable to speak. Then anger welled inside her. Did he really think it was that easy, that she would obey him without demur simply because after fifteen years he had finally come to offer her marriage?

She glared at him. "You may be emperor, Frederick, but your writ stops here! Do you think that I, too, can be commanded to do your bidding whenever it suits you? That I'll retract my word to God just because you have coerced Berard into issuing a dispensation?"

His eyes, those eyes she remembered so well, held her gaze. He opened his arms.

Bianca swallowed. Drawn by a force stronger than reason or pride or even faith, she stepped into his embrace. She laid her head against his chest. Tears welled in her eyes and spilled onto his cloak.

He closed his arms around her. "Don't cry, beloved," he whispered into the stiff linen of her wimple, "nothing except death will ever separate us now."

She raised her wet face to him. "But what will the world say if after having married a princess of Aragon, the queen of Jerusalem, and the king of England's sister you take a defrocked nun as your wife?"

"I no longer give the price of a rotten mackerel for what the world says."
He smiled.

She said, suddenly self-concious, "I . . . I have no hair."

"Then you'll have to wear a nightcap till it grows."

They both burst into laughter.

A WARM BREEZE rippled the waters of the Adriatic as the little cortège
walked from the castle of Trani across the palm-lined square to the white
limestone cathedral. Built above an intact Byzantine church and the Roman
catacombs beneath, this small cathedral by the sea had always symbolized
to Bianca the many layers of man's faith. Years ago, in the first glow of her
love for Frederick, when she still used to daydream of becoming his wife,
her dream's fulfilment was always set here.

Inside, a soft light filtered through windows of parchment-thin alabaster. A smell of the sea and the incense of centuries permeated the church.
The high altar stood beneath a gleaming canopy of white marble resting on
four columns of red porphyry. As she and Frederick walked down the
flower-strewn nave, the choir burst into plainsong.

They followed Berard's mitered figure. The church was only half full.
There were no foreign potentates or princes among those who stood clustered near the altar. As she moved forward, her hand on Frederick's arm,
dragging the train of her hyacinth-blue mantle, Bianca recognized those
standing in the front line. Her brother turned and smiled. Beside him were
Thomas of Aquinas, Piero della Vigna, and the archbishop of Magdeburg.
The four had earlier witnessed the marriage contract. In becoming Frederick's morganatic wife, she had renounced all royal and imperial privileges.
Despite this, Frederick had insisted, against Piero's advice, in giving her as
a wedding gift the duchies of Gravina and Montecarico, traditional dower
lands of the queens of Sicily.

For an instant, as she caught the chancellor's look, she felt a stab of fear.
She had always known that Piero disliked her. Yet what she had just seen
in his eyes wasn't the cool disdain of the past, the English marriage he so
skillfully persuaded Frederick to enter, or the recent opposition to their
wedding. The look cut into her like a dagger. She could still hear his voice,
shrill with fury, through a door left ajar by a careless servant as she came

along the passage. ". . . may cost you the support of Germany. Can you imagine what the French and English kings will say? A defrocked nun?"

She tightened her grip on Frederick's arm. He turned and smiled as if to reassure her. She touched the ivory cross on her chest like a talisman against evil. I won't, she thought, allow anyone to destroy this moment. She knelt down beside Frederick. The fringes of Berard's pallium quivered before her eyes as he bent down to hand her a lit taper. She took the candle with a steady hand and bent her head in prayer.

PALERMO, MAY 1243

Frederick rose like Neptune out of the water, his curly wet hair clinging to his head like that of an antique statue. How handsome he still is, Bianca thought. Despite his forty-nine years and a noticeable thickening around the middle, he was still as broad-shouldered and compelling as that first night so long ago, in Bari's sea-lapped castle.

He smiled up at her, a smile she had so often conjured from memory in her years of solitude. No matter how hard she had tried to devote herself to God, Frederick had frequently interposed himself between her and the Lord. Her prayers had often been clouded by his image.

She lowered herself onto the edge of the bath and untucked her linen towel. It fell to the turquoise tiles in a heap of creamy whiteness. Dangling her legs in the water, Bianca watched as he waded toward her. His wet arms encircled her. His lips sought hers, melded with them in a kiss that stirred all her senses. Against her belly she felt his hardness, prodding to enter the sanctuary within which she had carried his children, within which she had for so long ached with yearning. She yielded to him, encircling his body with her legs. Let him give me another child, a last child, she thought, closing her eyes.

The warm, rose-scented water in the marble basin undulated back and forth with the rhythm of their passion. The afternoon sun fell onto the water in the arabesque pattern of the carved window screens. In the distance, the bay of Palermo lay silvery below the dark outline of Mount Pellegrino.

*   *   *

A MONTH LATER, at the end of June, Palermo resounded with the pealing of bells. The papal interregnum that had afflicted the Church for three years was over. *"Habemus papam*—we have a pope!" priests proclaimed from every pulpit in Christendom.

Frederick rose from the chair in his study. "Well, my friends, Godspeed. We'll meet in Capua." He embraced Berard and Piero. "May you be successful." While the embassy's official purpose was to convey his congratulations to the new pontiff, its real objective was to negotiate the lifting of his excommunication.

Frederick stepped out onto the loggia. From where he stood, he could make out the bulbous orange domes of the Church of San Giovanni, a converted mosque. Despite its bells, it was distinctly un–Christian in appearance. Here and there, the first torchlights appeared on flat rooftops and street corners. In the twilight, the call of a muezzin was drowned out by the pealing bells.

He, more than anyone else, should have been elated. The cardinals had finally, after nearly three years of wrangling, elected a pope who was acceptable to them and to himself. Sinibaldo Fieschi came from a noble Genoese family. The Fieschis were shrewd pragmatists. They also had a long history of Ghibelline sympathies. Was his unease due to the fact that Sinibaldo had taken the ominous-sounding name of Innocent IV?

Frederick sighed. I am beginning to see black clouds where there aren't any. Innocent III was universally recognized as the most outstanding pope since Gregory the Great. What was more natural than that an ambitious worldly cardinal like Sinibaldo should choose a prestigious name for his pontificate? It didn't follow that his policies would be the same as those of his predecessor.

The negotiations, naturally, would be lengthy. Frederick was prepared to make generous concessions, such as restoring the confiscated properties of the Sicilian Church and releasing the remaining clerical hostages. In order to be closer to the negotiations, he would return to Capua. From there, too, he could continue his secret negotiations with the Frangipani family for possession of the Colosseum, which they had converted into an impregnable fortress.

He smiled. He would go and tell Bianca that the embassy had left. Although she never said so, he knew that she prayed daily for the ban to be lifted. While he himself didn't give it a second thought, its political effects were dangerous. The excommunication must be raised.

THE STARS HUNG like lanterns in the moonless sky. Frederick put his arm around Bianca's shoulders. They stood together, in the courtyard open on one side, gazing out over the terraced palace gardens to the city and the sea below. Here and there, a lonely light glowed in the distance. Palermo lay sleeping while the nightwatchmen went on their rounds, crying the passing of the hours.

The torches reflected themselves, flickering, in the long pool. A fountain murmured softly. In the gardens, the shrill calls of the peacocks had been silenced by sleep. The last guests had gone to their quarters. The musicians had been dismissed. In the port, the galley bearing Berard and Manfred toward Rome had long slipped her moorings. The night smelled of orange blossoms.

Frederick placed a kiss on Bianca's head. "How did I manage to be without you for so long?"

She nestled closer to his shoulder, without replying. There was no need for words. The years they had spent apart, with their solitude and calamities, had welded them together in a bond far stronger than ever before. He turned her to him. In the light of the oil lamps on the tables, her eyes, great pools of lustrous darkness, looked up at him. In these eyes, he thought, is mirrored my whole life.

Over a long bliaud of lemon-colored silk she wore a necklace of coral beads and large uneven gray pearls. Strange how the sight of that necklace, after so many years, caused him no pain, only a gentle tug of remembrance. Neither Yolanda nor Isabella had ever worn Constance's jewels. His only regret was that Bianca would never be able to wear his mother's crown. Yet her daughter would soon be empress of Byzantium.

"Do you know, Bianchina, that I thank God every day for having given you back to me?" He tightened his hands on her shoulders. "I couldn't bear to lose you."

A shadow clouded her eyes. She laid a hand on his chest. "Remember, beloved, that what God gives he may take, too. You mustn't cling to anything, not to Sicily, nor the Empire, not even to me, with such fervor."

TERNI, JUNE 1244

Frederick leaned against the battlements and peered into the Umbrian night. In the distance he could see the watch fires on the towers of Narni. There, tomorrow, he would meet with Innocent IV.

Nearly a year had passed since Berard and Piero began negotiations with the new pope. Innocent had proved a tenacious negotiator, extracting as many concessions as possible. Frederick had proposed that they meet in the Roman Campagna, held by his troops. Innocent suggested Narni instead, on the boundary of the papal lands. Why was the pontiff so nervous? Surely he couldn't think that Frederick would seize him at this stage. If he hadn't used force even against Gregory, why should he do so now? Innocent was known to be cautious. Probably the memory of the imprisoned cardinals loomed in his mind. Manfred was escorting the pontiff tomorrow from Civita Castellana to Narni.

Their meeting would culminate in the formal lifting of the ban. Six weeks ago, on Maundy Thursday, the text of a provisional treaty between himself and the new pope had been read before a cheering multitude outside the Lateran Palace. Piero had taken an oath on Frederick's behalf to maintain peace with the papacy. In the document, Frederick had once again become "A beloved son of the Church and a true believer."

The price for absolution had been heavy. Innocent demanded restitution not only of confiscated Church property, but also of large tracts of papal lands. Finally he had required of Frederick the penance of fasting. A bit of fasting will not do my waist any harm, he thought ruefully.

With a last glance at the clear starry sky, Frederick went back inside. Berard was resting in an X-shaped chair, his feet on a footstool. After months of riding back and forth between Rome and Capua, Berard looked exhausted. His eyes were ringed by dark circles, and his jowls reminded Frederick of an old hound.

He sat down on a chest. He, too, was weary, but also exhilarated. Soon he would enter Rome, this time as her master. The Colosseum was his. The people of Rome were awaiting him to acclaim him as their new overlord. He smiled. "What do you think, Berard, will he be content with the role I have planned for him?"

Berard looked up. "Innocent?"

Frederick nodded.

"Well, he's worldly enough to see the advantages. As long as you don't tighten your vise too much, he might accept the inevitable. I don't know," Berard scratched his white beard, "at times there's a light in his eyes that I don't like, a strange gleam . . ." Berard broke off. Loud voices could be heard in the passage. The door flew open. One glance at Manfred, still gloved and spurred, brought Frederick to his feet.

"God's teeth, what's the matter?"

"He's gone!"

"Innocent?" Frederick's eyes narrowed.

"He's gone. We've searched the castle from top to bottom. He escaped at dusk this morning, disguised as a soldier on a mule. He took with him only his nephew and two cardinals. We found the guard who let them pass. I've sent a detachment in pursuit. However, I fear they have too great an advantage."

"He's made for the sea, to take ship for Genoa." Frederick clenched his fists.

Manfred nodded.

"I know now what that gleam in his eyes was," Berard said, "the gleam of insane cunning. He planned this all along, driving a hard bargain in order to lull you into letting him leave Rome. With Rome in your hands, he knew he'd never get out." Berard sighed. "Never before in the history of the papacy has a pope willingly chosen exile. The Church of Peter, which has stood for more than a thousand years, has crumbled."

Frederick crashed his fist into the doorframe. "The son of a poxed whore!"

Rome without the pope was just an empty victory.

PALERMO, AUGUST 1244

"Hold still, Constance!" Bianca was combing her eldest daughter's long fair hair, entwining a rope of coral beads into the silky coils. Her other daughter Violante handed her two ivory combs. With them she secured the rope at both ends. Then she swept up the two sections of hair and secured them on top of the girl's head in a Grecian knot.

Bianca stood back to admire her handiwork, before handing Constance the hand mirror of polished silver.

"Why, mother, it's gorgeous! You're far better at dressing my hair than poor old Peppa ever was," Constance smiled.

Bianca, regarding her eldest daughter, thought, not for the first time, that of all Frederick's children, Constance was the only Hauteville. She resembled neither the Hohenstaufen nor Bianca's family. She was tall, with long limbs and golden hair, just as Frederick's mother, her namesake, was said to have been. She possessed a quiet dignity far beyond her years.

"Do you think the Basileus will like me?" Constance asked, turning her head this way and that, admiring her reflection in the mirror.

Bianca felt her heart contract. Constance was only fifteen, little more than a child. Yet she was of marriageable age. Frederick had arranged a match of unprecedented brilliance for her, even if the emperor was considerably older and had been married before. Next year she would have to part with her, perhaps never to see her again. Byzantium was so far away, and the perils of travel, of childbirth, of sickness so many. What trials did life hold in store for this beloved child she had carried and loved and had to forsake once, and whom she now had to give up again, this time perhaps for good?

"Of course he will, my duckling." She put her arm around Constance. At least, she thought, she'll never suffer the torments of love, unless she falls in love with her husband-to-be, which is unlikely. She'll never experience passion, nor will she ever know the ignominy of dishonor. She held her at arm's length and smiled. "You'll make a lovely Byzantine empress. You'll be even more regal than Theodora in the mosaics in Ravenna. She looked a bit of a harridan, although her pearls were unforgettable!"

Violante, who was a year younger than Constance, stuck her tongue out at her sister. "Fie, who wants a graybeard of an emperor for a husband? I've heard that he speaks through an intermediary, and receives ambassadors in immovable silence, as if he were a statue. I'm going to marry Richard. He may not be emperor, but did you see how he rode at the tournament on Ascension Day?"

Bianca glanced at Violante. "What makes you think that the Count of Caserta would want to marry you?"

Violante's eyes—Frederick's eyes—danced. She stuck her chin out and said with comical haughtiness, "The Count of Caserta wouldn't dare to displease the emperor's daughter."

So this was more than just meaningless banter, Bianca thought. Richard of Caserta stood high in Frederick's favor. He was the scion of an old Norman-Sicilian family. He was also handsome, almost excessively so. Violante, with her auburn hair and eyes the colour of the Tyrrhenian Sea, was in every way her father's daughter, except for her lack of interest in intellectual pursuits. Even as a child, Violante had resisted learning her psalter with every ingenious means her little mind could devise. However, she could ride like an amazon, fly a hawk with flamboyant skill, and beguile any male from eight to eighty. Her first conquest, in her tenderest infancy, had been her father.

Of her three children only twelve-year-old Manfred had inherited his father's studiousness. Manfred possessed charm and a keen intelligence. But he had another, rarer quality: he had depth of soul. Frederick, who doted on him, had taken him with him to Capua, for the final negotiations with the pope. Perhaps, Bianca thought with a surge of hope, the ban had already been lifted and they were in Rome.

"Oh, mother, dress my hair now, please!" Violante pleaded.

Bianca wiped her forehead with the back of her hand. She glanced outside. The sun burned down on the sea. She moved away from the window. The light, even inside, was too bright, hurting her eyes. She wished she could tell her maid to do Violante's hair, but she didn't want to disappoint the girl. Violante was already sitting on the huge cushion on the floor, looking at her. Her maid Zaïda held out a small casket of ornaments. Bianca selected a circlet of amber and turquoise. Standing behind her daughter, she set to work.

She was nearly finished. The circlet was secured on Violante's head. Just a few strands of hair remained loose at the back. Bianca turned to reach for another pin, when the room began to spin. Swaying, she stretched out a hand to steady herself on Violante's shoulder. "Mother, what's the matter?" Constance leapt up from her cushion. "Are you ill?"

Unable to speak, Bianca shook her head. She had gone a ghostly shade of white. They helped her to a nearby bench. Her forehead glistened with sweat.

* * *

A DULL RUMBLING could be heard outside the palace. Violante rushed to the window. A large cloud of dust approached. Drums beat and cymbals clashed. Banners flew in the hazy air.

Violante turned. "It's father! He's back!" she cried.

Bianca opened her eyes. "Thank you, God." She closed her eyes again.

Violante began to cry. If even their father's return from Rome did not raise her mother's spirits, she must indeed be very ill. She had been ill now for nearly two weeks.

FREDERICK KNELT BY Bianca's bedside. He took her hands and kissed them. Her skin felt searing hot and dry under his lips. "My precious swallow."

Bianca smiled weakly. Her hair was plastered to her temples. "Rome is yours?" she asked.

Frederick nodded.

"And the ban has been lifted?"

"No."

Bianca's eyes widened.

"Innocent agreed to lift the excommunication. A treaty was read to the citizens of Rome, to be signed by both of us in Narni. On the day he was to arrive there, he fled in disguise. He had planned it all in advance. A Genoese galley was waiting for him in Civitavecchia. He's now in Genoa."

"A pope would break his word?" Bianca whispered.

"I'm afraid so," Frederick said, "but don't worry. You need your strength to get well."

Bianca was about to reply when she began to cough. Two of her ladies rushed over to hold her upright while the cough racked her. She groped for a square of linen tucked under her pillow and pressed it to her lips. Frederick noticed that the linen was already stained with dark, dry blood. An icy fear shot through him. When it was over, she sank back onto the pillows. She closed her eyes, too weak to speak, and drifted into a hazy searing world of her own.

FOR THREE DAYS and nights Frederick didn't move from Bianca's room. Sleeping on a truckle bed beside her, he listened to the ramblings of her delirious mind, leaping up whenever she called his name. Racked by cough and burned by fever, she lay in the great bed hung with coral silk.

On the third day, Berard appeared in the doorway. "Frederick, you must have some rest." He glanced at the stubble on his face. "Have yourself shaved and take a bath. And eat something. I'll sit with her. There are urgent matters waiting. You must attend to them."

Frederick, his tunic stained and creased, pushed Berard back into the antechamber and closed the door. He stared at Berard, his eyes huge and feverish, his face haggard. "Berard," he said, swallowing, "tell me the truth. I don't believe the physicians. They're afraid . . . She is dying, isn't she?"

Berard laid his hand on Frederick's arm. "That, my son, is in God's hands. I have been praying for her, and so should you. Go now. I will remain with her."

"OH GOD, DON'T let her die! Punish me for my sins in any way You see fit, but don't take her from me!"

The palace chapel was cool and dim and empty. Above the altar flickered the sanctuary light in a little cup of silver filigree suspended on a long chain from the ceiling. Frederick lowered his face and rested it against the step. The inlaid marble felt cold under his cheek. "Here I lie, oh Lord, prostrated before you like the humblest of my villeins," he whispered, "begging for one life only. Out of all the teeming multitudes that are doomed, is it so much to ask for just one life? Just one life?"

The silence was vast. How did one bargain with God? The conventional method of promising a pilgrimage, a jeweled chalice, founding a convent or a hospital, all seemed commonplace, hackneyed. Could one in fact bargain with God? Could one offer one life for another?

Just then, steps echoed in the stillness. They halted for a moment in the vestibule, beside the baptismal font. Then the man, for they were the heavy steps of a man, entered the chapel and walked along the nave towards him.

"Frederick."

Frederick rose to his knees. He turned. For a fleeting instant he had a vision of another summer's day. The same voice, the same man, a dusty road, and behind, the steep cliffs and the blue gulf of Salerno.

Frederick looked up into Berard's face. "She's dead?"

Berard nodded. His eyes were moist.

Frederick rose slowly, steadying himself on the altar. He stared with the dull eyes of a blind man. A terrible desolation spread inside him. He saw the years stretch before him, empty days and nights, one after the other, each as devoid of her as the one before, culminating in the grey mist of a lonely death. He raised his eyes to the bearded Christ on the golden mosaics in the dome. "Why? Oh God, why?"

The Redeemer, gazing down at him with dark compassionate eyes, remained silent. The silence of eternity, Frederick thought, burying his face in his hands.

AFTER BIANCA'S DEATH, Frederick cloistered himself in the palace of his childhood in Palermo. Behind its high walls the halls were draped in black, the lutes and tambourines of the musicians lay silent in their caskets, while the sun burned down on the empty fountains in the courtyards and gardens, their gaily splashing waters stilled by his orders.

For hours on end, Frederick would sit in the window seat of his grandfather's study, staring out at the sea. He comforted his children as best he could. At times, when he pressed his son Manfred to him, tears stung his eyes as he looked down at Bianca's lustrous dark hair on the small head. He avoided Bianca's brother whenever he could. The sight of the brother, so alike her but alive, filled him with irrational anger at God's arbitrariness, an anger he was ashamed of but couldn't suppress. He worked every day from dawn till dusk in the chancery, eating his meals alone every night. He refused the company of everyone except his children and Berard. When the latter suggested a hawking expedition to cheer him, Frederick gave him a look as if he had uttered an unspeakable blasphemy. The old archbishop went away shaking his head in worry.

Finally, at the beginning of the new year, he came out of his seclusion. But he seemed to Berard a different man. The smile was there on occasion, but it no longer reached his eyes.

TURIN, AUGUST 1245

For nearly a year, the pope remained in Genoa. Beset by illness, he appealed for asylum to the sovereigns of Europe. England and Aragon would have none of him. Even Louis of France, as astute as he was pious, refused to shelter the pontiff on French soil. Instead, King Louis suggested the free city of Lyon. Traveling in a litter across the Alps and narrowly evading capture by Frederick's forces, Innocent arrived in Lyon in February. There he established his court in exile.

He immediately issued a call for a Church council to rival the fourth Lateran council held nearly thirty years earlier by Innocent III in Rome. Delegates from all over the world, as well as representatives of every ruling sovereign, were to attend the council, to be held in July. A welter of matters were to be dealt with, among them the renewed Mongol threat, but the crucial issue was to pass sentence upon the Emperor Frederick II, accused of heresy.

THE SUN DIPPED behind the red-roofed town of Turin, which controlled the passes over the western Alps. The moist heat of a northern Italian summer hung in a haze over the Po River. In the distance towered the snow-crested mountains, touched with a fiery glow by the setting sun.

In the bailey of the castle that the count of Savoy had put at his overlord's disposal, the torches were just being lit as Berard and the other emissaries rode through the gates. Berard was slumped in the saddle, his face gray with fatigue. He barely raised his head as a groom helped him off the mounting block. It had taken five days of hard riding to cover the distance from Lyon to Turin.

Within minutes of their arrival, word was brought to Frederick that his representatives at the Council of Lyon had returned.

FREDERICK CONTINUED CALMLY to work on the loose sheets of parchment. His book on falconry was almost completed. Dipping his quill into the inkhorn, he scratched out a word a scribe had misread and put the correct one into the margin.

Silence reigned in the long chamber with its smoke-darkened beams. Frederick liked to work here with his son before the evening meal, while the light was still good. He glanced at Manfred across the table, his dark curly head bent over an illustration showing how to fit a cap on a young falcon in training. Although he was only thirteen, his knowledge of falconry almost equaled that of his father. Tall for his age, he frowned as he completed one of Frederick's drawings, to be colored later by an illuminator. Despite his show of calm, the boy's hand trembled.

He, too, is afraid, like everyone else, Frederick thought. He felt a wave of love for this intense youth who so resembled his mother. Bianca, he thought, if only you were here, how much easier it would be for me to bear this. But she was beyond his reach, in a sarcophagus in Palermo's cathedral. There were days when he almost longed for the dark solace of the porphyry tomb he would one day share with her.

Before her death, in her delirium, she had rambled on about their son, jumbled words of warning, about death, about a crown falling on a field of battle. Try as he might to put her words out of his mind, as the natural result of the fever that consumed her, they kept on coming back. Was it a sign, Frederick wondered, that she had appeared to him in his sleep every night since the beginning of the Lyon council?

Manfred raised his head. "Where's Berard, Father? Why isn't he here yet?" he asked, his voice tight.

"He's over seventy, Manfred. He climbs stairs slowly. At his age, travel is no mean feat. I didn't want him to go to Lyon, but he was adamant. In his mind, no one else can defend me properly."

Manfred stared at his father. A knock at the door made him swing around.

Berard, leaning on the elder Manfred's arm, entered the chamber, followed by Piero.

"Berard!" Frederick went towards him with outstretched arms and embraced him. He shook his head. "You don't look well, my friend. I should never have let you travel so far."

Frederick gestured to the settles around the empty hearth. "Be seated." After they had eased their saddle-sore bodies onto the seats, Frederick frowned. "Well, what is the verdict? Guilty or innocent?"

Manfred was standing behind his father's chair, as if to protect him.

"Frederick, my heart grieves to be the bearer of such tidings," Berard began.

Frederick nodded at him, as if to encourage him to relieve himself of a burden that was too heavy.

Berard moistened his lips, "Despite all our efforts, and the protests of the representatives of the French and English kings, the council has found you guilty of heresy and sacrilege."

Silence spread through the room. "I see," Frederick said at last. "And the penalty?"

Berard raised an unsteady hand to the cross on his chest. "The pope has declared you deposed. He has called on the German princes to elect a new emperor."

Frederick steepled his fingers together. "I've been deposed, have I? And who does this pope think has given him the right to depose the sovereigns of this world? Are we kings by the grace of God? Or are we the pope's puppets? My brothers of France and England had better take care, or they, too, will be caught in this fisherman's net."

Berard stared at him. "You must do something, Frederick!" he said, his voice rising.

"Do something? I have no wish to do anything. Short of sweeping the entire papacy into the sea, there's nothing that would change the situation. I am weary. I have struggled with four popes in my lifetime. I have placated them and pandered to them and shown more forbearance than I ever thought myself capable of. To please them I've even issued laws against heretics and other harmless fools that today weigh heavily on my conscience."

"As for being deposed, let me tell you something." He leaned forward, his eyes burning. "No one but God is going to depose me! Fetch the imperial crown," he ordered his son, "and summon my household!"

Calm again, Frederick turned back to Berard. "This upstart priest has no army with which to enforce his decree," he said, "nor sufficient influence on the German princes. They, both lay and ecclesiastical, have stood by me for more than thirty years through my conflicts with the papacy. They'll continue to stand by me. I represent stability as well as a guarantee of their privileges, which," he glanced at Berard, "I have taken great care to extend over the years. The pope can rave and rant all he wants in his lair on the

Rhône, it'll avail him nothing. And what's more, now I can drop even the pretense of coming to terms with him. I'm finally free of the papacy, free forever!"

"Are you saying, Frederick," Berard asked, his voice unsteady, "that you are content to live as an excommunicate, perhaps for the rest of your days?"

"Anything is possible, dear friend. Popes change and so do their attitudes. I may still bring the Lombards to heel, in which case Innocent might be forced to change his mind, but it isn't of paramount importance. I don't fear the state of excommunication any longer. I have no doubt that if I died tomorrow, my soul would be received somewhere. The God of which Christ spoke sees beyond the fabrications of a church council. I've come to accept the pope's ban as a hazard of my calling."

He flung one arm over the back of his chair. "But this, too, will change. Men are weary of the Church's oppression and venality. Everywhere, there are orders and heretics preaching rebellion against this. So far, the Church has succeeded in integrating the former and exterminating the latter. Mostly they are foolish people without able leaders. But one day, a great man will rise against the Church and bring it to heel. It's inevitable. Within its trailing robes of shimmering samite embroidered with pearls and gold, the papacy carries the seeds of its own destruction."

Berard closed his eyes. This was heresy.

"But my lord," Piero put in, "even if you are willing to accept it, your people will find it difficult to obey you."

Frederick smiled coldly, "Most of the German and Sicilian clergy will side with me, won't they?" he turned to Berard.

Berard sighed. "Yes, many will choose allegiance to you over obedience to the pope. The sacraments will still be administered, justice isn't going to be impaired, but nevertheless, it's a terrible thing . . ."

FREDERICK OPENED THE silver coffer lined in faded crimson silk. He lifted the crown of Charlemagne up for all to see. An awed murmur ran through the room.

"As long as this crown rests on my head, I am emperor. Let him who dares take it from me!" he said, placing the crown on his head. He smiled,

"Now, let's sup, lest it be said that the rantings of a deranged pope have affected my appetite."

Berard, who had excused himself on account of his fatigue, stood leaning on the arm of his page. He watched Frederick, the crown still on his head, lead the others down the corridor at a brisk pace. The torchlit passage resounded with laughter. Frederick's lords, following his example, had chosen to cast the pope and his council into oblivion.

Berard watched until the last cloak had vanished around a corner and the voices faded into the distance. Silence descended on the passage. As he turned to climb the stairs to his apartments, he glanced back over his shoulder. It seemed to him as if he could still see Frederick, the crown of his forefathers on his head, bestriding the Christian world.

With sudden certainty, he knew that Frederick would prevail. A law onto himself, Frederick would continue to rule as emperor in total disregard of the conventions of men, obeying only the rules of a God of his own choosing.

FOGGIA, OCTOBER 1250

The white steed was restlessly pawing the dust in the piazza. Manfred, wearing his colors of green and gold, sat on his horse, waiting. As the fanfares sounded, all heads turned to see the emperor's favorite son enter the lists.

Frederick, presiding over the tournament, smiled as he watched his son charge, lance couched, thundering across the turf toward Rainald of Aquinas, who was flying toward him on a roan stallion from the opposite side of the tiltyard. A great roar went up. With effortless grace, without so much as leaning toward his adversary, Manfred unhorsed the count of Aquinas's son, famed for his skill at tourneying.

Berard saw the pride in Frederick's eyes as Manfred helped his adversary up with a mail-gloved hand. Fate, which had robbed Frederick of the women he loved, had been kind to him in the children it left him. They adored their father, who in turn loved them with an oriental fondness. Like many older fathers, Frederick reveled vicariously in his son's youthful successes.

He has aged, Berard thought, glancing sideways at Frederick. His hair, still short and curly, was steely gray now, his face clean-shaven and bronzed from the sun of Apulia. Slight jowls and some extra weight added dignity to his figure. He looked more than ever like the Caesar he had become, both in spirit and in flesh, down to the draped togalike cloak of purple Estanfort fastened on his right shoulder with a Roman fibula.

Five years had passed since Innocent IV pronounced his sentence on Frederick in the incense-clouded cathedral on the Rhône. Berard's mind went back to the terrible defeat of Victoria. Frederick, made careless by his success against the Lombards soon after Lyon, had gone hunting with his lords, leaving the imperial camp that besieged the city only scantily defended. His forces had fallen to a surprise sortie from the besieged garrison. The treasury was captured. Frederick's personal books, including his treatise on falconry, were thrown from mercenary to mercenary, to be sold as loot. The Saracen girls of his harem were dragged screaming through the streets, raped in the square, and then sold as slaves.

Since, Frederick had narrowly escaped two assassination attempts. The first, a conspiracy by some of his vassals to poison him at a banquet, had been discovered by Richard of Caserta in the nick of time. The second, also by poison, implicated Piero, and possibly the pope. The fall from grace of the most powerful man in the realm, who for years had had Frederick's complete trust, had been a terrible blow to him. Compromising letters from the pope's secretary, known for his knowledge of alchemy and poisons, had been found under the chancellor's floorboards.

Berard lowered his eyes. He remembered Piero's terrible screams. Frederick ordered the entire court to witness his punishment. His eyes were gouged out with red-hot irons. The blind man had then been cast into a dungeon. Shortly afterwards, Piero dashed out his own brains on a pillar. Had love, unrequited, turned to hate? Was it greed or sudden religious zeal? Had he really been guilty of an attempt on Frederick's life? While no one dared ask the question openly, many wondered about it.

Yet Frederick still ruled, just as Berard had known he would. The pope continued to live in exile. Frederick had been excommunicated for ten years. The world and his subjects had become used to it. The German princes and the Sicilian Church had, almost to a man, stood by him. Bianca's daughter Constance had married the emperor of Byzantium.

Three months ago, his son Manfred, in a ceremony attended by the princes of Europe, had wedded Beatrice, the Count of Savoy's daughter. King Conrad was proving if not a brilliant, at least a very adequate, ruler, counseled by his father.

However, two shadows darkened the autumn of Frederick's life: the Lombards and Enzio. He had been captured by the Bolognese. Despite Frederick's offer to lay a ring of silver around the walls of Bologna, the Bolognese refused to ransom him. He was imprisoned in a tower of Bologna's great fortress, where he composed melancholy poems and was visited by a beautiful Bolognese noblewoman who had fallen in love with him.

Frederick was planning another Lombard campaign in the spring, to liberate Enzio. How much blood, gold, and effort had already been expended in these Lombard wars. It was as if fate, which had smiled so generously on Frederick all his life, determined to deny him this last achievement: the destruction of the Lombard League, which the German emperors had been unsuccessfully attempting for more than a century.

Berard sighed. Age was beginning to weigh heavily on him. He closed his eyes again. His chin slipped down until his white beard touched his chest. The archbishop had fallen asleep. Around him the combatants clashed and the crowds cheered.

THE TWO MEN walked side by side through a path between the fields. Every now and then they'd halt, gesturing as if to make a point. Behind them rose rocky mountains, bleak and purple against a gray sky.

The lay brothers hoeing the fields paused at their approach. Removing their straw hats, they bowed to Frederick and the abbot before returning to their rhythmic preparation of the earth. They'd become accustomed to seeing him. Often, when his travels brought him to this mountainous part of Apulia, he would halt at the abbey for the night.

They reached the gate in the stone wall that fenced the fields. "I'll miss your chess, Matteo," Frederick said, opening the wattle wicket. In the courtyard, he could see the horses saddled and ready. The slow-moving baggage train had already left. "Thank you for your hospitality; I always sleep well under your roof."

The abbot inclined his head. He was tall and bony, in a gray Cistercian habit, his hair bleached by time. "Your Grace, it is I who thank you for your interest in my experiments, and the graciousness with which you eat the coarse bread of our house."

The abbey, built in the Cistercian manner of perfectly dressed blocks of stone, stood on a lonely plateau; its well-tended fields and orchards had been reclaimed from nature over many years of labor. They were crossing the open space before the church when a gentle tinkling grew and made them turn around. An immense flock of sheep appeared over a swell in the road, led by drovers and sheep dogs.

The abbot smiled. "The first flock of autumn."

Before Frederick and he could reach the courtyard, the sheep engulfed them, together with a tremendous ovine stench. They both stood still as the swirling current of dirt-encrusted sheep milled around them, bleating as they sensed fodder and rest.

Frederick raised his arms. He wrinkled his nose. "What a reek!" Yet despite the smell, he felt a sense of oneness with the earth as he waited for the animals to be driven into the sheepfolds behind the abbey. The Cistercian abbey of Santa Eufemia del Monte straddled one of Sicily's principal drover routes. He raised his voice above the bleating, barking chaos. "How many?"

The abbot shouted back, "Two, maybe three thousand. One of the larger flocks. The smallest number about three hundred, the biggest can reach five thousand."

Sheep were one of the great sources of Sicilian wealth. Frederick had revived the Roman custom of transhumance, fallen into disuse because of brigandage and lack of organized shelters. He regulated the use of common pastures and instituted two large annual fairs. Some of the main *traturri*, or drover routes, which led from the plains of Apulia to the summer pastures in the mountains, were hundreds of miles long. At regular intervals there were now shelters for animals and men, where fodder was available at fixed prices and guards provided safety in return for a tax. The sheep migrated to the mountains in May, after the fair of Foggia, and returned in autumn, to be blessed by the clergy.

The ovine turmoil finally subsided. Frederick swung himself into the saddle. "Farewell, Matteo. I'll await the arrival of the brother stonemason you've spoken of." He grinned. "And if your new lentils really are the size of chickpeas, send me some as proof!"

The abbot smiled. "I shall, Your Grace, if they turn out as I hope." He raised his hand. "Go with God, my lord."

The abbot's eyes followed Frederick's vermilion cloak until the cavalcade disappeared beyond a hill. The emperor's friendship was one of the treasures of his old age. "May the Lord protect him," he murmured, feeling suddenly apprehensive. The emperor's enemies were many.

The Cistercians had remained loyal to him through all his battles with Rome. For nearly thirty years, he had been their patron, granting them lands and encouraging their pioneering work to improve food production. He took a keen interest in their horse and sheep breeding and their experiments with new farming and building techniques. Cistercians had installed the plumbing in his castles, and the famous flushing privies, first used by them in their French mother abbey at Cîteaux.

FREDERICK, RIDING DOWN from Santa Eufemia over the rocky terrain, glanced at the sun that had chased away the early clouds. It was well past its zenith. Their next halt was the building site of a new hunting lodge. They should be there just after vespers.

The sun had begun to dip as they cantered along a river. As far as the eye could see, autumnal forests clothed the rolling hills. Flaming foliage mirrored itself in the river. On the opposite bank, the patched brick walls and Norman watchtower of a town came into view. A stone bridge with a keep in its middle spanned the river.

Frederick pointed, "Villafranca, fief of Odo of Villefranche."

Thomas of Aquinas, chief justiciar of Sicily, nodded.

"Odo's a good man," Frederick said, "and a sensible one. He continued to have masses said without having to be prodded by my senechals."

As they drew nearer, they noticed that the bridge was filled with people. The wind carried the loud clamor of voices across the water. Frederick, shielding his eyes against the setting sun, drew rein. The stone bridge reached only halfway across the river. From there, a wooden drawbridge joined it to the far side. The entire bridge was crammed with townspeople, shouting and shaking their fists.

"What's going on here?" Frederick asked.

Thomas leaned forward in the saddle. "Perhaps they're hanging a criminal." There were several men-at-arms in helmets clustered around the centre of the bridge.

"From the bridge?" Frederick frowned. Perhaps this one had already been executed and was now being suspended there as a deterrent to others.

"Officer," he called to the nearest Saracen, "find out what's happening."

The man spurred his horse forward. By now the people on the bridge, who had been facing the other way, had noticed the riders. Someone recognized the imperial eagle on its field of gold.

"The emperor! It's the emperor!" As they all turned around, a gap appeared in the crowd. At its center Frederick saw a woman, her coppery hair flowing down her back. She was standing, trussed up like a goose for the spit, rope wound around her from shoulders to feet.

Thomas spoke, his face eager. "An adulteress, no doubt. This one's obviously not going to be burned, but fed to the fishes."

Frederick shot him a searching glance. The count's tone had been gleeful, gloating almost. He had noticed Thomas's dislike of women before. Frederick asked himself, not for the first time, what his friend's sexual proclivities were. Perhaps, like Berard, he didn't have any. His disinterest in women had obviously been passed on to his heir, a brilliant scholar also named Thomas. The son, to his family's outrage, had recently taken holy orders. If credence could be given to the tales about him, young Thomas Aquinas was destined for sainthood.

"My lord," the Saracen officer reported, "they're trying a lady for murder. She's to be thrown into the river, bound. If she survives, they say God will have proven her innocence."

Frederick's eyes narrowed, "Trial by ordeal! I outlawed it years ago! Who's this woman?"

"The lord Odo's widow. The town's lord died recently. His wife gave birth to a deformed child a few days after his death, and is accused of having killed it."

"Superstitious fools!" Frederick gave spurs to his horse. He clattered across the bridge, scattering people and geese as he went. In the middle of the bridge he halted before a group of soldiers, a priest, acolytes, and a friar. The group was dominated by a tall, broad man with an imperious nose. Clearly a man of authority, this personage was dressed in a rich cloak of mustard yellow, a jeweled dagger at his side. The man bowed. "Count Tancred of Villafranca, at Your Grace's service." The smile reached only the lips; the hooded eyes were guarded.

"Don't you know that all trials by ordeal have been forbidden since the Constitutions of Melfi?" Frederick bellowed, jabbing a finger at the priest, who stood beside two acolytes carrying a silver crucifix on a long pole.

The count jutted out his jaw. "My lord, this is a matter of family honor, not of common law. The woman was my brother's wife. She has killed her own child, my brother's son. If she's truly innocent, as she claims to be, God won't let her perish."

"I didn't kill my child!" the bound woman cried out, "It died a natural death, poor deformed mite. My brother-by-marriage wants to do away with me for the sake of my husband's—" A brutal slap across the mouth from one of the count's guards silenced her.

Frederick looked for the first time properly at her. What a waste to feed such beauty to the fishes, he thought. Odo of Villefranche had excellent taste in women. His widow was a tall, willowy creature with milk-white skin and wavy hair the color of glowing copper, whose slender body was accentuated by the ropes that bound her. As she raised her eyes, wide with terror, in a mute plea, Frederick caught his breath. Her eyes were blue, a deep dark blue.

"Unbind the lady and take her on your horse," he ordered one of the Saracen officers who had ridden up behind him. The man dismounted and swiftly cut through the ropes with his eating dagger.

"I'm taking the lady into my custody," he said curtly to the new Count of Villafranca. "Present your case and your witnesses at my next assize in Melfi. Justice according to the law, and not your barbarous superstitions, will then be done. The offense of holding a trial by ordeal will also be dealt with by the assize." With that he jerked his horse around.

Thomas's eyebrows lifted. "What are you going to do with her?" he asked. Frederick frowned, chiding his foolish heart for beating too fast. "We'll take her back to Foggia and then we'll see. She must have kin somewhere. If I leave her here that mob will kill her before we're around the next bend. The new count may have good reason for getting rid of his brother's widow. Odo was wealthy. She must have received a large portion of dower lands."

THEY REACHED THE site of the new hunting lodge just after sunset. While Frederick went on a round of inspection with the chief mason, the stewards set up the tents, including the imperial pavilion of crimson silk.

As they walked back, Frederick threw his arm around Thomas's shoulders. "Share a cup of wine with me, I feel like company. Even if my physicians say I should be more abstemious."

The old count glanced at him, "Speaking of company, what are you going to do about that woman?" he asked, jerking his head towards the camp.

"To tell the truth, I had forgotten about her. There are no ladies here. We can't leave her at the mercy of the soldiers. We could ask her to sup with us tonight."

"She might be dangerous, my lord," Thomas of Aquinas said.

"I'll talk to her and see what she has to say for herself." Mirth danced in Frederick's eyes, "You're right. I have to be careful. Think, my friend, what the world would say if to my many other sins I should add that of dining in the company of a woman who has murdered her babe! No doubt I would be accused of having roasted the bairn on a spit and shared it with her!"

THE GUARD ANNOUNCED the lady Sibyl. She stood framed in the tent entrance, waiting. Frederick, glancing up, felt a catch in his throat. Everything about her, from her height to her coloring, was different, except for her eyes. They were Bianca's eyes. The streaks of soot across her face had vanished, the hair that cascaded down her back in a disheveled tangle had been braided into two thick glossy tresses wound around her head. Her gown of celadon wool, although stained and creased, fell to the floor in neat pleats. He noticed her small elegant hands. He had always found women with large hands unattractive.

He waved at her, "Come in."

She sank into a deep curtsy. Reaching for his hand, she pressed it to her lips. "I thank you, Your Grace, with all my heart," she said. "It was God himself who sent you." She had a deep voice that caressed his senses.

Frederick twisted his lips. "You'll still have to stand trial, you know." He gestured to a folding chair. "Have a seat, my lady. Some wine?"

She nodded. As he handed her the cup, she raised her eyes to him. For the first time, she smiled, a lovely smile that showed unblemished teeth.

Frederick sat down and stretched his booted legs. After a moment, he asked, watching her from under lowered lids, "Did you kill your child?"

She looked at him, unblinking. "No, Your Grace," she said. "How could a mother kill her own child? What would I have gained by doing so?"

Frederick cocked an eyebrow. "Perhaps," he said, holding her gaze, "it wasn't greed, but compassion, that motivated you? The child was deformed. Although the Church teaches us that all life is sacred, what kind of life would your child have led?"

She blinked. Her eyes filled with tears. Looking down at her lap, she smoothed the fabric of her gown. "That of a slavering monster, my lord, scorned by all." She raised her head and stared at the central pole that supported the tent. Tears ran down her cheeks.

Frederick sat and watched her in silence.

At length she turned to him. There was defiance in her eyes. "I smothered it with a pillow. One day its little soul will come back to earth in a perfect, healthy body, born to some blessed woman other than I."

Frederick caught his breath. By the beard of the Prophet, he thought, she's confessed to murder and she believes in the transmigration of souls! In Cathay, people believed that a soul was reborn many times. In Christendom, those who dared speculate openly about such ideas were burned as witches.

"You're a brave woman, Sibyl of Villafranca." Frederick raised his cup, "I salute you." He drained his wine and got up.

The blood left her face. Stunned by his reaction, she stared at him as she, too, rose. "What will you do with me, my lord?" she asked, a tremor in her voice.

"I'll see to it that you're reinstated in your rights. No one will ever know what you have told me."

Her eyes were wide and dark. "I had heard from my lord husband that you are a most unusual man, and a very just one. You, who do not know me, have looked into my heart with more insight than my own family."

Frederick undid his cloak and held it out to her. "Here, you can't go about the camp without a cover. Once we return to Foggia you'll be provided with waiting-women. Meanwhile, I shall have a tent set up for you."

He draped the cloak around her shoulders. As he did so, his hand brushed her cheek. "You're very beautiful, my lady Sybil. Did your lord husband also tell you that I still appreciate lovely women?"

She smiled, a sad little smile. "Yes, he did." With perfect naturalness, she raised herself up on her toes, offering him her lips.

Frederick felt a rush of desire. Her lips were full and inviting, the nearness of her body heady. He swallowed and took a step back. "Although I value beauty, I do not exact payment of this sort." He took her hand and kissed it. "You are, after all, my liegewoman. Will you sup with me tonight?"

The eyes looked at him levelly, with the same composure as those other eyes that would haunt him forever. She inclined her head. "It will be an honor, Your Grace."

Frederick watched her until she disappeared beyond the tent flap. He would give her time. . . . He went over to the trestle table and poured himself another cup of wine. He raised the goblet to an invisible presence. "You do understand, don't you, my swallow? I must go on living. Perhaps I'll find a shadow of yourself, and some of the peace that has been denied me since you went away." He drained the goblet and put it down abruptly.

CASTEL DEL MONTE, APULIA, DECEMBER 1250

The castle rose like a crown of golden limestone upon the barren Murge plateau, commanding the coastal plain of Apulia.

Neither castle nor hunting lodge, but a combination of both, it had eight octagonal towers joined to each other, with a classical portal of red breccia and gray marble. A balcony ran along the inner courtyard, overlooking a sunken marble fountain. Frederick had designed it himself, inspired by the Dome of the Rock in Jerusalem. It was his favorite castle.

One of the towers was a falcon mews, with a door onto the roof from where falcons could be trained. The rooftop was warm despite the season, bathed in the afternoon sun. Frederick picked up a piece of cheese from a bowl on the parapet. The falcon, a golden peregrine, snapped up the cheese with her razor-sharp beak. "Good girl," Frederick stroked her plumage. "They're just like women. Lavish affection on them and you can do anything you want with them."

He turned to Berard. "You don't know what you've missed. Life without women is terribly dull. Talking about women, I think I should like to marry again." To tease him, he added, "The Duke of Saxony's heiress. I hear she's comely."

Berard stared at him. "Frederick! At your age? You're nearly fifty-six."

"Well, my Saracen girls still enjoy my attentions. I don't see why my new wife shouldn't do likewise. It's true," he added, "that I can no longer accomplish what I used to, but even so, it's not too bad."

Berard smiled, revealing his gums. Most of his teeth had finally succumbed to old age. He shook his head. "I cannot say, having never experienced the joys of the flesh. But why the Duke of Saxony's heiress?"

"Because, dear Berard, I lust after her lands."

Berard laughed. "You're incorrigible. Why do you want more land? Soon, you'll be able to add Lombardy to the domains you leave your children. That is," he added, "if you don't go hunting again."

Frederick laughed. No one but Berard would have dared to remind him of the debacle of Victoria. He looked fondly at the octogenarian archbishop. "I've waited a long time for the final onslaught against the Lombards. I've learned from my mistakes. This time I'll wipe them out."

Berard nodded. The host that Frederick had been assembling over the last two years would be the largest army ever hurled at the Lombard city-states. This time, Frederick would prevail. Berard stared pensively into the distance, toward Andria and the sea.

Frederick fed the falcon another piece of cheese. "Did you know that ewe's cheese doesn't dull their keenness for the hunt? By the way, I've invited a famed troubadour, Raymond of Toulouse, just arrived back from Palestine. Will you join us tonight?'

Berard glanced up, surprised. After Bianca's death, Frederick banned music. He'd become almost a recluse, eating mostly alone in his apart-

ments with a few intimates or his son Manfred. He passed his evenings in
writing or drawing, in astronomical studies, or in discussion. Recently,
however, his spirits had revived. He had fallen in love again, with the
widow of one of his vassals, Sybil of Villafranca, whom many whispered to
be a murderess. Frederick, he was sure, knew the truth, but didn't say.

Berard inclined his head. "I'll be happy to." He gave a dry cough. "However, if I am not to embarrass you by dozing off, I had best go now and rest
awhile. I'm very old, you know."

Frederick smiled. "Nonsense. You're like an oak. You've outlived everybody. You'll outlive me, too."

Holding on to his nephew Richard, who acted as his page, Berard made
his way carefully down the steep stairs. He was glad to see Frederick so
cheerful. It was pleasant to stay in this isolated castle, far from the cares
of state.

THE SOUND OF cantering hooves filled the morning air. The ground was
carpeted with fallen leaves, still damp from the night's downpour.
Frederick, accompanied only by a small escort of Saracens, inhaled the
fertile odor of moist earth.

The frugal breakfasts of watered wine and frumenty he had been eating
on his physician's advice seemed to have improved his stomach. A smile
flickered across his lips. Well, he thought, I, too, must show some signs of
age. He shrugged his shoulders. So what. He was alive. His eyes swept the
expanse of moorland into which they had emerged, its harsh beauty reaching to the horizon. Sicily, he thought, you *are* the Promised Land.

He glanced at the low winter sun. It was nearly midmorning. Before
vespers he'd be in Lucera. He felt a flush of pleasurable anticipation at the
thought of spending a few days with Sibyl. She'd be waiting for him in the
apartments of the great keep amid the mosques and markets of the Muslim town he had created. The deported island Saracens lived there in
peace, following their crafts, cultivating the land, and serving the master
against whom they had once rebelled.

For reasons he himself didn't fully understand, he was conducting this
liaison with far more circumspection than any other. Why was he so reluctant for the world to know that he had a new mistress? Was it the fear of

seeing disappointment in his son Manfred's eyes rather than that of being associated with a woman who lived in the shadow of a terrible accusation? He found much solace in her arms, solace and a companionship both satisfying and undemanding.

They halted at noon. His servants erected a small pavilion of striped green and crimson silk. Frederick ate his favourite dish, escabeche, an Apulian stew of spiced vegetables, garlic, and onions in a sweet and sour sauce. He wiped his lips with a napkin and leaned back in his folding chair. Behind him, Giovanni, his steward, was packing the dishes back into panniers. Through the open tent flaps he could see that the men outside had already finished the bread, cheese, and onions that constituted their traveling rations. Frederick emptied the remains of the one cup of unwatered wine he now allowed himself a day. As he leaned forward to replace the cup, he groaned. A fierce, knifelike spasm contracted his insides. He clenched his teeth in an effort not to scream and slumped forward on the table.

They laid him on the Eastern rug that covered the turf. Abdul, the commander of his bodyguard, placed his own rolled-up cloak under Frederick's head. He stared at him, his dark eyes wide with anguish. Abdul cast a sharp glance at the back of the steward Giovanni, who was spreading another cloak over his shivering body.

Frederick, his insides churning with unbearable agony, caught the look. He shook his head. "It's just my stomach again, Abdul," he said with a grimace of pain. "Take me back . . ." Vomit spewed from his mouth. His head fell to one side. He had lost consciousness.

IN A TORRENTIAL winter downpour, late at night, a messenger hammered on the gates of Berard's country manor outside Foggia.

The man, wet and shaking with cold, was brought before Berard, who was already attired in a night cap and chamber robe, about to retire for the night.

"I beg your pardon for disturbing Your Grace at this hour. Orders of the emperor. You are to come to Fiorentino immediately."

"To Fiorentino?" Berard stared at him. What was Frederick doing in the village of Fiorentino? A dreadful presentiment filled him. "What's the matter?"

As the kneeling man raised his head, Berard saw his eyes cloud. "My lord, I bring evil tidings . . ." The man swallowed, blinking. "The emperor was taken ill at noon yesterday, on his way to Lucera. We carried him to the nearest castle, that of Fiorentino, and sent for his doctor from Lucera. He's very ill. He has summoned the great officers of the realm."

Berard stared at the man. He shook his head. His heart couldn't believe it.

YET AS HE stood by Frederick's bedside at dawn, having traveled through the night, Berard knew that it was true. Even in the dim light of the chamber, filled with people, he could see that the ashen grayness of death underlay Frederick's skin. The physicians thought it might be a slow-acting poison, administered over weeks. The pope or the Lombards, or both. They'd felled him just before he could finally defeat them . . .

Frederick's sunken features brightened as he saw him. "Thank you for coming so quickly. My time has come to say farewell to the temptations of this world." A smile, tinged with its former mischief, flickered across the cracked lips: "I enjoyed them greatly. . . . Will you administer the last rites so that they can't say I died a heretic?"

Berard kissed his forehead; it was clammy. His eyes fell on Frederick's sleeve. He was garbed in the white habit of a Cistercian monk.

Frederick caught his look. "A simple garment in which to depart. I've always admired the Cistercians. It'll also read well in the chronicles . . ."

Was this the last act in a life rich with calculated settings, or was it the final public expression of a private faith? Berard turned to his chaplain and the two acolytes behind him. They had brought a small traveling altar. With trembling hands, Berard administered the last rites.

". . . *ego te absolvo* . . ." Berard pronounced the words of absolution. He traced the cross upon Frederick's feet, forehead, eyes, and lips in chrism, completing the sacrament of the extreme unction. As he raised the host he saw a strange look in Frederick's eyes. Was it mockery or hope? The miracle of the transubstantiation, often denied by Frederick, was this time being invoked for his own benefit.

Confessed, absolved, and anointed, Frederick received communion. His soul would now be able to rise to heaven, escaping the talons of the

invisible devils clustering about the deathbed to carry the unprotected soul
off to their infernal abode.

A sob rose from the other side of the bed, where the two Manfreds,
uncle and nephew, stood side by side. Frederick's son flung himself on the
bed, ignoring his uncle's restraining hand.

"Father," he cried, "Father, you must live, live for those who love and
need you! Without you, the Empire will die!"

Frederick touched his wet cheek. "Manfred," he said in a voice straining with effort, "even I must obey God's summons. I leave Sicily and the
Empire in his hands. He will guide you and your brothers. Don't fret, my
son," he tried to smile, "I'm going to see your mother. Kiss me for a last
time and then leave. Deathbeds aren't for the young. Berard will stay
with me."

Manfred swallowed hard. He stood up and straightened his shoulders.
Bending down, he kissed his father's forehead. His uncle did likewise,
squeezing Frederick's hand before turning away, his eyes, too, filled with
tears. One by one the great officers of state knelt by the bed and took their
leave before filing out into the antechamber.

When all had left and the chamber was in silence, Frederick said, "Sit
by me, Berard, till it pleases Death to fetch me. He won't be long now. I
can hear him sharpening his scythe."

Berard sat on the coverlet. He took Frederick's hand.

The sea-green eyes looked at him, still clear and lucid. "I've failed,
haven't I? The new Rome has come to naught."

Berard shook his head. "I don't think so, Frederick. Nothing's ever for
naught in God's world. You're right, it was too late or too early, I don't
know which, to revive the golden age of Rome. But you gave men a vision
of enlightenment, justice, and tolerance. You gave them hope."

Frederick sighed. He took a deep rattling breath to give himself
strength. "At least," he said, "I've broken the papacy. Never again will the
popes wield the unquestioned power they've abused for centuries."

"Perhaps," said Berard.

Frederick closed his eyes. His breath seemed to come more evenly.
Berard's lips moved in silent prayer. Despite the logs burning in the fireplace, the chamber was icy. The pallid rays of the December sun slanted
onto the flagstones near the window, left open by Frederick's orders. A

smell of burning wood and winter filled the room. The winter of the soul, Berard thought, shivering suddenly despite his furred robe, the end of a full and glorious season.

Frederick's eyes flew open again. "Will the storks return to Haguenau?"

So he hadn't forgotten the old prophecy. Berard inclined his head. "The Hohenstaufen power remains unbroken." Even as he said it, he asked himself if that was so. His eyes rose in supplication to the crucifix above the bed. Someone had affixed it there in this guardroom hastily converted into a makeshift bedchamber. How strange, and how fitting. Never before had the symbol of our Lord in his agony blessed Frederick's chamber.

When he looked down again, Berard's heart contracted. Frederick was staring at him, unseeing. A great stillness reigned in the chamber. It was cold. Outside, a falcon skimmed over the wooden watchtower. The bird circled once, then dipped its dark wings and soared into the sky.

Berard closed the lifeless eyes. He raised the hand to his lips. It was still warm. "Farewell, my son," he whispered. He knew that he should get up and tell the others, yet he remained seated. He could not bring himself to leave him alone in that most desolate of all solitudes, death.

After what seemed like a very long time, a whole life, Berard rose. With bent shoulders, he shuffled to the door, to announce to those waiting outside that the Emperor Frederick was dead.

Epilogue

PALERMO 1296

The autumn sun slanted into the monastery's cloister. Fragrant, late-blooming roses rambled up the pillars in pink and crimson and yellow. The old friar sat against a column, enjoying the warmth. A scrawny tortoise-shell cat leaped onto the wall and rubbed itself against his habit. The friar stroked the animal absently. He was a tall man, of broad shoulders, with strong brows that had remained black where his hair and beard had turned white with age. His name was Richard of Castacca.

"So what happened? Tell me, uncle," the youth sitting beside him prodded.

Richard smiled. He, too, had been young once, and impatient, before God called him to the brotherhood of Saint Francis. He had been part of his uncle Berard's household and had spent much time at the Emperor Frederick's court, in the heyday of Hohenstaufen rule.

He remembered the emperor's death as if it had happened yesterday. They wrapped his embalmed body in a linen tunic embroidered with verses from the Koran. A purple mantle lay upon his shoulders. Boots of soft crimson leather clad his feet, and on his head rested a crown of Byzantine design, with two long jeweled pendants. Beside him lay a golden orb filled with the soil of Sicily.

In his mind's eye, Richard saw himself again as a young page, riding beside his uncle Berard's litter. An immense procession followed the dead emperor as he was borne across Apulia. To the beat of black-muffled drums, sixteen turbaned Saracens carried the coffin in relays on their shoulders, escorted by cavalry on mounts caparisoned in black and gold. In the villages and market towns of Apulia the people lined the roads in their thousands, removing their caps, weeping or simply kneeling in silence as the coffin passed by. It rested for the last night in Bianca Lancia's castle at Ghioa del Colle before proceeding by ship from Taranto to Palermo. There, in a sarcophagus of red Egyptian porphyry, the Emperor was laid to rest beside his last wife.

Richard marshaled his memories. So many upheavals had taken place since then, so much hardship for Sicily.

"Those were dark days indeed, my son," he began. "After Frederick's death, whom many said the pope had poisoned, one trouble followed another, both in Sicily and Germany. The emperor's son by his English wife Isabella died three years after his father. At the pope's instigation, a faction of German princes elected a new emperor to oust Conrad IV, Frederick's son, from the imperial throne. After years of fighting, Conrad abandoned the Empire and came to Sicily. Within a year he, too, was dead."

"And that's when Manfred became king?" his nephew interrupted.

The old man nodded. "Yes, my boy. For sixteen years Manfred ruled Sicily as wisely as his father. But the enemies of the Hohenstaufen were gathering like locusts in a summer sky. The pope offered the crown of Sicily to Charles of Anjou, the French king's brother. An evil man of ruthless ambition, Charles managed to raise the forces other pretenders of the pope's choosing had been unable to muster. He invaded Sicily, burning and pillaging as he went.

"At Benevento, on a large plain, the prophecy of Manfred's mother Bianca Lancia came to pass: The Sicilians faced the French. Manfred and his army fought valiantly all day, but in the end they were defeated by their enemies' superior numbers. Manfred was slain. As he fell from his horse, the crown of Sicily tumbled into the grass, just as his mother had predicted. His wife and sons were imprisoned in Frederick's most sublime castle, the Castel del Monte, where they starved to death.

"But that still was not the end. In the spring of 1268, a fair-haired boy of fourteen, Frederick's grandson Conradin, left Germany and crossed the Alps with a handful of followers. With the same precocious ability as his grandfather, he rallied Ghibelline loyalists in Italy to his cause. Many thought that again a Hohenstaufen prince had risen to fulfill the promise of a great name. It was not to be. His supporters were too few and his experience too little.

"Charles of Anjou defeated him at the battle of Tagliacozzo. On that day, the Sicilian chivalry that had lived to fight another day after King Manfred's defeat perished almost to a man. Conradin was captured. To the horror of Christendom and the everlasting shame of Charles of Anjou, the boy was beheaded like a common criminal in the market square of Naples."

Richard wiped his rheumy eyes. "And thus, the Hohenstaufen were nearly extirpated."

"Nearly, uncle? But they're all dead."

Richard smiled. "Almost, but not quite. You see, one of Manfred's daughters, Constance, had married King Peter of Aragon and Catalonia. In March 1282, at the hour of vespers, the people of Palermo rose against their French oppressors in a massacre called the Sicilian Vespers. From Palermo, the revolt spread to the whole island. On a moonless night, a galley left a cove near Palermo. Aboard was a group of Sicilian noblemen. In Barcelona, they begged King Peter to assume the crown of Sicily in his wife's right. Thirty-two years after the Emperor Frederick's death, his and Bianca Lancia's granddaughter Constance and her husband Peter of Aragon were crowned king and queen of Sicily in the cathedral of Palermo."

"You mean King Peter's son Frederick, our king, is a great-grandson of the Emperor Frederick?"

Richard chuckled. "Yes, but he's also, by a fateful coincidence, a great-nephew of the Aragonese princess who was Frederick's first wife. There's a curious story told about the royal palace in Palermo. It's said that at full moon, when the waters of the bay glitter like silver under the moonbeams, the ghost of a tall fair-haired lady walks the mosaic halls. The specter wears a crown just like the one with which Constance of Aragon was buried. A smile plays upon her lips.

"I wonder," Richard said, tilting his head, "if it is a smile of satisfaction that, after all, God's justice has prevailed?"

List of Characters

Historical:

CONSTANCE OF SICILY—Frederick's mother

HENRY IV OF HOHENSTAUFEN—German emperor and Frederick's father

WALTER OF PALEAR—First Chancellor of Sicily

POPE INNOCENT III

BERARD OF CASTACCA—Archbishop of Palermo

ALFONSO OF ARAGON—Count of Provence, Constance of Aragon's brother

CONSTANCE OF ARAGON—Frederick's first wife

JOLANDA OF JERUSALEM—Frederick's second wife

ISABELLA OF ENGLAND—Frederick's third wife

BIANCA LANCIA—Frederick's morganatic fourth wife

ALAMAN DA COSTA—Genoese admiral

OTTO OF BRUNSWICK—German emperor

MANFRED LANCIA—Bianca Lancia's brother

CONRAD VON SCHARFENBURG—German chancellor

ADELAIDE VON URSLINGEN—Frederick's mistress and Enzo's mother

HERMANN VON SALZA—Grandmaster of the Teutonic Order

DUKE HENRY OF BRABANT—Frederick's erstwhile enemy and later friend

WALTER VON DER VOGELWEIDE—Frederick's court poet and Henry's tutor

POPE HONORIUS III

JEAN DE BRIENNE—Jolanda's father
FAKHR-ED-DIN—Sultan of Egypt's envoy and Frederick's friend
AL-KAMIL—Sultan of Egypt, Fakhr-ed-Din's cousin
SAINT FRANCIS OF ASSISI
PIERO DELLA VIGNA—Second chancellor of Sicily
POPE GREGORY IX
MICHAEL SCOT—Scottish scholar at Frederick's court
THOMAS AQUINAS—Frederick's courtier and father of saint
POPE INNOCENT IV

Frederick's children:
HENRY—Constance's son (L)
ENZO—Adelaide's son (I)
CATHERINE—Adelaide's daughter (I)
CONRAD—Jolanda's son (L)
MARGARET—Isabella's daughter (L)
CONSTANCE—Bianca's daughter (I)
VIOLANTE—Bianca's daughter (I)
MANFRED—Bianca's son (I)

Fictional:
William—Frederick's tutor
Leila—Saracen mistress
Fakir—Saracen falconer
Juana—Constance of Aragon's maid
Mahmoud—Saracen servant
Ibn Tulun—Saracen physician
Catalina—Tavern dancer in Genoa
Von Falkstein—Governor of Trifels castle
Orbert—Frederick's master mason
Sybil—Frederick's last mistress
Matteo—Cistercian Abbot of Eufemia

Note: Very minor characters, both historical and fictional, have been
omitted from the above list.